THE TOMORROW SERIES #7

THE OTHER SIDE OF DAWN

JOHN MARSDEN

SCHOLASTIC INC.
New York Toronto London Auckland
Sydney Mexico City New Delhi Hong Kong

ACKNOWLEDGMENTS

Many thanks for ideas, information and stories to: Dallas Wilkinson, Ross Barlow, Lizzie Matthews, Roos Marsden, Jeanne Marsden, Charlotte Lindsay, The Farran family (especially Elizabeth), Barry Traill, Chris Kalff, Lesley Tuncliffe ("Write Inside the Mind"), Lachlan Monsbourgh, and Lachie Dunn

Special thanks to Anna McFarlane for editing the manuscript, and to Paul Kenny for his perceptive and generous support of this series since its earliest days.

The reference to the bell tolling on p. 236 is paraphrased from *Devotions upon Emergent Occasions* by John Donne.

ISBN 978-0-439-85805-2

12 11 10 9 8 7 6 5 4 3 2 1   10 11 12 13 14 15/0

Printed in the U.S.A.   40

First paperback edition, February 2007

AN AUSSIE GLOSSARY

bitumen: asphalt, tar
bludger: a lazy person
bole: the spot on a tree where two branches meet
bonbons: Christmas crackers or party favors
bonnet: the hood of a car
bowsers: gas pumps
bunyip: an imaginary creature
chewie: gum
chook: a chicken
cockies: cockatoos
crims: criminals
dag: an annoying person
dinking: carrying a passenger on a bike
dobbing: tattling
dropkicks: loser
duckboards: floorboards
dunny: a toilet
echidna: spiny anteater
eucalypt: a eucalyptus tree
fair dinkum: the truth, the real thing
fibro: a type of building material
flat chat: as fast as possible
footie: Australian rules football
fringe: bangs
goanna: an Australian lizard
goer: someone who gets things done
haka: a Maori war chant
header: a piece of farm machinery that harvests wheat and other crops
jumper: a sweater
k's: kilometers
killer: a sheep that's been designated as the one to be killed to provide the family with its next supply of meat
kookaburra: an Australian bird
maggie: a magpie
milk bar: a small corner store, a minimart
nicked: shoplifted
parkers: parking lights
Perspex: a hard clear plastic similar to Plexiglas
possie: position
postmortem: an inquiry into what went wrong
pressies: presents

rapt: delighted

rellies: relatives

revs: revolutions

rosella: an Australian bird

Rotorua: a town in New Zealand famous for its volcanic springs

scabbed: stolen

servo: a service station

snow gum: a kind of tree

soapie: a soap opera

spat chips: was angry

Stimorol: a brand of chewing gum

stuffed: exhausted

suss: suspicious

tackers: kids

Texta: a marker pen

toey: anxious to get started

torch: a flashlight

truckie: a truck driver

uni: a university

ute: a utility vehicle

whinger: a whiner

willy-willy: a dust storm

windscreen: a windshield

To the people of Tibet, East Timor, and
West Papua (Irian Jaya)

1

THE NOISE OF A HELICOPTER AT NIGHT FILLS THE WHOLE world. Your ears rattle with the sound. Your other senses haven't got a hope. Oh of course you can still see, and smell, and feel. You see the dark shape of the chopper dropping like a huge March fly, with just two thin white lights checking the ground below. You smell the fumes of the aviation fuel. They go straight to your head, making you dizzy, like you're a little drunk. You feel the blast of air, getting stronger and stronger, blowing your hair then buffeting your whole body. But you hardly notice any of that stuff. The noise takes over everything. It's like a turbo-charged cappuccino machine. You've got your hands over your ears but it doesn't matter; you still can't keep out the racket.

All sounds are louder at night, and at three in the morning a helicopter is very, very loud.

When you're scared it sounds even louder.

In the middle of the bush you don't normally get loud noises. Cockatoos at dusk, tractors in the paddock, cattle bellowing: they're about as noisy as it gets. So the helicopter did kind of stand out.

There wasn't much we could do about it. Lee and Homer and Kevin were at different points around the paddocks, on high spots overlooking gates and four-wheel-drive tracks. We'd scrapped our first plan, which was to leave Kevin and Fi in Hell to look after the little kids. We'd decided at the last minute that we needed everyone we could get. We were so nervous, not knowing what to expect. So Kevin came with us and Fi had to do the babysitting on her own.

I agonised over that decision. That's what this war seemed to be all about, agonising over decisions. We called it right more often than we called it wrong, but the consequences of mistakes were so terrible. It wasn't enough to score ninety-nine per cent in the tests of war; not if the other one per cent represented a human life.

If we'd called this one wrong we'd lose Fi, Casey, Natalie, Jack and Gavin. Pretty bad call. A few days ago we would have felt confident leaving Fi there. Not any-more. Not after the gunfight of twenty-four hours earlier. Not after spending the morning burying the bullet-torn and chopped-up bodies of the eight soldiers we'd killed.

So, the boys were watching for more enemy soldiers, but at best they'd get only a few minutes warning of any-one approaching. There were too many different ways the soldiers could come. Plus, we didn't know exactly where the chopper would land. Last time it had been about a kilometre and a half from its target, which was pretty good, considering how hard the navigation must be, but if it was that far out again our sentries were useless.

Actually the pilot did well. He didn't go where we landed last time. He came down where we should have landed last time. But that was OK, because it was still in the area we'd marked out. In the excitement of watching the great black shape dropping onto us, and with my ears deaf-ened by the clatter of the blades and the roar of the engine, I forgot for a moment about the dangers of gatecrashers.

Through the dark Perspex of the chopper I could see the glow of the dashboard lights and the green light on the navigation table. The storm of dust and leaves meant I couldn't see the people, only a few dark heads. I was hoping the pilot would be Sam, the guy who'd brought us over last time, because I liked him, and admired him. For a guy I'd met only once, and so briefly, he'd made a big impression. But there was no telling who was flying this helicopter.

It settled, like a pregnant cow sinking to the ground, and the side hatch dropped open straightaway. A figure in dark clothes leapt out, then he turned to help bring down a large container. I ran forward. Two other people, in uniform, jumped through the hatch, and the four of us, without a word, arranged ourselves in a line, passing out a heap of boxes and barrels. I found myself panting, like the effort of doing it was full-on exhausting; I guess it wasn't, but it felt that way.

Less than three minutes later, the first soldier, putting one hand on either side of the hatch, levered himself back up and disappeared inside; the next one followed, and at the same moment the helicopter lifted off. If Sam had been at the controls I'd have had no chance to see him, let alone say hello.

Anyway there was no time for anything really, not even thinking. I'd registered that with two people back in the chopper we still had one on the ground, but we also had a heap of stuff. There'd been no warning from Colonel Finley of what to expect, just that we'd have a visitor for twenty-four hours. My curiosity was running at maximum revs.

There was no time to satisfy it. The man and I started carrying the boxes towards a pile of rocks a hundred metres to the west. It was the nearest cover. We wouldn't be able to get all this stuff into Hell in one trip, and there wouldn't be time to go there and back before dawn. I heard a slippage of stones and turned around in time to see Lee coming up the slope, out of the darkness. For a moment it seemed he wore the darkness, was dressed in it, but he was moving so quickly that he was with me before I had time to think about that.

"How'd it go?" he whispered, looking around all the time, like he was having a bad trip and thought spiders were crawling all over him.

"Is it safe?" I asked, more worried that he had left his lookout post than I was about answering his question.

"No, what do you bloody reckon?"

We were all on edge. But I didn't like the way he kept looking around.

"Well, is he here?" Lee asked.

"Yeah. With a heap of stuff." I nodded at the crate I was dragging along. "Grab the other end will you."

We carried it between us, then went back for another one. In the meantime Homer and Kevin had arrived, so by the time they took a couple of crates, and the man got a second load, Lee and I could take it easy.

Suddenly the night was peaceful once more. The helicopter had long gone — the noise just a memory — and the air was clear and sweet. It was hard to believe in a war, or enemies, or danger. With the stuff safely stowed we found ourselves standing in a little group on the edge of the escarpment.

And we were all embarrassed. Well, I don't know about the others, but I was, and they looked it. It had been so long since we'd met any strangers. Apart from the feral kids — and I couldn't really count them — we'd been on our own a long time.

The man looked about thirty. He was dressed in camouflage gear, but without a cap. From what I could see in the moonlight he had black hair and quite a dark face; heavy eyebrows that met in the middle. Ears that stuck out a bit and an unshaven chin. He smelt like a smoker. That was all I had time to notice. We got engaged in a rapid-fire conversation that rattled along like an automatic rifle.

"How far's your hide-out?"

"Three hours."

"Will the stuff be safe here?"

"Should be."

"We could leave a sentry," said Lee.

"But a sentry couldn't do anything against a patrol," Homer said.

"We're a long way from anywhere," I said.

"If they tracked the chopper . . ." the man said.

I realised what he meant. The helicopter might have been picked up by radar or something. If a patrol had been sent from Wirrawee, they could arrive in two or three hours, long after we'd left the area.

"Damn," I thought, "we've got some hard work ahead." But out loud I said: "We'll have to move the whole lot."

"Where to?"

"Towards Tailor's Stitch. We could get it halfway up the road tonight. That way we won't have so far to carry it tomorrow."

"Which way is Tailor's Stitch?" the man asked.

"North-east."

"You might want to take it in a different direction after I've talked to you," he said.

That brought me to a dead stop. Obviously these crates weren't just full of Mars bars.

"OK," I said, rethinking. "You tell us."

The man suddenly looked cautious. "Anywhere in the direction of Stratton would be OK," he said.

But from the way he said it, I knew Stratton wasn't the target.

I paused, mentally scanning possible places, like I was scrolling down on a computer, but rejecting each one. "I know," I said at last. "There is a safe place. But we'll have to move."

We loaded up. The New Zealander pulled out a couple of backpacks that he suggested we take to our hide-out. Everything else had to be carried away. With five of us we could do it in two trips, but we each had to take a fair bit of weight.

The place I had in mind was the wetlands; a swamp on the eastern boundary of our property. My grandfather drained the wetlands, paying for it with a government grant that they were handing out in those days. He turned it into pasture. Before I was born Dad brought in the bulldozers and dug it all out again. It was a radical thing to do. Most farmers wanted to turn every square centimetre into productive land, and to hell with the natural features or the natural vegetation. But trust my stubborn father: he was determined to bring back those wetlands. Grandpa spat chips in a big way and the neighbours thought we were mad. But Dad reckoned it'd give us a good source of permanent water, and it'd bring back birds that keep the insects down, plus it'd be a huge firebreak.

He was right too, on all three counts. I remember how proud he was when the ibis started nesting on the islands in the middle of the swamp. The first season they came, there were eight or nine pairs, the next year twenty, and now we had a few hundred, returning every year.

It was quite good actually. Bit of a contribution to the environment.

The main reason I thought we should go there was that if a patrol brought dogs to chase us, the wetlands would stop them in their tracks. I didn't know what was in the boxes, but the way this guy was acting it must have been important. So I thought it was worth going the extra couple of k's to get the stuff onto the islands. The wetlands covered about eight hectares, so it'd take a few dogs a few days to search that little lot.

We got there pretty quickly. Grunting with relief I dropped the box I'd carried. In front of me, tied to a bolt in a tree stump, was an old yellow and green dinghy which I'd mucked around in when I was a kid. It only had one oar; I don't know where the other one went, but it had been missing for as long as I could remember.

We all wanted to row the stuff to the island but Kevin and I got the job because I knew the best hiding place, and Homer had to navigate the others back to where the chopper landed.

We got into the boat with a bit of difficulty, mainly because Kevin tried to push off and jump in at the same time. But after some wild rocking, with me clutching both sides, we managed to get clear of the shore.

As the others went back along the shoreline they couldn't resist. Lee had to chuck a handful of mud, and Homer bombed us with a rock. It was a very bad idea. The soldier went off like a car backfiring. "What the hell do you think you're doing?" he snarled at them. "Mother of God. Show a bit of sense."

Kevin and I giggled at each other. But I didn't really blame the man. He was probably wondering why on earth he'd been sent all the way from New Zealand to talk to a bunch of teenage dropkicks. He followed the two boys, watching them as he made his way through the grass. He sure didn't pick up any mud or rocks.

Distracted by Lee and Homer playing silly buggers, Kevin and I had got into a 360, and by the time we recovered and looked around at the bank they'd disappeared. I just got a glimpse of Lee's tall thin body disappearing like a shadow over the crest of the hill.

Suddenly it seemed awfully cold and dark and lonely, even with Kevin there.

We didn't talk much, just rowed in a clumsy zig-zag way till we grounded on mud. We carried the boxes and packs into the bushes, causing a riot among the birds, who probably hadn't seen a human visitor since Homer and I stirred them up a few years ago.

Yes, that first trip was OK. By the end of the second trip I was so tired that when Lee picked up a handful of mud, glancing around guiltily to make sure the New Zealander wasn't watching, I ripped off a string of words that convinced him to drop it back in the water.

"OK, mud-mouth," he said sulkily, "I wasn't going to throw it."

The trouble was, I was already thinking of the trek into Hell. We were heading for another late finish. After dealing with Gavin and the other kids all day, then hauling this stuff, I couldn't find my sense of humour at 4.45 in the morning. I tried to tie up the boat, but the rope was so thick and slippery that I kept losing one end, and then I couldn't get the knot to hold. The boys were bringing branches and brush to camouflage the boat and cover our tracks. Everyone was slipping in the mud and swearing.

The man from New Zealand was over at the point of

the wetlands, gazing into the distance, but I think watching us at the same time. Again I thought he would be less than impressed. Something about the attitude of these professional soldiers got so far up my nostrils it reached my sinuses. Oh well. I was past caring what anyone thought.

9

2

I'M NOT A BIG BELIEVER IN INSTINCT, BUT I FELT WEIRDLY anxious as we slogged our way up the spur in the last of the darkness. We didn't talk much. We were too tired and strung out. When we stopped for a breather the man did at least tell us his name. Ryan was twenty-eight, he lived just outside Dunedin, he was an engineer. He wouldn't say his last name.

"Why won't you tell us?" I asked.

"You'd never be able to pronounce it," he answered.

"No, really, why not?"

"Security."

I stood there in the semi-darkness, leaning against a snow gum, wondering what he meant. I figured it out soon enough: if we were caught and forced to tell everything we knew — well, the less we knew, the better.

It scared me to realise he was thinking in those terms. It made me feel we were too casual sometimes.

Lost in my thoughts I'd stopped listening to the whispered conversation; when I paid attention again I found Homer was in the middle of firing a bunch of questions at Ryan. He got a few answers. Turned out Ryan was in a New Zealand Army group called the SAS, and he had the rank of captain, which I think might have been fairly impressive for a twenty-eight-year-old.

He had a growly sort of voice, very strong and firm, like a tractor engine. You felt he was reliable. He sounded the way I'd like to sound, always knowing what to do, never being flurried or flustered. "Flurry and fluster, they sound like a pair of puppies." That was in a book I'd read once. What was the name of it? I couldn't remember. A year out of school and my brain was peanut butter.

Against Ryan's reliable voice was the way he'd snapped at Lee and Homer. He was entitled to be angry at them, sure, but what worried me was that maybe he would be like that whenever there was pressure. Fiery and unfriendly.

I got tired and stopped listening again. They were talking about conditions back in New Zealand. Ryan didn't want to say much about that either, but for a different reason. He just wasn't sure it was safe using our voices out here in the bush.

I wasn't sure either. We were well away from the drop zone, there was no sign of the enemy, and at this time of morning we should be the only people stupid enough to be out and about. And yet my tummy was rumbling like Rotorua and I was as nervous as I'd ever been.

So I listened to the music of the soft voices around me, but I didn't listen to the words.

We set off again. The hike up to Tailor's Stitch seemed endless. I couldn't remember it ever taking so long, even in the worst circumstances. The trouble was I hadn't had any real sleep since Colonel Finley told us we were getting a visitor. Not much more than twenty-four hours ago, but it felt like a fortnight. I knew every tree, every pothole, every bend of that track, but I could swear someone had taken the road and stretched it out like a piece of chewie, till it was a hundred per cent longer.

The light gradually got grey rather than black, then that sort of fuzzy grey before dawn. Shapes started to appear. Suddenly I could see trees a hundred metres up the track. We were nearly at the top, thank God. Everyone had stopped talking. I guess we were all tired, and a bit puffed by the last steep bit of the climb. I glanced at the crest that we were toiling towards. I felt like I was watching a black and white movie. And there were new actors in this movie. A line of them, three, then four, then five.

I was so tired that for a moment I didn't believe what I was seeing. They were like a line of ghost soldiers. I stood still, in shock. My body tingled and burned. Ahead of me Kevin had seen them, and he stopped too. I guess that's what convinced me they were real. Homer and Lee and Ryan plodded on with heads down. To my amazement, the soldiers on the ridge were still walking past in profile. Then Homer, now at the front of our group, suddenly saw them. He stopped like he'd been snap-frozen. That at last made the other two realise something was wrong, and they froze too.

The five of us were perfect targets. If the patrol went into attack mode we'd have to dive off into the bushes and hope we could find cover. But incredibly, the soldiers just kept walking. They looked pretty tired themselves. They were actually better targets than us, lined across the horizon like ducks in the shooting gallery at the Wirrawee Show. Maybe they'd been out all night too.

The last one moved across my line of vision and was gone. The bush was still and peaceful as though no humans had ever trodden through it.

We stared at each other in shock, then, without anyone needing to suggest it, we sidled like spirits into a patch of scrub on our left. We sneaked in about twenty metres, then gathered in a group. We were all trembling a bit I think. It had been so unexpected. There was just nowhere safe for us anymore.

The first thing that was obvious was Ryan's anger. I didn't blame him. He'd put his life in our hands and almost lost it. I suppose we'd been too tired, not thinking things through enough. But in the middle of the night, so far from anywhere, with one patrol dead and buried just hours ago, and us certain no-one would come looking for them for days, we'd convinced ourselves that we'd be OK.

I always had the feeling that the New Zealanders weren't sure that we really knew what we were doing. I just got the sense from talking to them that they thought we were a bunch of kids who'd done some crazy, wacky stuff and by a few lucky flukes got away with it. The first time I felt Colonel Finley finally, really, completely took us seriously was when we told him over the radio that we'd wiped out an entire patrol of enemy soldiers without getting a scratch. And now, such a short time later, it looked like we'd blown our reputation again. It was very aggravating.

Ryan said to all of us, "Well, that was a great effort," then he said to me: "Good call, Ellie."

Steam was coming out of every opening in his body — well, the visible ones anyway. He was flurried and flustered now. First he'd gone off at Homer and Lee for chucking mud, now his blood pressure was off the scale a second time. I was scared his moustache would catch fire.

It was funny having an argument in whispers, but we didn't have much choice. And for once I didn't buckle at this attack. I'd always struggled to cope with these army guys. Major Harvey and even Colonel Finley sometimes too. But now I looked Ryan straight in the eye and said: "We know these mountains backwards. In fourteen months they're only the second group of soldiers who've been up here. It was totally unpredictable."

All that was more or less true, although lately it seemed like the mountains had been swarming with as many enemy soldiers as a World War II movie.

OK maybe we had been careless. But they must have a lot more resources up here than we'd imagined. After all, not everything's foreseeable. Not everything that goes wrong has to be someone's fault. That's why I stood up to Ryan, and that's why I felt confident doing it.

He did gulp a bit. He literally swallowed his next words: I could see his Adam's apple go up and down. After a pause he said: "Well, it's no good having post-mortems. Let's decide what we do from here."

"We have to go on into Hell," I said. "Fi and four kids are down there. Kids we're looking after. I don't want to leave them any longer, with enemy soldiers running around the mountains."

Ryan didn't look impressed by that either. "Four kids? How old are they? Mother of God, it's a daycare centre. Where did they come from?"

He didn't seem like he really wanted an answer, and this wasn't the time or place anyway.

After another pause he said: "Do you all need to go on to — what do you call it? Maybe some of us could stay out here. I could go through what I need to and catch the midnight special out again."

"Is that the deal?" Homer asked. "You're only here for twenty-four hours?"

"Absolutely. Provided it's safe for the chopper to come in, I'm gone. I've got another hot appointment the next night, and I'm not missing that. If I judge it's not safe here I'll use the radio to arrange a new pickup point."

There was a sigh around the group. This was getting complicated.

Homer said: "I think we should go on into Hell. Once we're there we're safe. That's our base, it's where everything is, it's where we can organise ourselves for the job you want us to do. And it won't be hard to get in safely."

Ryan seemed about to disagree, but he looked around the group, at our faces, and whatever he saw seemed to persuade him. So in the end he just shrugged and said: "We're going to have to be bloody careful."

I thought that was one of the dumber comments of the whole war, but occasionally in my life I've been smart enough to hold my tongue, and this was one of those times.

As we set off again I was thinking of all the possible answers I could have given. "No, I've got a better idea: let's form a conga line and dance our way to the top." "Hey, Ryan, have I told you about my diploma in yodelling?" "By the way, guys, isn't it time for our morning haka?"

We did a bush-bash to the crest, stopping fifty metres short and sending Homer and Kevin to check it out. We could hardly hold Kevin back. I wondered if Ryan's presence made the difference. Maybe Kevin was so keen to make a good impression on a professional soldier that he didn't mind sticking his neck out.

They were away half an hour. The first I saw of them coming back was a glimpse of Homer in among the rocks at the top of the track. Just a glimpse of his black hair, before he bobbed down again. My stomach did a slow roll, a full 360 degrees, then fell apart. I knew this was bad news. If he was staying in deep cover it must be for a reason. I glanced round at the others. At least they were awake, and watching. I waved them down, like "Get out of sight." A second later they'd all disappeared.

Ten minutes later I saw Homer much closer, then

almost at the same time I saw Kevin coming down the hill on the other side. They were moving like daddy-long-legs, so delicately and carefully. I sneaked up the hill and met Homer behind a boulder. When I put my hand on his forearm I felt he had a thousand volts running through him. If we'd wired him up to the Wirrawee electricity grid they could have turned on the street lights and still had enough left over to heat the pool.

"What?" I asked.

"They're spread out along Tailor's Stitch," he said. "Just looking down into Hell. I don't know what they're doing. They're bloody suspicious though."

"Maybe they've seen something from the air," I said.

"Yeah, maybe." He was panting, then he added: "God, I can't take much more of this."

There was a rattle of stones behind me and I turned around. It was Ryan.

"What's happening?" he asked.

Homer repeated his news. We both looked at Ryan, waiting for him to say something brilliant. Instead he seemed a bit embarrassed. He said, "I haven't actually had a lot of experience in this kind of situation. What do you guys think?"

I felt my eyebrows go up, but got them under control again.

"We can't afford to let them start climbing down into Hell," I said. "Not with Fi and the ferals there."

"We're light on for weapons," Homer said.

"There's plenty of firepower in those crates," Ryan said.

"They're too far away now," I said. "How much ammo have you got for that thing?" I nodded at the rifle Ryan carried.

"Eighty rounds."

We all had automatic rifles, knocked off from the enemy, but with only thirty rounds between the four of us. It sounded like a lot, but I knew the patrol up on Tailor's Stitch would have a couple of thousand.

"Are there only five of them?" I asked Homer.

"I think so."

Kevin arrived, then Lee, from his position out on the flank. We told Lee the news.

"Let's get up closer and see what we can do," I said.

Ryan cleared his throat, nervously.

"Er . . . I don't quite know how to tell you this," he said.

We waited. I had no idea what he was about to say, but it was obviously important.

"I'm under strict orders," he said, getting redder with every word. "I'm not allowed to get involved in a combat situation. Not under any circumstances. Unless I'm being attacked, obviously."

"Oh," I said.

"Well, OK," Homer said.

"Unbelievable," Kevin said, which I thought was a bit rich, considering some of the performances he'd put on during this war.

Lee just gazed into the distance, up at the ridge, without saying anything.

"Well," I said, echoing Homer. "OK. At least we know. Better to find out now I guess."

With a big mental effort I made myself concentrate, not get distracted by negative feelings.

"You wait here," I said to Ryan. "We'll come and get you after we've checked things out. Can we have your ammo? If we leave you with, say, a dozen rounds?"

"Sure," he said in his gruff voice. "Look, I'm really sorry about this, but they seem to think I'm needed for a few more jobs yet . . ."

"It's fine," I said. I just wanted to get moving. I was very conscious of the patrol sniffing around at the edge of Hell, and in my overactive imagination I could see them already halfway down the sides of the crater, closing in on Fi and the kids.

We did the business with the rifles and started the long slow sneak up to the ridge. As I left Ryan he slammed his fist into a tree and muttered, "Mother of God, this is so unfair."

I suppose he meant it; I wasn't altogether sure.

The last thing I wanted was to go slowly but we simply had to be ultra careful. By the time we got to the top and set out for Wombegonoo the first heat of the day was starting to settle on us. The clear daylight scared me. We didn't normally fight in these conditions. We were nocturnal killers.

Five against four weren't good odds either.

We didn't see the first soldier until we were halfway to Wombegonoo. Homer, beside me, was really fretting. Anything to do with Fi had him on edge. "They were much closer than this," he muttered to me, meaning that the soldiers had moved farther along the ridge since he saw them. Either that or they'd already gone over the side and into Hell.

Then I saw one. He was standing on top of Satan's Steps, looking down the cliffs. He was holding something, but I couldn't work out what. Homer and I scanned the length of Tailor's Stitch, looking for the others. I could see Lee and Kevin, to my right, doing the same. When I glanced back at Satan's Steps, the guy had disappeared.

For a moment I thought he must have fallen over. But Lee, who was working his way along the side of the ridge quite quickly, waved Homer and me forward, and as I ran, crouched, to the safety of a tree, I got a glimpse of a rope trailing from a large eucalypt.

I realised then what was happening. They were abseiling over the edge.

After that things happened at a speed that allowed for no thought, no feeling, just the mad adrenaline rush to make the correct decisions, call the right shots, and stay alive. There was a commotion to my right, not a noise, just a sense of the air being disturbed. I snapped around to see what was happening. Lee and Kevin were doing something, under another tree. They had a body between them. I left Homer and sprinted over, rifle at the ready. But they didn't need me. They'd taken a prisoner. A young woman, in military uniform, was kneeling on the ground, her arms behind her head. Kevin had his rifle pointed at her face, from just three or four metres away. I was impressed, but then the problems hit me. Having a prisoner was a huge complication. But, like I said, no time for thought, we were in the middle of it now. Whatever happened in the next few minutes, we had to come out on top, we had to win. Second prizes in this war were handed out in the morgue.

The woman had been supervising the unwinding of the rope. She didn't have to do much I'd say, just stand there and keep an eye on it. It ran around the trunk, with a leather strap to stop any fraying. Lee pulled out his knife, and looking at me, made a gesture of "I'll cut it."

I shook my head at him and tried to think. God it was hard. I was too tired, not just from the events of the last day and two nights, but from the whole long exhausting war. Homer arrived. I was so glad to see him. Somehow his just being there helped me to focus my mind, clarify my thinking. "Look," I said, keeping my voice low, "leave the rope for now." I couldn't put it in words, but I knew in my mind I was right. If we cut the rope, anyone who wasn't on it would know right away there was a problem. They would melt into the bush in Hell and we'd never find them.

"Homer and I'll go down the track," I added, "and try to surprise them at the bottom of the cliff."

"I'll come with you," Lee said at once. "Kevin can look after her."

I didn't argue. I was too grateful for his company. I was wearing Lee's watch, so I hit the start button and said to Kevin: "Cut the rope in eight minutes."

I figured that if we moved fast enough we could get to the bottom of the cliffs in eight.

We went down that path like we had no fear. I guess the three of us were picturing Fi and the kids, those helpless kids who thought they were so tough. We ran silently, but we ran swiftly. Somehow I found myself in front. I hurdled logs, slipped on rocks, skidded round bends in the track, ducked under branches. I only looked behind me once. The boys were right there. That was all I needed to know.

Every time I hit another tree, or sharp edge of rock, I knew I'd collected another graze, or cut, or bruise. The sweat poured off me. It mingled with my blood. I ignored both the blood and the sweat, concentrating on the two important things, which were speed and silence. Nothing mattered beside them.

When I wasn't looking at the path, trying to dodge the ruts and bumps and huge mounds of wet leaves, I was checking the watch. In two minutes and forty-five seconds we reached the first bridge that the old Hermit had built. We made contact with Satan's Steps for the first time at three minutes fifty, again at four minutes forty, and again at five minutes twenty. We were cutting it awfully fine. Through the gap between the cliffs exactly one minute later. I guessed we'd need another minute and a half, which was horribly close to the deadline of eight minutes. We couldn't afford to be late. Surprise was worth lives in this race.

I heard Homer behind me cocking his rifle as he ran. I did the same. Kind of dangerous, running through bush at full speed with rifles cocked and loaded. I decided if I ever saw my dad again I wouldn't tell him about this. But it was good Homer did it. It made me remember that this wasn't just a race against the clock, a race against the bad guys, it was a battle, and I had to be in full combat mode, right now. No time for warm-ups or stretches or motivational speeches. I had to be ready to fire. To shoot. To kill.

The last glance at the watch showed seven and a half minutes gone. I reckon it probably was thirty seconds later that we reached the bottom of the cliffs, where I knew they'd be. It was only in the last twenty metres that we slowed down. Only for that little bit did I drop to a walk, then a fast creep forwards. I was so intent that I had no room to feel nervous. Talk about focused. All my energy, physical and mental and emotional, was on the job we had to do.

I saw them at the same time they saw me. The difference was that I was expecting to see them and they weren't expecting to see me. That gave me a moment. But a moment wasn't going to be enough, as I realised at once, with a kind of sick terror. There were six of them and three of us. Homer had been wrong about the numbers. Our little time advantage wasn't worth much when it was six to three. No way could we wipe out six of them in a face-to-face battle.

Despite that a reflex was bringing my rifle up and making my finger curl around the trigger. I started feeling very weird, like all the air had left my lungs, left my body. It wasn't a desperate feeling exactly, just the sensation that I'd been emptied of air. I didn't think about it particularly; it was just a very strange aspect to the whole thing.

Six against three. In fact that wasn't quite right. It was seven against four, only I didn't know it. Seven of them, four of us. The fourth for us was Kevin. The seventh for them was a woman soldier abseiling down the rock face, swinging out over the steepest cliff in Satan's Steps. As Kevin cut the rope.

I wonder how much warning she got. She must have known something was wrong, something was terribly wrong, as the rope began to ripple and shudder. The first I knew was the scream as she fell. God, that scream. Her voice filled Hell. It was a wail, it was a shriek, it was pure agony. Every time I think about it the skin on the back of my neck goes cold, like someone's put an ice block there. Time freezes over and I forget what I'm doing, I go a bit catatonic, reliving that scream.

Funny, that's what happens now when I think about it. At the time my mind worked a little better than that. Somewhere in my most primitive being I knew that the scream of the falling woman, a scream that would curdle milk and curdle blood, a scream that seemed to last half a minute, a scream that came from the deepest pit of hell itself, gave us our only chance.

While the enemy soldiers stood transfixed, as though a funnel-web spider had injected them with a paralysing venom, I squeezed the trigger with my right index finger.

The bang-bang-bang-bang of the automatic weapon, with the background of screams as the woman fell and fell, made the most horrible music I've ever heard.

It only lasted for a moment. The thump of the woman hitting the ground put an end to it. I hardly noticed that. Already other bodies were falling. They didn't have so far to go, but their destination was the same. Another noise joined in, as Homer and Lee began firing. I don't think they were more than a second behind me, but a lot of living and dying can happen in a second.

We kept firing for a bit longer but there was no need. Where a moment before there had been half-a-dozen soldiers alive and alert, now there were bodies torn apart by the force of bullets. Blood and pieces of flesh and scraps of uniform were everywhere, and my beautiful Hell had been destroyed forever. There was nothing but death in front of us. It truly was hell now.

Oddly enough the most intact body was that of the woman who fell.

Homer hurried to her, the one whose death scream had saved our lives, and checked her pulse. It didn't take long. But it was Lee who caught my attention. He swapped his rifle, which had jammed, for one of the dead soldier's and straightening up said to me, "One of them got away."

"Oh no."

"Yeah, he ran off past the cliff there. But he left his rifle."

"What the hell do we do about him?"

Homer came over to join us. "Leave him," he said

briskly. I was about to interrupt, to protest strongly, but Homer went straight on.

"He hasn't got a rifle. We could waste a week looking and still not find him. We'd be better off to get Fi and the ferals and join up with Kevin and Ryan again. In the long term that's the only way to go."

As so often happened, Homer had seen the problem clearly and figured out the solution. Well, maybe not the solution, but the best plan.

I was very conscious that Fi and the little kids would have heard the shots and the screams and be in a state of panic. Even Gavin would have just about heard the noise, and that's saying something. It seemed pretty important to get to them fast, before they did anything stupid.

I hesitated another moment then followed the two boys. One thing was for sure, there was nothing I could do back there at the foot of Satan's Steps.

We were only ten metres from the track. As soon as I met up with it again I swerved right and set off towards the clearing. Suddenly I heard a clamour of voices. Not girls' voices and not little kids' voices, not Fi and the ferals, but Homer and Lee and some other guy. The other guy sounded unhappy. Like, majorly unhappy. Like, crying and groaning and pleading.

I cocked my rifle again and started jogging. But I didn't have to jog far. In this thick bush sound only travelled a short distance. Two more bends in the track and there they were.

If they ever run a show on TV called *War's Funniest Home Videos*, with lots of amusing film of people getting wounded, blown up and killed, they'd have to find room for this one.

I'd never given a thought to the mantraps that Jack

and Gavin had worked on so busily. Fair dinkum, if Booby Traps was a school subject, those two should have given a presentation at Speech Night.

To be honest, though, I'd never taken them seriously. Even though I'd nearly broken my ankle in Jack's corrugations myself, I never believed in them.

Well, that had to change now.

Gavin's main contribution had been a hole for people to fall in. He'd covered it with leaves and stuff. The trouble was, being Gavin, he'd thought it was a fantastic idea, and started on it with huge enthusiasm, but after a few hours digging, spread over a few days, he'd given up. Even with Lee's help it hadn't ever reached its potential. The original idea was to have it so deep that an enemy soldier would be impaled on sharp sticks at the bottom. But it was only a metre deep and there were no sharp sticks in it at all.

Perhaps that was just as well, because I don't think I could have stomached seeing someone impaled the way Gavin planned.

What had happened though was that the soldier, running frantically from the massacre at the back of the cliffs, had dropped into it so heavily that it looked like he'd broken his leg.

Gavin was always getting the last laugh in this war. It was quite aggravating.

I wasn't totally sure the man had broken his leg. He might have snapped a tendon or something. Whatever, he was in agony, twisting and turning around, and talking nonstop in his own language. I don't know what he was saying. Half the time he sounded like he was begging, half the time like he was really angry. He'd dragged himself up over the edge of the hole but had stopped trying to get any farther. He was in too much pain. Pain's like that. No matter where it is on your body it still gets you in the gut.

None of us could be bothered with him. God I can't believe how brutal we were getting, how callous. Homer just said: "Well, he isn't going to give us any more trouble for a while." Lee and Homer started off again but I stopped them and said: "Look, hold the phone a sec, I think we'd better have someone go up the top, make sure there're no more soldiers, and that Kevin's OK."

They stood there taking that in, thinking about it, then Lee said: "Yeah, you're right, I'll go."

"What about Ryan?" Homer asked.

"He'll have to wait."

It was getting so confusing, people everywhere, but we had to stay calm. We were all ready to faint with weariness, but somehow the energy had to be found, to keep on keeping on. We agreed with Lee on a signal, his green T-shirt tied to a tree on Wombegonoo if things were under control, Homer's brown one if there was trouble. Homer pulled off his shirt with a primeval grunt and gave it to Lee who slipped away up the track, a phantom of the bush.

Watching him go, I felt that there was nothing out there that he couldn't handle, no enemy too smart or too strong for him. I had at last learned to trust him again, completely.

3

HOMER SAID: "LET'S TAKE IT SLOW AND STEADY ALONG the side of the ridge and watch out for the slightest sign of trouble."

We were all packing it pretty heavily. Fi had been beside herself when she heard the gunshots, and the kids were hysterical with fear. Even Gavin was the most nervous I'd ever seen him. When we went past the guy with the wrecked leg they stared at him like he had three heads and a bright-blue bum.

Fifty metres up the track we met Kevin and Lee, who were bringing the prisoner down into Hell. Lee had suggested that the two soldiers should be together, so they could help each other, but I don't think this woman was going to be much help to anyone. She looked off her head. It was like she wasn't seeing anything. Her eyes didn't focus on us. She had slobber drooling out of her mouth, and she was talking to herself in this strange sing-song voice. She was young and strong, but being caught by us might have done something funny to her mind. Or maybe she was like that normally. Maybe she was on drugs, I don't know.

I went back with Lee and we tied her to a tree, with constrictor knots. I had to harden my mind to do it, because there was always the chance that she wouldn't get out of them and I kept having images of her skeleton still tied to the tree, years after she'd starved to death. But I honestly believed that in a few hours she'd get them undone. That was all the time we'd need. She ranted and raved while we were doing it, and she was certainly aware of us then, because she hissed and growled at me like a feral cat in a corner. What with that and the bloke with the crook leg, moaning and crying and begging, it was an ugly scene all round, and I wasn't too unhappy about leaving them there and hurrying up to the top with the others.

No sooner had we got there, puffing and panting, than Gavin paid his way again. He was taking a leak against a tree trunk, half-a-dozen metres off the track. Just as he finished, he started waving urgently to us. A glint of metal, farther in the bush, had caught his eye.

We ran in there. In a neat circle were the soldiers' packs, along with two radio sets. There was no time to open anything. We carried the lot to a cliff and dropped them into the thickest patch of undergrowth we could see where they should be safe for a few hundred years.

We tiptoed along Tailor's Stitch, our nerves on edge and stomachs churning. There was just no telling what new treats this war might have in store: patrols, helicopters, snipers, who knows? I wouldn't have been surprised if a tank had come lumbering along the narrow track, blasting rocks and trees and wombats and us out of its way.

Every section of the track that we got through was a relief. To reach that gum tree. To reach that white rock. To make it around the next bend. To come at last to the turn-off, near Mt Martin, where the four-wheel-drive track started down to our property.

Ryan was waiting in there, not all that far from where we'd left him. He was holed up among a pile of rocks with a good view to the left and right of Tailor's Stitch.

To give him his due, he was genuinely ecstatic to see us

five. We must have bonded with him faster than we'd realised. He was about as ecstatic to see us as he was dismayed to see the feral kids. At least he had the good sense not to say anything, but every time he looked at them he shook his head like he was a deputy principal and they were on daily detention.

He had nothing to report though. He'd seen and heard nothing, not even our rifle fire. I was surprised that the walls of Hell sealed the place so well. It sure had been a perfect hiding place. Later, maybe, I'd have more time to feel sad about losing it.

I gave him a quick news bulletin.

"We need to get out of this area fast," I said. "If you're willing to trust my judgement, there's a part of our property that should be safe. We'll have to retrace our steps a bit."

"I have to trust your judgement," was all he said.

I found myself warming to him. Maybe it was the pressies. One of the backpacks he'd told us to bring was stuffed with goodies. Fresh bread, oh God, what a luxury that was. Avocados. Weet-Bix. Two bottles of Diet Pepsi. Kit-Kats. Iced Vo-Vos. Vegemite. We couldn't stand around having breakfast, but on the other hand we couldn't go any longer without food. We needed it for physical energy, and we needed it even more for emotional energy.

We grabbed whatever looked good, stuffing as much as we could into our pockets while looking around anxiously, then set off down the track, Homer and I leading, Lee and Ryan bringing up the rear, eating as we went. It was kind of messy. Every dozen or so steps I'd reach into my pocket for another smidgin of food, at the same time as I was keeping a lookout.

So I was scooping into my pocket, bringing out a couple of fingers-full of mushed avocado, or the crumbs of a broken Kit-Kat, or a torn piece of bread. I've often tried to picture what my stomach would look like after a meal of, say, pasta, with ice-cream and chocolate sauce for dessert, plus a glass of wine if my father was feeling generous. I mean, if you could see what was in your tummy, it'd be so utterly disgusting you'd never want to eat again. But I reckon if I'd looked into my pocket of food that morning I'd have found a pretty fair approximation.

It wasn't long before I was stuffed full. Jack was the ultimate chocolate mouth, but this time Fi and I gave him a run for his money.

I wondered as I licked the Kit-Kat crumbs from my fingers who'd packed these goodies. I bet it wasn't Colonel Finley. I don't know whether he would have bothered, and I also wasn't too sure that he cared enough about us to bother with luxuries. At least though he'd taken the trouble to ask on the radio what we wanted. Maybe he had more imagination than I'd given him credit for.

The kids were totally in awe of Ryan, in spite of the pressies. They were so shy they wouldn't speak to him at all for the first couple of hours. It had been a long time since they'd met any adults who were on their side. Gavin went into one of his furious sulks, refusing to go near him, or even to accept any food directly. It had to be passed on by Homer. I guess it was fair enough in a way, because the kids had been very suspicious of the food adults gave them in Stratton. Seemed like maybe the soldiers had put poisoned stuff out for them.

Casey hid behind me when she first met Ryan, and when we set off again stayed as close to me as I'd let her.

Natalie shadowed Fi in the same kind of way. Jack was a real dickhead for a while, showing off and being stupid, prancing around trying to be smart. We shut him up fast. We couldn't afford any noise.

I was embarrassed about the kids being so rude to Ryan, and disappointed in them. He seemed decent enough, and I think he really did feel bad about not being allowed to come with us when we went after the patrol. He certainly tried to make up for it in every way possible, helping with packs, and tying straps and encouraging everyone to take food.

When we got down the track a good way he even showed a bit of a sense of humour. Well, too try-hard at times, but basically decent, and you couldn't help laughing at some of the things he said.

We belted along at a hell of a pace, as fast as we could go without the kids falling over. I led, heading for our back paddocks. At least with the food inside us we could push it a bit. The first couple of hours were really fast, then we had to slow down. But by then we had covered a lot of ground, and felt safer. We were out of the mountains now and into the flatter country, where you could see for miles. Our danger in this area was more likely to come from the air, so we kept turning 360s, and scanning the hazy horizon. There was no time for relaxation. If we were no longer safe in Hell, we weren't safe anywhere.

When the ferals couldn't keep going any longer we stopped, in a dreary little patch of bush near the creek in one of our paddocks, Nellie's. At that point Ryan got very serious again. I'd hardly swallowed my last mouthful of Pepsi when he asked us to get rid of the kids. Homer and Kevin took them to a clearing a bit farther along the bank, so we could still see them. In my pack I always had paper and pens, so I gave them those and told them to write a story or draw a picture.

"Or go to sleep," Homer said optimistically.

They seemed almost relieved to have something normal to do. They'd been so pleased to see us when we came trotting into the campsite in Hell — I'd been moved by how pleased they were. Fi had got them to hide in the undergrowth, but I think they were all sure they were going to be killed. When we arrived and they realised it was safe they threw themselves at me like I was a gum tree and they were koalas.

Led by Homer and Kevin they trudged off along the creek with their pens and paper. As soon as they were out of range Ryan said: "Well, they're a real complication."

"Tell us something we didn't know," I said. I guess I sounded a bit unfriendly, but I didn't mean to be. I was still so off-balance after the terrible encounters with two patrols in as many days, plus I was nervous at what Ryan might want.

Anyway it was no news to us that the kids were a complication. They'd been a complication ever since we first had anything to do with them.

Ryan continued: "We'll have a chat about them later and see what's to be done."

I just shrugged and started picking up Kit-Kat wrappers. We didn't talk again until the boys were back.

"OK, let's get on with it," Homer said, as we sat down for the big conference. "Why are you here?"

By then we were busting with impatience.

"OK," Ryan began. "You want to know why I'm here? Basically, it's because Colonel Finley believes you can help us in the next phase of the war. Before I start though,

I have to say that everything I tell you is absolutely top-secret. I can't emphasise that strongly enough. If any of this reaches the wrong ears . . ."

I sighed, closed my eyes, and leaned my head against a tree trunk. Seemed like I'd been here before. I didn't blame Ryan though. Some stuff you just have to say, you feel you can't go to the next stage until you've said it, like teachers, when we stopped for lunch on excursions, and they'd say, "Make sure you pick up all your rubbish; don't go to the toilet on your own; make sure you're back here by half past one . . ."

So Ryan made his speech, only he got into some very heavy stuff which we hadn't been put through before, not so specifically anyway.

"If you get caught," he said, "your first line of defence is that you don't know anything. 'I know nothing.' You're just kids acting on your own initiative. You've never seen me. You may have noticed that I didn't bring any newspapers or magazines, and if you look closely at the food you'll find all the processed stuff has got labels from Stratton, and use-by dates that suggest it was made before the invasion. That's so if, God forbid, you get caught, there's nothing to prove you've had a visit from New Zealand. You could have picked up all this stuff locally.

"OK. Your second line, if they break that down, is that I dropped in here with the chopper, and I gave you certain tasks to carry out, without any explanation as to why you had to do them.

"Your third line, if you're getting desperate, is to change the details of what you're doing, and to change them in a way that will make them convincing. That needs a bit of imagination, but you could pull it off, and it might buy you time. If you've ever told a fib to your parents, and they tell me it's not unknown for teenagers to do that, you've probably used that technique already.

"And your last line . . ." He paused and looked at us meaningfully, like he was about to tell us where babies come from, or why we shouldn't use drugs, or the true reason Mrs Lance had to leave the school. "Your last line is to tell the truth. Obviously that's not something we'd welcome. But these people are tough and they're ruthless and the stakes are high. If they don't believe your other three stories they'll put extreme pressure on you. Mental and physical pressure. They're very good at doing that. So they might break you down."

I glanced at Fi who was white-faced, staring at him.

"If that happens, all we can ask is that you put it off as long as possible. If you know you're cracking up, try to hang on for another six hours. Or twelve. Or twenty-four. At this stage of the war every hour gained is critical."

He made us go through the four points, repeating them, to prove we'd absorbed what he said.

Only then did he get onto the big stuff.

"Have you had any news since you've been back here?"

"Not really."

"Well, I'm not sure where to start. Seems like I've got to be the NZBC. 'And now, here is the news.' OK. In the time we've got I don't think I'll be able to give you a full history of what's happened. But in some ways things have been going a lot better. The biggest difference is the international pressure. Sweden in particular: they've led the way. And France, and Japan. America, and the IMF too. They've been working away in the United Nations and NATO, and with the ASEAN nations. Gradually it's had an effect.

"Unfortunately though that's not enough. We keep

coming back to a military solution. For some time now we've been planting what the Intelligence people call 'dis-information.' In practice that means we've been conning them, getting them to think that we're weakening, losing our spirit, our heart, our resolve. Our Intelligence sources tell us that it's working. Mind you, if this information's up to the normal standards of our Intelligence Department it probably means that there's now a few thousand Scud missiles lined up along the coast pointing at us.

"Still . . . this time it seems like they might have got it right. And of course as you can now guess, the reality is the complete opposite. What's about to break in the next couple of days is our big push. It's the most important phase of the war. This is it. What happens in the next few weeks will decide the future history of this country. And ours. And theirs too for that matter. That's why you're being called into action. That's why we're using every resource we've got. That's why I'm here."

Ryan lit another cigarette. It was his third already since we'd stopped our mad rush away from Tailor's Stitch.

"And it's where you come in. Have you heard of D-Day, from the Second World War?"

We'd all heard of it but no-one knew quite what it meant.

"It's when you launch a big attack, isn't it?" Kevin asked. "I saw that movie."

"Yes, exactly. Come to think of it, I don't know why they call it D-Day. Why not A or B or Z? Anyway, our D-Day has arrived. Every soldier we can call on, every weapon we have, will be thrown into this. It's the counter-attack that we've been working on for nearly six months."

"Do you mean we're going for broke?" Kevin asked. "All or nothing?"

"Well, I wouldn't quite put it that way. But the consequences of our being defeated would be . . ."

Ryan searched for a word, but when I heard the one he chose, I wished he hadn't bothered.

". . . it would be catastrophic."

He stubbed his cigarette out on a rock and looked at us, waiting to see our reaction. I think he was disappointed. None of us said anything, none of us showed anything.

Eventually Homer broke the silence. "So we're one of the resources, huh?"

"Essentially, yes. Sounds a bit cold-blooded, doesn't it?"

He lit another cigarette. Fi wrinkled her nose and moved away, so she was upwind of him. "Sorry," he said to her. "I'm giving up after the war."

He continued. "The stuff we stored on that island is basically to let you live off the land for a few weeks, and inflict a lot of damage while you're doing it."

"Damage what exactly?" Lee asked.

For the first time Ryan looked a bit excited. He got a light in his eyes. I wondered if he really was a bit of a goer after all. It was hard to work out, after what had happened that morning. Did he really want to get involved, but was holding back because of orders, because his skills were too valuable to be risked? Or was he a wimp who used orders as an excuse to stay out of danger? I started to think it was probably the first, and the way he'd slammed his fist into the tree, up on Tailor's Stitch, was pretty fair dinkum.

Maybe now we were being asked to do the job he would have liked for himself.

"That's just it," he said. "You've got a record, and I

don't know everything you've done, only what I've read in the papers basically, but Mother of God you've got a record and that's why Colonel Finley sent me. And after what you've told me about how you ambushed that patrol this morning, I'm getting an idea why.

"What he wants you guys to do now is go totally mobile. Guerillas on the run. Bombs to go. You travel light, you pick your own targets, you hit and disappear."

"But that's not going to make a difference," Fi said. "Not a major difference, not the kind of difference you're talking about. The five of us aren't going to win back a state or two in a couple of weeks."

Ryan waved that away with his cigarette.

"Of course, of course," he said. "But for want of a nail a war was lost."

I don't think any of us had a clue what he meant.

He waved his cigarette again and said: "We'll be coming by land and sea and air. Like I said, we've led them to believe that we're too low on troops and equipment to do any more than hold our line. We're gambling that they've swallowed the disinformation. The truth is that we've been saving a lot of stuff for just this eventuality. I can't say any more about that.

"But your mission, should you choose to accept it . . ."

Lee laughed at that, and Ryan grinned at him, so I knew it was a line from a movie somewhere.

"Your mission is to spread chaos and confusion behind their lines, in every manner, shape and form that you can, so that while we're hitting them with heavy artillery from the front they have to keep turning round to see what's going on behind them. Not only that, but if you're effective, they'll have less hitting power. They'll be attacking us with softer punches. That's good news for us."

Now we did show some emotion. Ryan quickly added: "You don't have to win the war on your own. Even a few little attacks, like this morning, will help enormously."

"Little attacks," I thought furiously. "You should have been there." I couldn't believe he'd said something so patronising, especially after he'd just told us what a good job we'd done.

But he went on: "And you won't be a solo act. There'll be other groups doing the same thing in other areas. But you will be the only ones in the area I'll assign you. So you won't get in each other's way. And you're absolutely free to turn me down. Colonel Finley told me three times I had to make that clear."

Most of us laughed at that, me included. It was a sarcastic laugh. When was the last time we had a free choice, a really free choice, about anything?

For a minute Ryan looked a bit offended at our laughing, then he shrugged his shoulders. "Well, as free as any choice in wartime can be," he said.

"So let me get this right," Homer said. "We'd be running all over the place, wrecking everything we can? What we've been doing all along, except you want us to step up the pace? Is that right?"

"We want you to go for it, twenty-four hours a day. We want you to be totally destructive. To do it on as big a scale as you can manage. But with one critical difference."

"What's that?"

"Those cases I brought. The ones we hid on the island. They contain a few bits and pieces that I think you'll find interesting."

"Bits and pieces?" I asked.

"Specifically, grenades, automatic weapons, ammunition and plastic explosives."

"No wonder they were so heavy," Kevin said.

"What's plastic explosive?" Fi asked.

"It's very efficient, very adaptable, and very safe — if you can use that word in connection with explosives — and it'll blow up anything quickly and easily."

"But we don't know how to use stuff like that," Fi said.

"Hey, give us some credit," Ryan said. "We chose it because it's so simple. I could teach you in half an hour. In fact I'm planning to teach you in half an hour."

Fi looked worried. "I don't want to carry explosives around with us," she said. "It doesn't sound very safe. What if we fall over or drop it?"

"Wait a sec," Ryan said.

He went to one of the packs we'd brought. We'd already made quite a mess of it by digging into the food for our breakfast orgy. Ryan pulled out a cardboard box that had been pushed down the side. It must have gone the full depth of the pack. It had ORICA EXPLOSIVES in big blue and orange writing.

"This is it," he said.

The lid was taped down but Ryan ripped along the top and tipped out two big fat things that looked like salamis wrapped in plastic.

He picked one up and waved it in front of us.

"Plastic explosive," he said. "Powerpacks."

Suddenly he lost his grip. The salami seemed to slip from his hand. He made me grab at it, nearly got it, grabbed again, missed it, then threw himself backwards, as it dropped to the ground. I heard him yell: "Mother of God!" I didn't wait to see what the others did. I rolled across the rocks, covering my face as I went. There was a bit of a slope behind me, and that helped me roll. I went like a maniac, hoping to reach a tree I knew was there. I thought if I got behind it I might have a chance. I didn't know how long this stuff took to go off, but I'd seen Ryan's expression, so I knew this was serious.

About fifteen metres from the tree I stopped rolling, got up onto my hands and knees and scuttled towards the trunk, hoping to dive for it if I could get close enough. In fact I was almost into my dive when I heard the last sound I expected.

Laughter.

Laughter? I rolled over in shock and looked back. Ryan was sitting on his haunches, having a good old giggle.

"Bloody moron," I thought furiously, getting up and dusting myself off. To my left Homer was doing the same, and Fi was emerging from behind a tree. Kevin had gone for a sprint across the clearing. He'd covered a lot of ground in a short time. Lee had jumped down a series of rocks and was standing by the creek looking up at Ryan. If looks could kill, Ryan might as well have kissed his wife and kids goodbye.

I walked slowly back. I've never been a big fan of practical jokes — they always seem kind of boy-y to me — and I sure wasn't a big fan of this one. We'd seen enough real explosions in the war — a lot more than Ryan had, I'd guarantee that — and I for one didn't need any fake ones. We had been through a terrible morning while Ryan sat under the tree getting a suntan. We were exhausted, stressed about the past and terrified about the future. I decided then that I didn't like Ryan much after all.

He wasn't too bothered though. He didn't apologise, just proceeded to scare the life out of me again by bashing the orangey-yellow explosive with his fist.

Again nothing happened. Ryan grinned at Fi. "Does that answer your question?" he asked.

Fi shrugged. "You could have just told me," she said. "I'd have believed you."

"Oh well," Ryan said. "Nothing like seeing it with your own eyes. It gets hot quickly is all."

"So does anything make it go off?" Kevin asked.

Of all of us Kevin was the one most into scientific stuff, and he was getting interested in Ryan's demonstration.

"Of course something makes it go off," Homer said. "It's a bomb, isn't it?"

Ryan dived into the pack again and pulled out something I did recognise. It was a roll of fuse wire, fifty metres long at least, and with it came a box of what could have been fifty silver .303 shells, but weren't.

Plain detonators look a lot like .303 shells. I'd last seen plain detonators when Homer and I left some behind in the ship we destroyed in Cobbler's Bay.

Ryan also had new watches for all of us, and cigarette lighters that were like those trick candles for birthday cakes: the ones that don't blow out, no matter what you do. These lighters kept their flame even when we blew hard on them. We had a bit of fun playing with them and the watches.

His last little treasure was something I hadn't seen before, but as soon as I picked it up I knew what it was: a pair of special pliers for handling explosives. Metal on one side of the jaws and plastic on the other, so you couldn't accidentally strike a spark by having metal against metal.

They would have come in handy for our attack on Cobbler's Bay.

Those pliers reminded me again that even plastic explosive was still explosive. Maybe you could safely bash the daylights out of it with a baseball bat. But at the end of the day it was designed to blow big targets into shreds that looked like tissues after they'd been through a washing machine.

For the next hour Ryan gave us an intensive course in guerilla fighting. I have to admit, he knew his stuff. It wasn't just technical information about how to use plastic explosives and grenades. It was more general: tactics and camouflage, and overall cunning. He went on and on about something called the Pimlott Principles. The only problem with the Pimlott Principles was that the guy who invented them had been killed by a hand grenade he was playing around with in his own home, in 1997. I wish Ryan hadn't told us that.

Anyway, the Pimlott Principles are that first you achieve surprise, then you build momentum and keep the enemy off-balance, and you always go for objectives that can be achieved. You have to concentrate on the enemy's centre of gravity.

"What is their centre of gravity?" Fi wanted to know.

"Cavendish."

"Cavendish?"

"Yes, and the transport system around Cavendish. It's the hub of a rail and road network, as well as being the biggest industrial centre in the state. We've bombed it but without a lot of success. Their air cover's too strong. We lose too many aircraft."

"I've never been to Cavendish," I said.

It turned out none of us had.

"Well, I believe it's a nice place," Ryan said. "I recommend you pay it a visit."

After the hours of instruction Ryan finally got around to asking the big question. I suppose by then it had been established that we'd do it. We were all taking it for granted. So I got up as soon as he popped the question. I couldn't be bothered getting into that discussion. "I'm going to check on the kids," I said. "They've been there a long time. If you're taking a vote you can put me down as a 'Yes.'"

As I walked away I could hear them start up. "How long do you think we'd have to do it for?" Fi asked. "Would you come and get us if we got hurt?" Kevin asked.

That was all I heard. I was pretty impressed by Kevin's question though, and wondered what the answer had been. Then I realised that if Ryan said "Yes," it still wouldn't mean anything. How could we trust them to come and get us in an emergency? They might be dealing with other, bigger emergencies of their own. They mightn't have any aircraft available. They mightn't think we were worth the trouble. Again.

All the same, I was curious to know his answer.

The kids were bored and restless and keen to come back. I gave them a bag of Jelly Bellies I'd brought from Ryan's supplies, admired their stories and drawings, and convinced them to stay a little longer.

I didn't hang around for long talking to them though, because I suddenly realised I had to change my vote.

"I'm voting 'No' after all," I said.

"What?" Ryan said, staring at me angrily. "What the hell are you on about?"

"I can make it 'Yes' again," I said. "No worries. There's just one little condition."

"What?" he said.

The others were listening with interest.

"You'll have to take the ferals with you."

"The ferals?" he asked.

"The kids. Gavin and the other three."

"No way," he said, looking horrified. "I can't do that."

"Well, we can't go out and harass the enemy if we're baby-sitting a bunch of children," I said, glad that the kids weren't close enough to hear me describe them like that. "And we can't leave them behind."

"There must be something else you can do," he said. "Take them to a safe place somewhere."

"You don't know this area too well, do you?" I said. "There's nowhere safe anymore. This morning proved that."

He sat there thinking. "I agree they're too young to leave alone," he said after a while. "But I can't possibly take them back."

"Why not?"

He didn't answer that, just sat there a bit longer. Suddenly he said: "Look, you're not going to like this, but how would it be if they surrendered to the authorities? If they waited a day or two until I was well gone and you were safely out of the area? I don't think it'd do any harm. They probably wouldn't get asked too many questions. People would assume they're just kids who've been living rough. And they won't be prisoners for very long, because the peace settlement'll come before they know it."

I couldn't believe my ears. Ask Gavin to surrender? I could just picture his face when we told him.

I searched for the words to explain to Ryan why they couldn't surrender. Not after all they'd been through. And they wouldn't obey us if we told them to anyway.

But I couldn't find the words, so in the end I just said: "Look, you take them in the chopper, or there are no deals. It's as simple as that."

Before he could say anything else I added: "It'll be hard

enough for us to get them into the helicopter, believe me. It'll take all the influence we've got, just to achieve that."

"That's exactly right," Homer said.

I was relieved when Homer spoke, because no-one else had said anything and I didn't know if they were going to support me.

Ryan just shook his head again. "There's got to be another solution," he said. "Taking them in the chopper is simply not on."

After a long silence from us he added: "Let's leave it for a while. We'll come back to it later."

"It's impossible for us to help you in any way unless you take them," I said firmly.

"I can't!" he said. He almost wailed it. "Sweet Mary! You don't know what you're asking."

I pressed my lips together, folded my arms, and refused to say any more.

He tried reason then.

"The helicopter takes me straight from here to a base behind enemy lines," he said. "I'm there fifteen hours and then off again, to meet another group like yours. Put yourself in my position. How can I do anything with a bunch of kids?"

"There must be people going backwards and forwards to New Zealand all the time," I guessed. "You can send them on one of those flights."

"Those flights are always packed to the gunwales."

"They're only little kids. They don't take up much space."

Ryan's shoulders slumped and he said: "Colonel Finley's going to kill me."

Now no-one said anything, and I guess Ryan realised he was on his own. As a matter of fact I didn't envy him a trip in a helicopter with that bunch of monkeys. They'd probably hijack it and make him fly to Disneyland.

The meeting seemed to be over so I went back to get the kids. When I saw them sitting there with their drawing and colouring in, what I'd done suddenly hit me. I'd just arranged to send away these little ankle-biters, and what shocked me was that I'd gotten so fond of them I didn't know how I was going to survive without them. I stood staring at Jack and Gavin in amazement, till Casey looked up and said: "What's wrong, Ellie?"

"Nothing," I mumbled.

"Has that man finished yet?"

"Yes. Yes, you go back there. I'll be along in a minute. I'm just going to the toilet. Don't pig out on all the chocolate, OK?"

Before they went though they made me admire their artwork. Even the promise of chocolate wasn't enough to stop them wanting praise and attention. To make matters worse Casey kissed me and put her arm around my neck before running off to catch up with the others.

After she'd gone I sat there feeling like I'd been rammed in the guts by a boar with a blowtorch up his backside. How had this happened? How had I become so caught up in the lives of these little tackers? One minute they'd been a hopeless nuisance, marching off on their own, getting lost, causing Darina's death; the next they had wound fifty metres of baling twine around my heart and pulled it so tight that I wasn't sure I could survive the pain of losing them. I had an intense desire to rush back to Ryan and say, "Look, I've changed my mind again, sorry, but the kids'll have to stay, and we'll make other arrangements."

I knew I couldn't do that though. A little bit of it was my pride, but most of it was knowing that the kids would be better off safe in New Zealand — safe for the first time in over a year. I knew for the sake of the war I had to do this.

Another bloody sacrifice. Sacrifices suck. But you don't achieve anything without a sacrifice. Nothing's gained unless you give something up. According to Ryan we were on the brink of bringing this horrible war to an end. If that meant letting go of the kids for a while, then I had to bite back my feelings and say goodbye.

And the cold harsh reality was that with Hell lost to us there was nowhere safe we could hide them.

I looked at the scrub without seeing it. My mind was a mess. If I'd sat in the middle of a room with speakers all around, one playing Power Without Glory, one playing Beethoven, one Slim Dusty, and one the Stratton Municipal Brass Band performing "Advance Australia Fair," then I couldn't have been more confused.

Sometimes looking at the bush, sensing its strength, knowing how little it cared about the stupid squabbles we humans got caught in, helped me cope with the chaos of this war. Not this time though. The speakers in my head were going at maximum decibels. They were playing the howl of the falling woman, the voices of the feral kids, the explosion that killed Robyn, the last words my parents said to me, Corrie's cry when she saw her house destroyed, the sounds of the gunshots when I pulled the trigger in the barracks at the airfield, the cellophane-crackling of the flames in the barn the night when Lee betrayed me. I couldn't sit still, couldn't get my mind to be peaceful. An enemy patrol could have marched past with guns ready, and I might have nodded "G'day," but I don't think I would have noticed them.

It was all very well for Ryan to drop in on us for

twenty-four hours and announce that we had to become full-time guerillas. It was easy for him. He'd get plucked out of here again early tomorrow morning. If the war did end in a matter of weeks you could be sure he'd be all right. He'd be safe. But us: we had every chance of being cold corpses in our graves by the time the last shot was fired. What Colonel Finley and Ryan were asking us to do was incredibly bloody dangerous.

If the war did end, Ryan'd be somewhere close to a fridge, and you could guarantee the fridge would be full of champagne. And Ryan would have a corkscrew. He might drink a toast to us, as our bodies rotted away somewhere in Cavendish, but that was about all we could expect.

Then I remembered you don't need corkscrews to open champagne. I gave up then. Seemed like my brain was rotting away already.

4

Nothing in the war amazed me more than the reaction of our four ferals when we told them they had to go with Ryan. Basically they went off their heads. Natalie sobbed and sobbed, and clung to Fi so hard I think she left bruises. Casey lost all her colour and turned away. She walked across to a tree trunk and leaned against it, facing into it. Her good arm went around her back as though she were hugging herself. Jack sank into a little heap on the ground. He rocked backwards and forwards, whimpering like a baby.

Gavin, he was the biggest surprise. He exploded. He ran around the clearing then grabbed a branch that was twice his size and ran straight at Homer like he wanted to kill him, using the branch as a battering ram. If Homer had stood still I think the branch would have gone right through him. Homer at least had the sense to jump aside, but Gavin just gave a little cry of frustration and tried to turn around and have another go. It didn't work, because the branch stuck between two trees and he couldn't get it out without stopping and doing it patiently. He wasn't in the mood for that. He let it go and headed for the edge of the clearing, where we had piles of stuff sitting: Ryan's pack, and more food, weapons, and bits of clothing. Before we realised what he was up to he started kicking all this stuff around like he'd gone mad. I was upset about our stuff, and then suddenly terrified about the plastic explosive. Sure the explosive was tough and all, but that tough?

I rushed towards Gavin but Ryan beat me to it, grabbing him and swinging him off his feet before I'd got halfway.

Ryan was strong, but Gavin kept him honest. He kicked and punched and struggled and bit, until Homer helped by grabbing Gavin's arms. They held him for five minutes, Gavin rigid and swearing at us in his funny throaty voice. Ryan tried to reason with him, but of course he was behind Gavin and none of us had bothered to tell Ryan that Gavin was deaf. So all his calm patient words of advice were wasted.

In the end we decided to divide and conquer. We were getting nowhere arguing with them, our group against theirs. So we made a secret agreement to split them up. Homer scored Gavin. Fi got Natalie, Lee got Jack, and I ended up with Casey.

I don't know what tactics the others used. At first I was pretty unscrupulous with Casey. I promised her anything and everything. The war would end in a couple of weeks, I'd come and get her from New Zealand, I'd bring her back here, she could stay on our farm . . . I felt my heart sink lower with each promise, wondering what would happen if I couldn't keep them, which seemed more likely than not. I pictured Casey's tragic face as she sat in front of a hostel in Wellington waiting year after year for me to turn up . . .

I guess I'd read too many V. C. Andrews novels. But I was seriously worried about the future for Casey and her friends. I didn't know how well they'd be looked after in New Zealand, with so many refugees there and everyone frantically busy. And after the war, there'd be a whole new set of problems. How on earth I'd get back in touch with her, and what I'd do then, if she hadn't found her parents, I hated to think.

Making it worse was the little voice inside me saying, "You only want her here for your sake, because you'll miss her so much. You know the best thing for Casey is to go to New Zealand, even if she doesn't know it."

The whole time I was talking Casey sat there with the most miserable expression. It was all very well for me to imagine her looking tragic while she was in New Zealand: she was doing a pretty good job right now. I sat gazing back, wondering what on earth I could do. A strange memory came into my mind. It was of me at the age of seven wanting to know where Mum was. I knew something funny was going on, because when I got home from school Dad was in the kitchen looking at recipe books, trying to work out what we could have for tea. He was acting really oddly, and when I asked where Mum was he said she'd gone away for a bit of a rest. He stuck to that story till she came home a week later. And when I asked her, she said she'd needed some time off. I guess they'd had a fight, but what really annoyed me was that they didn't tell me the truth. I might have been only seven, but I knew something complicated was happening, more complicated than having time off, or going away for a rest. And I felt that whatever it was I could understand it, I could deal with it. What I couldn't deal with was being treated like a stupid kid who had to be fed a lot of lies and double-talk.

I think if you grow up in the bush you can deal with the truth. After all, you see it all around you, all the time. I stopped believing in Santa when I was still pretty young. I couldn't believe in a guy who gave you something for nothing. You never get that when you're dealing with Mother Nature. So I took a deep breath and told Casey the truth.

"Case, I love you so much that it's like you're my own sister. If it was up to me, maybe I would just stay with you somewhere safe until the war's over, one way or another. But the thing is, we all belong to something bigger than ourselves. We belong to our families, our friends, our country, our religion . . . oh, help, I think I put those in the wrong order. Anyway, I don't think it matters what the order is. The main thing is that life isn't as simple as me saying 'I want it, I'll have it.' While my parents, and your parents, and your brother and sister, and even your guinea pigs, are prisoners, while this country's still in the hands of our enemies, we can't put ourselves first. We can't even put ourselves second. About three thousandth'd be more like it. That's why you have to go back to New Zealand. I couldn't fight this war properly, do what I have to do, if I was worrying all the time about whether you were safe or not."

I walked her back to the clearing, telling her again how good life in New Zealand was: how she could watch TV and eat McDonald's and no-one'd try to kill her. It seemed like a pretty good deal we were offering, and although she was still teary I think she'd finally accepted that it was going to happen.

Our tactics had worked fairly well. By convincing each one individually we'd robbed them of the power to resist us as a group. Natalie and Jack were red-eyed, Natalie whimpering every twenty seconds or so, and Gavin was sulky, but the fight had gone out of them.

Casey's last comment on the situation was to walk up to Ryan, kick him hard in the ankle, and walk away again. She didn't look at him again from that moment on.

We had to reorganise our packs. In our scramble to get

out of Hell we'd grabbed anything and everything, and now we had to sort ourselves out. Every item we carried had to be carefully chosen, because by the time we added some of the stuff we'd hidden in the wetlands we'd have a lot of weight. So we spent half an hour doing that while Ryan kept watch. I smiled as I watched Fi carefully rolling a jumper and stuffing it deep into her pack. For a moment I thought back, remembering how Fi had been so hopeless about packing when we first set out for Hell. Had she really brought a dressing gown? I could hardly believe it, but when I searched my memory, there it was: Fi on the top of Tailor's Stitch, looking embarrassed as we gave her a lesson in outdoor living.

This time roles were reversed: Fi caught me sneaking in the rock Lee gave me for Christmas.

"Oh you can't take that!" she said.

It was such a beautiful rock though. The size of a tennis ball, but flatter, and green or grey or shades of both, depending on the light. And on the back, down in the corner, in impossibly tiny writing, a message that I had only seen a couple of days ago: Lee's initials and mine in a tiny heart. I'd been lying on my bed when I saw it, and fair dinkum, I prickled like I was wearing a woollen blanket against my bare skin. I felt myself go red and hot. If Lee had been there at that moment he might have got lucky, for the first time in a while. He hadn't said a word about the message when he handed me the rock.

So no way was I leaving it behind. But Fi caught me by surprise and I couldn't think of anything to say. Fi just sighed and shook her head. "This is the most complicated relationship since Romeo and Juliet," she complained. "You're both hopeless. I mean, what is the big problem?

You love him. He adores you. You get together and live happily ever after. Any questions? No, of course not. That'll be ten dollars, thank you."

"It's the war," I said.

"No it's not," Fi said.

"Oh really? Well, OK Miss Smartypants, you tell me then, if you're such a big expert all of a sudden."

Without so much as pausing in her packing Fi said: "It's because you're scared that this is for real, you love him to the max, and you're running away from that. This isn't just kidding around anymore, this is serious business."

I stood there with my mouth open like a baby maggie. After a minute Fi looked up from her pack, gave a little sly grin and said: "See? I'm not as stupid as you think. I'm right, aren't I?"

"I don't think you're stupid," I said automatically, trying to buy time, but not sure that Fi was as right as she thought.

Fi, who was obviously in an extremely aggravating mood, just shrugged and started rolling up her black T-shirt.

"I was in love with Steve," I said.

"No you weren't. Oh, you liked him, and you had a crush on him, and he got you hot, but it wasn't serious love like this."

"How do you know what I feel for Lee? I never talk about it."

"No, but you talk about him. Three-quarters of your conversation is about him. Even if you're criticising him, you're still talking about him. You're obsessed with him. Sometimes I wish you'd find someone else to talk about."

I stood there sucking on the corner of my sleeping bag. It was true that I thought about Lee a lot. I was always watching him. When he appeared on the scene I'd straightaway be distracted from whatever I was doing. When I was teaching the kids about question marks and all that punctuation stuff, in our homemade bush school, I'd lose the thread as soon as Lee came walking through the trees. I'd have one eye on the kids and one eye on Lee. If he brushed a fly away I'd be wanting to know what kind of fly it was.

Was that love? I didn't know. Maybe it was. It sure was something.

A lot of the time I was extremely irritated with him, but I'd learned enough to know that irritation could be just another symptom of love.

I felt like I was on my toes more when Lee was around. If I was half asleep and he wandered in from somewhere I'd snap wide awake. Every time he said something I'd respond, either in my mind or out loud. Usually by arguing with him, but sometimes I was moved, or deeply impressed, by what he said.

Sitting there thinking about all this I told myself not to be so silly: it was the worst possible time to be getting emotionally involved again, just as we were going out to fight. I needed my full concentration to stay alive; never mind this love stuff. It was no good thinking about love as a storm of bullets came at you.

That didn't work though. Shoving my sleeping bag into the pack I sighed. You couldn't escape your feelings. I just wished I knew what my feelings were. I thought again of the two steers on the ramp going up to the abattoir killing floor. One mounting the other; the two of them still trying to mate, even though the conditions weren't exactly ideal, in more ways than one. We were on the ramp to the killing floor too, but at least we weren't steers. I ought to be grateful for that much.

I finished the packing without much thought. After all the fussing I'd been doing, now I didn't care much what went in. Fi didn't say another word, which was lucky for her.

At dusk we plodded off towards the wetlands, on our way to the helicopter rendezvous, each walking in our different ways. I felt better, knowing that here in the paddocks, in the dark, we should be safe. The kids weren't happy though. They whined and whimpered and dragged their feet, except for Gavin who insisted on coming last, and in fact came so far last that we lost sight of him from time to time. Lee and Ryan, on the other hand, were so far in front that we almost lost sight of them too. Fi was very quiet and I think scared of what was to come. Kevin made stupid jokes and talked too loudly. Homer was serious, like he was miles away.

About halfway to the island, as we paused again waiting for Gavin, Homer said to me: "I think we're heading into big trouble."

I glanced at him. He made me nervous, the way he said it.

"Why do you think that?"

He shrugged. "Male intuition."

I thought for a moment, then decided to bite. It had been a while since I'd given Homer the satisfaction. "Male intuition? Is that like the Prime Minister before the war, when he said there was no threat of invasion?"

"That's different," Homer said, suddenly losing the distant look in his eyes. "That's politicians. Male intuition is what told me you were in trouble at the airfield. It's what tells me when a girl's melting with lust for me."

"When's a girl ever melted with lust for you? You're in fantasy land."

As Gavin arrived we started off again, but I couldn't resist saying: "It was the sound of the shotgun that told you I was in trouble at the airfield. And the only girl I've seen melting for you was that old black and white milker you had for years. The one you nearly killed with Ratsak."

"You don't understand guys," Homer said. "You're a typical girl; you think you've got us figured out, and I'm here to tell you that no girl has ever figured out any guy yet."

"This is in your wide experience, huh?" I asked.

We sniped at each other a few more times, but it was too much like hard work thinking of good comeback lines against Homer, as well as trying to stay on course and keep an eye on the kids. The trouble was, with all that happening I forgot about Homer's warning.

Maybe it did influence me a bit though. Suddenly I got sick of the sloppy way we were travelling. It wasn't the right approach for this all-important trip. So I called a halt, got Ryan and Lee back, waited for Gavin, then gave them a lecture about how we had to do it. Ryan and Lee in front still, me at the rear, Homer out on the left, Kevin on the right, and Fi with the kids in the middle, and the same code as usual: if one person stopped everyone stopped. Then if it seemed safe behind you, you started moving back. It was the way Ursula and Iain taught me in Wirrawee, even if it hadn't quite worked there.

They agreed, some of them kind of sulkily, but I got

my reward when Ryan said to me: "You just beat me to it. This is good now. You guys are pretty impressive. I can see how you got your reputation."

I blushed, wanting to tell him some of the other things we'd done, but knowing that'd be a bit of a wank. I knew he was patronising us, but I was still glad he'd said it.

It was a slow way to get along. By 11.30 pm we were clear of the wetlands again, our packs creaking at the seams with grenades and plastic explosive, detonators and ammo. Just past midnight we left the track and struck out across the paddocks. We were in Burnt Hut, one of the paddocks that used to be on Mr Cooper's place but was now ours. Well, before the war they were ours. I didn't know who the new owners were.

We're not very imaginative when it comes to naming paddocks. A hundred or so years ago a boundary rider had lived in this paddock, but the only remains of his hut were a pile of burnt timber, some roofing iron, and a ceramic stove thingy that sat in the ruins looking like it was six months old.

It was easy travelling through there: the ground was reasonably soft with the recent rain, and most of it was flat.

I had the luxury of being able to look around a bit more, to think about things, and daydream. Ahead of me Casey plodded on patiently. I could see all the ferals, and Fi and Kevin and Homer, but not Ryan and Lee. Our numbers sure were about to drop dramatically. It would be a relief not having to worry about the little kids; not having to fuss over grazed knees, or listen to boring descriptions of dreams, or admire pieces of art produced in Lee's art class, or watch plays written by

Casey, produced by Casey, and starring Casey, with minor performances by the other three.

I sighed. I was going to miss those grazed knees and the long plays that seemed to lose their way halfway through and start going in circles. Speaking of which, we seemed to be drifting too far to the left. We'd be going in circles ourselves before long, if we weren't careful. I picked up my pace and made my way forward, giving Casey a little pat as I did, until I caught up with Lee.

It was hard to navigate through this section. We were too far below the ridgeline to see the moon, and the ridgeline zig-zagged all over the place, making it tricky to stick to our route. As we moved out of the cleared part of the paddock, into light scrub, things would be even tougher. Lee realised how difficult it was getting. "You take the lead," he whispered. "I'll go down the back."

"Good," I said. He'd taken the words out of my mouth.

He disappeared into the darkness behind me. Now I could only see Ryan, who was out to my left, about forty metres away and back a bit. But I knew that as long as I kept going at the right pace the others would keep me in sight.

I started out again. We weren't that far from the landing zone now. I think when you're getting close to your goal like that, something happens: you start to look ahead more. You don't notice what's at your feet so much. Your eyes search the distance, looking for the signs that you've arrived.

In a lot of situations that doesn't matter at all. In a war, when you're in the middle of enemy territory, it can matter quite a lot.

I led the way to the gate, slipped the catch off quietly and opened it. It was funny how little things suddenly caught me by surprise, making me feel desperately sad. This gate had a homemade catch to secure it: Dad had used a bit of wire off a barbed wire fence, so the chain fastened straight onto the mesh of the gate. Touching that catch again reminded me of when he had made it. It wasn't any great moment or special occasion, it was just another day in the paddocks, when a rusty bit of wire that held the gate snapped, and Dad used his pliers to make a new one.

But I could see his face so clearly, so suddenly, as he cut the wire. Maybe it was a warning. Maybe he appeared like a vision or an angel or something, to tell me to watch out, to take special care. Unfortunately I didn't think of it that way. I left the gate for Lee to close, and kept walking. There was a slight downward slope and a track that led to the area where the helicopter was meant to land, but we hardly ever used tracks these days: I pushed through some long grass to my right, getting flicked by a low-growing blackberry, then straightened up again. Looking back and to the left I saw Homer and Kevin close to each other and Ryan moving across behind me. I walked forward, probably twenty paces, and stepped onto an enemy soldier.

He was lying on the ground with his feet towards me, facing the landing area. I actually trod on his boots, which meant I lost balance for a moment, although the shock didn't help me keep my balance either. I teetered over sideways and backwards throwing out my left arm to break my fall. It was happening so fast the fear didn't have time to reach my brain. If I'd died at that instant it wouldn't have been too bad, because I hadn't felt any terror yet. That was about to change though. The soldier was scrabbling around on the ground. Whatever shock I'd got, he was getting a worse one. Thinking back on it I wonder if he'd been asleep, or at least half-asleep. He seemed so slow to move. I got my balance first but he did something totally unexpected. He was starting to stand, but then he turned as he was standing. He twisted his whole body while he was still off-balance and dived onto me. I'd thought I had another half-second yet, so he caught me by surprise.

I went flying backwards, losing my hat. I should have landed flat on the ground but my pack was in the way. It gave me a bit of leverage to push up again. It was my turn to surprise him when I did push up. It was such a little advantage, but when you're fighting for your life, even the littlest advantage is worth something. I rolled him half-over but that was as far as I could get him; he was too strong for me, and he rolled me back. The whole thing was so shocking that I couldn't think what to do. It flashed through my mind that in this whole war I'd never grappled one on one with any of the enemy. I'd wrestled with Homer quite a lot when I was younger, and that was an even match, but once he got some muscle it stopped being even. I gave up wrestling him because I had no hope.

I had no hope now, as this guy got on top of me, held me down and drew his head back. I knew what was coming: he was going to headbutt me into oblivion. I closed my eyes and tried to twist my head to the side, to avoid the full impact. It seemed a long time coming. I'd been in situations before in this war where a split second was like ten minutes. This was one of them. I waited for the blow. When it came it was weird. It was more like a flop than a full-blooded smash. I felt I was in a dream. Nothing was happening. The man's head was lying on me but his hand still gripped my arms, like barbed wire. I had a flashback to Adam in New Zealand and felt sick, worse than sick, mad and hysterical. In a frenzy of fear I fought to get him off. Then he kind of lifted off. I realised I still had my eyes shut but I didn't want to open them. His hands still hung onto my arms but they were looser now. Then they slid away like wet seaweed. I felt a great hotness on my stomach. I heard Ryan's voice saying: "Get up Ellie, quick." I still thought it was a dream but Fi was whispering too, and both my arms were being pulled.

I opened my eyes. In the moonlight I saw Fi pulling at my left arm and Ryan my right. I suddenly decided it was incredibly urgent to get to my feet. I staggered up, staggered two steps to the right, and promptly half-tripped over a body in the grass. Then at last my brain cleared and I understood everything. I wanted to vomit but swallowed it again. When Ryan muttered, "We've got to get out of here," I was the first to start retreating. The others followed. They must have been more than happy to see me come to my senses. We left the body of the soldier there in the darkness. I don't know who killed him, but I guessed it was Ryan. He had been closest.

I couldn't move freely or easily but I stumbled along, trying to make as little noise as possible. Where there was one soldier there would be others. These guys never did anything on their own.

A dark shape loomed up on my right and disappeared again: Homer.

The pace got faster and faster. We were going uphill. I didn't know why I was going in that direction, then I realised Ryan was behind me, prompting me. Maybe I'd been hearing him unconsciously.

Someone shouted, from not far away, in the darkness. Then a whistle blew. I ran even harder.

We sprinted for fifteen or twenty minutes. God it was hard, going uphill. Before I could get my second wind, assuming I ever would, I ran into Lee, who was coming from my left. The kids were behind him. They must have detoured around my battle with the soldier. They looked like startled possums, their hair all frizzy and their eyes wide open. Even Gavin looked shocked. I wondered how much of the brief fight he'd seen.

"Is this far enough?" Lee asked someone over my head.

"Yes," Ryan answered.

Lee pulled his hand out from his pack, like Little Jack Horner, and there was the radio. Ryan grabbed at it. Faster than we ever could, he had it on and tuned and was broadcasting. I had the impression he'd used them before.

Once he made contact he only needed a dozen words.

"This is Fritters. Three-nine-three. Go to backup. Go backup."

He got his confirmation, then switched off fast.

"Fritters?" I asked, as he started packing up the radio. I was shivering uncontrollably, even though it wasn't that cold.

"I eat a lot of them," he said, without a smile.

He beckoned the others in closer, although we were packed in pretty close anyway.

"The second drop zone," he said to me. "Where is it?"

"Six kilometres that way," I said, pointing.

Casey gave a little whimper, realising she had a lot more walking ahead of her.

"OK," Ryan said. "Do you all know the place? Fi? Kevin?"

They nodded; so did Homer and Lee.

"All right. Keep an eye on the little kids, so we don't lose them. Homer, you lead. Let's go."

Ryan must have been prophetic. All through this war we'd hardly lost anyone when we were in enemy territory. Now, just when he especially said to keep an eye on each other, it went wrong. I'd say we'd gone less than a kilometre when I suddenly realised I couldn't see anyone anymore. It was my fault. I had been too busy reliving the horrors of the fight with the soldier. In my mind I kept going through it, wondering how I could have handled it differently, ticking myself off for the mistakes I'd made. I should have watched more carefully, I should have thrown myself the other way, I should have found more strength when I was rolling him over . . .

In going over the old stale mistakes I distracted myself so much I made new ones. Life's always playing tricks like that. But when I realised I'd lost sight of everyone I quickened my pace, eyes searching anxiously ahead for the dark familiar shapes. I stopped thinking about the fight with the soldier.

The dark seemed to swallow me up suddenly. From being in touch with my friends, linked by a net of complicated invisible cords, I was in a world of just me and the black night and nothing else. I felt like I was in zero gravity. I got faster and faster, trying to force the darkness apart with the power of my eyes, knowing I couldn't call out, but praying that the next step would show me a friendly human silhouette.

The only silhouettes I saw were of trees. Then I started

panicking, thinking, "Oh, I went too fast, I've probably passed them, they're probably waiting back there somewhere for me."

I paused, not knowing what to do. Stay there, go back, go forward? I tried to guess what the others would do. I got angry, thinking, "How could this happen? One minute I'm going along in a group, following the others, the next minute I'm totally on my own." I took a few steps back, then realised that was hopeless; I didn't know what route Homer was taking. I could search all night and still not get anywhere near them. I had no real choice after all. I had to head for the second landing place and hope to God they'd be there.

My target was a point where two creeks met in a Y shape. One was called Breakfast Creek; the other usually flowed only in winter and didn't have a name. The helicopter was meant to land between the arms of the Y. It was no problem for me to navigate there, yet it felt strange, hurrying through the dark night, like I was the only person on Earth. I felt like I was no-one, in a world of nothing, going to a place that would be empty when I arrived.

I climbed through a fence. The wire felt cold to the touch. I straightened up, but as I did I glanced down at my stomach, and realised a huge patch of blood from the dead soldier was on my shirt. A big sticky patch around the bottom buttons. A foul taste filled my mouth. I spat it out and hurried on. A series of dim grey shapes floated across the ground in front of me. A scream rose in my throat like a column of mercury. I stopped it but couldn't cut if off completely. Something still came out, a half-sob, half-whimper. The sheep plodded away into the darkness. I clutched myself around the elbows and kept walking.

More movement ahead: a willy-willy of mist where the middle of the paddock dipped. I walked through the white strands, feeling their cold touch on my face and hands.

The big row of pine trees on the other side had been planted by my grandfather as a windbreak. They didn't seem friendly anymore. They seemed to be moving from right to left. In primary school I'd read an old legend about a field full of stones. Every hundred years they uprooted themselves and rolled down to the ocean for a drink, before returning to their homes to lie undisturbed for another century. I wondered if the trees were on the move tonight. As I got closer they stopped moving and instead towered over me, like dark grandfathers themselves, looking down sternly. It was as if they wanted to fall on me. They didn't approve of me, roaming the country at night, lost, a feral creature, caught up in hunting and killing instead of caring for the Earth. Under their shadow, nothing grew. I felt my skin prickle as I squeezed through the next fence, the barbed wire grabbing at my skin.

The mist was swirling across the paddock, more of it, moving quickly and lightly. It seemed to dance, but with no aim, like it had nowhere to go. I wondered if the helicopter would be able to land if the mist got thicker. Someone had ploughed the paddock recently but it was a heavy clay soil and they'd ploughed when it was wet, so now it was a series of corrugations, a speed hump every pace or two, real ankle-breaking stuff.

All the time I was looking and listening for the others, but there was not a trace of them. My mind threatened to get out of control again, telling me that I was the only one left, they'd all been captured or killed, or they'd simply disappeared, and for the rest of my life I'd be alone.

Maybe they wouldn't arrive at the landing site, and I'd have to explain to the helicopter crew why there was no pick-up. Maybe not even the helicopter would arrive.

In spite of the untrustworthy ground I started to jog, knowing I was getting close, and scared that there was still no sign of life, good or bad, friend or enemy.

I heard Breakfast Creek before I saw it. It was running strongly, the water churning along with plenty of energy. I had a quick drink, trying not to think of how many dead animals might be upstream. Then I backed away again, knowing I needed my ears for other things than listening to the water. I went downstream for nearly a kilometre before I saw the second creek coming in from my left. Standing there I did a full 360, hoping that from some direction or other I'd see my nine most wanted people, marching out of the darkness and mist.

There was nothing. And there was nothing I could do except wait. I sat on a damp fallen tree trunk, crossed my legs under me, and leaned back against the roots of the tree. Only then did I realise how tired I was. God, would I ever have a decent sleep again? All this high-action stuff at night. I couldn't hack it much longer. Even when I did sleep, I'd wake up half-a-dozen times — half-a-dozen minimum — thinking something was happening or I'd heard something or I was meant to be on sentry. Not a very restful way to sleep. And after that terrible fight with the soldier, when I really thought he was going to smash me in the head: every time I got a flashback to that I felt sick right through my stomach and into my bowels. His blood was still damp on my shirt. I couldn't bear to have it on me and I couldn't bring myself to wipe it off.

I woke up when Homer gave me a punch in the arm.

"Great lookout you are," he said. "Have you seen the others?"

There was an urgency in his voice that I hadn't heard too often.

"No," I said, as glad to see him as I'd ever been to see anyone. "Haven't you got them with you?"

"I've got Natalie and Jack and Fi," he said. "But I'm buggered if I know what happened to the others. One minute they were there and the next thing they were gone."

I glanced over to the creek and saw the two girls and Jack. They had spread out and were gazing back across the paddock, trying to find the rest of our group.

I glanced at my new watch.

"Twenty minutes before the helicopter," I said.

"What are we going to do if it comes and they're not here?"

"I guess we give them Natalie and Jack, and then start worrying about the others."

But I was worrying about them now.

"I haven't heard any shots."

"Me neither."

I peered into the mist and darkness. A flurry of mist looked like a person, and I gasped and moved forward and started to point, then realised it was nothing.

The twenty minutes passed with painful slowness. I hoped the helicopter would be late, but eventually I heard a faint buzzing to the east.

"It's coming," I said.

Homer nodded. He'd already heard it.

By now we'd moved into a rough semicircle, facing out looking for the missing five people. I had some vague idea that if I stared hard enough I'd bring them into view. No such luck. Behind me the buzzing got louder, the fast thrashing of the helicopter blades sounding more and more urgent. The louder it sounded the worse I sweated.

Finally it got so loud I couldn't ignore it anymore. I had to turn around and check it out. Already it was lowering into the little clearing, spot on with its navigation: not so surprising I guess, because the intersection of the creeks made it easy to find. The two thin white lights were shining, but just as I turned around they switched off. The pilot must have decided he was close enough not to need them. The chopper came slowly down the last few metres, leaning to one side, like they always seemed to do. Just as he touched he straightened it up. As he did so I heard Homer's excited yell: "Here they come!"

I looked back. And there they were. Dark shapes, big and small, running and stumbling towards us. Thank God for that. I sprinted to the chopper. The engine had been throttled back, so the noise was quite bearable. Already the hatch was open as Fi arrived with Jack and Natalie. The two kids were so shocked and overwhelmed that they just stood staring at the dark hole above their heads. A man in a flying suit was grinning down at us. "What have we got here?" he asked.

"Your first two passengers," I said, handing up Natalie. Poor Natalie looked terrified. Her big eyes stared back at me. I felt awful. "See you in New Zealand," I said optimistically, squeezing her hand as the man swung her into the cabin. I grabbed Jack. He was a lot heavier but I got him under the armpits and did the big lift. "Be good, little buddy," I said. Then he too disappeared. It seemed terrible that we couldn't say proper goodbyes. Before I could even think about that though I got grabbed from behind, two little hands latching around me like ratchets. It gave me a hell of a shock actually. I thought I was being attacked. And in a way I was. At the last second Casey had decided she wasn't going anywhere. I'd seen her running towards the helicopter just a minute before, so I hadn't expected this. I guess she was just caught up in the flow of the moment until now, when she suddenly realised what it all meant. She was hysterical with grief and fear. It was no good reasoning with her: there was no time and it wouldn't have worked anyway. I tried to prise her off but she had such a grip I couldn't do it. Ryan pulled her away, a lot less gently than I would have done, and lifted her up through the hatch. There was a dim green light from the control panel, and it made her face look diseased. She was holding out her arms to me and screaming, "Ellie, Ellie, I want to stay with you."

It was awful. She was tearing me apart. My heart was a pounding pain in my chest. For the first time I understood how those cows felt when we separated them from their calves. I didn't cry, because I thought she would get even more hysterical. One of us had to keep some self-control. I called out: "I'll come and find you, Casey," but I don't know if she heard me. And then she was gone.

I hardly noticed Ryan follow her. He said something to me but I didn't hear it. Probably "Good luck." As he hauled himself up through the hatch the chopper was already lifting. A second later it was out of my reach. Another few seconds and it was just a distant black dot.

Only then did I understand what the others were saying. They were talking to each other so urgently that I started to realise something was wrong. I heard Lee say, "I reckon he's done it deliberately."

"Well, it doesn't matter now whether he has or not," Homer said.

For a minute I still couldn't work out exactly what the problem was. Then it suddenly hit me. We'd only put three kids into the helicopter.

"We don't have time to look for him," Kevin said.

"We don't have to look for him," Homer said. He pointed.

I squinted into the darkness where he was aiming. A dark little figure was marching straight across the paddock towards us. I didn't know whether to laugh or cry. We waited in silence. I sneaked a glance at Homer. He looked furious. Then I caught Fi's eye. She was trying not to laugh. That gave me the giggles then. But the boys looked so serious that I don't think either of us dared to crack up in front of them.

Of course it wasn't funny at all. Gavin had done it again. He'd put us in a terrible situation. I think my getting the giggles was more nervous relief after the desperate sadness, the grief, of having Casey ripped out of my arms. Anyway, I managed to control myself, for the second time in a couple of minutes, and look as serious as the boys.

Gavin arrived like a soldier reporting for duty. "I got lost," he said.

It was such a joke. There was nothing any of us could do except laugh. Fi and I didn't hold back at all. Kevin rolled around like I hadn't seen for six months. Lee laughed quietly, turning away like he'd noticed some private joke that no-one else had picked up on. Homer just shook his head. He grabbed Gavin's hair and pulled it, enough to hurt. "You're a liar," he said. Gavin had taught us a few signs that he used, that were like a shorthand. I don't know whether he'd made them up or whether all deaf people used them, but one of them was a sign for lying, which was pulling your index finger across your lips. So now, when Homer said, "You're a liar," he made that signal too, to emphasise the point.

Of course Gavin was really worried by that. We'd undermined Homer completely by laughing, so Gavin just grinned cheerfully at us and ignored Homer.

"Let's go get 'em," he said. Honestly, he was hopeless.

5

WE GOT TO STRATTON WITH OUR NERVES JANGLING. I know mine were going like wind chimes in a thunderstorm. We would have been nervous enough already, but making it worse was the last piece of information Ryan gave us: "The starting signal should come in the next forty-eight hours. Be ready. Check with Headquarters twice a day, every day till you get the green. The moment the weather's right, we go."

His words snuck through my ears like little worms, parasites, then crawled into my brain, so that by the time we got to Stratton they were playing around freely in there, doing a lot of damage. I was so keyed up that if a convoy of tanks had come at me I would have charged into battle with a tennis racquet and a shaken-up bottle of Coke.

Luckily we had a bit more than tennis racquets and Coke. We'd travelled there via the wetlands, and we were loaded up.

We camped at Grandma's house. I wasn't happy about being there at all. As soon as I walked in the back door I hated it. It seemed too empty now, too much part of our past. A few of our bits and pieces were still there, but other people had visited too. A window was broken and a bottle of beer had been dropped on the kitchen floor and left to soak into the lino. Stuff had been chucked around, as though someone had searched the place.

I got less happy with every passing hour. It was like

being on the high diving board, your toes over the edge, your muscles quivering as you prepare to dive, then the coach yells: "Oh, just hold it for a couple of hours thanks, I have to go make a phone call."

You can't put adrenaline on hold.

I wished we could go back, to those happy days in Hell. Stratton seemed suffocating. Unlike Hell it wasn't safe to go into the streets. Not that Hell had a lot of streets. In fact it only had one, and that had stopped being safe in recent days. Stratton, on the other hand, had always been dangerous and was getting worse. The motorbike patrols were uglier and more frequent. Every twenty or thirty minutes they roared past the house. The only warning was a sudden blast of sound that hit your nerves and ears at about the same time. There were usually six riders in each group, and they were on big powerful bikes that I guess they'd scabbed from shops and houses. Judging by the fumes and smoke farting from the exhaust pipes I'd say they weren't being looked after too well.

Quite often they were dinking someone. Maybe they ran a taxi service on the side, I don't know.

I prowled around the house, feeling toey and itchy and restless. The others didn't seem as bad as I was. Fi curled up in a tree to do sentry, but she took one of Grandma's books called *Tangara*. Lee was in an upstairs bedroom, drawing. He didn't often let anyone see his work, but this time he gave me a glimpse. Like everything Lee did, the standard was somewhere between breathtaking and fantastic, even if the picture was kind of dark. Some people would call it sick. Satanic figures, burning babies, aliens crawling out of people's mouths, giant black beetles crushing houses as they rolled across the landscape. I wouldn't call it sick, just brilliant. Anyway, what else would he draw, after the stuff we'd seen?

Kevin and Homer and Gavin were playing Hearts, with a pack of Grandma's old cards. I was glad the two older boys were entertaining Gavin, as Gavin wasn't much into reading or drawing, and he didn't handle sitting around too well.

All these different activities looked so nice and harmless. But Lee had that dark look on his face, and Kevin jumped a metre when I dropped a glass, and the boys got into furious arguments every ten minutes about the card game. It wasn't just me. The strain on our nerves from the stuff that had happened lately — the terrible encounter with the patrol in Hell, the mad scramble to get out of there, the frightening journey to the helicopter pick-up, the loss of the three kids, the waiting for action — was working away steadily on us. The atmosphere was so terrible that Gavin must have wished he'd caught the chopper after all.

Late in the morning I went out of the house for a while. I know I shouldn't have but I couldn't stand it any longer. I was going crazy. And no-one tried to talk me out of it. Maybe they thought it was one less person to snap at — or to have snap at them.

I figured if I walked across front lawns as much as possible, keeping out of the streets, I could avoid the motorbikes.

I planned to be half an hour, and in fact I told Fi that, but just as I turned to come back I realised I was only a block from the newsagent in West Stratton, the one near the big house where I'd seen Casey and her friends playing. I'd never had a proper look in there, but I thought I might find something to read or do. Anything to take my mind off what lay ahead. And as I zig-zagged towards it, I thought I might be able to find some pens Lee could use in his drawing. I liked the idea of bringing him a present.

I pushed open the door and slipped inside, checking straightaway that no-one was following.

Quite a lot of the shop was intact. Everything around the counter, the sweets and cigarettes and pens, had gone, but the rest, where they kept the books and magazines, hadn't been disturbed much. After all, when bombs are dropping, do you really want to read about a Hollywood marriage breaking up?

I collected a couple of novels, and half-a-dozen magazines, and a bit of other stuff, then found some Crayolas that I thought Lee would appreciate, before I headed back to Grandma's.

I delivered my present, and got a grunt of thanks from Lee, and a "Where have you been?" from Fi, then climbed a tree with Homer to do the radio check. At least my little walk had succeeded in one way. For a short time I'd been able to put off thinking about this moment, this critical moment. Climbing the pine tree though, with Homer's big hairy legs above me, and the radio bumping against his hip, I had to face it: this might be the beginning of the end for us. We were about to become serious, like professional soldiers, in this horribly serious war.

I was panting when we got to a good possie, not from the effort of climbing, but from tension and fear. I tried to say something but my mouth was too dry, and I had to use a trick Andrea had taught me, scratch the underneath of my chin with the tip of my finger, to get some saliva flowing and lubricate my throat. After a few moments of that I was able to croak: "There's a patrol coming."

We waited silently. Would have been silly to wait any other way. The motorbikes snarled past, sounding louder than ever. It was like they had a mind of their own, like they were alive, like one of them might come crawling up the tree and grab my legs and drag me down. I clutched the trunk tighter and closed my eyes and prayed.

When they'd gone Homer switched on the radio and in his familiar low rumbling voice began transmitting our call code.

"Charlie Baker Foxtrot. Charlie Baker Foxtrot."

Ryan had given us a list of the possible responses we might get from New Zealand. Each of them had a separate meaning. Within a minute and a half we got one.

"Pineapples," repeated three times.

Pineapples meant: "D-Day postponed twelve hours. Give us a call some time if you're not doing anything, and we might be able to go out, catch a movie, whatever."

Well, maybe I didn't get that last bit quite right.

Anyway, like it or not, we'd got ourselves a twelve-hour reprieve.

And it was the last thing I wanted! My nerves were screaming for action. In some ways the best message would have been Wallaby, which meant D-Day post-poned indefinitely: "Abandon all plans." But that wouldn't have been the best news in the long run. The tough reality of our situation was that the best message for us now was to go straight into action. Get it over and done with.

Instead we had more of this awful waiting.

In a temper I threw myself on a bed and started reading the magazines from the newsagent, hoping to find something I could get into. It was impossible to concentrate. I turned page after page, not noticing whether I was seeing ads or articles or horoscopes or crosswords. Then suddenly I did take notice. In *Who Weekly* I was looking at a photo of a bike racer flying through the air. The bike was somersaulting over a wall with the rider somersaulting in the opposite direction. The headline said "Isle of Man Tragedy."

It gave me an idea.

Homer was on sentry so I climbed our lookout tree again to talk to him. Unfortunately I made the mistake of giving him a tractor magazine before telling him my idea, which meant that from then on I had to work extremely hard to get his attention.

I got it eventually though. "You know those motorbike patrols?" I asked.

"Motorbikes? Sure."

"And how scary they are?"

"Uh huh. Look, that's the John Deere 8300, the tracked one. Dad wanted to buy one of those before the war."

"Beautiful. Very sexy. Well, while we're waiting, waiting for the green light, I reckon we should do something with these patrols."

"Yeah, fair enough."

He still wasn't concentrating.

"I want us to start attacking the patrols."

"Attacking the patrols? Are you serious?"

At least now he was listening.

"We have to do something. I'm like an addict waiting for a fix. I'm jumping out of my skin. I think this war's made me into an action junkie."

He laughed.

"And we're all the same. We've got to do something tonight. I mean, what else is there? Go to bed early and get a good night's sleep? I don't think so. No-one's going to sleep a wink. All we have to do is work out ways to attack which won't put us in danger."

"Like, drop something on them from a rooftop?"

When Homer did catch on he was quick.

He added: "What we really need is to sabotage them and make it look like an accident."

"Yeah. That'd be better still."

We sat in the tree, talking over ideas. It was funny: there we were, held by the strong smooth white arms of the gum tree, stopping every few minutes to watch the little green and yellow birds with their black and white crests as they ripped at the bark, listening to their noisy confident babble, and working out how to kill people. Is there any comeback after a war? Can normal transmission ever resume? I didn't know the answers but I guessed not. After World War II my grandfather had come back to the old way of life, right away resuming the yearly cycle of drenching, crutching, lambing, shearing, dipping, selling. But I had no idea of what he'd really done in the war. I knew he'd gone overseas, to Italy and Malaya, that he'd been in the Artillery, firing huge guns like cannons, and every year he went to reunions with his mates. But I didn't know the answers to the big questions. Had he killed anyone? Had he seen their faces? Did he kill in cold blood? I suspect he probably had, but I never got to know him very well, so I could be wrong.

Anyway, what I'm trying to say is that there's quite a difference between strangling someone with a belt, and firing a shell into a distant patch of jungle.

When Lee came out of the house to take over sentry from Homer we included him in the discussion. Right away he added a new element. As soon as he understood what we were talking about he said: "If we kill them all they won't know if it was an accident or what." I was trying to figure out what he meant, so he added: "Like the first patrol up on Tailor's Stitch. If we set a booby trap that kills one soldier, the others will see it and know how he died. If we set a booby trap that wipes out the whole patrol, no-one need know how they died. As long as we get rid of the evidence."

Trust Lee to come up with a savage twist like that. It shocked me into silence.

The boys talked about how they could do it, but they didn't have any ideas, and neither did Fi or Kevin when they got involved. In the end we decided to try for something a bit simpler. After all, it's often the simplest things that work best.

As soon as it was dark we left the house. We had to do it early, to be back in time for the next radio check. Only Homer and Fi and I went. We decided to do it that way in case any of us were caught. It was one of those tough hard-nosed decisions we had to make so often these days. If we three were caught, Lee and Kevin would still be available to carry out Ryan's orders.

We snuck out while Lee entertained Gavin, so he wouldn't know what was going on.

What we did was to get under a diesel bus parked outside a truck depot in Brougham. We drained the sump into four plastic half-buckets, then went down the hill towards the city centre.

It was too dangerous to go all the way into town of course. We got as far as the Safeway carpark in Morris Street. The Safeway was trading again in something — clothes I think, judging by the huge pile of empty cartons out the back — but it was closed at night. We hung round for twenty minutes, watching, until Homer finally said:

"Well, there's no point sitting here waiting to be caught. We better do it and get clear."

So we used the shadows of the carpark as cover, skulking around the edges like alley cats afraid of dog packs, until we were standing under the elm tree on the side of the road. Fi had two buckets, I had the other two. When the street was quiet, we stepped out into the wide-open spaces of Morris Street. I felt very exposed. It reminded me of the first moment when I'd taken a real risk in this war: outside the Wirrawee Showground, when we realised our families were prisoners there. Then I'd darted out of the safe cover of trees, across some clear ground to the next tree. At the time I felt like I was doing something dramatic, that would change my life forever. I was right about that.

Although there was power in this part of town, they had no street lights. They had no street lights anywhere; so New Zealand bombers couldn't see them. A lot of buildings had heavy curtains over their windows, to make sure no lights showed at night. But there was a bright moon shining when we stepped onto the road, enough for me to feel we were in the middle of a footie ground with a large crowd watching. A day-night match.

We trotted up to the corner, Fi and I on opposite sides of the street. We started pouring the oil. I wanted to look around, to see if anyone was coming, but I had to discipline myself. There was no point and it would waste time.

The whole thing only took twenty seconds. I watched the oil pour out onto the warm black bitumen. It seemed to lie there invisibly, black on black. I sprinted on soft feet back to Homer and Fi.

We decided to wait a while, in the hope of seeing some fun. We waited so long I started getting cold, but when I suggested to the others that we give up, Fi, who could hear the blink of an owl's eye, said: "I think they're coming." So I shut up and huddled in closer to the smelly overflowing Dumpmaster, trying to hear what Fi had heard.

In fact I didn't hear anything until they turned into Morris Street. As usual the first sound was sudden and loud. There was the rasping roar of a half-a-dozen engines, and down the road they came. I stood up a little and peered between the cartons. Two of the soldiers nearly caught me because they unexpectedly swung off left and came burning through the carpark. I shouldn't have been surprised; after all, this was exactly the kind of stuff they did all the time. But the big rowdy black bikes both accelerated past where I was crouched. In long curves they arced away from each other. I think they were more interested in doing some freestyle riding in the wide-open spaces of the carpark than in seriously looking for enemy agents. They seemed to be having a good time, going pretty damn fast.

They were way down the other end of the carpark when I heard the chaos from the road. To my left Homer gave me a thumbs up. Beyond him Fi watched with her hands to her face. There was a gleam in her eyes though, that was just another of the confusing things I'd noticed about her during this war.

I quickly peered through the cartons again. Two bikes were down already, and stopping, as their riders struggled to their feet. A third was on its way down. Its rider was flying, helmet aiming at the footpath ten metres away, arms in front of him. His bike slid away in the other direction. The soldier spun over onto his back, bounced on the road, and skidded along until he hit the gutter with a dull clunk. Then he lay still. The bike crashed into a telegraph pole with a ripping, smashing sound that must have echoed for a dozen blocks. Homer grabbed my shoulder, giving me a hell of a shock. I hadn't realised he'd moved so close to me. He looked demented with joy. "Time to go," he hissed in my ear. I backed away. The two bikes that had been in the carpark were now out on the road, the riders rushing to help their friends. So we had clear ground behind us. We turned and ran.

We ran nearly the whole distance to my grandmother's. It was funny really, that we did that. It was like a cross-country race. At first it was natural enough, rushing to get clear before the reinforcements arrived. But even when we were far enough away to be safe, we kept running. After a couple of k's I stopped thinking about patrols and concentrated on getting my breathing right. Glancing across at Homer and Fi, on the other side of the street, I saw the same expression on their faces that I'm sure was on mine. Kind of concentrated. Panting away, skin getting paler as the streets rolled by, keeping the legs going, keeping the arms going.

But it was fun too in a way. It was the kind of dumb thing we did before the war, running for the hell of it: because we were young and didn't need an excuse to be stupid. In the old days you'd see little kids in the main street of Wirrawee holding their mum or dad's hand, and because their mum or dad was walking too boringly the kids would skip and hop and dance. It was like they had so much energy they had to work it off somehow.

We were a bit old for that but we still had some energy and there were still times when we felt like skipping or dancing. Not so many of those times lately but once in a while . . .

Back at the house we waited while Kevin and Lee did the next radio check. They came back with the same message. Pineapples. Nothing doing till tomorrow. At the earliest. Twelve hours more waiting.

We were revved up, like city kids going out to start nightclubbing at one o'clock in the morning. Lee went outside to do sentry, and Kevin came in, so we talked to him about the attack on the motorbikes. He was in a good mood: sensible and interested. He was a lot better these days.

"I want to go out again," Homer said. "But not with the oil."

"Why not?"

"Well, face it, what damage did we do? Stuffed up a few bikes, gave at least one of them a headache, but that's all."

"Do you think we only gave him a headache?" I asked. "He looked worse than that."

"No way," Homer said. "He didn't hit the gutter hard enough to do any real damage."

"But," Kevin said helpfully, "there's a place on your temple, on the corner here I think, and if you hit that it'll kill you stone cold dead straightaway. You don't have to hit it hard at all."

"He had a helmet on," I said, not liking this kind of gory detail. "OK, geniuses, if we're not going to spread oil again what can we do?"

It was actually Kevin who came up with our next idea. It was his fault that three-quarters of an hour later I found myself lying in wait on McManus Street. I was behind a tree on the west side of the street, Homer was behind a telephone box on the other side. Kevin was lurking somewhere farther along, doing nothing in particular, just being a back-up.

Two patrols had passed already but we had to let them go. I was getting bored and, although I'd said to Homer earlier that none of us would sleep tonight, I was tired now. I wandered across the street to talk to Homer. "Let's wait for one more," he said. "If it's no good we'll go back to the house."

I heard yet again the buzzing noise of a patrol. Like a big slow wasp. In this street, more open than Morris Street, you could hear them coming. These guys were still a distance away but they moved so fast sometimes, and I was on the wrong side of the road. I ended my conversation with Homer in mid-sentence and ran back to the flowering gum. I picked up my end of the wire.

A minute later they came into McManus Street. The throbbing of the engines reached me loud and clear, no longer muffled by houses or trees. But unless my ears were lying there was something different this time. They did sound more spread out. Maybe our chance had come. The first two were already halfway along the street, almost level with me. The other four were quite a way behind. I tensed even further, if that was possible. The first two passed quickly. I saw their bright red brake lights come on for the corner, before the others had even reached me. Three more came past. I knew this was it now. There was one still coming, and he was the one we wanted. He was fifty metres behind, but as the others got to the corner he accelerated, to catch up with them. Big mistake. Huge mistake. If he'd been going slowly he would have fallen more gently and probably not have done himself much damage. But a few metres before he got to us he went for it.

With a roar from the engine he powered into a wheelstand. I couldn't believe our luck. As his rear wheel reached our wire I was already grabbing my end and pulling as hard as I could. Homer was doing the same. I'd been thinking of wrapping the wire around my wrist so I could get a good grip on it. Lucky I didn't. I think I would have lost my hand. The wire whipped out of my grasp like it had been electrified. But it did the job. The guy flew through the air, almost in slow motion. The motorbike banged and slid its way towards Homer. It definitely wasn't going in slow motion. The man hit a tree with a dull thud, the same sort of sound you'd make if you hit the trunk with the back of an axe. The tree shook and leaves fell. The man dropped to the footpath and lay there sprawled out, completely lifeless. I'm not saying he was dead, I'm just saying he was totally unconscious, and he may have been dead. I don't know.

While I'd been watching this frightening sight Homer was already out of his hiding place and gathering the wire. He wasn't even looking at the rider. I was annoyed with myself that Homer was doing the work while I was being a tourist. Lucky I didn't have a camera; I'd probably have been taking photos.

So I ran to help. We had to get the wire out of the way so they would find no reason for the crash. We wanted it to be a mysterious, inexplicable accident.

The wire was in two parts. The impact had snapped it. Already I could hear the other bikes coming back. All of this had taken only five or ten seconds. The previous three bikes had just got around the bend when we tripped the last guy, so it was taking them no time to return.

"Come on," I said to Homer. I was badly scared. We had almost a hundred metres to get into safe cover. We wanted to be down a driveway and into the next block before anyone started looking.

Homer took off and I followed, trailing about ten metres of cable and trying to roll it up as I went. It caught on something behind me and nearly ripped my hand off again. I pulled fiercely, determined to make it come free, determined that the sheer strength of my willpower would get it free. No way in the world I was going to go back and get it.

Unfortunately my willpower wasn't enough. The bloody thing wouldn't move.

Like it or not, I had to do something. I started charging towards it, then saw, even in the darkness, that it had caught around a tap. I yanked it from a different direction and felt it come loose at last.

I turned and followed Homer again, reeling the wire in as I ran. He was as good as out of sight, down the end of the driveway, getting ready to climb the fence. He didn't seem worried about me. Maybe he thought I was right behind him. Maybe he didn't think about me at all. I went at that fence as though I was at the school sports day and running the last leg in the relay. A beam of light came down the driveway, lighting my legs. I understood that it was one of the headlights, either searching the driveway or a bike turning round and accidentally lighting the place up. Whichever, I felt totally exposed. I didn't know whether to stop, so that my movement didn't attract their attention, or to keep going to outrun their bullets. I kept going. I figured they'd already had heaps of time to see me.

The fence seemed an awful long way off. Homer was lying along the top of it like an old-fashioned high jumper rolling over the bar. He seemed to have realised at last that I wasn't breathing down his neck. I leapt at his outstretched arm and grabbed it, chucking the wire over into the darkness, then using my left hand to scrabble my way up the fence. I gripped the crossbar and hauled myself to the top, Homer rolling over just before me, so that I landed on top of him, in someone's garden.

"Do you think they saw you?" he panted from underneath.

"How should I know?" I said crossly.

I could feel him trembling. We couldn't take much more of this, I thought. Even simple little operations were riddled with danger now, like old timber rotten with borer.

"Where's Kevin?" Homer asked.

"Will you stop asking silly questions?"

That was probably a silly question. Anyway, Homer didn't answer it. At the same moment a slight rustling told us Kevin was coming from the next-door garden. He crouched down beside me.

"Do you two want to be left alone?" he asked.

I'd been in a bad enough mood already and he'd just made it worse.

"What happened?" I asked coldly. I disentangled myself from Homer.

Kevin must have got the message because he didn't try any more jokes.

"I think we're OK," he said. "The guy's badly hurt.

Might even be dead. They didn't see anything. And the bloke himself, if he does survive, won't remember a lot."

"Fair enough," Homer said, then, to Kevin, "do you want to go back and have another look?"

He meant, to go back and get their thrills by perving on the body of the motorbike rider.

"I'm going," I said, standing up and looking for the wire. I was disgusted with both of them.

6

After that ugly moment I can hardly believe what I did next. But then again, who said humans are meant to be smart?

I think I'll take the gutless way out and blame hormones. You can't control your feelings, just your behaviour. And sometimes you can't control your behaviour.

OK, here goes. I went to bed when we got back from the second raid on the motorbikes. It was close to three o'clock in the morning. Like I'd predicted, I couldn't sleep. I couldn't have forced my eyes shut with a pair of pliers. I was lying there thinking about my great-grandmother Tommy, then about Ryan, then about the huge unexploded bomb we'd seen cordoned off in a street on the way back to the house, then about the soldier thumping into the tree, then about the wild and sickening race down the driveway to the fence.

Each thought was so vague, they were just wisps of smoke through my brain, no beginnings and no ends, one wisping into another.

I heard Lee's voice next door, saying goodnight to Homer. Their voices rumbled away for a while but I couldn't hear the words. I think I did then drift off into a little half-sleep, my daydreams mixing in with my sleep-dreams. I had a woollen blanket over me and it was prickling my skin, but I quite liked it. I started to feel warm inside and out, then hot and restless. I knew what I wanted, and for once I couldn't be bothered analysing it or thinking about the negatives. My skin was so sensitive I could feel every little point of contact between my body and the blanket. I felt like my body was swollen, like everything was a little bigger than usual, though some parts more than others. I felt I was sailing in some sort of strange hot sea.

I knew Homer had gone when I heard him stomping downstairs, mumbling to himself, sounding like a tractor down a gully. I waited ten minutes or so, then got up, wrapped Grandma's biggest towel around me, and padded down to Lee's room. I slid the door open quietly. The room was quite dark: the only light came from the moon through the window. I liked the dim light. It laid a kind of golden touch on the carpet. Lee was sprawled across the double bed on his back and his skin looked kind of golden too. I smiled at the pyramid he'd erected under the old cotton sheet. Seemed like this wasn't going to be too difficult. I let the towel slide off me, and even the sensation of that — the fabric touching me — gave me goose pimples.

I slipped in under the sheet. I had a feeling Lee was awake and when I felt the tension of his body I knew it. I rubbed his chest.

"How would you like to find a gorgeous naked babe in your bed?" I asked.

Without opening his eyes he said: "Well, I'll settle for you in the meantime."

I bit him sharply on the shoulder and he opened his eyes then. We wrestled like animals, twisting and turning and biting and growling, like kittens or puppies. Then there was a bit of a pause while I got the condom onto Lee. He said in surprise: "Where did you get that?"

"Newsagent," I answered.

After a few minutes I got my legs around his hips and pretended I was squeezing him, but I knew I was just giving him his chance, letting him in. He was quick too. He had me pinned in a moment. I cried out so loudly I gave him a shock, but then he realised it wasn't a cry of pain. It seemed like only seconds before we were both totally out of control, in convulsions.

Then, almost straightaway, we did it again, more slowly. It was nice. I heard myself whimpering as the moment approached, and although the convulsions were slower to start they seemed to go deeper. Like the foundations of my being were stirring and shifting and rumbling. Lee sounded kind of happy too. He kissed me so fervently afterwards that I was astonished. But pleased. It was like I'd been doing him a favour, when I was really doing myself a favour. I suppose we'd done each other a favour.

I let him slip out of me, then I snuggled into him and had a proper sleep, a comfortable sleep, about the best sleep I'd had since the war started. About 7 a.m. I snuck back to my room, just to avoid the embarrassment of being busted by the others.

A couple of hours later, as Fi and I changed sentry shifts, Homer gave us a big spiel about how if we got another "Pineapples" message at lunchtime he'd organise the next motorbike attack. He was absolutely determined to try this scheme where he'd run a live electrical wire into a puddle, so a soldier who stood in it would be electrocuted. Then he'd pull the wire out, run off with it, and they'd never know how the guy died. They'd think it was another accident.

There were at least two problems with this brilliant idea. One was that a doctor would be able to tell with one glance that he'd been electrocuted, which might strike them as a bit strange. If we were stuck in Stratton for weeks, and they realised guerillas were in town, things might get a bit hot.

The second problem was that even Homer couldn't think of a way to make the rider get off his bike in the middle of a puddle. He didn't have to get off his bike, just put his foot on the ground, so he was no longer protected by his rubber tyres. Sure we could easily drag stuff onto the road to make a roadblock, and that would stop them, but it would obviously be an act of sabotage. You could try to make a roadblock seem natural, but how? Saw-marks on a tree or a telegraph pole would be a bit of a giveaway, not to mention the noise we'd make cutting it down.

So it was probably lucky that we didn't get the chance to try Homer's idea.

Instead the time came for our last big adventure together.

When we called at lunchtime, instead of a coded message we got a straightforward statement: "Call back at twenty-one hundred."

It sounded ominous — or promising, depending on which way you looked at it.

The codeword to trigger us back into action was "Oodnadatta," deliberately chosen because it didn't suggest anything too dramatic. Homer had wanted "Blast-off," but as Ryan pointed out, if anyone was listening in and heard that, they'd know something big was about to break. Even a detail like that could be important.

At 8.59 Kevin and I attempted the radio check. Reception was poor and we didn't make any contact on the first try. The standard procedure was to try again an hour later, but at ten o'clock, although we made contact, we got so much static we couldn't be sure what they were saying. That was really annoying, because it meant we had to go all the way out into the country for the third one, at eleven o'clock. There was no other way we could be sure of getting a good signal.

It also meant that if we did make contact we'd be doing it at the normal time anyway, which made the idea of the twenty-one hundred gig a bit of a joke.

Light rain was falling. We sneaked through the streets again, but relaxed when we were out in the paddocks. Walking along with my head bowed, feeling the water trickling steadily down the back of my neck, I heard Kevin say: "I think she said 'Oodnadatta' on the last call."

Suddenly the water trickling down my back turned to ice. I shivered from head to foot. I reckon my body temperature dropped ten degrees.

"Why didn't you say so before?"

"I'm not a hundred per cent sure. I'm not even fifty per cent sure."

I searched my memory of the conversation, which had had more snap, crackle and pop than a bowl of Rice Bubbles. After a minute or so I convinced myself that the woman in New Zealand had said nothing but Oodnadatta. It was like "Count to ten without thinking of a rabbit." Once someone's put a word in your head it can stay there for hours.

"Gee, I don't know," I said to Kevin.

I was pretty anxious when we set the radio up again. I couldn't stop shivering.

Now that we were away from the suburbs we got a good signal. It's that fresh clean country air. Works every time.

I couldn't believe how fast everything happened after that. It was like those sprint races at school sports days, where you do all the mucking around, taking off your trackies and getting down in the blocks and flexing your legs and the starter says, "On your marks," and you muck around some more, and then it's "Get set, BANG," one following the other before you have time to react to the first one.

The next thing you're going like mad down the track, making your legs go faster and faster, wondering how so many of the other runners can already be twenty metres in front of you.

Within a minute of making contact with New Zealand we were shutting down the radio again, staring at each other. Kevin had this terribly serious look on his face.

"Oh God," he said. "I don't know if our luck can survive this."

"We haven't been that lucky," I thought. "We've had three of our friends die already."

But I didn't say that, just hugged him. We ran, jogged and walked all the way back to Grandma's without talking again.

Of course the five of us — plus Gavin occasionally — had swapped lots of ideas about what we should do to carry out Colonel Finley's and Ryan's orders. None of our ideas were going to be easy and none were going to be safe. Plus Gavin was a major complication. We'd made a few attempts to convince him that anything he wanted to do to help us was bound to be a bad idea, but I guess we all knew that we were stuck with him now: when it came to Gavin there was no Plan B, C or D.

We also knew that he could die in the weeks ahead. I didn't let myself think much about that either, except to tell myself I would never forgive this terrible war if that happened. I mean, I wasn't going to forgive it anyway, but I didn't think I could survive myself if this cheeky little brat with no neck, built like a cane toad, ended up like Robyn or Corrie or Chris. Or Darina.

Needless to say though, when Gavin got the news that we were going into action he wasn't intimidated at all. In fact he did a series of handstands down the corridor. I thought it was amazing. The more I saw of war the less I liked it. With Gavin, who had seen some awful things and had had terrible experiences, it was like he couldn't get enough. He said he wanted to get back at the soldiers, and I'm sure that was part of the story, but I think he also was thrilled by the danger and adventure. Maybe he thought he was indestructible.

Funny, I'd once thought that about myself.

We packed carefully. Thanks to Ryan we had more weaponry than ever before. It seemed like next time we were caught there wasn't going to be much point pretending we were just innocent teenagers who'd been having a sleepover at a friend's while the war raged around us. No, this time we packed the explosives and the ammo and the weapons, knowing that trying the first of Ryan's cover stories would be a waste of time. We'd never get away with a lie that big. If things went the way Ryan had predicted, we were heading into the grand final. You can't fake it in a grand final.

By 1.30 a.m. Lee and I were ready. We sat outside the house, being lookouts waiting for the others and at the same time talking about our first target.

"I don't want this war to end," Lee said suddenly.

"You what?"

He shrugged, and looked away. I was annoyed with myself. I'd jumped on him too quickly, without waiting to see what he meant. You couldn't do that with Lee, except with sex maybe. Now I'd have to draw it out of him.

"What, are you worried about how it's going to end?"

"No, not that."

"After the war? You're worried about that?"

I realised what it would be.

"You mean with your little brothers and sisters?"

Now that the end was vaguely in sight it started to dawn on me just how it was going to be for Lee. When the war was over, he would have an awfully big gig, coping not just with the stuff the rest of us would have to confront, but more, with the fact that he didn't have parents anymore. Of course we all might have to deal with the deaths of close relatives — we didn't know yet — but with Lee it was a certainty. We could still look forward to reunions with mothers and fathers; he couldn't. Hope wasn't part of the equation of his life.

I took his hand and studied his lean brown fingers. "Have you thought about what you're going to do?"

"Nuh. How can I? How can anyone? In the last year I reckon I wouldn't have spent two seconds thinking about life after the war. Might as well think about having a holiday on Jupiter."

I began to feel afraid that he was not planning on being alive at the end of the war. It would be terribly, horribly, like Lee to go out in some huge heroic blaze of glory, hoping to say in that way what he'd never managed to say in words.

"What about your sisters and brothers?" I asked nervously, wanting to remind him of them again, to remind him of the importance of staying alive.

He broke away from me impatiently, standing up and walking across the lawn, with his hands pushed into his pockets. I thought he was going to keep walking away, but instead, when he got to the front fence he kicked the gate then turned and came back. He stood in front of me, scowling, still with his hands in his pockets.

"It's so unfair," he said angrily. "I don't want to be a parent. There are things I want to do, places I want to go. And you know what'll happen instead? I'll be stuck with the kids, packing their lunches and wiping their noses and wiping their bums. Great, isn't it? Great future. If only I had grandparents." He laughed. "'If only.' I've never trusted those words. I never thought I'd start using them. They're useless words, but right now . . . See, if I had grandparents, at least they'd take care of all that day-to-day stuff and I could get on with my music. But as it is . . ."

He kicked out again, at a tree this time. "It's like I'll go back to being a peasant, with the older kids looking after the younger kids. I'm not a peasant. And I'm too young to be a parent."

I searched my memory. "Didn't you say that the people who looked after your mother when she came to this country . . . weren't they like grandparents to you?"

"Yeah . . . yeah, that's true. I thought about them maybe helping out. But I don't know. They're pretty old now. And it's like everything else, you don't know if they're alive or dead or somewhere in between. The trouble is, you don't know anything, you can't plan anything, your whole life's sitting in the freezer."

Homer came out of the house, struggling to put on his pack as he lurched towards us. We all had huge packs, with a lot of weight, but Homer's was the hugest. Sometimes when I was handfeeding stock I'd load the ute with so many bales of hay that you could hardly see the vehicle. That's what Homer looked like when he got the pack on.

"Ready boys and girls?" he asked.

"Been ready for half an hour," Lee answered.

"Any chance you'll ever say 'girls and boys'?" I asked.

"None at all," he said cheerfully.

We had to wait twenty minutes before the other three were ready. Gavin and Fi were last. I laughed at Gavin, who zig-zagged across the lawn like an old drunk. We'd put every gram in his pack that we thought we could, without having him tip over. It was touch and go. The slightest tail breeze and he'd fall flat on his face.

"Is it too heavy?" I asked. I was teasing him really. But he didn't see me ask the question, because my face was in darkness, so I had to move a little to where he could see.

When he did work it out he just turned down his lips and shook his head. "No way," he said. "I could take more."

Little bugger. I was never going to get him to admit to any weakness. He was as tough as my father, and that's saying something. As tough as my grandmother, and that's really saying something.

Five hours later no-one was feeling too tough though. We made good time, because there was a half-moon, and that was easily enough light for us to go across country, instead of having to use roads or tracks. The range of light you got at night was amazing. It could be so black you could hold your hand in front of your face and not see it — and I did this often enough on dark nights to know what I'm talking about, especially early in the evening — or so light you could see every blade of grass and every rabbit hole you were about to put your foot into. So in one way it was good having a bit of decent light this particular night, but bad in another way because it meant we could travel at a tooth-rattling pace.

The night was humid and I was soon sweating, at the speed Homer set. I could hear Gavin grunting and puffing behind me, but typically he didn't complain, and what was more important, he kept up. No-one talked, even though there were stretches when it would have been safe enough. But not only did we need all our energy for walking, I imagine the others were doing the same as me: thinking.

Tiring stuff, thinking. Mental aerobics are always tougher than physical ones. For me anyway. I'd rather walk than think, but to do both at the same time is a big task.

Of course there was only one thing to think about. The war. What it had done to us, what it continued to do, what it would do in the future. I ranged between the extremes of light and darkness: from imagining the reunion with my beautiful parents and our return to the farm, to imagining the moment before my death as the bullet erupted from the gun. The pain as it tore into me, the terrible pain as my life spurted out and flowed away.

It seemed that life was heading towards one extreme or the other. That was another thing I'd learned about war — it was big on extremes. Maybe that's why the old men struck me as kind of excited when they talked about their wars. Sure they talked about the suffering and the fear and the grief, but you felt that underneath was a secret, and the secret was that the war was the biggest and most exciting thing in their lives.

I knew that whatever else happened I would never feel that way about this war. Maybe if no-one I knew had been killed, but this war had cost me so much that I could never think of it as exciting, or an adventure. It would always be the worst time of my life, and with all my being I longed for it to end.

Eventually I got into a kind of rhythm with my walking, and as the k's passed I was able to escape to a daydream where all my rellies survived the war and we had a big reunion at home, like the family Christmases we'd had once in a while. The sun rose, but I barely noticed it, although it was a relief not having to worry about where I put my feet.

Lee, who was leading at that stage, called a halt, and I realised with a shock that it was nearly 8 a.m.

"Where are we?" Fi whispered.

"That's the Russell Highway," Homer said, pointing down the steep slope that ran away from us.

The highway was a ribbon of black, lying across the countryside like a strap of licorice, before climbing a series of steep hills.

"It's quiet," Fi said.

"Too quiet," said Lee, the movie fanatic, always fast on the clichés.

We decided to hole up and take a rest. I was hungry, but couldn't be bothered opening my pack and searching for food. Fi said she'd do sentry, so I lurched off to a hollow full of bracken and wire grass and crawled into that. Gavin wriggled in beside me and snuggled into me like a chicken getting under its mother's wing. Inside a minute I heard his breathing slow down and in another minute I'd say he was sound asleep. I envied him. If only it was that easy for me.

But as I lay there listening to him I think I must have dozed off myself, because the next thing I knew the sun was high in the sky and it was after eleven.

It wasn't surprising that I'd woken. There'd been a dramatic change in three hours. The quiet road, stretching out lifelessly earlier in the morning, was now almost unrecognisable. The noise alone would have been enough to wake me. Vehicles growling and grunting, vehicles whining and straining as they took the bend and tackled the steep climb. I could even feel a slight vibration in the earth as the big trucks rumbled up the hill.

Beside me Gavin was still asleep and to my left I could see Fi equally out of it. But Homer's broad back was just ten metres away, and he was obviously awake, watching the convoy. I wriggled over to him, feeling sluggish and crotchety, like I usually did after these restless naps.

"Why didn't you wake me?"

"I made an executive decision. There's nothing we can do at the moment, in broad daylight. And I figured sleep could be pretty rare in the next few days."

"How long have they been going past?"

"Ten minutes. Nearly fifteen."

"God. That's a lot of vehicles."

"Yeah. There've been a few breaks but . . . Hey, have a look over there. What do you reckon that's all about?"

I looked where he was pointing, to the south-east. For a moment there was nothing, then I saw what he meant. A series of flashes lit up the sky, first a big one, then three or four little ones.

"You know what it looks like?" I said.

"Bombs?"

"Yeah, exactly. Could even be Cobbler's Bay. Wow. I guess Ryan was serious when he said there was going to be a counter-attack. D-Day."

"Fits in with this convoy. They're going flat chat. Check out that car for instance."

A large grey-green car, maybe a Fairlane, was overtaking a string of trucks. The driver sure had his foot down. Even on the blind bend at the bottom of the hill he stayed on the wrong side of the road.

"He must know the road ahead's clear, to risk overtaking like that," I said.

"Yeah. I guess they've got radio contact all the way along the convoy. So they could tell him if there's a car coming."

"It'd be great to wipe out a car like that. It'd be a general or someone. If we could get them, we might make a big difference."

This was what Ryan had talked about, by the water, as we ate Kit-Kats and avocado. "If you take out one truck, one load of fuel, one soldier, if you slow down one convoy for half an hour, who knows what difference that could make? 'For want of a nail a war was lost.' Every target's a big target. Grab any opportunity. Somewhere out there, one of our soldiers, someone you'll never meet, someone who doesn't even know you exist, will have cause to be grateful to you."

Kevin crawled over to join us. He lay watching the trucks, without a word. When I pointed out another series of flashes towards Cobbler's he just grunted.

I had given up trying to guess what Kevin might be thinking. After a while though, still staring at the convoy, he said, kind of nervously: "If we blew up that cliff with the plastics, we'd block the road big-time."

I gazed at the cliff he was talking about, feeling quite impressed. It dawned on me as I looked at it that it would be a lot safer for us to blow up a cliff than to fling ourselves at a long line of army vehicles.

But Homer said: "I don't think we'd handle that too

well. Remember, Ryan said go for stuff we know we can achieve. Like, how would we know where to put the charges, and how much to use? We could waste a lot of explosive and not have anything to show for it."

"Well, you got a better idea then?" I asked.

"I think we should have a look along the highway a bit. I know we're meant to be going at it full-on, but that doesn't mean we have to rush in and attack the first target we see."

I woke Fi and Lee up and we left Fi on sentry while Lee and I walked along the escarpment looking down over the road and Homer and Kevin went the other way. We stayed well back of course, in among the trees, but there wasn't a lot to see. The best target was a small bridge, but it wasn't much. Even if we blew it up they'd fix it in no time.

Homer and Kevin had done a bit better though. They arrived back busting with excitement.

"There's a truck stop about three k's up the road," Kevin said.

"And they all stop there," Homer added.

"For fuel," Kevin said.

"And food. And to go to the dunny."

"It's a real centre of gravity."

They were like a comedy act, doing the lines backwards and forwards.

"The trucks stop for about twenty minutes each."

"And there're guards, but if we wait till tonight, we should be able to get around them."

Kevin looked anxious when Homer said that. I was still nervous about Kevin, would always be nervous about him now, wondering if he would crack up again.

Gavin, who was awake, was following the conversation

keenly. I was never sure whether he picked up every word, but he certainly seemed to understand enough to get the sense of things. I'd tried a few times lately to lip-read, when I could see the others talking too far away for me to hear, but I couldn't work out any of it. I just did it for fun, to get a sense of what it would be like for him, but I was glad I didn't have to rely on it.

"So what are you suggesting?" Fi asked. She was pale, and her finger was tracing the scar on her chin.

Homer sat on a rock and we all drew in closer. In the short time they'd had, walking back after spying on the truck stop, he'd worked out a whole complicated plan. And ten minutes later he'd talked us into it.

7

It started pretty well. The later the night got, the more time the trucks spent at the servo. I guess everyone slows down at night. Some of the small convoys sat around for thirty or forty minutes. That was good for us, because we would have more time to sneak up on the vehicles and plant the explosive charges.

We'd set up an assembly line, back in the bush, out of sight of the road, where we spent two hours putting twenty small bombs together. Gavin organised the raw materials, Lee and I did the actual assembling, then Fi checked them, then Kevin. Homer stayed on lookout.

It wasn't difficult doing the work. If they'd been bonbons, which I'd always made for Christmas instead of buying cheap nasty ones in the shops, I'd have done them quite quickly: no sweat, no worries. These weren't any more complicated than bonbons. But knowing I was working, not with cardboard tubes and tissue-paper hats, not with handwritten jokes and homemade nougat, but with detonators and fuses and high explosive . . . well, it did make a difference. It was yes sweat, yes worries. The memory of Ryan's cute demonstration didn't mean much now. I had to stop to wipe my hands on my jeans every few minutes, and I brushed my hair out of my eyes so often that Fi got sick of it and tied my hair back with a bit of her ribbon.

After that we armed the grenades.

We finished at 2.30 in the afternoon then suddenly

realised we had hours ahead with nothing to do. It was a bit of an anticlimax after the tension of leaving Stratton and travelling through the night. Ryan had told us so strongly how we should use every minute, every situation, every opportunity, and now here we were settling back for a long lazy afternoon, getting a tan. I felt too guilty, so I said to Homer: "We should find another target."

"Yeah, I was thinking the same thing. But where do we find one? We're still fifty k's from Cavendish, easy. We're not going to find an enemy airfield behind the nearest gum tree."

I knew he was right. But I was restless. No way could I sit and wait till dark.

"Do you want to just come and check out what's over that way? It might help us tonight, if we have to do a runner."

"Oh yeah, if you want. Nice day for a walk."

Of course Gavin had to come too. He roamed ahead like a young dog, zig-zagging through the bush, following one scent then another. I mean, I think he really might have been following scents. With no hearing he probably had developed his other senses more strongly. They say blind people can tell who you are by your smell. After a couple of months without a shower, they certainly could have smelt me.

The bush was very quiet. I saw one small bird with a green-gold breast, and way ahead of us a black wallaby suddenly broke cover and bounded across the hill, head down, putting as much distance between himself and Gavin as he possibly could. I sympathised with him.

We were on an animal track, probably made by roos or foxes. It was lucky we could follow it, because all around us wire grass had taken over and was slowly covering the trees and bushes and fallen logs. It seemed a bit eerie. All the living things were shrouded, like mummies, or furniture with dust sheets. But one thing you could guarantee: there was life here, even if we didn't see it. Just as I was thinking about how ghostly it was, we passed a new hole in the ground, under a rotting stump. It looked like it had been dug that very morning. Caramel-coloured earth, little granules like sugar, forming a mound as big as Homer's boot. We stopped and peered down the hole but of course we couldn't see anything. It was too small for a rabbit though. Probably a bandicoot, or maybe an echidna. A bit farther on was a whole area of earth, about ten metres by five, that had been worked over really thoroughly by something. Homer said that definitely was an echidna.

Over the third ridge we found a different form of life. Very human. It looked ugly: raw and artificial, stretching across bush that had been there a long time.

It took us by surprise. We hadn't realised we were so close to the railway line. It shone in the afternoon sun. Stratton to Cavendish, city joined to city by a silent cold ribbon of steel. Well constructed too, and well maintained, built up with gravel and timber, neat and clean and tidy.

Gavin, little idiot, was already right down at the tracks, inspecting them with great interest. God knows how he'd survived so long in Stratton. Talk about fools rushing in. We couldn't attract his attention to get him back, so in the end I had to go down there. I pulled him away, crossly, but he wasn't bothered.

We went up the hill to where Homer was waiting. My mouth was watering, and when I saw the gleam in Homer's eyes I knew he was thinking what I was thinking.

"Let's blow it up," I said.

"Sounds good to me."

Gavin, watching our lips avidly, giggled.

"Sounds good to me too," he said.

I took a swipe at his head but he ducked away easily.

"Cheeky little brat," I said.

"Cheeky little brat," he echoed, ducking again. But this time I'd bluffed with my right arm and I got him nicely with my left. It was hard enough for me to hurt my hand, but neither of us showed any pain. That's what growing up's all about, isn't it? Not showing your pain.

Now, as we talked about blowing up truck stops and train tracks, Gavin thought his dreams had come true. To him this new world we lived in was a violent and exciting place, where you could destroy anything and not get in trouble — in fact, far from getting in trouble, you got praised. It was a long way from being yelled at on the beach when you kicked over some kid's sandcastle.

Homer and I tried to ignore him as we picked our way along the ridge above the railway line, looking down for a good place to attack. The only time we paid him any attention was when he started chucking rocks into the gully, probably hoping one of them would derail the next train. We paid him a lot of attention when he did that.

We only found one place that was a possibility. A bridge nearly a hundred metres long, across the gully. The line went underneath. We didn't go too close, as it was fairly exposed, but we went back into the bush and found the road that led to the bridge. It was bitumen, but it seemed quiet. Not the kind of road where you'd expect to find convoys, or even patrols.

"So what's the plan?" Homer asked me.

"The ideal thing would be to drop the bridge on it. But I don't know, maybe they could clean that up pretty quickly. Or we could blow up some of the tracks. But again they might be able to fix that."

"We could do both," Homer said, looking about as doubtful as I felt.

We started walking back towards the line. "Where's Gavin?" Homer asked.

"God, I don't know," I said anxiously, looking behind me as though I expected him to jump on my back.

"He's probably ripping up the tracks with his bare hands," Homer said.

"Homer, it's not funny. He can't go missing all the time. He's got to learn, before he kills the lot of us."

We walked much faster, searching the trees with our eyes. From the top of the gully we saw him easily enough. He was back down at the tracks, but he was crouching beside them. I couldn't see what he was doing.

"What's he up to?" Homer asked crossly.

Gavin saw us, but he didn't muck around like he often did these days. Instead he looked very serious. I realised he had his hand on the tracks. Then, running with incredible speed, bent close to the ground, he raced up the slope.

We both faded back into the bush as he reached us. You didn't need a huge IQ to know something was going on.

With Gavin very much in charge, waving us into position, we hid behind trees and a rock, where we could still see the railway line. Nothing happened for quite a while. I'd say, four minutes. Then, just as I thought Gavin was having us on, a strange vehicle appeared around the bend. It took me a few secs to figure out what it was. But I soon got it. One of those old-fashioned things you see in Westerns sometimes. It was the size of a little Japanese car. Two men pushed a level up and down and made it go along the tracks. Four others, two men and two women, were perched on its corners. They held automatic rifles and as the truck came towards us they peered into the bush on both sides. They were the lookouts.

Gavin must have felt the vibrations on the track. Lucky he had, because the thing was practically noiseless and I don't think we would have realised it was coming until it was right on top of us. That was another favour I owed Gavin. What with that, and the way he'd swung the door open at the Whittakers', I was losing count.

We crouched even lower. There was no chance they would see us, but you feel so naked when there're people with rifles who'd love to use them on you. I had my hand on the back of Gavin's neck, not because I thought he'd do anything stupid, just for security. I could feel his bristles stand up, like the stubble on Homer's chin. You could actually feel the goose pimples. Or maybe I was getting fingers as sensitive as his.

The truck continued silently on its way, the two blokes in the middle still pumping, until it had gone under the bridge and disappeared around the next bend.

I felt Gavin slowly relaxing, but we still didn't say anything for a few minutes. Then we eased ourselves up from our cramped positions.

"Nice little surprise," Homer grunted. "You're not safe anywhere these days."

We faced towards the tracks and I'll be damned if Gavin didn't do it again. Without even going down to the line. A look of intense concentration came over his face, like a baby pooing its nappy. He held up one hand, then pointed towards the bend again, from where the little truck had come. A moment later Homer and I heard it.

But Gavin had beaten us by a good five or ten seconds. I don't know how. He must have felt the vibrations in the air. I can't explain it any other way.

There was a slow chugging, then a big diesel locomotive came around the bend. Not just a locomotive either. It pulled a row of trucks and it was a long row.

We ducked down again, but this time I made sure I got a good view. I needed to see this. The noise got louder as the engine hauled its way past. It was a beautiful thing, a bit greasy and streaked, but so graceful, so powerful. Then followed the carriages. I started counting, like a kid at a level crossing. "Five, six, seven, eight." They were all crammed with soldiers. "Eleven, twelve, thirteen, fourteen." A couple of soldiers lay on the roof of each carriage, rifles ready, gazing around looking for people like us. "Seventeen, eighteen, nineteen." Then the guard's van, which seemed to be packed with more soldiers. Ryan had been right. Big stuff was happening. That train must have held a thousand soldiers. They were peering out of windows, standing in corridors. One was even perched on the couplings between two carriages taking a leak, a sight that had Gavin nudging me and giggling, and which I tried to ignore.

"Wow," I said to Homer.

"What a target," he said.

"Let's blow them up," said Gavin.

"Do you reckon it's going to Cavendish?" I asked Homer.

"Well, yeah, obviously, right now. But that doesn't mean they'll stay there."

We went back to the other three, thinking hard all the way. If troops were being moved around the country in their thousands it was more evidence that some heavy action was going down. I didn't know where the New Zealanders had launched their attack — Ryan wouldn't tell us a syllable more than he had to — but wherever it was, they'd triggered a huge reaction. I hadn't seen this much movement since taking the lid off a grain bin in the last mouse plague. The bin had rusted through at the bottom and the mice had taken full advantage.

Fi and Lee and Kevin were stressing out big-time at us for being away so long. Kevin started it, which was just like his style. "Where the hell have you three been?" It was like being nagged by your parents. "You've been hours. No-one had a clue where you were."

All he needed to add was "Your mother and I have been worried sick about you," and I would have felt right back at home.

But the other two were equally annoyed. "Honestly," Fi said, "as if we weren't stressed enough already. How were we supposed to guess where you were? For all we knew you could have been caught."

The one I hated hearing it from most was Lee. I didn't want Lee telling me I'd done something dumb. I wanted him telling me, "Good one, El, you're a legend." Instead he said: "We can't afford this kind of goofing off. We've got to be disciplined twenty-four hours a day."

That was a bit rich coming from him. But it was true, we had been away a long time. We hadn't told them which direction we were going, which was slack.

They were so worked up about the attack on the truck stop that they were half off their heads. They would have been stressing about a broken shoelace, let alone us going missing for most of the afternoon. So we had to stand there feeling guilty while they got stuck into us.

Once they'd got that out of their systems we told them

about the train line. They were interested, and even impressed, but they were so focused on the truck stop that they immediately forced us back to that. The best I could get was a lot of mumbles about how "We can have a look at it after this, if we get a chance."

We went over the plan of attack again and again, working out all kinds of possibilities. If they did this, we'd do that; if this happened, we'd make that happen; if they went this way we'd go that way.

The trouble was we had too much detail, too many plans. We could have done with three weeks to memorise them, instead of a couple of hours.

The other trouble was that we didn't give much thought to escape routes. The only plan Lee and Kevin and Fi had was to race back to our packs and get the hell out of the place. But we made them agree that after the petrol station we'd head to the railway, and use any remaining charges on the bridge and the tracks. It was another enemy centre of gravity.

As people started to get mentally tired the energy levels dropped. Without much more talk they started drifting away to have a rest, or get something to eat.

Lee and I sat down and made some charges for the bridge. We were getting quite good at it. With each new one we took less time. By the end our hands smelt like old cheddar, and felt cheesy too. I don't know what plastic explosive is made from — plastic, I guess — but I wouldn't be surprised if it was from something they'd found in the basement of a Kraft factory.

We used most of Ryan's precious explosives, but we had a good little arsenal, and I felt confident that we'd do some damage before the night was out.

I went for a walk to clear my brain. I had a headache

from the tension of working on the charges. Kevin was doing lookout and at least this time I told him the general direction I was going. I mooched along feeling suddenly depressed. I hated the way these moods crept up on me with no warning. Of course it was no great surprise that I'd be depressed, when we were about to start a night of violence that might end in our deaths. It'd be a bit strange if I was feeling hysterically happy. But I don't know if my feelings were really to do with what lay ahead. I wasn't actually thinking about the servo or the train tracks. I was thinking about other stuff: the days before the war, where my parents were now and what they might be doing, the horrible awful empty way I missed Corrie and Robyn.

The last news I'd had of my parents was when Lee told me my father was still under guard in a pavilion at the Wirrawee Showground, and my mother was working as a servant in the Holloway area somewhere. That was such a long time ago. They could be anywhere now. And even if they were at Wirrawee and Holloway, I couldn't be farther away, fifty kilometres or more from Cavendish. It was in totally the wrong direction.

I was walking pretty slowly and I'd gone up the hill only a short way when I came across a sight that stopped me in my tracks. Funny, I don't know why it took me so completely by surprise. After all, Homer and Fi had been interested in each other since the first day of this war, even a few days before that. They'd started quite passionately, then cooled off as we got more absorbed by the battle to stay alive and found ourselves with less time or energy for relationships.

But something had set it flaring again now. Flaring? They'd poured a tank of petrol on it then chucked in a detonator. It was bigger than the fire at Wirrawee Airfield.

They were sitting — half lying — on a soft green slope, kissing so hard they were in danger of reincarnating as leeches. They still had their clothes on, but it was kind of like they didn't. Homer's hands were all over Fi, and I could see the whites of her knuckles as she pulled him farther and farther into her. For a moment I was so fascinated I couldn't turn away. Then I came to my senses and quickly went off to the left, down a steep gully. I was embarrassed it had taken me that long. I felt like a voyeur.

But embarrassment was only one of a whole lot of feelings squeezing my insides. I shouldn't have been so disturbed but I was. I felt hot and giddy. I didn't know which emotion to have, which one to let out first. I picked up a stick and started bashing the trees, not caring how much noise I made. My face burned. I just hoped I didn't meet the others. I didn't want them to see me like this; didn't want to have to talk to Lee or anyone else.

I sat on a rock and stared dumbly at a big tree trunk that had grown through a hole in a rock overhang. Why was I feeling such a mess? Or to go back to basics, what was I feeling anyway? Come on, Ellie, get a grip, what the hell is this electric blender in your stomach, churning up your intestines? You haven't actually been ruptured, so what is going on? Think about it. Work it out. List your emotions in order of importance from one to ten. Attach an extra sheet if insufficient paper is provided.

OK, there was jealousy. No, not jealousy, envy. Well, maybe halfway between the two. I was pretty sure I didn't love Homer, not in that way, but I liked him in truckfuls. I certainly didn't want to share him, not even with Fi. And to make things worse, I didn't want to share Fi either.

Especially with a boy. I liked the way it had always been: me getting involved big-time with Steve then Lee, plus a couple of other minor crushes along the way, and Fi liking boys from a distance. That way I could go and tell her all the stuff I was doing and she could tell me what I should do, and who she was rapt in, and we didn't get in each other's way. That suited me fine, and I didn't want it to change.

Gradually I started to realise that envy accounted for most of what I was feeling. The rest of it was called loneliness. I was a bit obsessed with Lee, like Fi had said, but we still didn't have the kind of relationship I wanted. There were great moments, moments of real friendship, moments of sex, moments of caring and looking out for each other. But it wasn't on a full-time enough basis for me. We kissed occasionally, we held hands, we went for walks and talked about our lives, we'd even had sex the night before last, but we didn't have the intensity of those days when we were hiding in Robyn's music teacher's house. So often I longed to be hugged by a guy, to feel strong bony arms holding me, to feel rough skin on my face, to smell that guy smell. At most of those times Lee was nowhere to be found, or he was in one of those moods when you knew it wasn't a good idea to approach him.

Seeing Homer and Fi brought it home to me that I was missing something, something I never wanted to be without. I like guys and I like being around them. I feel more complete if I'm with someone. I wanted a relationship that was closer to a hundred per cent than forty per cent.

When they drag me off to the nursing home I'm going to demand a twin room, in the co-ed wing.

I didn't bother to search for any other emotions; the ones I'd identified already were more than enough. I trudged back to the place where we'd dumped our stuff. Lee and Gavin were on sentry, watching the road. Kevin was asleep, snoring like a steamroller.

I told Lee and Gavin that I'd do sentry. It suited my mood. I still didn't want to talk to anyone — especially Lee — but I didn't want to sit around feeling sorry for myself. Watching the road took full concentration, because there was so much happening, and we were so dangerously close to it. If one soldier decided to walk up the hill to take a crap, we'd have to react fast, and withdraw silently towards the train tracks.

The trouble was that I couldn't concentrate. I sat there wondering about Homer and Fi. Was this the first time? Had they been kissing like that for days or weeks or months? How come they hadn't told me about it? Didn't they trust me? Did Fi enjoy it? Would we still be friends? And the big question, that I guess you always wonder about until your friends tell you, how far had they gone?

All in all I wasn't much good as a sentry.

The other thing distracting me, apart from my own stirred-up thoughts and feelings, was the occasional rumble in the direction of the coast. It kind of echoed Kevin's snoring. Whatever was going on over there, it was big. Gradually a line of black seeped along the horizon, like God had taken a big Texta and tried to draw a straight line along the edge, only he was a bit old and doddery and the pen kept wobbling.

I just hoped the New Zealanders were blowing stuff up, and I hoped they were winning.

I was worried that the convoys would eventually stop using the road, that the enemy commanders would have moved all the soldiers they wanted, and our attack would come too late. And there were times when the road got very quiet. At one stage there was no movement for half an hour. But right on dusk another long line of trucks came past, this time with a couple of tanks. We hadn't seen many tanks in this war. They looked like crocodiles, not in their shape, but in their tough hides and the slow nasty way they rolled along. Behind me, Lee, whom I hadn't even heard approach, said: "I hope they don't have some rule that the convoys after dark get tanks."

I hadn't thought of that. It gave me a shock. Made my tummy rumble for about two minutes.

Fi and Homer came back, walking way apart, as though they hardly knew each other. In my envy even that annoyed me. I felt they were pretending about their relationship, instead of talking to me about it, sharing it with me, like in the past. I was cranky and unpleasant to them both, and even to Lee. In fact the only ones I was nice to were Kevin, which must have surprised him, and Gavin.

Unlike other attacks we couldn't wait till three or four a.m. to make our move. Now that the big battles were on we couldn't afford luxuries like that. We had to go as soon as it got dark. That doubled the danger: not just doubled it, trebled, quadrupled, whatever the next one is. Quintupled. But for all our good intentions it was nine o'clock before we started. It was probably dark enough before then, but we kept hesitating, putting it off, imagining we could still see a bit of light along the horizon. It reminded me of being with Iain and Ursula on Tailor's Stitch, ages ago.

Finally the moment came. "Let's do it," said Homer, picking up his daypack. Like kids on a school excursion we grabbed our stuff and followed him down the hill. I was suddenly too tired to resent the fact that Homer was telling us what to do yet again.

At least we didn't have heavy loads; we'd hidden our main packs, to collect after the attack.

I found myself side by side with Lee and suddenly felt an urgent desire to connect with him, to weld myself to him. It was the complete opposite of the way I'd been a couple of hours before. I grabbed his hand and squeezed it tight. And when I say tight, I mean I drew blood. Well, nearly.

I was surprised at my feelings but I don't think Lee was. He just made a face at me. He didn't actually say, "Are you in a state of total terror?" but he knew what was going on. My insides were liquid from the neck down. I could almost hear them sloshing around.

I kept my grip on Lee's hand until we were fifty metres from the road. Then I let go, wondering when I would get to hold it again. And if I ever did, would it be warm and comforting, like now? Or would it be cold and clammy, lying lifeless in mine?

We said goodbye to Kevin. This was one part of our plan that made me incredibly nervous. The others seemed too willing to forgive and forget. I was happy to forgive. But forgetting, that was the hard part. As long as our plans involved Kevin I was going to keep seeing in my mind's eye the blubbering wreck at the airfield. When we needed five people that day, we only had four. No, worse, we only had three, or two, because Kevin wasn't just a zero back then, he was a minus number.

Maybe that's too harsh, but that's the way I felt, and to me Kevin had to prove himself again. Just being more involved and friendly wasn't any kind of proof that in an emergency he'd stand tall and straight and strong. I thought we were a bit mad to put our trust in him.

Anyway, it was too late to say or do anything. I kissed

him, same as Fi, but feeling like a hypocrite, giving a Judas kiss. And I waved as he hurried away. At least he looked focused. I had to hope that was enough.

We paralleled the road for a bit, till we could cross at a point we'd chosen earlier, between a bend to the right and a bend to the left. One by one we scuttled over the bitumen. I felt very exposed. We should be safe: we should hear any convoy or patrol as it approached, but I still three-quarters expected a bullet between my shoulder blades.

There was no bullet, for me or anyone else. When we were safely in the bush again we set off in single file, keeping a good distance apart. We were now only a k at the most from the servo. My nerves were screwed up, like a Sumo wrestler had taken a wrench and put all his strength into tightening them. The trees got thinner as we approached the outbuildings. We spread out to find cover. It was safer that way. Made it harder for a soldier with an automatic weapon to kill all of us at once.

Carefully we picked our way through the ghost gums. They were well named. There was something eerie about the way their white trunks shone at nighttime. Never more than this night. My heart throbbed painfully as I saw the dark outlines of the main buildings. They had lights on inside, but like most places they had heavy curtains to stop those pesky New Zealand Air Force bombers seeing the lights and dropping little Valentines down their chimneys.

Well, heavy curtains weren't going to stop us.

We were coming in towards the back corner of the service station. I saw and smelt a Dumpmaster. There was the usual collection of litter you find round the back of those places. A couple of 44s, a derelict car, a few rusting engines, and an overhead tank that had been abandoned a long time ago.

Unfortunately the toilets were there too. I could see a shabby fibro building with a battered white door. Someone had left the door slightly open, and the light on inside. It wasn't much light, probably only forty watts, but enough to see the little black man on the door with his top hat and walking stick.

Kind of weird when you think about it: a guy looking so elegant and dressed up, on the door of such a cruddy building.

We got a couple of steps closer, then stopped and crouched low as a bloke came round the corner and disappeared into the dunny.

I knew there was no danger from him so I huddled down and hugged myself while we waited. "No-one else is going to hug me," I thought, being a bit pathetic, but remembering again Fi and Homer passionately kissing each other. To stop myself getting too gloomy I went over the plans again. It seemed neat enough, the way we'd worked it out. Trouble was, it didn't allow for things like soldiers acting unpredictably: doing their jobs extra well for example, or going for a bushwalk. It certainly didn't allow for one of us failing.

The bloke finished in the toilet and went back to the main building. Without needing a signal we started moving again.

We were closer to the servo than I would have liked, but there was no choice. The bush behind the place was too thick and the hill too steep. It would have taken ages to get up there and down again.

Just after ten o'clock we arrived, at the other back corner.

Stretching away beyond us was the carpark, which looked like it had been extended since the start of the war. Guess these convoys were keeping them busy. They might have been a regular event. We should have paid this place a visit a long time ago. To my right was a billboard advertising KFC, but it looked tattered and weatherbeaten now. The bowsers were around the corner, out of my sight.

After the tension I'd been through to reach this point, it would have been a relief to go straight into action. No such luck. If it took all night we had to wait for a convoy. There wasn't much value attacking an empty truck stop.

Homer and Fi and Gavin said goodbye. Somehow here, so close to the danger, it didn't seem appropriate to embrace or kiss or whisper nice comments to each other. I patted Gavin on the head and mouthed at him: "Be careful. Take care." He just shrugged and made a face. I don't know if he even understood what I'd said. They moved away so quickly that I got a shock at how fast they disappeared. They went into darkness, like it was a kind of death. They were swallowed up.

I looked at Lee. He seemed affected too. Maybe we were both wondering if we'd see them again in this life. He touched my elbow and we moved farther down the slope. We found a hollow where we could see the bowsers. I crouched behind a bottlebrush, shoved my hands into my armpits and waited. My rifle was on the ground beside me and my daypack of explosives on the other side. For this little effort I was useless without these weapons. In fact I was only needed here as the means to activate them. Tonight I had no real value as a human being.

I amused myself by trying to remember the Pimlott Principles that Ryan had raved on about. We were certainly using surprise. And if we could go on and get the railway line, that would be momentum: keeping the enemy off-balance. And both were centres of gravity.

I couldn't remember the other Pimlott Principle, but trying to remember it gave me something to think about, until nearly 10.45. Then a low hum in the distance told me that a convoy was approaching.

Our time had come.

At the same time I finally remembered the other Pimlott Principle. Go for targets that are achievable. I gulped, with a dry mouth. I could only hope we'd got that one right.

8

When I tried to stand I was alarmed to realise how much I'd stiffened up. I could hardly move. This wasn't a good start. I desperately stretched my arms and legs, as much as I could without doing a full range of aerobic exercises behind the bottlebrush.

I soon realised though that we were way too early. We had to wait for most of the trucks to refuel before we could do anything. So in spite of my cramped muscles I crouched again, and tried to keep my limbs in working order.

I didn't need to look to tell what was happening. The sounds were enough. Tough on Gavin, who was with Homer and Fi, and who relied on his eyes quite a lot.

The trucks came pouring in. It got noisy. Engines revving, people shouting orders or instructions or abuse, horns blaring. There was no sign of tanks, but there were quite a few cars.

Our first problem was unexpected though. First one man, then another, then another, then another, came past, all with the same idea: to get a bit of relief after being jolted around in their trucks for hours.

The constant hissing and splashing, and the bitter smell, got unpleasant after a while. Worse, it made me want to do the same thing, and I found myself squirming, wishing I could duck into the bushes.

Lee whispered: "Maybe we should get a couple of them," meaning the men using the lavatory.

"But what would we do with them then?" I whispered back. Funny, after all this time, I still hated to think of killing anyone in cold blood.

Lee didn't answer.

The action around the bowsers continued without a break. I counted fifteen trucks rolling towards their parking area one by one, after they filled their tanks. I hoped they would meet Homer and Gavin and Fi there. Then at last there was a break in the toilet action. Without needing to tell each other we both got up at the same time and darted through the shadows, in and out of Dumpmasters and piles of drums and stacks of old tyres, towards the parking area.

There was no sign that Kevin was doing his job. I knew it was tricky for him, because we had no accurate way of working out the timing, but even so, by now he should have struck. I wished, not for the first time in this war, that I had followed my gut instinct and told Homer we shouldn't use him. But as much as anything, I hoped for Kevin's sake that nothing had gone seriously wrong. It would have been bad enough if the charge hadn't gone off, or hadn't been strong enough, but what would that matter compared to him being hurt or captured or killed?

Or — and this was the real issue for me — compared to him losing his nerve. What if he was now curled up in a ditch sobbing and shaking and wetting himself with fear?

I wriggled again. At least this way I was getting some exercise.

Then the lights went out.

Even with the curtains covering the windows it was instantly noticeable. I hadn't realised how much light there had been over the whole place until suddenly there was none. And I heard the bowsers die. With a kind of "Urrrrr" noise they stopped pumping. Kevin had come good after all.

I struggled to my feet and took a step out from behind my bottlebrush. Lee did the same, but on the other side. God it was dark. There'd been just a few calls and cries when the power first went but now it was getting noisy. I heard one voice start to emerge above the others, a guy who sounded like he was in charge. The way he talked, I think he was quite efficient, which was bad news for us. But we had to ignore him and get to work. Getting a good grip on the pack of explosive charges and the rifle, I crept along the side of the building. I saw a couple of dark shapes go past, heading in the other direction. It made me realise how visible I must be. I glanced across at Lee. He was farther towards the shadows and a bit harder to see.

Already we were closing in on our target. I was startled to see how near we were. We were heading for the little parking area for cars, at the other end of the servo to the truck section. I strained my eyes trying to see how many cars were in there. I could see some dull reflections, off metal and glass, and thought there were maybe three or four.

Lee loomed up beside me. He used his shoulder to push me towards the left, and I let him do it, knowing he must have a reason.

He did. Somehow he'd seen one car a little away from the others. That's what we needed. A bit of privacy.

We circled around behind it, moving as fast as we dared. I felt the fear rise inside me, so much of it that I put my spare hand on my stomach to try to keep it down. We came up behind the car, Lee on the right and me on the left. Through the back windscreen it looked like no-one was inside. I confirmed it by checking through the side windows. Same result. It didn't surprise me. Anyone in his right mind wouldn't sit inside a car during a blackout in the middle of a war zone.

We kept moving forward. At last I saw Lee's target. A soldier was right ahead, his hand cupped over his eyes: that familiar gesture of someone searching darkness, trying to see better. We'd agreed before that we'd go for a pair of soldiers, that we needed two. That's what we'd said in the easy peace of the bush, up on the hill, when we'd been working this out. Now it felt a bit different. We'd settle for one, no worries, and sort out our next move afterwards. I glanced across, caught Lee's eye, pointed to myself, made a series of beating gestures with my fist, pointed to Lee and made little tiptoeing motions. He nodded and I had to hope he'd got the message.

I dropped my pack and rifle, and we both sneaked up on the man, me still on the left, not sure when to start making some noise, when to act as the decoy. The timing was kind of crucial. My life depended on it.

I was maybe a dozen steps from him when it was decided for me, because I made a noise without meaning it. The side of my boot scraped on a split in the bitumen. The man turned around quite slowly, as if he was curious but not yet suspicious. I started moving faster, hoping Lee would move faster still. The man reacted then. With a 360-degree leap he jumped and spun onto the bonnet of the car. I had no problem seeing his next move. A flying leap straight at me. Already his legs were tensing, about to drive off the metal and into my guts.

I was completely out of my depth. I wouldn't have the slightest idea how to do that Jackie Chan stuff. Might as well ask me to do open heart surgery on a bandicoot. I had my rifle, but I didn't dare fire. I was relying on Lee. Maybe that was lucky, because I glanced across, beyond the man on the bonnet, to see if Lee was going to do anything in the near future. I guess it was like those old movies where the goodie pretends to see cops coming up behind the baddie, to trick the baddie into turning around. Only this was no trick. And I think the soldier realised it. Maybe it was because I did it so unconsciously, kind of naturally, like I wasn't even thinking of how it would look to him.

So he drove off the bonnet, straight at me, but with a little less momentum, because he hesitated for a fraction of a second as he half-glanced backwards. And that meant Lee, diving after him, got a hold of his foot and tried to twist him in mid-air. The man landed on top of me, still twisting around. I fell, and then Lee came slithering after the soldier and he landed on top of me too.

It was a shambles. The man fought so desperately. It was like when you're marking steers that are getting pretty big, and you don't get a proper grip on one of them, and you know it's more than your life is worth to let go, but at the same time you know that by hanging on you're likely to get your face kicked in. And worse.

This was more like trying to hold down a tiger. The three of us were writhing around, and although two against one should have been enough, I began to panic and think he was going to get away. He was hitting me so hard that I felt I couldn't hold on any longer. Then he got a hand up to my face and scratched my left cheek with sharp fingernails. He dug so deep. I screeched with the pain, feeling like half my face had been torn away. A moment later Lee hit him with the butt of his rifle. I felt the shock of the impact right through my body. But the arms suddenly went limp and fell away.

Trying not to sob, trying to hold myself together, ignoring the stinging in my face and the bruises to my body, I staggered up. Already Lee had fallen on the body and was tugging off his tunic. I picked up the cap, which had rolled away in the dust, and then helped Lee get the jacket off.

"What do you think we should do?" I asked. "I can't go through this again."

"No," he agreed. "And there isn't time. If I wear the jacket and you wear the shirt, it should be enough."

I didn't know what to think. It seemed a huge risk. But there wasn't a choice.

"All right," I muttered.

It was so difficult to get the shirt off. The jacket had been easy, by comparison, even if his floppy, heavy arms did keep getting in the way. Lee got the tie undone while I worked on the buttons. It was a revolting job. I think the guy was dead, although I kept telling myself he wasn't. A couple of times my hands touched his skin, which made me feel nauseous. He felt sticky, clammy, like he was still sweating. Almost worse was having to put my arms through the sleeves. I kept my T-shirt on, to save time, and I was glad I had, when I felt how my skin crawled with the touch of the damp cotton.

Lee gave me the tie, but I had to get him to tie it. That's one thing I've never learned. Then Lee pulled on the jacket. With the cap on his head he did look pretty authentic. I just hoped I looked the same.

Neither of us discussed getting the soldier's trousers. We both would have heaved big-time if we'd so much as tried. Besides, I'd quite often seen soldiers with jeans and scraps of uniform. In fact it wasn't often you saw one with a full uniform.

I had no idea how much time we'd wasted, but it seemed like a hell of a lot. Without any more conversation I grabbed my pack and rifle, and we headed out fast towards the front of the truck stop.

It was like coming from a suburb into the city. We'd been out in the suburbs, in the little carpark. Now we stepped into the CBD.

We'd worked out that the trucks would turn on their parking lights. We weren't too bothered by that. We knew they wouldn't risk turning on full headlights. But we didn't realise how much light parkers would create. And stupidly, we hadn't thought of torches. There must have been a dozen of those. All in all there was a hell of a lot more light than I would have liked.

We were coming around the front of the main building. I kept close to the buildings and at the same time stayed in Lee's shadow. It was quite a balancing act. I needed a good choreographer. If I ever got back to school, back to my drama class, this would make a fantastic dance routine. But Lee's shadow kept me out of the range of most of the parking lights. It didn't save me from the torches though. Some of them were waving around out of control, like the people holding them were way over .05. I'm not sure what was going on. I'd say from their voices that they were definitely nervous. They probably suspected sabotage. They'd be mad if they didn't. A couple of soldiers holding rifles ran past me at a good speed. Maybe they'd been posted to do sentry. A torch-beam suddenly ran across my face. It seemed to burn. I felt my skin go red where the light touched me. It was like some really sleazy guy had stroked my cheek with the back of his hand.

I kept walking. It was more than my life was worth to hesitate. The light seemed to linger on my face. My eyes half closed, expecting the challenge, the shout of discovery. It didn't come, and a moment later the beam of light wandered off again.

I tried to get even closer to Lee's shadow. I had to, with him in the tunic and cap. He had to ride shotgun for me. But as we approached the front of the truck stop the time came for tough decisions. I couldn't skulk in the shadows anymore, scuttling along like a rat.

I veered out from the wall. Already we were nearly at the corner. In another moment we would reach it and turn right, into the main refuelling area. What would we see? Would they notice us? What would happen if they somehow fixed the power supply when we were right out in the middle, dropping explosive charges into their fuel tanks? I gripped my pack tighter and turned the corner.

My mouth was dry as a dam in a drought. And I felt so strange in the unfamiliar shirt. Uncomfortable. Not only because it was a foreign uniform, but because they were the clothes of a dead man. I didn't hesitate any more though. I was so set on doing the job that I didn't think of hesitating. Anyway, hesitation would have been fatal. We had to act with total confidence.

We kept walking, but now, as we moved out from the line of the buildings, I scanned the ground, searching in the darkness for the little metal lid. I didn't know where it would be. We'd all compared notes, back in the bush, trying to remember where service stations kept the covers for their underground tanks, but no-one really had a clue.

"Out of the line of the bowsers," we all thought. We based that idea on the fact that when tankers arrived at service stations to refuel them, they seemed to park a bit away from the bowser area. That was the best evidence we could come up with. Suddenly it didn't seem like much.

Nevertheless we kept walking. There was nothing else to do. I felt like I was in a music video, with spotlights and noises all around. As if things weren't tough enough already, we had to find the lid fast, before Homer and Fi made their mark. The timing on this gig was crucial, but so much was up to chance.

I heard a shout and looked around guiltily. Damn, that's exactly what I mustn't do. They'd notice something like that. I had to be more — what was that word? — -circumspect.

I ducked my head. At the same moment I saw the dull shine of the little cap in the ground. God, was that ever a relief.

Now I had to look around. There was no choice. I could hardly kneel down and prepare my bomb if there were half-a-dozen enemy soldiers watching closely. I kept walking, feeling my boot grind on the cap, giving quick glances to right and left. It seemed clear in both directions. Away in the darkness to my left was a row of trucks waiting to be fuelled. I couldn't see where the line ended, but I think it went right out into the road. For all I knew it could have gone a hundred metres farther.

I could see a few blokes around the trucks but they were far enough away for me to have a fighting chance of not being noticed.

I looked behind, a furtive peep. It was hard to get a good view. It seemed OK, kind of. There sure was a lot of movement, but I couldn't see what exactly was happening.

Just people trotting everywhere, some with torches, some without.

Well, I had to take the risk and get on with it. Homer said he'd give us twenty minutes. I couldn't be sure how much time had passed since Kevin blew up the power line but it seemed like an hour.

I hissed at Lee, who was about ten metres away, then dropped to one knee and put my pack on one side and my rifle on the other. From now on, whatever happened, I had to concentrate on the charges and nothing else. It hardly crossed my mind that I could blow myself up. I was dealing with a fairly potent mixture: plastic explosive, fuse cord, lighter and petrol. But I wasn't thinking about that. The fear dominating my mind was of the soldiers behind me and to my left. If they saw me I was dead. I had to stay cool. Nothing else mattered. Cool and steady. Calm mind. Calm eyes. Calm hands. I had to rely on Lee to deal with any problems that came along.

The cap came out fairly easily. Not like that terrible moment at Curr's fuel depot in Wirrawee when we tried to put sugar in the fuel tanks for the planes at the airfield. I could still see the huge padlock they'd stuck on that tank. It probably hadn't been that big a lock; it was just that in my memory it had grown to the size of a rockmelon.

I didn't see why we actually needed explosive in these underground tanks, but Kevin, who was our science expert, said it was the way to go. He said petrol doesn't explode when you drop a match in it, just combusts rapidly. Very rapidly. But he said a few sticks of Ryan's plastic would turn it from a big blast into a volcanic eruption.

I was fairly well organised. The explosive charge was on a bootlace. I lowered it into the tank, holding on to one end of the fuse. The smell of petrol made me nauseous, especially as I hadn't eaten all afternoon. I'd been too nervous. From behind me came another yell; it could have been of discovery. I froze. I was so tempted to let go of the fuse and run for my life. Instead I clenched my teeth and pulled the cap of the tank towards me, dropping it into its hole. I had to be gentle, so I didn't break the fuse. I sat it at an angle.

As I was adjusting it I heard one of the worst sounds in the world. At least, one of the worst sounds when you're separated from your friends.

A series of shots came from behind me, like the putt-putt-putt of an electric motor starting up. They sounded like they came from the other end, from the truck parking area. Exactly where Fi and Homer and Gavin were meant to be creating the big diversion.

I grabbed a quick, desperate look at Lee. He looked back at me. It was hard to figure his expression, but horror wouldn't have been too far wrong. He turned towards the sound and moved half-a-dozen uncertain steps in that direction.

Starting to panic I stood and ran away backwards from the tank, trailing out the fuse as I went. A glance showed dark figures running in all directions except towards us. Some were heading for the truck park, some were racing to the trucks in the queue, some were bolting into the restaurant area.

I got about fifty metres, quite close to the safety of the gardens between the servo and the bush. I heard a yell from my left, from among the sheds, the one direction I didn't expect danger. Shrinking as much as I could I took a peep over there. A man in uniform was walking straight towards me, pointing and asking something, in his own language. I shrugged and dropped the fuse, wishing I'd brought my rifle. It was still back at the tank. Lee had his, but he was too far away from me now and surely couldn't realise what was happening. The man seemed unarmed, but one yell from him and he could have me surrounded by his mates in seconds.

You could see him start to work it out. Even in the dark you could sense what was happening in his brain. "What's she doing? . . . rolling wire along the ground . . . she doesn't look like one of us . . . there's gunfire over by the carpark . . . HEY!"

He was opening his mouth to yell the "Hey," when suddenly he got interrupted. An explosion from the carpark shook the air. There were cries and shouts from all around. Anything this guy yelled would be lost in the confusion. I saw his face more clearly now, lit by the red glow from the blast. Behind me trucks were starting up by the dozen. The man's face was shocked, uncertain, angry, frightened. He screamed something at me, gesturing at the same time, as if to say "Get away from us." I had to take the risk. Watching him, I bent down. I hoped he couldn't see me take out the lighter. It was the special one Ryan had given me. Guaranteed to ignite in a snowstorm, a cyclone, a flood. First time, every time.

I tried to disguise what I was doing. There was another explosion from the carpark. I grabbed the chance and flicked the lighter.

It worked.

At the same time I yelled at the man: "Watch out!" I didn't do it because I wanted to save his life, I did it to confuse him even further.

I lit the fuse.

He could have been a hero and attacked me. He could

have been a hero and stamped out the burning fuse. He could have at least warned the others.

He turned on his heels and ran.

So did I. I didn't even pick up the daypack. We figured the fuse would only last two minutes. We'd deliberately made it short so there'd be less time for them to react and put it out. When the tank blew it would blow big-time. I wasn't going to hang around.

I'd taken only half-a-dozen steps when a shot rang out really close to me. For one ghastly sickening moment I thought I was about to be shot. But the opposite happened. A man fell forward in slow motion from the other side of the concrete apron. He had been standing, but now he dropped straight down "smack" onto the concrete. He landed on his face, bounced nearly a metre, then lay still. To my left Lee stood up again. Only then did I realise what had happened. Lee had caught up with me, just as a soldier lined me up in his rifle sights. From a kneeling position Lee got him with one shot.

Well, we were in trouble now. I suppose maybe we should have gone towards the truck park, to help the others. To be honest it didn't enter my mind. It would have been pretty stupid. The truck park wasn't nearly far enough from the underground tanks to be safe. And it would have been impossible to work out what was happening, in the darkness. We'd have been more hindrance than help.

As if to prove we should go in the other direction I heard and felt a whole new series of explosions from the truck park. I don't know how many. At least a dozen. Some small ones, but mostly big.

By then we were in among the first line of trees. With each shock wave from the explosions I felt I was being helped on my way. Like a sail on a yacht, catching the wind. I ran kind of madly, ignoring the dangers of the bush. If I'd tripped on one of the rocks or logs or stumps I would have been cactus. Behind me the explosions continued. Homer and Gavin and Fi must have done all right. With each one, another red light lit the sky.

There were three or four loud bangs, too.

Then I understood what loud really meant.

The first sign that my bomb had worked was a fizzing noise like a giant heating furnace at full blast. That lasted maybe a full second. I heard a human scream from somewhere behind me. Then the earth lifted.

It actually lifted! I felt it shift under my feet. It rocked backwards and forwards, quite gently. Like those tectonic plates were having a grind. Like they were partying, deep underground.

At the same time the sound hit. It filled the whole universe. Nothing else existed. There was no sky, no earth, no people and no life. Just noise. I thought Heaven would drop on me.

It probably only lasted ten seconds but time doesn't have any meaning in a situation like that.

Then came the shock wave. It wasn't just a rush of air. Someone had turned on a giant vacuum cleaner and put it on blow instead of suck. Bits of wood, bits of rock, bits of concrete, bits of paper even. It was a blast of every solid object between me and the service station.

I became one of those solid objects. I had no chance of staying on my feet, in control. I tried to keep standing and for a dozen steps I did it. I was kind of running but my legs weren't doing what I wanted. All my concentration was on not falling over. Trying to find places to put my feet where I wouldn't go sprawling. I couldn't control my direction; no hope of that. And after a dozen steps I lost it. The force blowing me along was too strong to resist. I had to take too many quick steps, all in a row, but my feet couldn't keep up with the rest of me.

I tumbled down the slope, knocking myself against a rock and a couple of logs, and being hit by a few more of those solid objects at the same time. I don't know what they were. They hurt though. But it was no time for emotions. I was in survival mode. When you're in huge danger your mind gets focused. You don't think about a bruise or a cut or a scratch. It's just the search for life, the struggle to stay alive. At the bottom of the slope I rolled on a few more metres, deliberately, to get clear of the bushes, then staggered up to my feet. The noise of the explosion had passed. It was booming on in the distance as though it would travel across the countryside, on and on, mile after mile, until it crashed to a halt against a cliff or a hill.

The ground seemed to have stopped rocking. A new noise washed across me. A roaring whooshing roar of flames, and almost at the same time a wave of heat. I could feel the leaves suddenly wither and dry on the trees. I turned to my right, in the direction of freedom, the direction of the road, looking to go uphill to the place where we'd left our packs.

That was as far as I got. I didn't even take a step before I heard the rush of feet from behind. I started to turn, terrified, crouching already, lifting my hand against the attack. There were four of them. They were still twenty metres away, coming down the slope. They'd sounded even closer.

I came to my senses then, as suddenly as I'd lost them. I turned and ran.

It was a blind, mad race. There was no time to zig-zag

or do anything tricky. All I could do was put my head down and sprint. The scrub was thick and getting thicker. Branches lashed my face a dozen times in the first hundred metres. Each one stung more than the others. I hardly noticed. I was in a cross-country race for life. I wasn't making any ground on these guys, but I didn't think they were gaining either. I wished for help but there was none coming. I had no idea where Lee had gone. It was just me and them.

Suddenly, with no warning, I came out on the road. The trees were so close to the bitumen that I only had to take another couple of steps and I was on the warm lifeless tar. It was no good going right or left. And if I went straight ahead I didn't know if I could get across the road before they burst out of the scrub behind me and shot me down like a fleeing rabbit.

So I ran a few metres to my left and cut back into the bush again, on the same side of the road. I crouched in among the bracken, trying not to breathe. To my right the crashing through the trees stopped abruptly. It was replaced by the flat pounding of boots on the road surface. I didn't know what to do. If I moved they'd hear me. If I stayed where I was they might catch me. Farther to my left I heard more trampling through bush. Seemed like there were soldiers everywhere. To my right came a shout. Boots galloped past.

My brain couldn't have been working too well because I still hadn't figured out what was happening. It took a shot to wake me up. The shot was horribly close, but somehow I knew it wasn't aimed at me. Only then did I realise. The noises down the road on the left were from Homer or Fi or Lee or Gavin. They had become the targets, instead of me.

I burst out of my hiding place, onto the road again. I tried to be like those champion tennis players who cover a court in four steps. No matter how far away the ball is, they get to it easily. They make the court look like it's two metres square.

Well, that's the way I tried to cross the road. So fast, with such big steps, that I could reach the other side in three-quarters of a second. I had a quick glimpse to the left and saw half-a-dozen grey uniforms. All with their backs to me, which was good news for me but bad news for the others.

A couple of metres away from the bush I gave a huge yell. Sort of a cross between a cooee and a haka. I knew I could get into cover before they had time to turn around, aim and fire. With one last leap I made it into the scrub. I just hoped it had helped Homer or the others.

I zig-zagged madly through the trees. The short rest, crouched on the other side of the road, had let me get some breath back. I knew where I wanted to go but I didn't want to be followed by enemy soldiers. And I was keen to get there without any bullet wounds.

I headed off to the right for a while, hoping to confuse them. A freshly fallen tree was ahead and I took a minute to get over it, because of the branches and leaves in the way. By then I had proof that the soldiers were following. Not only could I hear the puffing and panting, one of them yelled an order. He had a high-pitched agitated voice, but he sounded efficient and aggressive. I didn't like my chances if they were going to be organised about this.

I came to a track, quite wide, and paused. Which way? Would they expect me to go uphill or downhill? I realised the answer and crashed straight across, into the bush again. But I'd left it too long. A bullet stung the air. It sounded horribly close. The only good thing it did was give me a fresh hit of speed. Suddenly I seemed to be running twice as fast.

I started curving, in a big arc. I wanted to get back uphill, to our meeting place, to my pack. I didn't like the idea of being cut off from the others for too long, in the bush, in darkness. If we got separated here, how would I find them? Only then did I realise that stupidly, we hadn't made any plans for that. We didn't have a fall-back position. That's what Fi and Homer should have been working out this afternoon, instead of having such a good time.

I couldn't believe I was getting angry at them even then, as I was running along trying desperately to save my life. What a waste of energy.

It was only for a second though.

I felt I'd gained a few metres again, and I looked for somewhere to hide. Whatever I found had to be a certainty — I'd only get one chance. And it couldn't be too obvious. It was a tough call. Any hollow trees or big bushes that applied for the job would need good references. And no good trying to squeeze into a tree that wouldn't fit me. That was a sure way to get a bullet up my bum.

I skipped a couple of candidates because I thought the soldiers would expect me to duck into the first ones I passed. But I knew I had to find somewhere. I couldn't outrun them forever. I couldn't outrun them for very long at all. I'm just not that fast a runner. If I didn't use my brains here I was going to be dead. Dead as a smoked fish.

Then to my surprise I came to our meeting spot. I

hadn't realised I was so close. I hesitated, not sure which way to go. I knew our packs were hidden in the bushes to my right. I called out softly, "Homer! Lee! Kevin! Fi!" There was no answer. I still had to wait for them though, I had to take the risk of hanging out there for as long as possible. I didn't want to lose contact with my buddies. I crawled into the bushes, between the packs, and crouched, trying not to pant too loudly, hoping my friends would turn up before my enemies. I clutched my pack like it was a big teddy, feeling it was the only friend I had right then. My breathing was nearly out of control; I concentrated as hard as I could on making it regular: in, out, in, out, in, out.

At last it was reasonably even again. But it had taken a few minutes. I hadn't realised how on the edge I was. Sure I was puffed from the running, but I was a lot more puffed from the terror of being chased around in the dark by people wanting to kill me.

I crouched even lower, still holding my pack, and peered into the clearing. At best I hoped to see someone like me, a teenager with head rolling from side to side with exhaustion, eyes staring as if trying to see the bullet before it saw her or him, mouth open in a silent scream.

No-one arrived. Instead the crashing through the bush got closer and closer; men who didn't seem to care if they were heard or not. All around I could hear their cries. Sticks breaking and branches flailing. For once these guys were prepared to chase us through the bush. For once they were taking the risk of hunting dangerous guerillas in darkness, putting their own lives on the line. Either they were desperate to get us, or they'd seen we weren't armed. I'd left my rifle at the servo, but the others should have theirs. Maybe they'd lost them too. If the enemy knew that, we really were in trouble.

Or maybe the others had already been caught and I was the only one left.

I slipped the shirt off, and pulled the tie over my head. I didn't want to be caught in these clothes, especially if the guy in the carpark was dead, which seemed very likely. Wrapping them in a little ball I hid them under a pile of leaves and bark.

Now I couldn't wait any longer. And to help me make up my mind, a shout came from only metres away. I couldn't believe how close it was. He hadn't seen me yet, I knew that, just from the sound of his voice, but we were about to get closely acquainted.

There was no point in being subtle. He was bush-bashing at speed, one line of trees away. More men were on my right, and they were close too. I grabbed my pack, wriggled it onto my back, and went straight uphill, not caring too much about the noise I made.

The chase was on again. I realised within a few metres that I was in trouble. The slope was steeper than I remembered, the pack heavier, and I was stuffed after the terrors of the night. I didn't seem to be making any progress. Sometimes at the school sports you'd see kids running as fast as they could, and getting absolutely nowhere. Like they were running on the spot. I used to wonder why they were like that, whether they were born that way or whether they just hadn't learned how to run.

Now I had a good opportunity to understand how they felt, because I wasn't going anywhere either. I panted and floundered. It was like trying to run when you're up to your waist in quicksand. I was sorry now that I hadn't been quieter when I left the clearing. The startled cry behind me was all the evidence I needed to know that they were after me again.

The broken ground made it too difficult. I wanted so much to get to the top, because then I could charge down the other side, with a chance of gaining a break on them. But at this stage the only break I'd get would be to my ankle.

I saw a ridge coming but as usual it was a false summit. Seemed like every summit in this war was a false one. I just hoped the one Ryan had promised, the big one, wasn't another illusion.

Of course I could have ditched my pack. I had it in my mind that I'd do that in a big hurry if the soldiers got too close. But what a tough call. If I dumped it, I was dumping my life. Not only because it held my few precious personal possessions, but also because it had the last of my weapons, including one grenade and a kilo of plastic explosive. I had to give myself every chance I could, not just of surviving the next few minutes, but of surviving for days after that.

I ran over a fairly open patch with just a gentle slope. It was the kind of ground you often get when you're approaching the top of a climb. I had to hope this wasn't another trick. I pounded through a single line of peppermint gums and arrived at the top.

Behind me I could hear them puffing and panting up the hill. Away to my left came the whistle of a train. Just in front and downhill slightly was a scuffle in a tree, as though something big, like a powerful owl, had grabbed something small, like a ringtail possum. I still didn't know which way to go but I knew one thing: I couldn't stay here. There was no cover at all.

I plunged down the bank, bearing to the right. A chatter

of voices followed: they were so loud and clear that the soldiers must have been on the ridge already. It sounded like they were arguing about what to do. That was good. It gave me a couple more seconds. I slithered down a slippery grass slope, almost losing my footing, then ran full speed across the face of the hill.

Now I couldn't tell if they were following or not. I was starting to feel more confident, like I had a chance, but that was a bit premature. They had another tactic that hadn't crossed my mind. A stream of gunfire suddenly opened up. Although it was way over to my left, it was coming my way. They were traversing the whole slope with an automatic weapon.

I ran another half-a-dozen steps, then dived to the ground. I lay clutching myself round the waist as though I'd been hit already. It was terrifying. The shots were rapidly coming towards me. Funny, before the war, if I'd thought about it at all, I would have said that bullets through the bush wouldn't do much harm. Might break a few twigs, not much more than that. But these bullets were like chainsaws. You could hear them smashing the bush apart. The noise was awful. It wasn't just the unbearable banging of the gun, it was the branches falling from trees all over the place, splintering and breaking and thumping to the ground. It was the confused screaming of cockatoos, woken from their sleep. It was the screeching of ricochets. The quiet bush had suddenly turned into a wild, out-of-control fireworks display. There wasn't much to look at, apart from the showers of sparks when a bullet hit a rock, but there was enough noise for an Olympics opening ceremony.

And all the time in the background the steady chugging of the train got louder and louder, closer and closer.

I'd never heard such an orchestra of ugly mechanical sounds in my life.

But I think the train might have actually saved me, at that moment anyway. The firing stopped as suddenly as it started, when the bullets were cutting swathes through the bush just ten metres away. I guess they figured that in another few seconds they would be shooting holes in their own train. I heard them yelling, up on the ridge, and I think they were spreading out and coming down the hill. I didn't wait to find out. Keeping low I sprinted off to the right again, losing height all the time.

In less than a hundred metres I hit the bitumen road that Homer and Gavin and I had been on earlier. I was pretty sure that I was a bit ahead of the chase, so I turned left and ran along the bitumen. Being out in the clear was such a relief, not having to worry about branches or rabbit holes. For the first time that night the air felt fresh and bubbly on my face. Again I had a surge of hope, like a quick hit with an electric prod.

I should have known better. It was so hard to work out what was happening, but I think a second lot of soldiers were coming along the road, looking for me or the others. The first I knew of them was when I heard a clattering of feet, as though a mob of horses with new shoes was belting along behind me. For a second I didn't get it, but when one of them yelled, in his high-pitched voice, I had no more problems understanding.

"Oh God," I gasped. I didn't know if they'd seen me: I suspected they hadn't. But they would in the next few seconds. I really felt that this might be it. There was no cover at all. I put on a burst of speed but I knew it wouldn't last long. My reserves were gone. I was coming to the bridge over the railway line. The ground was shuddering in sympathy with the train. Most of the carriages had already passed. I could see them stretched away to my right. It seemed like a long train, pulling a heavy load, and it was struggling to get up the hill. As I ran over the bridge the last dozen carriages, all identical open trucks and all empty, started going under it, on my left. I could feel them beneath my feet. A couple of moments later the first of them started coming out the other side. It seemed to come out faster than it went in. But I didn't hesitate.

9

THANK GOD THERE WERE NO SOLDIERS ON THESE CARriages, riding shotgun. I guess because it wasn't a troop train. There were passenger carriages way up ahead, but at least a couple of dozen goods trucks between me and them, and I couldn't see any soldiers on the passenger ones anyway.

I landed pretty heavily. The train was grunting away at a slow pace, but it was quite a drop from the bridge, and there wasn't much to break my fall. Just a layer of coal about thirty centimetres deep. I dropped vertically but at the last second twisted sideways, and put a hand out, mainly trying to save my bad knee. In point of actual fact, as Dad says sometimes when he's trying to be funny, I don't think there was any brilliant way I could have landed. I didn't do much damage. Just a heap more bruises and aches and pains to add to the ones I'd already collected in this war. In some ways the worst thing was the sharp jabs from the lumps of coal, each leaving its own individual bruise.

For a minute I stayed down in among the coal. If anyone had seen me from the bridge they'd be firing at me right now. Like people at a wedding throwing rice; I'd be saturated with bullets. All I could do was pray two big prayers: one, that they hadn't seen me, and two, that if they did, no-one had a mobile phone or a walkie-talkie, for calling ahead of the train, or maybe even talking to the guys on it.

I didn't hear any bullets, but that didn't mean a lot. The train was making such a racket getting up the gradient that I mightn't have heard them anyway.

Just as I couldn't rely on the first prayer being answered, so too I couldn't rely on the second. I waited a few moments until the train reached the top of the cutting, when it started surging forward. It had new energy as it came out of the hills and approached the flatter country. I dragged myself up and went to the front of the truck. With the greatest of caution I put my nose over the top and had a look. Ahead, the long line of the train curved away like a giant snake lying across the land. It had no lights. Just a dark shape in the darkness.

I took a look behind.

And wished I hadn't.

At first I thought I was seeing things. It was the slightest movement that caught my eye. As I gazed anxiously, my heart so big in my chest that it felt like it was suffocating me, I got the proof I didn't want. A soldier flung himself over the side of the truck two away, and dived headlong into it.

I knew he wasn't the only one, because the movement I'd seen a moment earlier was the hand of another soldier in front of him, leading the way in the chase to capture me and become a hero.

At least I hoped he was leading the way. If there was another one — or more — in front of him, I had no hope.

I flung the pack off my back and knelt beside it, ripping the straps out of the buckles. The soldiers looked like they were unarmed — they'd probably abandoned their rifles when they jumped into the train, or maybe they'd damaged them — but that was too bad for them.

I grabbed my grenade from the dark musty inside of the pack. We'd armed the grenades back in the clearing, the previous afternoon. I'd been nervous of it when I was running through the bush. We only had one each, but one would have been enough to blow me to smithereens. And one should be enough now, if I did this right. I just hoped I'd be more successful with them than Mr Pimlott, who'd blown himself up.

I ran to the end of the truck. I ripped the pin out with my teeth, the way Ryan taught us, and stood up to throw it.

A soldier was staring into my face.

He was climbing out of the truck behind mine. Only the coupling between the two carriages separated us. It wasn't much of a gap. I could see his face clearly. He wore glasses, which really threw me off-balance. I always associate glasses with serious, gentle people. Not logical, but that's what I do. In the act of throwing the grenade, I hesitated. I knew I could lob it over his head, into his open truck, but if I did it would give him huge encouragement to make the leap into mine. I didn't want him in there with me. But on the other hand I couldn't stand around holding a live grenade for much longer.

I threw it.

There was no other decision I could make really. I'd waited long enough. I threw it, then turned and ran. This time I didn't pick up the pack. I figured if I was still alive after the explosion I could come back and get it later. I got to the end of the truck and started scrambling up it, then realised I'd waited too long for that as well. So I dropped down and huddled into the corner. At the other end the guy with glasses took the leap and dived into the diagonally opposite corner to me. For about one second we huddled into our respective corners, both covering our heads with an arm, waiting for the explosion. I took a little glance at him. The grenade went off.

By then the train was choofing along at a fair speed. I'm not very good at estimating speeds, but I'd say it was doing nearly a hundred. The air was cold and the train was thundering, rocking backwards and forwards like a rodeo bull. When the grenade exploded it made a bang, sure, but not as loud as I'd expected. There was a big heavy thud and I felt my carriage twist and shudder, but it stayed on the rails. It seemed to drag for a bit, that was all. What did happen though, and what I didn't expect, was another fireworks display. Not a nice pretty one where you sit in your deckchair and watch, going "ooh" and "ah," but a bloody dangerous one. Bits of hot metal went scorching into the air and started falling. You could hear the wild whooshing sound as they went up, then a scary wailing noise as they fell. Some of the pieces were big; most were small. The small ones were the biggest problem though. Only a couple of big ones fell near me, and I avoided them easily. But the little ones fell like snow, and were as hard as snowflakes to dodge. At least four bits landed on me and two of them burnt through to my skin. I gasped with the pain of it, but at the same time I knew I couldn't sit around waiting for Savlon and Band-Aids. The moment the worst of the shower was over I was up and racing for the wall again.

I didn't waste time looking behind. I knew he'd be there. There was a chance I'd got lucky and he'd been dropped on from a great height by a hunk of molten steel, but it wasn't much of a chance. I wasn't going to sit around relying on it.

I shinned up the metal and rolled over the top.

For a moment I hung, looking down. It was a horrible sight. The couplings were rocking and rolling. Below those I could see the dark track racing along. It'd be all gravel and sleepers and steel rails. One slip and I'd lose a leg. Another slip and I'd be ripped apart, crushed to a pulp.

There was nowhere stable to stand. But I had to get across. I let myself down onto the narrow step, and turned, facing the gap. With my arms out on either side I took a hesitant step. My boot landed on a big buffer thing that was grinding against another buffer. I couldn't get a good platform. "Look," I told myself sternly, "this is hopeless. You won't get anywhere being nervous. Just charge across and be done with it."

It was like jumping a creek that you thought might be too wide.

I took a deep breath and put all my weight on the buffer, but not for long enough to rely on it. With panic threatening to pull me apart I made a nervous leap, as big as I could manage, to the little step at the end of the next truck. Then, while I was on the roll, I kept going and reached for the top of the metal wall, pulling myself up till my head was over it.

At that moment, just when I thought I was getting somewhere, I felt a terrific pressure on my left leg. Like it was being pulled out of its socket. Hanging on to the top of the wall I looked down. The soldier, still wearing his glasses, was glaring up at me. He looked like a crazy man. He was on the buffers, and he had the fingers of his left hand around the side of the carriage and his right hand on my leg, pulling it down like a truckie tightening a rope on his load. I gripped the edge of the wall even tighter but as I did I thought, "There's no future in this." I mean, what was I meant to do, hang on there till the end of the war? The guy with the glasses had all the advantage. With my back to him and no hands, I was helpless. If I was going to beat him I had to use my brains. But how?

The pressure increased and I felt my fingers start to slip. He was strong, no doubt about that. Still not quite sure what I could do, I let my body relax, hoping to bluff him into thinking he'd won already. I think it did surprise him. I felt him change his grip, letting go slightly and then grabbing me again, a bit higher up. At that moment I kicked out with all my strength.

I must have used a bit of force, because my body came right away from the wall. I know that, because I slammed into it again a moment later. But at the same time I felt my leg free of his grip. I scrambled up that wall as fast as a rat across a roof. At the top, as I went over, I took a quick look behind, hoping to see nothing, hoping the man had slipped through the couplings and was now lying in a mash of flesh and blood and bones on the track. I wanted him out of my way, and fast. I felt so panicked by him, desperate to escape. But as I rolled over into the next truck I saw him come back up, grabbing at me. Bad luck for him, he couldn't get a good enough grip before I was over and running for the front of that carriage.

Up, over, run, up, over, run. I did it through that truck and two more, getting glimpses of him each time I scaled the next wall. He just kept on coming. As I ran and climbed I tried to think. I knew I'd soon be out of carriages. Each time I got to the top of another one I could see the passenger ones getting closer. There seemed to be about a dozen of them, and only seven or eight more trucks between us. This guy chasing me was tougher and stronger than me; well, tougher, anyway. I'd have to use my brains, I just had to.

When I got into the next truck I didn't do the sprint across its lurching surface like before. This time I crouched under the protection of the wall I'd just straddled. And waited.

It wasn't a long wait. Only a couple of moments later I heard his boots thump into the wall on the other side. His hands scrabbled at the dark steel. I looked up. His fingers were already over the top, gripping the thick edge. I got ready. I tried to think of my tired legs as springs, tried to imagine they were on springs. I summoned up all the energy I could find.

The timing was everything. There would be that crucial instant when he would be, should be, balanced on the top. It would be the only chance I'd get. I had to take it.

I saw his head appear, the moonlight glinting on his glasses. He wasn't looking down, thank God. He was looking at the edge that he had to roll over, looking at his fingers. Then, as he got his body up on the top, just before he rolled over, he looked down the length of the truck, searching for me I guess, trying to see if he was narrowing the gap between us.

That was my moment. I pounced, driving upwards like those springs were in perfect working order, using the platform of my legs to give me all the strength I could muster. I went for the shoulder and the hip, not through any logical plan, but because instinct told me they were the main points of balance for his body. His centre of gravity. Thank you, Mr Pimlott.

I lifted him clean off the wall, except for his hands. It was such a powerful position to come from, driving up underneath him. I had most of his body back over the other side before he knew what hit him.

But he clung desperately with those fingers. I could see the knuckles whiten as he took a tighter grip. Worse, I felt him start to come back up. I could hear his boots through the steel, kicking at the wall again, trying for a toehold.

My mind seemed to work at massive speed, like a Pentium processor. I sorted through about a hundred options in half a second. Then I remembered.

I reached into my pocket. Would it still be there? If not I was out of options, out of ideas.

My fingers closed on Ryan's nifty little special issue lighter. I brought it out of my pocket. Quickly, do it fast, before he recovers his balance. Quickly, quickly, faster, faster.

These things were designed to be operated with one hand. They were designed to be used by people like Ryan: saboteurs and guerillas. People like me.

I flicked the lever. I didn't have to look for long to see if it was working. The little hot circle of light told me it was. I held it to the man's hand.

It was horrible. He actually held on for a moment. Until I could smell his flesh burning. Then he let go with that hand.

When I applied the lighter to the other hand he didn't hold on for so long.

He gave a scream, the only sound he'd made up till then, and I heard his feet scrabbling at something, on the other side of the steel wall.

Then, nothing. Just the roaring rushing noises of the train, and the cold moon high in the sky.

I had a good view of the moon, because I was lying on

my back looking up at it. The bare steel floor of the truck was cold, but I didn't mind that. I'd collapsed gratefully onto it when the man let go. All that unnatural strength and energy left my body in a rush.

But I couldn't stay there. I had to find out what had happened to him.

I forced myself to my feet and tried to climb the wall. Suddenly I didn't have the energy. I ran across to the corner and waited for the train to lurch in my direction. As it took a curve to the left it pushed me into the corner and I used the momentum to get up the wall again.

Hanging on to the corner, resting on my elbows, with my feet up high on the wall and my bum sticking out behind, I at last got a look down at the couplings between the carriages. I don't know what I expected to see. I think, probably nothing at all, just a smear of blood and a space empty of people.

If that's what I expected, I was disappointed. To my horror, the man was lying there, on his back across the couplings, unconscious, one arm trailing down into the darkness.

He must have hit his head when he fell. It seemed like his hand was only inches from the gravel of the track that rushed by under the wheels at a million k's an hour. I stared in horror. It sounds terrible, but I guess I had wanted him to be killed. All I'd thought about was wanting him out of my life: the quicker the better. But realistically, the only way that could happen was if he went over the edge, and at the speed we were doing, that meant death.

I couldn't think. To give myself time I shinned up to the top of the wall and went over it. I stepped gingerly across the man and jumped the couplings. I figured at least now I could get my pack back. I knew I had to get it, and not only because these days I was more bonded with it than the Notre Dame guy with the hunch on his back. No, the main reason was that I still had the plastic explosive, a kilo of it. No matter what else was happening, right now I was in a unique position: on an enemy train rocketing through the darkness, with a burning opportunity to do exactly what Ryan wanted. Somehow I had to find a way to do some major damage while I had the chance. Preferably without doing too much damage to myself.

At least I had no problems getting to the pack, and no problems getting it on. I couldn't see any enemy soldiers back here. The hand grenade must have done its job. And if there was anyone in the guard's van, he was keeping quiet. Smart thing to do, when saboteurs blow up your train bit by bit. Or maybe he'd been chasing me, along with the soldiers.

I still hadn't made up my mind what to do about the unconscious guy with the glasses. But when I climbed over the front wall of the truck where I thought I'd left him, he wasn't there.

"I must have miscounted," I thought. "Must be the next carriage."

But as I crossed the couplings I realised I'd been right after all. On the steel step, to the left of my foot, was an unmistakable smear of blood.

What happened? Where had he gone? I didn't know. But there were only two possibilities. Either he'd rolled over the edge, or he was somewhere on the train ahead.

I had to keep going forward, but now my mood was very different. A moment ago I'd been keyed up and keen, determined to do major damage to this train, win a medal for being brave, and make my parents proud. Now I was thinking, "I'll swap the medal and anything that goes with it for a clear run up to the front of this mongrel thing."

And I made another half-a-dozen goods trucks without a problem. The last two had lots of stuff in them: hundreds of empty five-gallon drums in one, with their lids in a dumpbin at the rear. At least there was a good passage down the middle, so it was easy to get through. The second was half-full of wooden crates. I didn't stop to look at them, but I think it was machinery of some kind.

My nerves were more and more keyed up. Not only because I didn't know what had happened to the bloke with the glasses, but also because I was approaching the business end, the part with the passenger carriages. I still hadn't figured out how to destroy the train but I knew there was no point having a go at the empty trucks. The farther up the front I got, the better. I kept thinking what I needed to do. Wreck the train sure, preferably the engine. Try to find out if anyone was in the passenger carriages. Then decide if I had the brutality or courage to blow them to high Heaven.

One more truck along, past a dozen coils of wire, and I thought, "What I really want is to put the whole line out of action, so they can't use it at all."

But I didn't know how to do that.

There was only one truck between me and the passenger carriages. It was three-quarters full, with drums of chemicals. The writing on them was in a foreign language, so I couldn't read it, but I could see the little "flammable" symbol on each one. It meant that the train could become a pretty toxic bonfire if it crashed.

I made my way along the top of the drums. It was the only way to get over them. The train slowed down again quite suddenly, as we climbed another hill. With every kilometre I was going farther and farther from my friends, but I hardly gave that a thought. If I didn't focus totally on this job I'd have no chance of surviving. Homer and the others might never know what happened to me. Assuming they'd survived.

I got halfway. I felt like a ballet dancer, stepping daintily, and getting more confident by the minute. I was convinced that at the speed I was moving I would have caught up with the soldier whose hands I'd burned. I assumed now he had been shaken off the couplings.

It was like a bad dream, a very bad dream, when he reappeared from behind the drums. He was like a ghost, a gaunt staring face, waiting for me. He'd seen me coming, and he'd hidden behind the drums at the front end.

I stopped dead and stared. I felt my own burns from the hot metal smoulder on my skin as he started towards me. They were like sensors, warning me. But I couldn't move. Just kept staring, unable to think of a thing to do.

He wasn't much more than twenty drums away. Then fifteen, then twelve, then ten.

At last I did something. Backed up. Not a brilliant career move, but I was grateful that my limbs were working again. For a full minute I'd been so paralysed by his ghastly white face that I couldn't move anything. The rims around his glasses, the moonlight gleaming off them, made him look like an alien wearing goggles. One lens had cracked badly, which wasn't surprising. It made him look even scarier.

I kept backing up till I bumped into the cold hard steel of the wall. I stood there trying to make my mind work, trying not to get hypnotised by his slow approach. I had to look away for a moment, to break his grip. I was helped by the train accelerating again into a sharp left-hand bend. We were both thrown off-balance, but him more than me, because he was standing on the drums. He had to crouch down and grip on the drums with his hands.

As he did that I reached into my pocket and brought out the most useful weapon I had. That cigarette lighter was paying its way. If I got out of this I'd buy it a 44 of fuel and give it free drinks for the rest of its life.

But to have any hope of getting clear I had to pull off a giant bluff.

The drums just had the standard screwtop lid. I grabbed the nearest one and turned the cap. Thank God it didn't have a childproof lock. I don't think I could have coped with that. It resisted for a moment, until I broke the seal, and then it came off easily.

I heaved it over and started tipping the stuff out. It sure smelt strong. One of those intense smells like petrol or creosote or Texta. It might have been some kind of resin. It was thick like honey, but it poured easily.

As the train belted down a hill, the pool I'd created ran down the floor of the truck, disappearing among the other drums.

And it had an effect on the soldier. Maybe he'd read the writing on the labels and knew what it was. Or maybe he recognised the smell. He stood up again to get away from it, one foot on one drum, one on another, his arms spread wide to balance himself against the rocking of the train.

Then I showed him the cigarette lighter.

It worked quite well. The way he put his hands up and started stepping backwards, looking behind to see where it was safe to put his feet, made me wonder just what was in these drums. I squatted down, as if to light the fluid, and he retreated fast, this time not even bothering to look. He shouted something to me, but I couldn't hear it above the clattering of the train, and I wouldn't have understood it anyway. I stood up again, and gestured at him to keep going. He slowed a bit, kind of sulkily, like he'd decided I wasn't going to light the stuff after all. I used the drums to take a leap to the top of the wall and leaned down, showing him the lighter, as though I was going to ignite it and drop it. He moved faster then. As he got to his end of the carriage I dropped down out of his view, onto the couplings, and jumped to the next truck. I knew I didn't have much time. I'd run out of bluffs.

Three carriages farther I came to my destination. By then I had no energy left. I'd taken each carriage at the run: the sprint down the middle and the scramble over the wall, till my ribs were aching, my legs had no drive left, and my arms wouldn't lift anymore.

I got to the truck with the five-gallon drums, and more importantly, the container with the lids. For a moment I just hung on to it, panting. The lids were my last chance. If this didn't work, I was finished. I had nothing left to continue this fight: no strength, no energy, no spirit.

I glanced in the direction I'd just come, the direction where he'd be appearing. He was already there! I couldn't believe it. I thought I'd run so fast and so hard. Nobody could have kept up with me. But unmistakably his two white hands, like long pale spiders, showed up against the black of the railway steel as he climbed over the other side.

I tried to steady my beating heart, steady my heaving chest, steady my trembling hands. I grabbed a lid, turned a little to get the right rhythm, and chucked it, just as his scalp bobbed up over the top.

It was too high. Missed him by a metre. And I realised at once that I'd been too early. All I'd achieve would be to drive him back into cover. He'd just go back and find a weapon, or get reinforcements.

My good luck was that he was so busy climbing the wall he didn't see my frisbee. So now I waited. At least I'd got the range, and at least I knew the lids would fly. They were heavy, much heavier than the ones we had at home, but that was good. I needed them to do a lot of damage. I wanted him to be balanced on the top, and I wanted a lid to smash him in the face, and I wanted him to fall off the train, even if it meant he was crushed to death under the wheels. I was too tired to fight him anymore. It was either him or me, and I still didn't want to die.

As he reached the top I let fly. For a second I thought I was going to wipe him out there and then. The lid looked like it was going to hit him right in the nose. But just like a frisbee it curved gracefully away and missed by a whisker.

He noticed that one. He looked up, startled. The next one was already on its way. He saw it coming and ducked. It missed by quite a bit I think, but I didn't get a good view, because I was already grabbing at another one.

As I went to throw it I had to hesitate. It was too late. He was dropping off the top of the wall, not on the other side where he'd be safe, but on my side, where I wouldn't be safe. My stomach felt like I'd done a belly flop from the high tower. Suddenly my arm got its strength back. I let fly with a throw that I knew was about the most violent I could ever do; maybe the most violent I'd ever done. He was just straightening up from his landing. This time it did hit him in the face. God it hit him hard. I'm glad it wasn't me. His arms flew to his face and he fell backwards, staggering against the drums to his right. Blood flew from between his fingers. I knew I'd hurt him bad. I picked up a U-bolt that was in the drum. It was a big one, the size of a shoe. I gritted my teeth and flung it as hard as I'd frisbeed the lid. The man was turning away, bent over, with his hands still to his head. The bolt hit him on the temple, with a heavy hard thump. He went down without a whimper, like he'd been hit by a baseball bat.

I approached carefully. He was still moving, lying on the floor of the truck, his hands jerking and his legs twitching like a dog in its dreams. I was scared that maybe he was faking it, but when I stood over him I could see his eyes had rolled right back in his head and his eyelids were fluttering uncontrollably. I remembered Kevin saying there was a spot on the temple, where if you hit someone you could kill them.

I took another step, to get around the man, and felt something scrunch under my feet. His glasses. I'd completely smashed them, lens and frame. That's the trouble with boots. They're kind of unforgiving.

I still hadn't solved my problems. I wanted to destroy the train and destroy the tracks, but I couldn't risk leaving the man. If he recovered and came after me again I wouldn't have a chance. He'd be so determined the next time. He wouldn't underestimate me again.

I looked around, unsure of what to do, wanting a clue, a sign from somewhere.

And I got one.

Strangely enough it came from the train itself. I think all the time I'd been frisbeeing the drum tops at the soldier the train had been slowing down, but I hadn't noticed it. I'd been concentrating too hard on staying alive. But now I became aware that the train was making the grinding noises trains make when they're coming to a halt. We'd been running through a pretty level part of the country, and going at quite a speed, but suddenly the wheels gripped the track and I heard the squeals of metal on metal.

I didn't know if this would be good or bad. At first I crouched beside the soldier, almost expecting to be attacked. But I knew as soon as I did it that I had to find the energy to fight on. So I went to the end of the truck and climbed on a drum, peering over the top of the wall to see what was happening.

I couldn't see much. Sure there was plenty of moonlight, but that's not the reason I couldn't see much. The reason was, there was nothing to see. Just trees, trees and more trees. We were slowing right down in the middle of the bush. Maybe there was a red signal up ahead. Maybe there was a problem with the engine. Maybe the driver needed to take a leak.

I glanced back at the soldier. He had rolled onto his side but he didn't look any better. I thought it was safe to leave him a bit longer. I shinned over the wall and crouched on the coupling, just as we came to a complete halt. There was a chance that someone would come along, either looking for me, or making a general check of the train. I had to take that chance. I knew what I wanted to do. I just didn't know if it would be possible. But I couldn't believe how easy it was. Once I'd removed the pin the coupling lifted straight off, easier than taking the trailer off the tractor at home. All I had to do then was pull out a couple of cables.

It took thirty seconds. I sat back, feeling relieved, excited, and annoyed that I hadn't done it ages ago, when we were still going. I could have saved myself a lot of trouble.

Now I just had to wait, and hope the soldier didn't recover in the meantime. I snuck back over the wall, keeping my profile as low as possible. The man was still lying there, but was on his back again. His breathing was more peaceful, more relaxed. He'd stopped blinking. He looked like he might wake at any moment. I picked up a drum lid, wondering if I'd have the guts to hit him again. I didn't think I would somehow. The fury had gone out of me; I'd calmed down. I suddenly felt cold.

I went back to the wall to see if anything was happening. Peering over the top, looking at the silent grass shoulder of the track, I had another idea. Maybe I could kill two birds with one stone. I hitched my pack up tighter and just about vaulted over the wall. Ignoring the separated coupling I jumped down onto the track. I peeped out, first looking to the front of the train, then to the rear. Still no movement. As stealthily as I could, I ran around to the gap between the next two trucks. Then, when no-one reacted, I ran straight out from the train to the trees.

It seemed a long way. It probably wasn't: about thirty metres I think. But I felt pretty relieved to get into the protection of the bush. Trouble was, I didn't have time to feel relieved. I had to race the train. I took off without caring much about the noise I made. The train engine revving away, waiting for the signal to start again, was noisy enough. With luck it would cover me.

I crashed through the undergrowth. It was darker in here, because of the tree canopy. I couldn't see any details of the obstacles, just their outline. There seemed to be an interesting range of vegetation, including wire grass and blanket leaves and of course blackberries. I think there was even some holly. Whatever, I collected so many scratches that my skin must have looked like red mohair. Some of the wood I hit was rotten and broke easily; some wasn't. I tried to protect my bad knee but I couldn't very well. It was just madness, running as fast as I could, through heavy bush, keeping one eye on the train, hoping the next dark shape was a soft shrub, not a solid tree trunk . . .

After I'd tripped and rolled for the third time I tried to make myself slow down. It was no use. A kind of madness had got control of me. If I'd been cold a few minutes earlier I was hot now. I crunched full length into a patch of broom, then brushed through some nettles. When your blood's up you don't feel a lot of pain. It's only later that the stinging sets in. I slowed a little though, running at what I hoped was a safer speed, not even able to see the train now, but sure from the lack of noise that it was still sitting where I'd left it.

I angled back towards the track. It was a relief to get out of the bush and into the clear ground alongside the line. A slight bend hid me from the train driver. I kept going. My idea was to blow up the track farther along when the train had gained speed and would derail properly. Otherwise the driver might see the damage and stop in time. I wanted maximum effect.

I reckon I went a kilometre and a half. The good thing was that I'd reached a steepish downhill slope. That was pretty much perfect. When it flattened I stopped, took off my pack, and as gently as I could, tipped out the contents.

All I had was the last of the plastic explosive. The charges I'd made with Lee were in his pack, but I still had enough left. It would be nice to blow up the track and the train simultaneously but I couldn't hope to be that lucky. The train might arrive in thirty seconds or it might sit where it was for a day and a half.

I cut the fuse to about fifty centimetres and wrapped the explosive around it. At least there was no need to waterproof it when it was going off this soon. I used my super-duper little lighter again and without even looking around, lit the fuse.

From then on everything happened so fast I'm not even sure what came first, what came second, what came last. I only know that suddenly things got very ugly.

10

THE TRAIN WAS THERE WITH NO WARNING. I STILL CAN'T believe I didn't hear it, but then in peacetime I could never understand how people got killed on railway crossings. Like, how could you not hear a train? Well, at least now I knew the answer to that. I guess I was concentrating too hard on the job at hand. Dad would have been pleased with me. He was always saying I didn't concentrate enough.

Anyway, I'd just stepped back from lighting the fuse, when I felt a push of cool air against me and realised a milli-second later that it was the train. Only then did I hear it. It still didn't have any lights. I sprang back, grabbing my pack, then did a sort of half-turn and a dive down the bank. It wasn't graceful but it got me clear of the engine. I deliberately kept rolling till the ground levelled out and I couldn't roll any farther.

I got up to run but at that moment the bomb went off. God the fuse had burned fast. Maybe the rush of air from the train caused it to go faster; I really don't know. So just as I was getting up I was bowled over again. Bowled over and blown away.

By now I should have been used to the power of an explosion. I'd been in enough. But nothing can get you used to them. They're such a shock to the body, the mind, the place where you have your emotions. It's like you've been chucked into a coffee grinder and someone's turned it on at full speed. You lose all control over everything.

"Jump down spin around pick a bale of cotton." That's a line from a song. You're like an epileptic cotton-picker. You've been wired with electrodes and your limbs go into a dance you didn't choreograph. It's horrible.

The only good thing about it is that it doesn't last very long.

I ended up on my back in a dump of bark and leaf litter, my bones loose in my body, my skin stretched and sore. I didn't know where my pack was. I just knew that I didn't have it anymore. But at least I got a good view of the anarchy above. Bits of bark and branches were flying in all directions. Behind them were lines of white smoke, no patterns to them, just going where they felt like. I saw a thick huge white cloud billowing up in the centre of the wreck, then it started rolling, very fast, towards me. Suddenly I was in a fog and couldn't make out anything anymore.

It gave me the kick up the backside I needed. Before the fog I'd seen enough to know that the engine and the first couple of carriages had gone over the bomb before it blew up. So the people in them were probably OK. But they'd be madder than a staff room on Year 12 Muck-up Day. They'd be swarming after me with every weapon they could find.

I started groping through the fog. While I'd been lying on the leaf litter I thought the fog was ideal; I could make my escape in safety. But now I realised it wasn't such a bonus after all. I had to go too slowly, and the so-called fog was already lifting. Within a minute it cleared as quickly as it had arrived, and I was still within a hundred metres of the train wreck.

I heard yells from behind, and I didn't need an interpreter to know what they meant. "There she is!" was the general drift. The bush was straight ahead and I'd never been more glad to see it. I bolted into the treeline like a rosella in a wheat crop. I felt a big attraction to the smell of eucalyptus at that moment.

As I started down a slope which I knew would take me out of sight of the train I risked one glance behind. I got the shock of my life. What looked like a squad of soldiers had fanned out across the top of the hill, and in the light of the burning trucks I could see that they were armed to the teeth. A couple of them were in the act of kneeling. They obviously thought they could get a good shot at me before I scurried into the deeper bush.

Unfortunately by looking back I'd lost my momentum. I'd like to have accelerated down the slope, maybe diving through the bracken to throw them off their aim. But I wasn't going fast enough. All I could do was swerve, and try to get up more speed at the same time. So I swerved to the left, and came almost immediately to a bank I hadn't seen in the darkness.

I plunged down, thinking, "Well, at least I'll be out of their sight for a little bit now."

I was overconfident about that.

I ran another six paces before I was shot.

It was a feeling I'll never forget. If it was some other pain, I guess I would have got over it. At first it wasn't even the worst pain I've had in my life. In some ways being winded was worse. But one difference was that you soon start getting better when you're winded. With this I soon started getting worse.

Another difference was the psychological one. When you know you've been shot, it hurts all over.

For a moment I actually thought it was a snakebite. I know you don't expect to be bitten by a snake at night, although I'm sure it's very possible. I've seen quite a few snakes out at night when it's hot enough, once even on our verandah at home.

This wasn't such a hot night. But I still thought it was a snakebite. There was a terrible stabbing pain in my left calf, like a red-hot three-inch nail had been driven in there. Right away a burning feeling spread up my leg, like a hot coal was lodged inside.

I looked around frantically, expecting for a moment to see a quick swerve through the grass as a tiger or a brownie took off in a hurry. But it was too dark and I didn't see anything.

I hopped along on one leg for about six paces, then the pain virtually went again. I mean, sure, there was still an ache, but nothing worth writing home about. I put my foot back down, ran three or four more steps, then, bang, the leg went from under me.

This time it really hurt. Jeez did it hurt. I knew then that it was no snakebite; that I had been shot. The whole leg was screaming at me. It had no strength at all. It was a mass of pain from the toes to way up my thigh. Virtually to my waist.

It didn't strike me at the time but I'd been shot in pretty much the same place as Lee; my left calf.

I opened my mouth to scream, then realised I couldn't do that, and it was a waste of time anyway. Not only was there no-one to come to my rescue, to offer sympathy and Band-Aids and Panadeine, but a few dozen soldiers were chasing me at full speed with rifles blazing. If there'd been time to think I'd have had to acknowledge that they were good shots, too. One of them was, anyway. Or incredibly lucky.

I put my hand to my leg, as if holding it would ease the

pain, but it didn't help at all, and when I took my hand away again I realised it was sticky with blood. My blood. I started to feel funny all over. Shock, I guess. I was dragging myself along, not at much speed, but trembling and shaking, and just feeling totally weird. Like I wanted to faint and throw up and go to sleep, all at the same time.

What I did instead was crawl another twenty metres towards a big patch of bracken. Twenty metres. That was the longest journey of my life. I knew I was making little whimpering noises, like a tired baby, and it's funny but I distinctly remember having a vision of my mother at that moment. I felt a sudden intense desire to be a baby again: to be held safe against her, to rest in her arms, to feel the heat of her body and to breathe in her warm smell.

The last six or eight metres I did a centimetre at a time. I heard, or thought I heard, the voices of the soldiers following me, looking for me. I heard both men and women, but I don't know if I really heard them or if I imagined it. There was another volley of shots, and I know I didn't imagine that. Bullets ripped through some leaves quite near me. Branches snapped and fell slowly, from limb to limb of the trees, until they thumped to the ground. The bush was taking a pounding tonight. I thought, "One of those bullets hit me, one of those bullets that are so powerful they can break big branches. What has it done to my leg?" I started shaking again and was afraid to look down at the wound, afraid of the damage I might see.

Gradually though I felt calmer. I seemed to stop shaking and drift away. Like a dream where I was awake and could see myself having the dream. Almost like there were two of me. Then it got weirder and I saw myself lying in the bracken, as though I was in the high branches of a tree and looking down. I saw the top of my own head.

Although it was a cold night I felt surprisingly warm. I prickled all over, like I'd been injected with something radioactive. I had pins and needles, but they were hot needles. I couldn't hear anything. Maybe I'd been identifying too closely with Gavin, but a huge cotton wool muffler had been placed over the world and there were no sounds any more. I don't know how long that lasted. But as I lay in the bracken, buried under its fronds, a strong voice from somewhere inside started making itself heard, and it said, "Come on, fight back, be strong."

"Don't disturb me," I begged it. "Don't wake me. I'm feeling quite nice now, quite comfortable. Let me stay like this."

But it wouldn't be silenced. It got louder and louder, and more demanding, and even though I got cross with it, suddenly the fog in my mind cleared and I could see and hear everything clearly again.

And I could feel everything again. That was the bad news. My leg was agony from top to bottom. If I could have torn it off and thrown it away I would have done it. Burns of pain ripped through it, wave after wave after wave, with almost no pauses, no relief, no chance to draw another breath and get my mind ready for the next hit. Such a tiny thing, a little lead bullet, to do so much damage. Just a couple of centimetres long. I vowed I'd never shoot another living creature again. I was shocked to think I'd put animals through this torture. Then my mind cleared even further and I remembered all the people I'd shot during this war. I decided not to think about that anymore.

Even through the pain, even as I clasped my leg and sweated and sobbed, I could hear the soldiers. The voices were getting closer all the time. They were calling to each other continuously, I think so they didn't get out of line, keeping themselves organised, but maybe also to intimidate their target. Me.

Well, that worked all right. I was intimidated. They sounded so professional, so disciplined, that I couldn't think of anything to do against them. They sounded so strong that they made me feel weak.

About the only thing I could do was stop myself groaning. That was quite an achievement. I bit my bottom lip, so hard my teeth nearly went through it. I pushed the heel of my right leg deep into the soft earth. I arched my back and twisted my head from side to side, all the time keeping the tight grip on my left leg.

The only distraction I had from the pain was when a pair of boots crunched past my face. He or she, whoever it was, had a torch, so I was at risk of being trodden on or seen or both. But neither happened. The boots strode on, less than a metre from me, but for that couple of seconds I stopped thinking so much about my leg. As soon as the soldier disappeared down into the gully a new blaze of pain ran through me, going higher now, up my side into my armpit.

The next time the pain ebbed it was such a relief that I lay back gasping. I dared to hope that it might stay like that. Oh, if only it would. I didn't make the slightest move, in case I set it off again. But I did start to think: "How am I going to get out of this?" I wanted to respond to the voice in my head I'd heard — or imagined I'd heard — earlier, but the way I was going, just staying alive might be more than I could manage. I might bleed to death here, in among the bracken. I knew I was bleeding but I didn't know how much. Finally, reluctantly, I ran my hand down my leg and patted around on the ground. It felt pretty dry. That was lucky. But it didn't mean I wouldn't die. I remembered the feeling of calm and peace that had stolen over me just a few minutes before. I shuddered. Suddenly that feeling didn't seem so peaceful after all. I realised it might have been death, stealing around me with its peaceful fingers. I didn't want that kind of peace, thank you very much. I wasn't ready for it.

Judging from the noise there were soldiers everywhere. If they stayed around I had no chance. With a bullet in my leg, and the sun coming up, I'd be as easy a target as a scarecrow in a paddock.

Experimentally I slid a metre to my right, towards the edge of the bracken patch. Right away the pain came back, so violently that this time I did cry out. I could still hear the soldiers. Funny, considering how long it had been since the boots trampled past. I thought they might have been well gone by now.

As I lay listening, it struck me that they weren't getting any farther away. In fact they seemed to have stopped. I didn't know what that meant, but there was every chance it was bad news for me.

Then things did get worse. The search party started coming back up the slope.

My leg now felt like someone was cutting it open with a blunt chisel heated red-hot. I hated being so helpless. I knew I had to move but I didn't know if I could. I tried another experiment, going in the opposite direction, but that was even worse, as it meant I was trying to roll over on the wounded leg. I thought, grimly, "Well, at least it's the same leg as my bad knee. If they cut it off I'll have solved two problems at once."

The way the soldiers were now casting around, not far

from me, I was pretty sure they knew I was close by. I wished so much that I still had my pack, and that it was full of Ryan's explosives. Or that I had a weapon of any kind. I bet they knew I wasn't armed. They'd had too good a view of me, even in the dark, as I raced away down the slope. If I'd had a weapon they wouldn't be this confident, searching the bush at night.

I began to realise that this time I really had no chance. Daylight couldn't be far away, and if they hadn't found me by then, it wouldn't take them long once the sun came up. The drops of blood would be a dead give-away. "Dead" in every sense of the word.

For a while the soldiers were fairly quiet again. I'm not sure how much time passed. I think I might have drifted into a bit of a blear. The next time I registered anything was when I heard the bark of a dog.

It gave me such a shock. Not at first though. At first I heard it while I was in a dream. Somehow I was back home, before the war, with Dad giving me a lecture. Again. One of his favourite sayings was: "The gate's always open, the bull's always angry, and the rifle's always loaded." He was telling me that again, because I hadn't checked the cows every day, assuming that because they'd been all right on the days I did check, they'd be all right on the days I didn't. Mum had actually told me she thought this cow might be calving — I can even remember her number, 132 — but I never noticed her in a dip in the long grass of One Tree Paddock. And we'd had such a good run with calving that I'd become over-confident.

When we did find her we were about a week too late. The calf had been dead a long time. I'd say the cow had been in labour a full week. We started pulling the calf out from the cow, but it was rotten and it disintegrated.

Meanwhile the cow was burping and farting totally noxious gasses. Dad and I were both dry-retching. The smells were overpowering, as if the sight wasn't bad enough. We got the legs of the calf out, one by one, then Dad got a chain around its head, but when we started pulling on the chain we pulled its head off. We got most of the bits out eventually but, surprise surprise, the cow died of shock, about a minute after we'd finished.

That's when Dad gave me the lecture, as if I didn't feel guilty enough. I mean it wasn't really because I hadn't checked the cows every day. She was in such a deep hole in the corner of the paddock that I must have missed her at least three times. But I guess I could have checked more carefully.

Maybe it wasn't so surprising that I'd dream about that, as I lay there with my leg feeling it had been shattered and shredded by the bullet, and me knowing that it was because I hadn't kept a good enough lookout. "The gate's always open, the bull's always angry, and the rifle's always loaded." Yeah, and I could add to that. The train's always loaded with soldiers. And they're always armed and dangerous.

And if you hang around for long enough they bring dogs.

I heard the first few barks while I was still in my little dream and thought it was Millie, our old dog. Then suddenly I was wide awake. The sun was shining hard into my eyes and the barking was very close. It was sharp, aggressive, and loud. A few moments later there was a volley of shots, smashing into the earth and vegetation three or four metres from me.

They started there anyway; then they moved away. I

saw the grass and bracken being blown backwards and forwards as though a great wind was rushing through the undergrowth.

I could see what was happening, and what I couldn't see I worked out. When the dogs got excited the soldiers started firing. Why not? Saved a lot of mucking around. Less time and less danger. Let the rifle do the work for you, instead of having to rake through the bush looking for a dangerous terrorist with your bare hands. The taxpayers paid for the ammo anyway.

The firing stopped and there was a bit of silence. Then I heard voices again, men calling to each other, and then, unmistakably, encouraging the dogs to have another go. The barking started, only it quickly became an excited yapping. I could hear them coming straight towards me. It was time for me to give up. I might only extend my life by a few moments, but when it comes to the end, even a few moments seem precious.

"All right, keep your shirts on," I called.

I tried to get up, but it was hard, with my leg in raw pain. I couldn't put any weight on it; not when the slightest movement had me gasping with shock.

But I levered myself up on my right knee, enough for them to see me.

And for me to see them. There were half-a-dozen lounging around in the background, leaning against trees, smoking, just hanging out. They sure were confident. Then there were four doing the actual business of searching. Two had dogs on leashes; and each had a soldier with him. These soldiers seemed like the hatchet men, because they had automatic rifles at the ready, and they looked ready themselves. I got very cautious when I saw them, raising my hands slowly and deliberately, staring them down in case they felt like testing their aim on me.

The dogs were cute. I wished I could have patted them and played with them and scratched their stomachs, like in the old days. They were beagles, both quite young, and very pretty. Lovely alert heads and shining eyes. They looked pleased with themselves, and of course they had every right. They'd caught the vicious enemy guerilla. Caught her without a fight.

It wasn't a very dignified surrender. I tried to stand on my one good leg but I lost my balance. I guess being so tired didn't help. I fell in the bracken and just lay there, not caring very much whether they killed me on the spot. It seemed like ages before they came to get me, but it probably wasn't. A whole lot of boots suddenly surrounded me. I looked up and there they all were, staring down at me. For the first time I noticed that the grass was quite badly bloodstained, smears of it everywhere, so I guess I'd bled more than I realised. I wasn't sure what I was expected to do. I'd only been caught once before, and the circumstances had been different. Now four rifles were pointed at me, so I lay waiting for them to do whatever they wanted. I felt a strange kind of peace, not the same as a few hours earlier, just an acceptance that this was the end of the road; I'd done everything possible; I couldn't carry out any more of Colonel Finley and Ryan's programme of sabotage. The soldiers would take their revenge. I would pay the same price I had made their friends pay.

It didn't quite work out like that. They prodded me with the barrels of the rifles to make me stand. I got up slowly, awkwardly, this time being more careful not to fall over. It went OK, until I was nearly upright, then they seemed to lose patience. Maybe they thought I was being deliberately slow. One of them shouted and swung his rifle so that it hit me across the back. I kept my balance, but only just. Another one pushed at me to get me moving, then the first one swung with his rifle again. I put up a hand to block him but as I did someone from behind kicked me in the left leg, on the exact place where I'd been wounded.

I went down like a beast with a bullet between the eyes. The only satisfaction I can claim is that I didn't make any noise. I don't know whether that was self-control or unconsciousness, because I sure saw stars. I had a blurred view of the bracken as though someone had put heavy black glass in front of my eyes.

I copped a few more boots. At first the pain was crippling; beyond anything I'd experienced, anything I could possibly bear. I curled into a ball and protected my leg as much as I could. The blows rained down. I couldn't stay silent anymore; I cried out, then I screamed, but it didn't lessen the pain by the slightest degree.

After quite a while the pain seemed to go away, and although I felt the thuds of their boots it was like they were doing it to something else, to a block of wood perhaps. I heard them, and felt the impact, but the pain had faded into a blur of darkness. It was weird.

At some stage it stopped but I think it was a long time before I realised why. Someone was grabbing me and lifting me by the armpits. "Don't," I cried out, like a baby. They didn't take any notice. Instead they dragged me, heels bumping over the ground, for quite a distance. The pain came back, ten times worse. Every bump to my left leg sent agony racing up my side, like someone had ripped my leg open with his bare hands and was now pouring kerosene into the wound. I started screaming. I wanted it to stop, and I didn't care what price I had to pay. If someone had offered me death at that moment, with a promise of no more pain, I'd have taken it, no problems, no complaints.

I had no power left. If the hands had let go I'd have dropped to the ground like an imploded building. The pain had taken over. I was drunk with it. No other part of me functioned.

Then things changed again. The hands suddenly got more gentle. Instead of dragging me along they were holding me up. I still didn't realise what had made the difference. I don't think I realised until I was in the back of their truck. Through the haze of pain and sweat and terror I sensed that someone was directing the whole operation. Someone was in charge. Before, it had just been a rabble.

I couldn't see him but I became aware of his voice. He sounded calm and quiet. It was a relief after the yelling and screaming of the soldiers. I couldn't understand what he was saying to them of course, but after a minute I suddenly heard his voice right at my ear. He was speaking English, easily and confidently, with only a faint accent.

"You will be treated properly now. I have made sure of it. I will get a doctor for your leg. For now, you go to a holding area."

I tried to nod, to show my thanks, but I couldn't move my head. Sensing that he was moving away, desperate not to lose my chance, I croaked, "Water."

"What is it you want?"

I tried again but the word wouldn't come out.

"What is it you want? Something to drink?"

"Yes. Yes. Please."

I think I only made meaningless sounds, but he got the drift, because a minute or two later I felt a water bottle at my lips. I couldn't get much of it into my mouth. I didn't care: the feeling of it running down my chin and onto my body was enough. The man was patient though, and held it to my lips, pouring in little sips, one by one. I was very grateful to him.

My eyes seemed stuck together. I tried to open them but then gave up and just lay there. Sensing him still near me I had another go at speaking, and this time, thanks to the water, did a little better.

"Excuse me . . ."

"Yes? What is it now?"

I wanted to ask about Homer and Lee and Fi and Kevin and Gavin. I tried to formulate a question about them. But even in my blear of pain and fear and exhaustion I had enough instinct left to avoid talking about them to an enemy soldier. With a groan I gave up and let my head roll away.

11

The first time I saw myself was as a reflection in the sunglasses of a soldier, when they took me off the truck. By then I could open my eyes, but straightaway I was sorry I had. At first I had absolutely no idea I was looking at myself. What I saw was a head the size of a Halloween pumpkin, and about as attractive.

A pair of black eyes stared at me out of the mask of a face. They were like squash balls, so big that I couldn't understand how they could still fit in their sockets. My whole face was bruised and black and swollen. There were red and purple streaks across it. I've never seen a human face like it. I couldn't believe it was mine. But army boots are pretty hard of course.

I don't know how long I'd been on the truck. A long time. A lifetime. It had jolted and swayed and bumped for hour after hour. I didn't know where we were going and I didn't care; I just wanted to go somewhere. I wanted to crawl into a hole and stay there and go to sleep and never wake up. All my ambitions had come down to that. No more dreams of going to uni or traveling the world or marrying some gorgeous guy. Just a hole and no-one to disturb me. I wanted nothing more. A kind of grave I guess.

When I saw myself reflected in the sunglasses and finally registered it was me, I shut my eyes again. I didn't want to know what was happening. I didn't want to know anything.

It actually hurt my eyes to close them.

I lay on the ground. After a while I heard the man again, the one who'd saved me.

"The doctors are coming now," he said. "I have arranged this. It was very difficult but it is arranged. I will come and see you later, in a day or so. You understand?"

"Yes," I said. I didn't understand a single solitary thing but it was easier to go with the flow than to ask questions.

Then a couple of doctors were crouched over me. I heard their soft voices murmuring away. They were like waves of sound, quite gentle, washing across my body, slipping back into the sea again, fizzing and foaming.

I think I slipped away like the waves. The next thing I knew I was being lifted onto a bed. I cried out and groaned with the pain, clutching for someone to hold, begging them to leave me alone. No-one answered. There was no-one for me to hold. They just kept lifting, then arranging me on the bed. Although I had protested so much, it was a relief to feel the firm mattress under me. Every part of my body throbbed with pain, but at least the bed gave some kind of support.

Later a woman was standing next to my bed giving me an injection. She didn't say anything. Neither did I.

I think they operated on me then, because when I woke up the pain in my leg was virtually gone. The rest of me still ached almost as badly as before, but I was grateful that the pain in the leg was better.

I was desperate for a drink. My tongue felt as big as a whale, and about as good as a dead fish. I tried to groan for water, without success: this time not a sound came out. But I kept trying, and eventually some sort of mangled noise emerged, like Kermit the Frog with a bad case of flu.

At first I thought no-one had heard, so I kept making the noise, and after a few minutes someone came and put a hand on my forehead. It felt soft and small and cool, a woman's hand. She made a remark to someone else, but not in English. I tried again: "Water," and in English she then said: "Can she have a drink, Doctor?"

He replied in English: "A hundred mils only."

This time when the cup was held to my lips I took great care not to spill a drop. It was too precious. A hundred mils wasn't much, but it did make my lips and mouth feel better.

I tried to open my eyes while I was drinking, but they hurt so badly. When I'd emptied the little metal cup I let my head fall back onto the pillow.

A few minutes later the pain in my leg came back, worse than before. I gasped at the fierceness of it, and started panting, like I was going uphill in a cross-country race. After a while I got the idea that if I moved my head backwards and forwards it would somehow ease the pain. The trouble was it hurt my head, but it still seemed better than just lying there. Then there was another injection, in the fold of my elbow, and I roamed away into a nothing world again.

How long did I lie there for? I don't know. There weren't many highlights. In fact the only highlights were the breaks from the pain that the needles gave, and there were never enough of those.

A few moments stood out though. One was seeing my face again, reflected in a stainless steel bowl that the nurse used to wash me. It was still a horrible sight, only now the bruises had changed colour, from purple and black to red and green and grey. Once again I looked away. The swelling had gone down a bit; that was the only good news.

Another memory was asking the doctor if he had cut my leg off. I'd read a book a few years ago about a guy whose leg was amputated but he didn't know until days afterwards because the phantom pain in his missing leg was as bad or worse than real pain.

The doctor said: "We think we can save it," which wasn't very confident, and sounded like he was answering a different question to the one I'd asked.

I didn't have a clue what they were giving me in the injections, but it was potent. I spent so much of my time somewhere up around the ceiling, bumping gently against the light fittings, my mind held there by millions of cotton wool balls. Then one day it all became too much. I had the weirdest feeling that if I didn't stop this right now, if I didn't cancel the drug, I'd never get off it; I'd be hooked forever. So when the nurse came along with another needle I waved her away. She said, in poor English: "Doctor saying you have." I said: "Send the doctor here — I want to see him," and she hesitated then went off again.

I soon regretted turning down the injection. The pain got so bad that I took to biting the blanket so I wouldn't bite my tongue or lips instead. Everything hurt, minute by minute, hour by hour, with no relief. My leg was the worst. I panted and moaned with it, and I think I upset the other patients in the ward, because three times the nurses tried to get me to have the shot and three times I refused, getting quite aggressive, trying to make them scared of me.

At last a doctor turned up, a small serious man with tiny rimless glasses.

"You know you must keep having the pain-killers," he said. "You are still in quite a dangerous post-operative state. You are putting too much strain on your body."

"I don't want any more," I said. Talking was difficult; my mouth and teeth and jaws and neck all hurt. "It made me float away."

"You are keeping the other patients awake."

"I'm sorry. I won't make any more noise."

"You know, we are not putting anything bad into the injections, if that's what you're worried about."

"No. I never thought that." I had, briefly, but my gut feeling was that they weren't doing anything sinister.

I didn't say any more, and after a few moments he said: "I will try you on Panadeine Forte tabs. But if they are not strong enough, or if you can't keep them down, I will put you back on pethidine."

A couple of minutes later a nurse arrived with two white tablets, which I swallowed. They did make a difference, I think. Anyway I didn't go back on the injections.

The medical staff were fairly good to me, I have to say that. I was given good care, even if it didn't come with chocolates and flowers. They treated me a bit like I was a robot, but overall I had no complaints. Considering what I'd done to their soldiers, they would have been within their rights to chuck me straight in the nearest cemetery.

It seemed like I owed my life to the mysterious man who'd intervened to save me, back in the bush. He kept his promise to come and see me, too. He was an officer, with three gold crowns on his shoulders.

He was around thirty-five I'd say. A balding man with a sharp nose and old acne scars. He had the thinnest moustache I've ever seen. His English was excellent, but he pronounced "hospital" as "hospitable," which always made me want to laugh.

I don't know how many times he visited, but I'd say at

least three or four. He even woke me if I was asleep, as though he was anxious to let me know that he was still around, protecting me. I had no idea why he'd be doing such a thing, why I wasn't being hauled away for interrogation, punishment, execution, but I sure wasn't going to complain. This guy seemed my best hope of staying alive.

A few times another man in a suit came to interrogate me, but I just made like I was too sick, which didn't take a lot of acting, considering how hard talking — even thinking — still was. At least I had the sense to give him a false name. I told him my first name was Amber — I got that from the word ambulance, because I could hear them squealing and wailing as they arrived at the hospital at regular intervals — and I gave my family name as Faulding. That came from a bottle of tablets I saw on the nurse's trolley.

I quite liked it as a name. It sounded glamorous. Sounded like a character in a soapie.

At first I didn't realise that they had me under guard, but I shouldn't have been surprised. By the time I worked it out I was starting to make a bit of a recovery. I'd learned I was on the second floor of a hospital in Cavendish that had been taken over for the military. I'd become aware of the other patients in the ward, five of them, all women, all enemy soldiers, although their faces kept changing, as different ones were admitted and discharged. None of them seemed anxious to make friends with me.

The people doing the dirty jobs around the place, the cleaning and bed-making and meal serving, were my own people, prisoners I guessed, although they weren't allowed near me. The nurses made my bed. Still, one hot afternoon, a lady who looked a bit like my mum, and who was mopping the floor of the ward, gave me a big cheesy smile and a wink, when no-one was looking, and that was the nicest thing that happened the whole time I was there. I watched for her each day, hoping she'd do it again, but it was difficult, because she could only catch my eye when everyone else, staff and patients, was distracted, and that didn't happen often.

The first really ugly moment came when I was sitting up for the first time, helped by a nice young nurse who could have been younger than me. As I struggled up onto the pillows, trying not to cry with the pain, determined to get upright, one of the other patients in my ward, a middle-aged woman who looked like a dung beetle in a body-building contest, glared at me as she walked past and yelled something accusing and spat, hitting me on the forehead, just below my fringe. I know I went red, and I stared at her, trying not to let any tears come into my eyes. She stared back, even when she got to her bed, and kept staring at me as she flung herself onto the mattress. There was nothing I could do. The nurse looked embarrassed, but she didn't say anything. How could she? Siding with the enemy wouldn't be a good career move.

I realised the nurse wasn't going to wipe off the gob of spit so I took a tissue from her trolley, tensing my hand to stop trembling, and wiped it off myself.

Two days after sitting up I walked for the first time, ten or twelve steps across the ward and back to my bed. It was a big moment, even if it took a quarter of an hour and I moved like an old lady with arthritis. But for a long time I hadn't known if I would ever walk again.

Each day I tried to go a little farther, and that was how I learned I was under guard. On the day I got to the door of the room and took my first step through it a young sulky-looking male soldier got up from a chair outside the door, and pushing his long black hair away from his forehead told me to go back inside.

When I turned around I noticed for the first time the bars on the windows, and realised that I was in every sense a prisoner.

I still didn't figure out the full extent of the situation straightaway though. The next day, when the doctor with the small glasses came in, I asked: "Can I walk up and down the corridor outside?"

"That's not up to me," he said. "But I doubt if they'll let you. No-one else is allowed."

It took me a moment to connect with what he'd said. Then I asked: "You mean no-one in here?"

"That's right."

He was looking through my charts, and not really concentrating on my questions. But I kept asking. I had the feeling he was quite proud of the progress I'd made. Considering how limited the facilities in the hospital seemed to be, he probably had done a good job on the operation. Anyway, I sensed that he felt friendly towards me, so I took full advantage by asking him questions whenever he came in.

"But aren't I the only one under guard in here?"

He gave me his full attention then, lowering the notes and looking at me in surprise.

"No. Oh no, whatever made you think that?"

I still hadn't made all the right links in my brain. "Is everyone in here under guard?"

He gave me a strange look and glanced down at the charts again, made a brief note, then left. But I already had the answer. We were all prisoners. I couldn't figure out why, but I was sure I was right. The next time the young nurse was changing the dressing on my leg I said to her, as quietly as I could: "Is this like a prison ward?"

She looked at me sharply.

"Prison, yes."

"What did these other women do?"

She shrugged and ignored me, concentrating on the dressing. I gripped the base of the mattress, knowing how much pain I was in for. To help distract myself I asked her again, "What did they do?"

"All different," she answered, not looking up from my leg.

"They did different things?"

"That right."

"Like what?"

I paid the price for being inquisitive as she ripped the dressing off. If the ceiling had been any lower I would have hit it. I took a sideways glance at the wound. It was big and ugly but at least it was clean.

"Any infection?" I asked.

"Little bit. Not too bad."

"So what did they do to get put in here?"

But she wouldn't answer, just bent her head over the dressing and ignored me.

I couldn't imagine what crimes the women had committed, although I guessed that I was probably the only one who'd blown up trains and ships and planes and service stations. But it helped explain the bad moods of the other patients; the way they lay there sullenly. I didn't know what injuries or illnesses they'd suffered to put them in hospital. I don't think they'd been beaten up like me. Most of them seemed sick, with bronchitis or heart problems, stuff like that. I guess prisoners can get sick just like anyone else. Probably more than anyone else.

Being prisoners together didn't create any good feelings between us though. Like, we didn't exactly bond. There were no "getting to know you" games. The one who spat in my face was the extreme but the others weren't much better. Come to think of it, they didn't show much friendliness towards each other either.

As I got better physically I paid a price that I didn't welcome. The thoughts about my friends, that I'd pushed behind me while I was semiconscious, started to take over. I'd lie on the bed, holding my head with both hands, wishing with every molecule that I could see and feel and hear and smell them, and be with them again. I ached with loneliness.

I still hoped I could find a way to ask the officer who had helped me what had happened to Homer and the others. But I couldn't figure out how to do it without giving away my identity, and I knew that no matter how friendly the man was, I'd sign my death warrant if he associated me with the teenagers who'd been doing so mach damage around Wirrawee and Cobbler's Bay and Stratton.

When he came in the next time I tried to get a line on why he was being so helpful, and, more importantly, what more I could get out of him.

So I said: "Thanks for saving my life out in the bush that day."

It was the first time I'd been lucid enough to have a proper conversation with him.

"That right," he said. "I saved your life. You are the enemy to my people. What you did was very bad. All the same, I saved your life."

"Yes. Thank you. Thank you very much."

He gave a brief grin. He was sweating a lot, as though

this conversation was important, but at the same time it was making him extremely nervous. I was about to find out why.

He glanced around, then sat in the chair beside my bed, moving it a little closer. "I have saved your life," he said. "Is very hard work. Even now, is very hard work. A lot of people say, 'Why is she in one of our hospitals? Why do we not just shoot her?'"

I said carefully: "I guess I owe you."

Seemed like he was pleased to hear that. He gave an eager little nod, and moved his chair even closer.

"For me, I am realist. I love my country, yes, of course, but also I have myself to think of, I have a family, I have a wife, two children, also mother and father, all depend on me."

I nodded, trying to look understanding and sympathetic.

"This war soon be over. Soon be finished. United Nations, be here soon."

I felt a gleam of excitement come into my eyes, and tried to hide it. It was the first good news I'd had since coming into hospital.

"Lots of bad things happen during war," the man said, giving me a sudden sharp glance. I realised we were getting to the point now.

"Lots of bad things. In war, sometimes things happen, everything quick quick, bang-bang. No time to think."

"Yes, that's true," I said.

"After war, sometimes reporters come, judges come. Inquiries, commissions, trials. Things get, how you say, raked up?"

"I guess so. Like Nuremberg."

"Yes. That not good."

His face shone with sweat and his English was starting to break down under the pressure.

"I been very good to you. Saved your life. You say that to me. I save your life. That true, no?"

"It's definitely true."

"Good. Good. After war, you say that too? Anyone ask you, Colonel Long very good to you, save your life."

At last I could see what this was all about. At last it made sense. "You crafty bugger," I thought. Choosing my words carefully I said: "After the war it'll give me heaps of pleasure to tell everyone you saved my life, you were very good to me, you should get maximum praise for treating me so well."

Colonel Long leaned back in the chair. He took a neatly folded tissue from his pocket and wiped his face. He obviously felt he'd done a good day's work. I had to admire his cunning. Maybe he'd been looking for someone like me for a long time, or maybe he just thought of it on the spur of the moment when he saw the soldiers beating me up, but either way he was satisfied that he'd bought himself an insurance policy.

I was his protection if and when a war crimes tribunal got to work. For the moment at least I didn't want to know whether he'd actually committed war crimes. Obviously he had something pretty heavy on his conscience, but I'd worry about that later. If I survived that long.

What I did want was to use him now, to get information about my friends. So I said: "The night you caught me, was there anyone else caught that night?"

He didn't like the question. He scowled and looked away. "You don't want to be asking about those people," he said. "They very bad people. Anyone think you know those people, I can't save you. They do very bad things, at gas station."

I understood what he meant. Somehow he'd managed to separate me from the attack on the truck stop. As far as the authorities were concerned, I was only wanted for one offence, blowing up the train. If they knew any more it would get too heavy for Colonel Long to protect me. Even as I lay there working this out, the Colonel whispered in my ear: "Amber Faulding, I don't think that is your real name. I think I maybe know your real name, but I not going to say it here. But you be very careful. If you who I think you are, no-one can save you, I cannot save you, no-one can save you."

I felt the blood drain away from my face. There was a long silence. Without looking at him, staring straight at the ceiling, I forced myself to ask again: "But just between us, were there other people caught that night? Quite a long way from the train wreck? Like, at that gas station you mentioned?"

"They all dead," he hissed. "All killed at gas station. Four teenagers, all dead. Don't ask about them ever anymore."

"All dead?" I repeated stupidly.

"All killed. I see their bodies. They all killed. No more about that. No more never."

By the time I could bring myself to look at him again he wasn't there. He had left the room.

I wriggled down under the sheet and lay there shaking, out of control. It was all too much, too devastating. I remembered Mrs Slater when her garden was destroyed by bushfires, the garden that she'd built from nothing, the garden she'd spent fifteen years developing. When it happened, she told my mum that it was too big to take in. "If I'd lost just the rhodies, or just the hydrangeas," she said, "if I'd lost just the David Austins."

I sort of felt like that now. I was a desert inside, a garden that was black and burnt and desolate. I felt I had no blood. A kind of numbness crept through me. My fingers were playing with a tear in the sheet, a small slit. Without even knowing what I was doing I tore it a little further. It felt kind of satisfying to do that, so I tore it some more. Then I tore it back the other way. Slowly I began to tear the sheet to shreds. It wasn't too difficult, because it was an old sheet, and fairly thin. I don't know how long I lay there doing that. The night duty nurses never seemed to come near us if they could help it, and I guess this night they could help it, because I didn't notice — or I don't remember — anyone coming in.

Methodically, carefully, inch by inch, hour after hour, I tore that sheet into tiny pieces.

By the time the first grey light of dawn soaked into the room the sheet was like shredded coconut. I lay in a mess of cotton and all that was left was a piece the size of a handkerchief.

Outside the ward I heard the bustle of the day shift arriving, the night shift passing on their messages and saying goodbye. Calmly I reached for the bin beside the foot of my bed and scraped the million or so fragments into it. I lay back not caring whether anyone noticed that I was now one sheet short.

No-one did. The day continued. I gazed at the ceiling, making my mind numb, carefully anaesthetising every feeling that threatened to interrupt, turning myself into a robot.

But it didn't work. I could control my mind for a few hours, but after a while the thoughts and feelings came creeping back like ashamed dogs, heads down, tails tucked under them, as if to say, "We know we shouldn't have killed that wallaby but we couldn't help ourselves."

I felt the grief crawl from my limbs into my stomach and up through my chest into my head. It was like a cold fluid gradually creeping through me. I was drowning from the inside out. The worst thing seemed to be the knowledge that my friends had deserted me. They had gone off together, leaving me all alone. They must have known I couldn't cope with that. They must have known how I'd feel. How could they do that, without including me? It was the cruellest thing they had ever done, the cruellest thing that had ever happened.

The odds had been too heavily against us that night. We had disobeyed the Pimlott Principles. We'd gone for a target that was too big, a target that wasn't achievable. The way those soldiers had searched, the sheer number of them: it would have been a miracle if any of us got away. The train provided me with a miracle, and I'd still been caught. In the middle of my central nervous system, I'd known they couldn't have escaped.

By night-time I felt that my brain was being eaten away by these terrible thoughts. I lay there quietly, aware of the damage being done inside me, but powerless to do anything about it. The cold fluid in there was acid.

Not all my feelings were as selfish as my first ones. But there were certain things that were particularly bad. One was the thought of the pain of dying. I hoped, oh how I hoped, it hadn't been too bad. That it was quick, sudden, instant. Having felt the agony of the bullet in my leg, and everything afterwards, I didn't want my friends to have gone through anything remotely like that. Because if it had been that bad for me, when I was only injured, how much more must it hurt when you're killed, when you're being killed, when you're dying.

Another was the frustration, that the world could be deprived of Fi and Kevin and Lee and Homer. All that personality, resourcefulness, courage and sense of humour: all snuffed out with a few bullets. The world would never know the music Lee's fingers made as they danced with the keyboard, the beauty of Fi's butterfly mind, the strength of Homer's honesty, Kevin's rough-and-ready rural style. I wanted to be their ambassador, to travel the world telling everyone what it had lost, but I knew it was too big a job for me, or anyone else. No-one would ever know.

Of course this must have been the way the enemy felt when we killed their soldiers: that sense of unique talented individuals vaporised in an instant, but not knowing them personally I couldn't feel the way for them that I felt for our group. You can't understand anything unless you personalise it. You can't love or appreciate or mourn for anything unless you personalise it.

I sure personalised Fi and Kevin and Lee and Homer. They were the beats of my heart, the skin of my body, the breath that entered my mouth and nostrils. They were the beautiful friends who had taught me that love was the life-force.

No-one noticed that I didn't have a top sheet anymore. That night as the long hours of night started to send me over the edge I tried to tear up my other sheet. But I didn't have the energy for it. Instead I began to count. Through the darkest time I kept going: three thousand eight hundred and thirty-one, three thousand eight hundred and thirty-two, three thousand eight hundred and thirty-three . . .

I know it doesn't make any sense, but somehow I felt it stopped me from losing my mind completely. I got up to eight thousand four hundred.

It wasn't until the morning that I realised Colonel Long hadn't mentioned Gavin. I did sit up a little when I thought of that; feeling the first sensation of pleasure or excitement that I'd had since being caught. Surely he hadn't got away again! Impossible!

But if anyone could do it, it was Gavin.

There were many times in the days that followed when I saved myself from total despair by thinking of Gavin maybe still alive, still out there somewhere.

Generally though despair seemed to be the only feeling I had.

One thing that upset me too was that I might one day have to face all those parents and tell them that their sons and daughters were dead. And the siblings as well. I didn't think I could cope with that job.

I stopped thinking about my own future, my own survival. Not because I was being heroic, "putting myself last," but because I just didn't think about it. Certainly, and illogically, there were moments when I still thought I'd survive. I must have done, to imagine facing all the different parents after the war. But most of the time, if I gave it any thought, I just assumed something would go wrong, Colonel Long's protection would fail, I'd go through a trial sooner or later, and then they'd take me out and shoot me. Especially if they managed to link me to any other attacks. Like Colonel Long hinted, if they knew about those I'd get a one-way ticket to the morgue.

I felt like a dead person already. Everything that happened, everything I saw, was through a greyness, like I had died and gone to some limbo place, somewhere so like death it might as well have been death.

I didn't try to walk again. I just lay there.

It was three or four days before a nurse got me moving. She pushed me out of bed like I was a rag doll and stood me up. She was a lightly built, delicate-looking girl, not much older than me, but she was strong. And after lying on the bed for so long I had no strength. For the first time in the hospital I cried as she pushed me around the ward. Even my crying sounded like a dead person: I could hear it as though it were someone else, a thin wailing, empty and hungry. If not like a corpse then like a baby.

Over the days that followed I started to become more aware of my surroundings again, like I was being forced back into life.

Gradually the pace in the hospital was picking up. For a while the change was subtle, then it accelerated. The doctors and nurses got busier and busier, patients admitted one day were gone the next, my doctor looked harassed and had less time to look at my charts. There were more emergencies. I was woken in the middle of the night by trucks in the courtyard, people rushing past the door of our ward, voices yelling in agitated tones. If I hadn't known already that it was related to the war I could have worked it out by the way I was treated the next morning. And it didn't happen just once or twice. It soon became a regular event. Suddenly I was copping bucketloads of open anger and hatred. A nurse changing my dressing ripped it off as roughly as she could. My fellow patients shouted abuse at me, especially when a nurse was treating me. Their tone was like: "Don't waste time on her. Why should you help one of them?" For prisoners, these women were pretty patriotic. Or maybe they were just naturally feral.

I don't think there'd been any battles in the suburbs of Cavendish since I'd been in hospital, because I hadn't heard any planes or explosions. But at last the night came when I was woken by the familiar low growl of bombers overhead. They made a sound like a long loud tummy rumble. As they got closer the windows shook, rattling the glass so loudly I hoped the bars would fall out. No such luck. The planes kept going and after a few minutes I heard the bombs start to fall. Only two or three kilometres away. "Crump, crump, crump."

Outside our room the hospital still seemed to be asleep. At no stage did I hear the slightest noise from the corridor, and certainly no-one came to check our health. Inside the ward it was a little different though. I felt like I was in a zombie nightmare. Women screamed and cried, sobbing like they were at a funeral already. Someone turned a bedlight on and someone else screamed at her to turn it off. Someone went to draw the curtains closed but the others wanted them open. A couple of women — the only two who could walk — staggered to the door and tried to open it. But it seemed we'd been locked in. The women pounded on the door, yelling for help. No-one came.

I lay in my bed, very quietly, nervous about the air raid but more nervous about the people in the ward. I felt I was in a lot more danger from them. On the one hand I was proud of the New Zealand Air Force, if that's who it was, and pleased that they must be doing well. On the other hand it seemed unfair that I might get a bomb dropped on me by my own side. I guess if you're blown up, it feels the same whether you're blown up by your friends or your enemies.

The raid lasted nearly twenty minutes, then it was over

as suddenly as it began. The silence filled the night sky. I could see half-a-dozen stars through the hospital window. The women stopped screaming, but there was still a fair bit of sobbing and crying. I just kept as quiet as a guinea pig. I definitely didn't want to attract attention.

Half an hour later the staff returned. I don't know where they had gone, but obviously they'd put their own safety well above ours. I was a bit shocked by that. I thought nurses were meant to be more concerned about their patients.

I was glad to see them, because things in the ward were getting ugly. One woman had made a speech to the others, and I seemed to be the main subject of the speech. She stood at the foot of my bed, facing the rest of the room, and addressed them in a throaty voice, waving at me every now and then. The light of the night sky shone through the window, right on her face, making her look like a witch. I just lay there, not that I had any choice, and stared at her, determined not to show any weakness. I tried to work out ways to defend myself. If I'd had a bedpan I'd have thrown it at her. I was sorry I didn't have one; preferably a full one. I didn't want to look away, because she might think I was scared, so I had to try to remember what weapons were within reach of my bed. I had my own box of tissues now but somehow I didn't think tissues would be good for much. For a few days I'd had a desk-lamp, but it had walked. I knew there was a little kidney-shaped stainless steel dish that the nurses dropped dressings and stuff in. If I hit her with that it'd probably be better than using my bare fists, but not much better. For the first time I realised that there was a deliberate policy of not leaving stuff in the ward that could be used as a weapon. Of course. They'd be crazy otherwise, but it hadn't crossed my mind before, when I'd been so sick.

The woman wound up to the big climax. No doubt she listed every atrocity committed during the entire war. At the same time she gave me the hate stare, her whole face shining with rage, like a big old full moon. She got so excited that she suddenly grabbed the end of the bed, the rails, and shook them, like a monkey rattling the cage at the zoo.

It was the final straw for me. I pulled myself up by the grab bar above my head and let rip. Wow did I let go. I gave her the works. I made my voice as deep and loud as possible, because I thought that would sound tougher, and I told her everything I didn't like about her, her friends, her country and the invasion. I knew she was strong, but I knew I had to be stronger. If I couldn't stare her down I was in big trouble. So I went on and on, feeling my throat get sorer, hearing my voice get hoarser, but knowing that she couldn't get a word in edgeways. Every so often I stared around the room at the other women, knowing some of them wouldn't see me very well in the dark, but knowing they would feel my gaze directed at them, and hear my voice coming full-blast in their direction. When I ran out of all the things I wanted to say about the war I shifted to a few older subjects that could get me fired up, like the continuous assessment policy at school, and the lack of any entertainment for people my age in Wirrawee, and the ways boys' sport in our school attracted so much more attention and funding than girls'. I was kind of gambling on these people not having a huge understanding of English, and gambling that the way I was yelling would stop them making out the words anyway.

The trouble was, I didn't know where I could go after

this. Like, when I got to the end of the speech, what would I do?

In the middle of my telling them how I was fed up with the way the school bus driver wouldn't wait for you even if he could see your car coming down the driveway, the door burst open. A senior nurse, one I'd only seen occasionally, stomped in, shouted at me to shut up, charged across to the window and drew the curtains closed.

I sank back onto the pillows. I wonder if she knew how pleased I was to see her. My energy levels had been nonexistent since the news about Homer and Lee and Kevin and Fi. My big speech was the most exercise I'd had. A new kind of physiotherapy. Funny, it was almost like it had brought me back to life.

But from then on I felt seriously threatened in the ward. I didn't even feel safe going to sleep at nights, never knowing if I was going to be attacked. The big woman showed no signs of being discharged, so I started putting pressure on the doctor to kick me out. I didn't know where I'd be going but I figured it couldn't be any worse.

The doctor didn't take a lot of persuading. I think they realised the tension in the ward had become a bit over the top. When I asked him outright if I could go he just shrugged, but twelve and a half hours later I got my marching orders.

They didn't give me a lot of time to pack, but that was OK, seeing I didn't have anything to pack. What I did need was time to get used to the fact that my life was about to change dramatically again. Even that weird ward had become kind of comfortable. Taking another plunge into the unknown wasn't necessarily what I wanted. They gave me a pair of khaki trousers and a lighter khaki shirt, and I was allowed to draw the curtains around the bed for a minute to get changed, but a minute was all I got. It wasn't enough of course: I was quite worried at how stiff and sore I felt, and how much time it took to do simple things like getting dressed, but it seemed like I'd unmade my bed and I'd have to leave it.

The next minute I was limping out, still doing up buttons, while the other women lay in their beds watching. Not surprisingly I didn't get any smiles, any waves, any calls of good luck. I was glad to be going. Since my last visit from Colonel Long I'd felt I was in a morgue, not a hospital. Maybe if I knew what I'd let myself in for I wouldn't have been in such a hurry.

12

My escort was pretty full-on. I kept forgetting what a dangerous terrorist I was. Lucky they didn't know the full story. But even in the middle of the war they found four soldiers to guard me, plus I got handcuffs on my wrists, which was embarrassing. I thought stuff like that only happened on TV.

In spite of the handcuffs I managed to wave goodbye to a couple of the nicer nurses, and one of them waved back. I hope she didn't get in trouble for it, but it made me feel a million times better. I just wished there was some way of telling her what it meant to me.

The handcuffs quickly became uncomfortable but when I complained to the guards they ignored me. The trouble was the cuffs were put on too tight, and they cut into the bone, and squeezed my skin. But no-one seemed too interested in doing anything about it.

Instead of a prison van I got a minibus, one of those Toyota things that take about twelve or fifteen people. On the door was the logo of the West Cavendish Cricket Club, so I guess that's where they'd flogged it.

I got in without making a fuss. Apart from complaining about the handcuffs I hadn't tried to speak to the guards. I couldn't be bothered. Partly because I didn't want to give them the satisfaction, partly because I knew it wouldn't make any difference. What would happen would happen. These guys wouldn't have any say in whether I lived or died. Someone else would have made that decision; probably some faceless person who I'd never meet.

As if one pair of handcuffs wasn't enough they put me in a seat halfway towards the back, and handcuffed me to the seat frames behind and in front. My left arm behind and my right arm in front. They sure weren't taking any risks. They waved their rifles around and made it clear they'd be happy to shoot me if I tried to escape.

As if, when I was wearing three pairs of cuffs.

Then there was another of those endless meaningless infuriating delays that seem to happen so much more in wartime. It lasted about forty minutes and was broken in an unexpected way. The door into the van suddenly slid open and there was Colonel Long.

"Ah, good," he said, smirking away like a pig who'd just been offered some Chocolate Bavarian. "There you are."

He closed the door behind him and sat next to me for a confidential chat.

"I have fixed everything," he said. "You see, I am still looking after you."

"Yes, thank you," I said, swallowing about six different emotions all in one gulp.

"You will see," he said. "I am sending you to a very good place. Not a bad place. As long as you keep sensible you will be all right."

I nodded.

"But you must be very careful," he said. "Say nothing to anyone. Not even your own people. Not even your friends. Your name Amber Faulding. You don't know anything except train. That way, you will be fine and one day soon the war will end and you will be back with your family and you will remember Colonel Long and how good he was to you."

"Yes," I said, "thank you very much. Thank you for all you have done. I'll definitely remember you after the war."

He nodded, satisfied.

Then he put his hand on my leg, just above the knee.

I felt like I'd had a hot brand applied to my skin. I felt it burn through to the bone. I sat there in shock. I hadn't realised what his sleazy looks really meant. I'd thought he was only interested in our conspiracy and when he sat close to me it was because we were partners in his plot to save his skin. Suddenly it seemed like there was a second agenda.

I must have been so red that I couldn't imagine he would fancy me, unless he was into tomatoes. I'd just turned into Tomato Head. I didn't know how to stop him. I was completely in his power. But when he moved his hand farther up my leg, I couldn't stand it anymore. To distract him, I asked again, "Colonel Long, the people at the truck stop, they were only kids, like me, are you sure they were . . ."

His eyes burned holes in me. "I told you," he hissed. "I told you already. Don't talk about that place. They all dead. I told you that. You very naughty girl."

"OK, I'm sorry. I won't ask again, I promise."

He scowled at me again, threw open the door of the bus and got out.

I sank back into my seat, feeling as much relief as if I'd just escaped death.

The driver and the guards got in, and we went for a little scenic drive. I didn't know this country at all, so I had no idea where we were going. We headed pretty much in a straight line for an hour and a half, roughly north-east. Then we turned west for about ten minutes, and that was it. We'd arrived.

I still felt so shaky after my chat with Colonel Long that I hardly took in the view from the bus window. But my first thought when we drove through the main set of gates, and I could see the whole place, was, "Heaps better than Stratton Prison."

For one thing it was in the open. Fresh air. Light. Real weather. The things that you don't even notice normally. The things you realise are the essence of life when you lose them. It all looked quite good, and I felt pleased to be out of the hospital. "Looks like I made a good call for once," I thought.

I still hadn't learned not to judge from appearances.

It was a clever set-up. I never saw any other prison camps, so I don't know what they were like, but Camp 23 was set in a quarry. And it was some quarry. You could lay out half-a-dozen football fields and still have room for a pony club. From top to bottom must have been a hundred metres, sheer cliffs all the way. I looked at them, wondering how it would be to climb them, at night for example, with the guards looking for you with rifles and spotlights. Thinking of my other climbs in this war, into the Holloway Valley, and more recently, down steep rock in search of the missing feral kids, I shuddered and looked away. I'd have to be full-on desperate to go up that cliff.

The camp itself was rows of tents, with two wooden buildings in the middle and a couple more around the perimeter. Soon enough I found out what the wooden buildings were: offices for the staff, mostly, except the ones in the middle, which were dining halls for us, the prisoners. Two high-wire fences stretched around the whole place, with fifty metres between them and guard towers at each corner. The ground between the fences had been cleared and raked: like it had been designed as the no-go zone, a good place to hang out if you were tired of life.

The tents seemed to go forever, in their neat lines, stretching away to the other end of the quarry. They were grey, with flies tightly stretched, and taut white ropes to the pegs. It was all perfectly symmetrical. After the jungle I'd been living in for so long it was kind of comforting.

Of course what I most wanted to see, what mattered most to me, was who was living in those tents. If I had to be locked up, I wanted it to be with my own people. The worst thing about the ward was not the injuries and the injections and the pain. The worst thing was being alone. You can survive anything if you're with friends. If the last year or so hadn't taught me that, it hadn't taught me anything.

Unfortunately I couldn't see the prisoners. The smell of food made me think they might be eating but I didn't get time to think about that. Instead I was un-cuffed from the bus seats.

I got up and stepped out, wanting to stretch my legs after the long trip, wanting to be free of the squashy little bus. But there was no time for that either. A guard from the camp, a man in an immaculate grey uniform, grabbed me by the left elbow and pulled me across in front of him, then, while I was still off-balance, pushed me hard towards the gate.

I went sprawling into the dust. I lay there, wanting to

give up, feeling the dust on my lips, feeling my heart turn to dust. Suddenly I realised this place might be pretty bad news.

I heard a voice yell, "Leave her alone, you mongrel." I looked up. A dozen or so prisoners, all men I think, had appeared, and were pressed against the inner fence, watching through the wire. At least my main question had just been answered. There was no doubt about the nationality of these people. It helped give me some strength.

The guard grabbed me by my hair, at the back of my head, and lifted me by it. The prisoners were all yelling now, but I couldn't make out the words through the pain that filled my head. The guard marched me along, into a small wooden building. As soon as we were in there he threw me against a wall and yelled: "Stand there! Stand up straight! You wait!"

Then he went into an office.

Nothing happened for a long time. I stood there, standing up as straight as I could, but leaning against the wall when I thought I could get away with it. Occasionally one of the guards kicked me in the shins to make me stand up again, but I was very tired and each time they pushed me off the wall I'd look for my chance to slump back against it. My main concern was to protect my wound, by keeping it away from the soldiers. I made sure they hit and kicked me on my good side.

I could still feel the place where Colonel Long had touched me, like a dark mark on my leg. I fantasised getting some soap and scrubbing it for an hour or two, to remove the shadow of his hand. But I had a feeling I wouldn't be getting too many bubble baths in this place.

People came and went, most of them guards in ordinary grey uniforms, plus a few officers with red trimming on their jackets, and different shaped hats. Phones kept ringing but they didn't get answered often. No-one seemed to be working too hard. One young guy sat at a desk typing some stuff into a computer, but he wasn't breaking any speed records, and judging by the way he kept cursing and using the backspace key I don't think he had much idea of what he was doing. I had a strong urge to go across there and take over, show him how to do it.

Some time in the middle of the afternoon, around three o'clock, a bloke came out of an office and gestured for me to go in.

I shuffled after him. It was hard to move with all the bruises I'd picked up that day. My leg and face were throbbing and I had a bad headache.

To my surprise the officer was quite polite. He asked about my bullet wound, but not about the other injuries. Maybe he didn't want to know that soldiers in his army beat up on girls. He didn't seem too interested in my answers anyway. I was in the middle of a long rambling description of the medical care in the hospital when he cut me off, and handed me a sheet of paper. It looked official but I couldn't read it.

"You don't know our language?"

"No."

"It is the result of your case. A military court met on the 28th and found you guilty of sabotage, terrorism and murder. You have been sentenced to thirty years imprisonment."

There didn't seem to be anything to say. I nearly laughed. If anything I felt relief, that apparently they weren't going to kill me. Anyway, thirty years seemed such a ridiculous figure. How did they arrive at that? Why not say forty? Or fifty? They were all equally meaningless.

The officer, as if trying to read my mind, said, "You are very lucky to avoid the death sentence. You committed your crimes at the right time."

When I looked puzzled he added: "It's all politics. Death sentences are not regarded as good politics at this moment."

I think he decided then that he'd said too much, because he stood up suddenly and went outside, where I could hear him talking to someone.

Two new guards came in, both women. They escorted me outside and marched me towards the first row of tents. No-one seemed to be around. We marched all the way along until we came to another barrier, which the guards unlocked, ushering me into a small compound at the north end of camp. When I saw a few women in the distance I realised this must be the female section. It was the end of my journey. One of the soldiers unlocked my handcuffs. God that felt good. The skin was raw in a few spots, where they'd been rubbing. I shook my hands to get the blood moving, then held them under my armpits. The guards headed out through the gate, but already another pair, a man and a woman this time, were marching towards me, their eyes focused hard on me.

I waited nervously. My introduction to this place had been so bad I didn't know what to expect. Ever since I'd been caught I felt I'd just been passed from one set of bullies to the next.

They pulled up in front of me, their boots raising a little cloud of dust. They were both overweight, both about thirty-five, both with soft baby faces. Before the dust settled the man started to shout at me. Or scream, I should say. He had a piercing voice. They would have heard him back in Stratton. I couldn't work out for a minute what he was saying. I was too tired. I didn't even realise it was in English. But eventually I understood it was the rules for the camp. Every time he yelled another one he came a bit nearer, until I felt really uncomfortable with his closeness.

"You not be late for meals! You not be late for roll-calls! You not be late for jobs!"

I took a step back and straightaway he slapped me, making my face sting and my eyes water. From then on he slapped me with each new rule. "You be polite to soldiers." Slap. "You not go over red line." Slap. "You not talk on rollcalls." Slap. "You keep tent neat and tidy. You not be outside tent at night. You not make up lies about soldiers." Slap slap slap.

My face became numb, but I could feel my jaw hurting more and more, like he was pushing it out of shape. I didn't dare back away again. I just had to wait till he'd finished.

He stopped as suddenly as he'd started. He yelled: "You stand there till I say," slapped me again, and the two of them marched away. I had thought he was giving me another rule, so it took me a moment to register that the speech was over. I waited, my face feeling swollen and sore, thinking, "I don't know whether I can hack thirty years of this."

I stood there for a while, I'm not sure how long, probably about an hour, then I started getting dizzy. It was weird. My stomach and chest seemed to have nothing in them but air, and my vision got really blurry. I thought I was swaying but maybe I was swaying quite a lot, because suddenly I did a Robyn, and fainted.

It's a strange feeling, fainting. Not that you have any feeling while you're doing it, of course. But when you wake up, you're still far away, floating, like something's gone wrong but you're not sure what it is. At least that's how it was for me. I've never fainted before so I can't be sure if that's the regular reaction. I woke up slowly, and knew I was lying on a bed but knew I shouldn't be, at that time of day. I struggled to get up, but immediately a couple of people held me down, which just made me struggle all the more.

"Let her go," someone said. It was a friendly voice, and I sat up, feeling stupid, trying to look around, to see where I was. I was in a tent. There were eight stretchers, four on each side, all neatly made up. I was sitting on the first one. They weren't hospital stretchers, just old-fashioned camping ones, like my grandmother kept in her shed. There was no other furniture. In the grey-green light everything seemed old and quiet and calm, but then my aches and pains gradually returned, reminding me that they were still there, and I didn't feel too calm after that.

There were three women watching me, one sitting on the next bed and the other two standing beside my stretcher.

They looked pretty grim. They made me nervous.

"Welcome to Camp 23," one of them said.

I didn't answer.

"I'm Judy."

I wasn't sure if I had any broken teeth or not, but somehow I mumbled, "I'm . . . I'm, um, Amber." Only at the last second did I remember my new name.

Judy nodded. I closed my eyes again. It hurt too much to have them open.

I became aware that there was a bad smell in the place. Like the chook shed at home when I hadn't cleaned it out for ages and the hay was rank and mouldy and rotten. I felt my nose wrinkle but tried to ignore it. I could hear the women talking but I was too tired to make out the words. I got the general idea that they were trying to work out where to put me. I wanted to say, "I can't move, I don't want to move, I'm too tired," but I was too tired to say it or anything else. Then they virtually rolled me off the bed.

I staggered back outside. It felt cold out there. They were prodding me along relentlessly. Even my own people didn't seem to have any mercy. When they'd lined the fence before, and yelled out support, I'd hoped I was coming into a friendly, kind environment. This didn't feel too friendly or kind.

They prodded me all the way to another tent that seemed the same as the one I'd left, even to the bad smell. I collapsed onto a bed and fell straight asleep without even getting under the rough grey blanket. I must have slept pretty heavily; when I woke up I had the pattern of the blanket embedded on the side of my face.

From the moment I woke I felt desperately scared and insecure. I didn't know the rules for this place. I was in a limbo, and had no points of contact with anyone. The only thing I knew for sure was that this camp was ugly and violent and frightening. The stiffness and soreness of my face and body were evidence of that.

Two girls a bit older than me were already rolling out of their beds. They'd slept in their clothes, in the rough-and-ready kind of stuff that everyone here seemed to wear, like they'd raided the dump bin behind an op-shop.

"You'd better hurry," one of them said. "You don't want to be late for rollcall."

The way she said it made rollcall sound a fraction worse than an iceberg warning on the *Titanic*.

I sat upright then somehow got off the bed and made myself stand, ignoring the throbbing in my neck and jaw. The other two were already hurrying out of the tent, and I stumbled after them, catching up with the last girl as we passed the next tent. Ahead of us were a couple of dozen others, heading in the same direction.

"I'm Issa," the girl said.

"Hi, I'm Amber."

It was too cold, and I was too tired to say any more. A few moments later we were on the parade ground.

The guards arrived. Even as they marched towards us I felt the tension rise. There wasn't a single thing you could point to that showed it. No-one screamed or fainted or fell to their knees. No-one hugged the person next to them or begged for mercy. But I felt a fear that was different to anything I'd felt before. It was a fear like a breeze, chilling the whole place. It sure brought my skin out in prickles.

Yet nothing really happened. We had to stand in the places we were allocated, while they read out the names. They were organised enough to have my name already, and in alphabetical order. Maybe that guy had been smarter with the computer than I'd thought. We had to yell "Present" in a loud voice, and then they counted us, to make sure we weren't answering for each other. It should have been easy, but because there were people in the camp hospital, or missing for some other legit reason, like working in the camp kitchen, the numbers wouldn't balance.

We stood there for three-quarters of an hour. In the cold light of dawn it wasn't very funny, but at the same time I loved to see the sun rising. It looked like it was floating above a bank of clouds, sitting on them even: a huge red soft sun that looked like it might melt onto the clouds.

Then suddenly it was just a normal clear day, bright, and the sky was all blue.

I stood in line for breakfast with the two girls from my new tent, Issa and Monique. Feeling a stir of energy at the end of the queue I glanced around. The men were coming in, from their side of the camp. They crowded into the meal hut, outnumbering the women by at least five to one.

We got our food on battered stainless steel trays that were scratched and dented and warped. The food was complete crap. A mouldy orange, with white powder over half the peel and the inside soft and oversweet, a bowl of water with some kind of weak beef flavouring in it, and a slice of toast that was soggy and unbuttered. I nearly threw up when I tried to eat the orange. I went to push it away, but Issa leaned over to me and said, "If you want to survive, eat everything. You'll need all the strength you can get."

So I made myself. I forced the orange down by tearing it into small segments. At least none of the stuff hurt my sore mouth.

Men and women weren't allowed to sit in the same areas, but there was a boundary and you could talk across it if you had the energy.

I didn't go near the men. I didn't want to. I felt too sick and scared and tired and old. Hearing those male voices reminded me so fiercely of Homer and Lee and Kevin that I felt terrible physical pain, a sickness that twisted my gut.

I was relieved to get out of there, but less relieved when I found what the day had in store. I went to the dunny, which was foul, but no sooner was I out of there than Issa was hurrying towards me: "Quick, you can't stay here. The work parade starts now."

"Work parade?"

But she was already trotting away, between the lines of tents. I followed her to the place where we'd had the roll-call before breakfast. After the little panic to get there we had an anticlimax, waiting for another three-quarters of an hour while orders were yelled and cancelled, lists were checked, long lines of men were marched away from their section to different locations, and we got colder and hungrier.

Issa stood beside me, huddled into a holey old purple rollneck jumper, with big holes and lots of loose threads. It looked like the moths had held their annual convention in it, but it looked warm, and I envied her that. She said to me: "What's happened to your leg?"

Even though I'd been asleep so much of the time I'd still done a bit of thinking. I didn't like my conclusion, but I knew it was the right one. This was a huge camp; maybe a thousand prisoners. Anything I said was going to travel the length and breadth of the place.

"I hitched a ride on a train," I said. "And just after I got off, the train derailed. So they thought I'd sabotaged it or something. They came chasing after me, and I decided it wasn't too healthy, so I ran. And these soldiers starting firing at me, and I copped a bullet in the leg."

She nodded sympathetically. "I heard you'd been accused of wrecking a train. See, there's no secrets in this place. You're lucky though, a few months ago something like that would have put you in front of a firing squad."

"Why's it changed?"

She looked at me in surprise. "Don't you know? They're

getting nervous. Since D-Day they've been backing off a bit. They're worried that if the Kiwis win, they'll get busted for war crimes."

I sat up. "So are we definitely winning? What's been happening?"

"God, where have you been?"

"I've been living rough. I haven't heard any news. I've been hanging out in the bush."

"So did you nick off from a secured area? Or a work party? Don't they take reprisals if you do that?"

"No, no," I said uncertainly. "We live way out, and they're pretty slack out there. They left us alone. We could get away with just about anything."

I figured Issa wouldn't know any better. I hated lying to her, but it was a matter of life and death for me. If word got out that I'd been involved in stuff like bombing Cobbler's Bay or wrecking Wirrawee airfield, I'd get the firing squad then, no worries, D-Day or no D-Day. In fact with what they'd do to me, I'd probably be begging for a firing squad before they'd finished.

To change the subject I started asking Issa about herself, and Monique. "I got twelve years," she said, "for sabotage."

"What kind of sabotage?"

"They put me in a factory in Cavendish, making hydraulic hoses, for aircraft mainly. It was so boring, you've got no idea. A couple of us started organising everyone to sabotage them. Pricking little holes in them, deliberately making them a couple of centimetres short, that kind of thing. When they got onto it, they pulled some of the weaker girls in for questioning, and within half an hour they had my name and two others they reckoned were the ringleaders. The other two confessed, and got eight years, but like an idiot I denied the whole thing and got twelve."

I thought, "There's more than one way to fight." I asked her: "So is the war really going better?"

"Well, you know how it is, one rumour after another, you wouldn't know what's happening. But they say there's a chance now. And the Administration and the senior guards have changed their attitude. The others haven't, but I guess if you're a true sadist you don't like to give it up.

"Still," she sighed, "you can't imagine how a little country like New Zealand could win a war. I don't see how they can."

"If they get lots of help though . . ."

"Yes, they say Japan's backing us. Never would have picked that, hey? According to Monique they don't even have an army of their own. Well, who knows, we may get up yet. God I hope so. Can't stand much more of these bastards."

We were on the move at last, marching through the gates and out onto the road, away from the quarry. Well, everyone else marched. I limped. We went about three kilometres, to a smaller quarry. My leg was killing me by then.

We were put to work shovelling mud. This quarry hadn't been used for a long time. I don't know how deep the mud was in the middle, but at the edges, where we were working, it was up to my knees, awful black sticky stuff, that sucked you in like quicksand. Every time you took a wrong step you sank down into it, and if you weren't careful you'd lose your boots trying to pull yourself out. By the fifth or sixth time I was utterly exhausted, and it was only eleven o'clock.

I swapped with Issa, wheeling the barrows instead of shovelling, but it wasn't any easier. Gradually the mud dried on my legs till it caked like a plaster cast, and then fell off, leaving shells of mud along my tracks. But that was the least of my problems. I thought I was strong, and normally I would be, but now, still recovering from all that had happened, I had no strength at all. The vital thing, on each trip with the barrow, was to get it moving. The first part was the worst. As the weight of mud built up, its legs sank deeper and deeper. If I could pull it out of the mud and start it rolling, I had a chance to push it up onto the drier land. It was all to do with momentum. If I couldn't keep it moving through the first fifty metres of muddy stuff I was in real trouble.

It wasn't just the weight of the barrow and the sticking power of the mud. It was the guards standing around watching, laughing at your efforts, then bashing you every time the barrow tipped over. You had to get the barrow upright again before the guard came striding down, truncheon swinging, and you felt the heavy smack of it against your shoulder blades.

The other bad part was at the end of each trip, pushing the barrow along a plank onto a kind of loading dock, then tipping it into a truck. The plank looked easy from the bottom but once you got a few metres along it started to bend and sway like it would break at any moment.

My main motivation in keeping my balance on the plank, in not letting the barrow tip over, was seeing a middle-aged woman lose her barrow over the edge when she was halfway to the truck. A guard hit her across the mouth with the full force of his truncheon. She fell from the plank onto the barrow. She opened her mouth, in slow motion, and I saw a pool of blood run from it and then she spat out a sprinkle of teeth, like little diamonds. I wondered how bad things had been before D-Day, if things were so much better at Camp 23 now. Maybe this guard was just one of the sadists Issa had mentioned.

Lunch was as many cans of peeled tomatoes as you could eat. It was a strange meal. A four-wheel drive came down and dumped about fifty cases of the stuff, and a couple of can openers. Remembering what Issa said about eating everything, and figuring I needed the vitamin C, I ate as much as I could — three and a quarter cans — then brought half of it up ten minutes later.

The afternoon was a nightmare. I thought it would never end. I trudged in and out of the mud a hundred times, my legs aching, cramping, knotting, until I couldn't lift them, and had to slide along like I was wearing skates. My back was so painful from the baton hits that I couldn't lift my arms above shoulder level, which made it hard to shovel. To make things worse, they'd moved us to the western side of the quarry, and every time I pushed my barrow along the track I had to pass the body of a young woman who looked like she'd been there a week or more. She had obviously been a prisoner, but I didn't like to ask anyone who she was or how she died, because I didn't want to upset Issa and the others. But she lay there with her eye sockets empty and her skin blackened and peeling from the sun, and all the signs that rodents or birds or foxes had been doing what scavengers do. It didn't help me keep the peeled tomatoes down.

What did help was the attitude of the other prisoners. They were gutsy. All morning they'd kept me going with encouragement, jokes, advice. As the day wore on and their energy levels dropped, they didn't have so much to say, but every grin through cracked and bleeding lips was worth another half an hour to me.

At last it was over. We gathered up the tools and dragged them to a little shed. Then we began the march back. I didn't think I would make it. I fell over four times in the last kilometre, and each time Issa or Monique helped me up. I remember how I used to be the strong one, and wondered if after a few weeks of this I'd be as tough as these women. I wondered if I'd ever get any strength from a diet of mouldy oranges and canned tomatoes. I remembered how I'd almost laughed when the officers said I had thirty years. I wasn't laughing now. I didn't see how I could survive six months of this, let alone another day.

We got back to the tent. I collapsed onto my bed, and I mean collapsed. But I did have enough energy to ask Monique: "Are there any showers?"

She and Issa both looked at me.

"Didn't you notice the smell when you moved in?" Issa asked.

I blushed. "Well, yes, I guess . . . but I don't really notice it now."

They laughed, but like all the laughter in Camp 23, it wasn't very funny. Not a lot of sweetness in it.

"That's because you smell so bad yourself, with that mud. We're all pretty rank." Issa was like that, direct and honest. She'd been studying architecture before she got arrested.

"So aren't there any showers?"

"There are. If you want to use them."

"Why wouldn't I want to use them? Are they cold? Right now I wouldn't care if they were melted ice."

"We keep ourselves smelling bad," Issa said. "It's the only contraceptive we've got."

It took me a bit of time to work out what she was saying, then I started to figure it. "You mean . . . the guards?"

"You got it, baby," Monique said.

"You deliberately make yourself smell bad?"

"There are women here who rub cow shit over themselves," Issa said, staring straight at me, like she was daring me to say it was disgusting. Or maybe she was seeing how tough I was, whether I was going to be tough enough to survive Camp 23.

"These guards are bad news," Monique said, joining in. "Don't ever get in a situation where you're on your own, if you can help it. They're dangerous."

"But most of the ones I've seen are women."

"Yeah. But there're eleven males. And some of the female ones don't mind helping them. You're young and good-looking, and that's a dangerous combination around here."

I shivered, feeling again the stain of Colonel Long's hand on my leg. That was another thing I hadn't mentioned to Monique and Issa. I was glad that I hadn't. Compared to what had been happening in this camp, Colonel Long sounded pretty small-time.

I felt very shy with Monique and Issa. Apart from the ferals, and Ryan, who didn't really count, I hadn't been with any new people for a long time. I certainly hadn't been with any girls near my age, except Fi.

They started telling me the facts of life in Camp 23. They could see I didn't want to say much, so they did the talking. They explained the camp was for "recalcitrants," which seemed to mean "hardliners." I knew that by now most of the population on the outside were back in normal houses, even if they were small and crowded. They were doing all the boring and dirty jobs for their new bosses. So I'd already figured out that anyone in this camp was likely to be special in one way or another. When I'd arrived I thought they might be crims; like, bank robbers and rapists. But as I listened I realised that they all seemed to have done stuff like me, but in different ways.

I already knew Issa's crime. Monique's had been to crash a car when she was the driver for a general. The general got two broken legs, Monique got three broken ribs and a fifteen-year jail sentence. She was twenty, and had a baby boy who'd been killed in a New Zealand air raid. She cried in her sleep every night.

Monique had been a trainee journalist on a little country newspaper in Malton.

I'd been lucky in my tentmates. But in the middle of their conversation I fell into a sleep so heavy that they had to pull me off my bed onto the floor to wake me for tea. I don't know why they bothered. The entire meal consisted of dry white bread with spots of mould all over it. Oh, and sorry, I forgot to mention the hot water with a few tea-leaves at the bottom of the cup.

13

The thing about Camp 23 that was different from any thing or any place else I'd been in my life was that here soldiers were vicious and cruel all the time, without any reason. Just for the hell of it. Sure, there was a group of boys at school who could be horrible to someone they didn't like. But it was a quantum leap (whatever that means) to the guards of Camp 23. They bashed and battered people because . . . well, that was it, there was no because. They just did it.

I saw terrible things. On my second day at the quarry, shovelling mud, a girl near me got mud pushed down her throat by a guard who decided he didn't like her attitude. He made her swallow, I don't know, about a litre of the stuff, until she lay on the ground spewing and choking. He walked away laughing.

I took my lead from the others, like the day before, and didn't try to interfere. I asked Issa that night: "Why doesn't anyone do anything?"

"Because we don't want to get our arms broken."

"OK."

Sometimes "OK" is the only thing you can say.

"You know that tall girl on crutches? Vanessa? The reason she's on crutches is that she tried to stop them raping a friend of hers. So the guards broke her leg by holding her down with her head on one chair and her feet on another, and then jumping on her leg till the bone snapped."

The next day, when a girl was pistol-whipped across

the face until her mouth was a red hole in a bleeding mess of flesh I kept my head down. I felt sick, I felt sweat break out all over my body, I felt tears fill my eyes until they dropped one by one into the sticky black mud, but I kept my head down.

Issa and Monique kept me going. Nothing else could have. I was just about ready to give up, not once but a hundred times. While I was in 23 Issa and Monique were stronger than me. Indomitable.

It showed in a hundred ways. A hug when you'd just walked past something brutal and awful. A quick comment like, "Come on, Amber, don't let them get to you," when I was struggling to keep my wheelbarrow moving along the plank. A joke when you looked at your plate and saw the crap that the guards called food.

We didn't have a lot of laughs though. There weren't many merry moments. The only truly fun episode I saw was when a guard accidentally shot his foot off. A rabbit suddenly sprinted across the floor of the quarry where we were working, and the guard tried to get his pistol out of his holster so he could have some target practice. Unfortunately for him he was in such a hurry that the gun went off while he was still pulling it out. God he screamed. That was what we called entertainment in Camp 23: someone shooting himself.

For once, the bleakness I felt inside matched the bleakness around me. The pain I felt over the deaths of my friends got lost in a more general pain, the pain of being alive in this terrible wasteland, a desert of the human spirit.

Nothing here was fun. Nothing. The food, the work, the mud, the guards, even the toilet facilities. The Hell I'd lived in for more than a year was a distant memory now. This place was called Camp 23, but it really was hell.

All week I looked forward to Sunday, the day of rest. In fact Issa and Monique and I spent a lot of time planning how to spend the precious spare time.

One thing we didn't need to worry about much was washing clothes. I hated the smell of my clothes and my body, the salty musty smell, and I hated the deep grime in my skin, that looked like it was sandblasted in there, but I realised the others were right: better to be dirty and smelly than the alternative.

My first Sunday all I wanted to do was sleep. God I looked forward to it. But instead, just after breakfast, Issa came and got me.

"Judy wants to see you."

"Judy?"

"You've met Judy. She's the one who brought you to our tent. She's the Senior Prisoner. That's one of the changes they've brought in recently. We were allowed to appoint someone to be in charge of us, and to be our spokesperson. She's the one the Administration deals with now."

Judy turned out to be a tough proposition. Issa and Monique had accepted my story about the train wreck so easily it hadn't occurred to me that I might have trouble with anyone else. But Judy was different. I told her the same stuff I'd told Issa, but right away she started picking holes in it. I suddenly realised I'd have to be very careful. I didn't know then that she'd been a lawyer before the war, but I should have guessed.

"So you left the train and it derailed a few moments later?"

She didn't need to add: "That's some coincidence." It was in her eyes and the tone of her voice.

"Well, yes, not just moments later. It was a few minutes after I'd got off."

"It must have been very close if the soldiers from the train chased you and caught you."

"I guess it was close, but not that close."

I was embarrassed by such a lame answer.

"What made the train derail?"

"I don't know. Maybe it was an accident, maybe it was sabotage. I think there have been some Kiwis operating around Cavendish, blowing up stuff."

"Was there an explosion?"

"Ah, yeah, I think there was, yeah, well a sort of explosion. It was hard to tell."

I knew I wasn't doing this too well, but I was so mentally exhausted, and this woman had taken me by surprise. She'd derailed me.

"Something blew up, but I'm not sure if it was before the thing derailed or as it derailed. Like, whether something in the train blew up when it left the line. Look, does it really matter?"

"Well, it could. I deal with the Administration here, and they're very different to the guards. If a prisoner's been unfairly convicted we prepare a submission to try to get them released again. We're actually making some headway on a couple of cases. Anyway," she smiled, "at the very least we're annoying them, and keeping them busy in another area. It's part of our campaign of harassment. Which of course is why most of us are here in the first place.

"Now tell me, you say you were living out in the country, ever since the invasion?"

"Yes."

The interrogation was back on again.

"Where exactly?"

"Uh, sort of, through Wirrawee."

"Really? That's funny, I thought that area was very strictly controlled."

"Oh yeah, closer into town, sure, but where we were, it's pretty slack."

"When you say 'we,' you mean you and your parents?"

"Yeah."

"So you were all allowed to stay out there? Together?"

I suddenly realised how stupid I'd been. Not only because my story was falling apart but by what I'd just said, and by sticking to my false name, I'd missed out on the one thing I was desperate to do: ask for information about my parents. I sat there like an asthmatic in a basketball game, gasping for breath. Judy just watched, her head cocked. It was impossible to tell what she was thinking.

"Well," I said finally, "we got separated a while back. I was actually looking for them when I took the train ride."

"We might be able to help you there. We have people from all over. We could find someone in the camp who's seen them."

I groaned inwardly. This was getting worse and worse. My big chance to track them down, and I was making a mess of it.

All I could think of was the old line I'd used so many times at Wirrawee High.

"Can I be excused please?" I mumbled. "I don't feel well."

"Of course." She stood up. "I can see you've been through a lot. This war's certainly taken its toll on all of us."

I really did feel awful as I left. She seemed like a nice and capable person. I hated having to lie to her.

Back at the tent there were more questions. "What did she want? What did you say to her? What did she say about your sentence?"

Too many questions. I was sick of questions. Suddenly I felt sick of everything. I turned my head into the pillow and scrabbled and kicked my legs until they were under the blanket. I suppose it must have looked pretty stupid. Like an echidna digging itself into the earth. But the questions weren't over yet. A few hours later, just before lunch, I got another message to go see Judy. I went with a lot of reluctance, dragging my feet like I was in the quarry pushing mud uphill. And no sooner was I sitting in her office than she went on the attack.

"I've made a few enquiries, Amber. There seems to be no doubt that the train was sabotaged using a high-powered explosive."

I didn't answer, just sat staring dumbly at her.

"There's also a rumour that you may have been involved in an attack on a truck depot, where they suffered heavy casualties.

"I don't understand, Amber. If you managed to blow up an enemy train, at such a critical stage of the war, you would be regarded as a hero in this camp. Why do you think we're all locked up? In our different ways, we've all opposed the invasion, resisted it, fought against it. Most of us haven't done something as spectacular as destroying a train, but we've each done what we can."

She sat back, waiting for me to say something. It was like she was inviting me to trust her. I couldn't make my mind work. I kept pressing every button in my brain, but it was totally dead. I got no response. This wasn't like a tractor with a flat battery in the middle of winter. Even that'll turn over slightly. Even that'll give a tired little whirr. I got nothing.

I'm not sure how long Judy sat there. I could see she was completely baffled, and I actually felt sorry for her, embarrassed that I was giving her such a hard time. But what could I do?

Finally she put both her hands flat on the desk in front of her, palms down, and gazed at me. "Amber, I don't know what else I can say to you. We have occasionally had spies and informers planted in the camp. I certainly hope you're not one of them. I don't think you are, but I'm bound to warn you, if you are, you're in a very dangerous situation, and I suggest you get out of the place again, as fast as you can arrange it."

I shook my head slowly, and keeping my voice expressionless I said: "I'm not a spy or an informer."

"No," she said. "I can believe that."

It seemed another interview was at an end. I got up to go. Still facing her I asked: "If I wanted to get information on some friends, people I knew before the war, how would I go about it?"

"We've just opened a tracing service, in Tent 29, with the help of the Red Cross. Go and see them."

"Thank you."

I still didn't know how to do it. If I turned up at Tent 29 and asked about my parents, Judy would hear about it within three minutes. All those media appearances we'd done in New Zealand, about a hundred years ago it seemed like, meant that my name was too well known. To be honest, one of the weirdest side-effects of the war was that we'd become famous. When I'd dreamed before the war of being famous, I'd never thought of it being for this kind of stuff.

What it meant was that Judy, and anyone else who could even spell IQ, would work out who I was. And if one person knew, as far as I was concerned, a thousand people would know.

I worried about it all through lunch. But it was still too hard to concentrate. It wasn't just my own state of mental white-out; it was the noise of the dining hall. I guess anytime you get one hundred females and nine hundred males in a small space it's likely to be noisy.

So I kept walking, past the last line of tents, to the first fence. I was now at the extreme end of the camp. Beyond the fence was the bare earth of the fifty-metre no-go zone, with a guard tower to my right, and another to my left. I stood gazing out at the wall of the quarry. I wanted to be alone but I knew the guards were watching from their towers. If I looked up I could see them: automatic carbines pointing towards me, bored faces over the edge of the railing, eyes hidden by dark glasses. I didn't dare go right to the fence, even though I think it was legal, but I hadn't been there long enough to know all the rules.

Suddenly the sense of loss for my friends overwhelmed me. I'd been fighting it, denying it, ignoring it, but I couldn't any longer. I didn't know who to mourn most, and my feelings got torn between the four of them. Growing up in a small community, like we all had, everyone and everything becomes so significant. There's nothing that doesn't matter. A tree falls, a garden grows, a baby's born, an old person dies. And it all goes to the heart of you. It rearranges you. The bigger the event, the more you're rearranged.

But somehow that wasn't enough for Homer, Lee, Fi, Kevin. It wasn't enough for Chris or Robyn or Corrie. It wasn't enough for me. Old people could accept the way things happened, but we couldn't.

When I set out to write what we'd done in the war, it was like a public thing. We wanted to know that we'd made a difference on a big scale. I wrote it because we wanted to be remembered, because we wanted to believe that our lives had some meaning. We wanted to know that we hadn't passed through the world unchanged, and that we hadn't left the world unchanged. We didn't want to come and go from this planet without leaving a mark. Looking around me sometimes, even before the war back at school, I'd had the feeling that the only mark some people were going to leave on the world was a skidmark.

As time went on, writing became my private thing, done for myself. A habit, a compulsion, a way of remembering and understanding. Writing it down made it real. But now I thought, standing at the fence, that I had to put it on paper because that was how I could tell other people about my friends, their lives and their deaths.

I'd changed my mind quite a bit about what it meant to have a big audience. The only people who really matter are the ones who are close to you, who know you as you are, and love you as you are. It didn't really take seven deaths to teach me that. But I still think it's wrong the way people who live and die quietly don't get noticed. I don't know why we mourn the death of a celebrity more than the death of a postman or a Papuan baby or a Bolivian widow. "Any man's death diminishes me. Never send to know for whom the bell tolls; it tolls for thee. No man is an island." The instructor on Outward Bound kept quoting that.

When I was much younger I'd been reading the paper over Mum's shoulder. I pointed to a little paragraph with the headline: "Over the Limit." It said something like: "A brewery worker in Osaka Japan drowned yesterday in a vat of beer. Police said the man may have already been unconscious when he fell into the vat. It was some hours before his work-mates noticed he was missing."

I giggled when I read it. My mother didn't giggle. She said: "That's terrible, and sad."

I felt that I'd done something wrong by giggling. "Why?" I asked.

"A man died. His family will be crying for him today. His friends will be missing him. There is a great emptiness in their lives right now. It's wrong for the newspaper to try to turn it into a joke."

Sometimes I think my mother is the wisest person I've ever met.

The last thing that died on our farm before the invasion was Boris, this feral peacock who had flown in one afternoon, decided he liked the place, and stayed. It wasn't quite as unlikely as it sounds, because there was an old retired guy a few k's down the road who had heaps of peacocks and quails and pigeons and stuff like that, and Boris had obviously done a midnight flit. Dad rang the guy and told him we had one of his escapees, but the guy didn't care.

Boris was a complete lunatic of a bird. He had an obsession with houses. Every time we left a door open Boris popped inside and pooed all over the floor. I hated cleaning it up. I hated Boris. One evening I found him in the house and chased him out but a bit later I realised he'd roosted on the lowest branch of the pine tree outside my window. I mean, we're talking about a metre off the ground. I thought, "Well, that's no good, because a fox'll get him," so I tried to lift him and put him up higher. He was incredibly heavy, but somehow I got him to the next branch. As soon as I let go he crashed straight to the ground. It was terrible. I've never seen a bird do that, before or since. Maybe at night he just shut down all his systems, including his sense of balance. I thought he'd broken his neck. He hadn't, but it took two of us, Mum and me, to get him into a bole in the tree where he wouldn't fall out again.

Anyway, to cut a long story short, one morning I saw a trail of Boris' feathers leading across a paddock. I followed them for a while, until I got to the ones that were red with blood, and then I knew I wasn't going to see Boris ever again. It must have been a huge struggle for a fox to get him away, but the fox had won.

And I felt terrible about it. I felt so sad for Boris. Even though I didn't like him, even though he was a complete dag, I wanted him not to be dead. Why? I don't know. Just because he was such a proud, stupid, beautiful bird, with his own annoying personality and his own weird lonely lifestyle.

Life is just so precious and strange and beautiful and sad and special, I guess that's all I'm saying, and I hate to see it thrown away or taken away or crushed and destroyed.

I still couldn't shed any tears that day for Homer and Fi and Lee and Kevin though. I gradually found myself sinking lower and lower on the ground until I was a little ball lying there. I suppose I must have looked like those ultrasounds of babies in the womb, the way I was curled up. Weird. I don't know how long I was there. Two or three hours maybe. I really don't know.

Suddenly it seemed like Sunday was over, and I felt furious that I hadn't enjoyed it. I'd wasted my day of rest.

But my Sunday wasn't quite over. That night I had a visitor. Judy had decided I needed a medical, so Dr Muir made a house call.

He took me by surprise. I'd never expected to see a male prisoner in our area, but he had the freedom to wander around. Likewise the guards let us go through the male area if we were going to the camp hospital, and if we were escorted by Judy.

Dr Muir was quite nice actually. Young guy, very blond, with pale skin and pale eyes and ginger eyebrows, slow and careful in the questions he asked and the way he examined me. He spent a lot of time checking my eyes and ears and mouth, in particular. He didn't have much equipment, just a stethoscope and a thermometer and a rubber hammer for belting my knees, to test my reflexes.

"So will I live?" I asked, when he'd finished.

"You're in better shape than you should be, considering what you've been through. Your hospital records arrived today, much to my surprise. You can never tell what'll turn up in this war. Judging by your test results, you should be dead. But you're very fit. That would have helped."

He looked at me curiously. "Judy is quite puzzled by you. Calls you the mystery girl."

"Nothing mysterious about me."

"Well, I don't know about that. You've been in this place nearly a week, and still no-one knows anything about you. I'd call that pretty mysterious, the way the grapevine works around here."

He made me even more nervous, saying that. I glanced at Issa, who was sitting in the entrance to the tent, her back to me. I didn't know if she could hear or not. The last thing I wanted was for people to be talking about me. That was terribly dangerous, in a place that thrived on gossip.

Issa and Monique had gone through a stage of being really curious, asking a heap of questions. When I survived that, they pretty much gave up, like they realised I didn't want to talk and wasn't about to start. That would have been all right, except it put a wall between us: I felt left out, like I couldn't be admitted to their friendship full-on. They were great to me, and I tried hard in every other way, like doing most of the work to keep the tent clean, but they were a bit reserved with me.

A week later I was sweeping the area around the back of the dining hall. It was a nice day and sweeping was quite a good job. For the previous six days we'd been loading bricks onto trucks. My hands were blistered and raw and bruised. The skin had been rubbed off them in a dozen different places. Every half an hour or so one of my fingers got crushed or pinched or scraped, until they were twice their normal size, looking like colourful pork sausages.

Maybe the biggest problem was that the bricks were ideal for the guards to use as weapons. A girl working right next to me had been hit so hard on the side of the head with a brick that her eye had been pushed out of its socket. She was still in the camp hospital. If the guards didn't like what you were doing, they'd chuck bricks at you from ten metres away. You had to watch them the whole time.

I'd volunteered to do the sweeping. It was Judy's policy for everyone to do some work on Sundays to keep the camp neat and tidy. I didn't mind, except holding the broom hurt my hands. Judy said a clean camp was good for morale, and it probably was. At least this was one of those mindless jobs where you could think about other stuff. For once I was thinking more about the future than the past. I was dreaming of being back on the farm with my parents, after the war, when everything would be back to normal. I'd be on the motorbike, accelerating through wet cowpats to splatter my father as he followed on his bike, I'd be creosoting the new pots for the cattle race and ignoring the warnings on the drum about how carcinogenic it was, I'd be winching the Land Rover out of the river as fast as I could, before Dad found I'd taken it "where I should have known better."

Of course in dreaming about the future I was really dreaming about the past. Sometimes it's impossible to separate the two. I guess it's always impossible. It's like the future is a building you put up on the foundations of the past.

I'd been sweeping for half an hour or so, and had worked my way around to the front of the dining hall, where already a few dozen people were waiting for lunch. Although the food was utterly disgusting, meals were still a big deal in the camp. Partly because they broke the monotony, partly because you got to see the men.

Suddenly my past caught up with me. A woman's voice screamed: "Oh my God! Ellie!"

My head whipped up like a Jack Russell that's seen a rabbit. I felt my eyes almost pop, the hair on my head stand up like a willy-willy had hit it. I stood holding the broom and gazing at the woman as she advanced on me. I didn't even recognise her. That was the biggest joke.

"Ellie," she kept saying, as if once wasn't enough. "Ellie Linton! Oh I don't believe it! Ellie! Oh, everyone's been talking about you! And you're actually here!"

She had been a big woman once, you could see that,

and it hit me then who she was. Mrs Samuels, who'd done the mail run out past our place for years. The trouble was, you rarely saw the person behind the wheel of the little station wagon delivering the letters, so it was no wonder I hadn't recognised her. Plus she'd lost weight of course, like everyone else in this war.

I dropped the broom and held out my hands to stop her. But it was too late. Already curious people were moving in on us, including Issa and Monique. I heard someone say: "Her name's Amber." Mrs Samuels rounded on her with all the pride of someone who's just bought the most expensive heifer at the annual sales. "Oh no," she said. "Don't you know who this is? You know the young people who blew up the ships in Cobbler's Bay? And the ammunition factory at Point Nelson. You've got a famous person here."

She turned to me. "How long have you been here, Ellie? How did you get caught? I've been sick for a few weeks, and in the camp hospital . . ."

I fled. It was all too much. I could no more have stopped her than I could have stopped a stampeding bull. Now that she was wound up I knew she'd go on for an hour and a half. And what on earth was all that about an ammunition factory? I'd never seen an ammunition factory in my life, let alone blown one up.

The trouble with being in prison is that there's nowhere to run. I went back to the tent, not because I felt safe there, but because I had no choice. And of course it wasn't at all safe. Three or four minutes later Issa and Monique arrived. They were absolutely goggle-eyed.

"Why didn't you tell us?"

"We knew there was something funny about you."

"Oh my God, this is so amazing."

"We heard all about you guys, on the pirate radios."

"That's why you never said anything about yourself."

"I tell you what, girl, if I'd done half of what you've done, I'd have been blabbing it all over the camp. You couldn't have shut me up."

"I don't know what to call you now, Amber or Ellie. I still think of you as Amber."

"How could you have done all that stuff? Weren't you shitting yourself from start to finish?"

The only good thing I heard among all the babble was Issa saying: "We told everyone to leave you alone. They've gone into lunch."

A minute later they got sent away. Judy had arrived.

14

My first instinct when we got back to Judy's office was to collapse in a blubbering heap on the floor. Unfortunately that was a luxury I couldn't afford. Things were too desperate.

"I wish you'd told me," she said crossly.

"I couldn't take the risk."

"Well, it's no good crying over spilt milk. We've got to decide what to do about this." She paused, and I guess she decided she was being a bit ungracious, because, getting quite pink, she added: "It is wonderful what you and your friends achieved. I suppose you did blow up the train after all?"

I nodded.

"Yes, I knew you had. That was just one of the confusing things about you. What happened to your friends? Are they all right, do you know?"

"They got killed, the same day I was caught."

I felt my face break up as I said it, and had to fight to get it back under control.

"I'm very sorry."

She stood and said: "Look, I'm going to go and see Joachim, my counterpart in the male section. We have a real problem now. Everyone in the camp will know about you already and in my opinion a number of prisoners are far too friendly with the guards. So our challenge is to keep your identity secret. In the meantime you'd better stay here, and I'll make sure none of the other prisoners are allowed in."

"How can you keep my identity secret?" I asked. I felt she had no hope. My future was looking disastrous.

"I don't know. It may well prove to be impossible."

I appreciated her honesty, even as I felt sick at the implications of what she said.

Then she really shocked me by adding: "There is another option. We can try to get you out of here, before the authorities discover who you are."

"How could you do that?"

"With great difficulty. There have been four escapes from the camp, in twelve months, but only two of them succeeded. The other two were caught before they'd gone half a kilometre."

She was about to leave, then she stopped and looked at me and said: "Is that what you'd like? Would you be willing to take the risk, if we come up with a plan that looks possible?"

"Do I have a choice?" I asked bitterly.

Strangely enough at that moment, I wasn't thinking so much of the risks, but of how awful it would be to leave the security of the girls in my tent, the comfort of having my own people around me. The outside looked lonely and dangerous from where I was sitting. But of course I knew the inside was now even more dangerous. It looked safe enough, but that had always been an illusion. Now it was an illusion that threatened my life.

Judy was gone nearly two hours. Someone brought me lunch, rice that must have been cooked two or three days ago. The grains were like hard little seeds. I never felt less like eating, but remembering what Issa had said I forced the food down. When Judy returned I was half-asleep, hanging over the back of the chair, but I woke up fast enough when she walked in.

"We have an idea," she said, "but I have to ask you again: is this what you want? Do you think escaping is better than staying here?"

"What do you think?"

"The truth is that if you stay here the authorities will know your identity within twenty-four hours, and after that your life won't be worth . . ." She snapped her fingers.

She was only confirming what I already knew. I just needed to have her spell it out. It was time to get out, and the sooner the better.

I didn't have to answer. She worked it out, from the expression on my face.

"All right," she said briskly. "This is what's been suggested, by Dr Muir actually, whom you've met. Now you may or may not know that at the other end of the camp are a few tents we are allowed to use as a little hospital."

I nodded. I did know that.

"Most of the patients are people with relatively minor illnesses, or injuries caused by the guards. We usually persuade the authorities to admit more serious illnesses, cancer and the like, to their hospitals."

I nodded again. I was very anxious to hear her plan. My life depended on this.

"The exceptions are four men who have AIDS. They've been here all along, although two of them were very ill indeed. They should have been hospitalised long ago, but we're forced to keep them, because the authorities are so paranoid about AIDS. I suppose in some ways they're better off here.

"Anyway, I'm sorry to say that one of the men died in the early hours of this morning. That's a very sad thing for those of us who got to know him well, and who came to admire his courage, but something good may yet come out of it, and I know he would be delighted by the plan I'm about to suggest. Three days ago he told me he wished he could have donated his organs for transplants. Well, obviously he couldn't do that, but in a different sense I think his death may give you a chance at a new lease of life.

"What Dr Muir has suggested is that we take advantage of the soldiers' irrational fear of AIDS. If you agree, he will go to the prison authorities and tell them that everything Aaron owned or used will need to be incinerated, to prevent the spread of the virus. That's not medically accurate, but we're sure the guards will believe it. He is the first AIDS death we've had in the camp, so we can make up our own rules. The doctor will offer to oversee the burning. There's an old truck that they employ for trips to the tip, and I assume they'll use that. And as you've probably guessed, we plan for you to be aboard that truck."

"How?"

"We're not sure yet. Dr Muir has gone to talk to a few other people who we're hoping will have some ideas."

"So it all depends on them not searching the truck too carefully . . ."

"Which we're fairly optimistic about because of the AIDS thing."

". . . and me finding a way to escape when we get to wherever they do the burn-off."

"Yes. We can't plan that part of it. You'd have to take whatever opportunity suggested itself."

When I didn't say anything she added: "It's a question of the balance of risks. Which is more dangerous, to stay here or to attempt an escape?"

I knew there wasn't a choice, as I'd known from the moment Mrs Samuels busted me. The only reason I hadn't committed myself straightaway was that I didn't want to say the actual words, to condemn myself to this huge risk. But now, before I could stop myself, I said: "I'll do it, of course."

I know the words sounded confident. I only wish I'd felt a fraction of that confidence.

Before I had any second thoughts Judy nodded and was gone. I guess it was better that way. If I didn't have a chance to reconsider I couldn't reconsider.

During the afternoon Judy came and went. I only got glimpses of what was going on. But it seemed that there was plenty of action outside. Prisoners had been banned from talking to guards unless another prisoner was there. They couldn't ban them altogether, because it would make the guards suspicious, but this was the best compromise they could come up with. I was touched that they were going to all this trouble for me.

Late in the afternoon Judy told me that the authorities had agreed to Dr Muir taking the dead man's possessions to the tip, and burning them.

I'd been doing some thinking and I asked Judy: "There might be someone in the camp who'd have news about my father and mother. I couldn't ask before, because it was too dangerous, but would you be able to spread the word? You mentioned that tent where they help people trace relatives."

"I'll do what I can," she said crisply, and was gone before I could go into any more detail.

I dozed a little at her desk, my head on my arms. It was Judy who woke me when she burst in, at about 6.30.

"We're going with it tonight, now," she said.

"Now?"

I struggled to my feet, trying to wake up.

"Yes. It's worked all too well. They're so nervous about the virus that they want everything associated with Aaron burnt immediately. I think Stuart's managed to convince them that the virus escapes from the body when someone dies."

I realised Stuart was Dr Muir.

As we headed out the door Judy said: "I've arranged for Mrs Samuels to meet us. I believe she has some information about your parents."

I felt giddy, and had to grab the doorframe for support. "She does?"

"Apparently." She glanced sideways at me. "Don't get your hopes up. This war's such a mess, a lot of information doesn't check out too well. You can't rely on much."

When we got to the hospital tent Mrs Samuels was waiting. She was very emotional. She blamed herself for blowing my cover. She didn't know I was going to try a break-out, but she knew she'd put me in a heap of danger.

I wasn't interested in a big discussion about that. I wanted as much information as I could get, in as short a time as possible. Ever since Judy had told me Mrs Samuels might know something, I was in a fever of excitement. Even in the middle of all the fear about escaping, I was distracted, wondering what I was going to hear, and when.

So I stopped Mrs Samuels' apologies short. Judy was

hovering in the background and I knew time was running out.

"Mrs Samuels, I'm sorry to cut you off, but I think the doctor's waiting for me. What I want to know is, have you seen my parents?"

At once she dropped her eyes. I felt my stomach sag, like I'd swallowed half a tonne of cement.

"What?" I begged, grabbing her arm.

"No, no, I think they're all right," she said. "As far as I know they're all right."

"Are you sure?"

"Yes," she said, but again I felt there was something she wasn't telling me. "Well, at least I've seen your mum quite recently, but I haven't seen your dad for ages."

"Where are they?"

"They were separated quite early in the war. So I'm not altogether sure where your dad is. But I can tell you where your mum is."

"Where? Where?"

A tiny hesitation, then she said: "She's at Simmons' Reef. There's a whole lot of them there from Wirrawee, and other places too of course. They're kept in the big blocks of flats, and they work in different shops and factories and places like that. I must say, it's a shame to see a lady like your mum, been on the land all these years, and now having to live in one of those awful flats. They're crowded in like sardines. It's terrible."

"Is there anything else you can tell me?"

"Well, not really . . ."

"Come on," Judy said.

There wasn't time for anything else. Judy ushered me away, at the same time pushing Mrs Samuels in the opposite direction.

You had to hand it to her. She was the right person to have in charge of prisoners. She had a knack for organising people.

Inside the tent Dr Muir was waiting. To me he said: "We'll have to be quick. The truck should be here at any second." To Judy he said: "Have you told her?"

"No."

"There's only one way we can do this," he said to me. "It won't be very pleasant I'm afraid."

"What?"

"I'm going to sew you into a mattress. We've already opened it up and pulled out enough of the stuffing. You'll have to get in there, then I'll stitch it up again."

I started to feel claustrophobic, just thinking about it. "Is it the mattress of the guy who died?"

"No," he said. But just like Mrs Samuels, he seemed to hesitate. Everyone was hesitating tonight. It made me very nervous. With Dr Muir it was incredibly obvious that he was lying. With Mrs Samuels I didn't have a clue.

I followed him and Judy into the next tent. The mattress was waiting, like he said. There was a pile of horsehair stuffing pulled out of it, and a big slit for me.

Unlike everyone else I didn't hesitate. There wasn't time. I started wriggling inside. As I did I thought of something. Now I did hesitate. I said to Judy: "Won't there be reprisals for you, when I'm not at rollcall?"

"Leave that for us to worry about," she said.

I felt an immense wave of gratitude, realising how much they were doing for me.

"Thank you," I said.

"See you after the war."

"After the war. Yes."

Inside the mattress felt strange. There was light coming

through, and I could breathe, but I had to struggle not to panic. The stuffing was so uncomfortable; prickly and scratchy, bits of it sticking into me every time I moved. We had a couple of old horsehair mattresses stored in the shearers' quarters, but you'd never dare offer them to shearers nowadays.

Without turning my head I sensed that Dr Muir had started the stitching up. It must feel strange to him too — I bet his time in Medical School hadn't prepared him for a suture job like this.

Being in the mattress reminded me of something, and I tried to think what it was. Eventually I remembered. When I was a kid I'd snuggled down deep into the bed, with the blanket over my head, imagining I was in my own little world, all outside influences cut off — that was the feeling. I could have been in a space shuttle.

Less than five minutes later I heard heavy footsteps clumping in on the duckboards of the tent. I felt myself lifted. They struggled to get me up. It was lucky I'd lost weight in this war. I felt hands come in underneath me, to stop me falling through the fabric of the mattress. "Don't move," someone whispered.

Even through the mattress I felt the coolness of the outside air. A few more metres and I was lifted again, then dropped onto a metal base. I heard the occasional shouted comment, but nothing else seemed to happen for quite a time. Then there was a series of thumps, as other stuff was dropped next to me. Almost immediately the truck started, and sat there rumbling, a big diesel engine. Doors opened and shut, there was a lurch, and we were off.

We didn't get far before we stopped again. There were more shouts, and I could hear Dr Muir's voice. Several times I heard the word "AIDS." I was sweating so much I was making the stuffing of the mattress damp, and the air around me felt more and more stuffy and smelly. We seemed to be waiting an interminable time.

It was too long. Something must have gone wrong. I've never felt more helpless. I was totally in the hands of other people. I don't like that; have never liked it.

The truck rocked as someone got up on it. Sweat broke out of me like never before. I just spontaneously sweated from every pore. The automatic sprinklers had come on. I was rigid with fear. Boots clumped past me and stopped. I could hear loud breathing, then something scraped, as though a heavy metal object was being moved. There was a bit of scuffling, then a boot kicked the corner of the mattress, hard. I felt a rush of vomit come into my mouth, just a first taste, but I pressed my lips tight and kept it in. A sharp stick, or a rifle more like, jabbed fiercely into the middle of the mattress, about a ruler's length from me. My stomach knotted up like a huge bunch of fishing line in a gigantic tangle.

There was silence for — well, I honestly don't know how long. Between thirty seconds and four minutes, that's the best I can do. Time goes into a new dimension when you're waiting to be killed.

The truck lurched underneath me. I gasped, then with no warning we were underway again.

I could tell when we left the actual camp, because we started climbing out of the quarry. I didn't dare move, because I hadn't heard the man on the back get off. I wasn't sure if I had a soldier riding with me.

We travelled only ten or twelve minutes, then bumped over a poor bit of road for a while before coming to a halt, with a squeak of the brakes. The engine was switched off. Suddenly everything felt incredibly quiet. I heard the tailgate rasp open. A pair of boots clanged across the metal, and stuff was dragged past me. A few minutes later the boots returned. I heard Dr Muir's voice, whispering: "They're keeping their distance, Ellie. But I've got to get you off the truck on my own, so it could get pretty rough."

"OK," I whispered back, but I'm not sure if he heard me.

I soon found out what "pretty rough" meant. Dr Muir dragged my mattress to the tailgate and then half-dropped me, half-slid me, to the ground. I landed on my hip, which hurt. There was a bit of padding under me, which protected my bum, but my hip had no protection.

Then I started sliding along.

Poor Dr Muir. Not only did he have to drag me to the incinerator, but I guess he had to do it in a way that looked reasonably effortless. He couldn't afford to have the guards think there was anything odd about the mattress.

I could smell the burning even through the fabric and the stuffing, and knew we were getting close. I just hoped Dr Muir wouldn't have to chuck me in the flames.

He dumped the mattress and I think left it for a while. Then I felt a little breeze through the side and looking around realised that a thin sharp knife was cutting through the stitches. The doctor's voice murmured: "Slide out, quick. The guards can't see you."

I obeyed at once, although it was hard to move. I was cramped from being still for so long, especially in my wounded leg. But I got out OK and lay on the asphalt.

The incinerator was a few metres away. It was huge: a full-on industrial size. It smelt pretty bad, now that I was out in the open and able to get the full effect.

I kept lying there until Dr Muir appeared from the truck and threw two green plastic garbage bags full of stuff into the fire. Without looking at me he said: "Sneak around the back."

I wriggled round where he said, and huddled into the warm back of the incinerator. It felt nice and safe and I almost forgot the danger. I remembered pretty fast when I heard a soldier's voice suddenly very close to me, saying: "Hurry up."

"Yes, yes, won't be long now." Dr Muir sounded calm; his voice was steady.

I could hear someone, I assume the soldier, poke around with a stick or a metal rod. I could hear it scraping on the concrete base the incinerator stood on. It sounded horribly close. I shrank even smaller, crowded into the incinerator even more closely. The warm bricks were making me sweat.

"Careful," Dr Muir said. His voice seemed less calm now, slightly higher in pitch. "The virus can survive for quite a while."

It didn't sound too convincing to me, and the soldier just grunted. He must have been only a couple of metres away, but the circular shape of the incinerator kept me from his view.

I heard the truck start and the horn sound. Someone was getting impatient. The soldier said a few words to Dr Muir, something I didn't catch, but the doctor said, "Yes, fine." I had a wild flicker of excitement, the first real thought of "Yes! Maybe I'll get away with this."

As though God wanted to punish me for that moment of relaxation, a second later the guard appeared around the side of the incinerator.

He got such a shock that he froze, staring at me, his eyes getting bigger and bigger. He carried a rifle, and he started fumbling with it, lifting it to his shoulder. I unfolded myself and stood and turned and tried to run. I was desperate to make my legs work. I was like a drunk trying to win an Olympic sprint. I remember I had my arms stretched out like I was reaching for something, a tape, that was nowhere to be seen. Deep within me I knew I couldn't bear to be shot again. I couldn't go through it a second time. I didn't feel like I was moving but I must have been because when he finally got a shot off it whistled away to my left, missing by a ruler's length I'd guess. I realised I was enough of the way around the side to be almost out of his sight again.

But it would only be for a moment. In front of me was the opening to the incinerator. It was bigger than I'd expected, twice the size of our fireplace at home, with flames licking out. It was a mess, with stuff scattered between it and the truck: all the things the doctor was shifting to be burnt. There was no sign of Dr Muir. But I got a glimpse of the soldier coming around after me, lifting his rifle for a second shot. In desperation I picked up a burning length of wood that seemed to be part of a bed frame, and turning, flung it like a spear at the soldier. It got him on the right hand. With a shout he dropped the rifle and darted back, grabbing his hand where it had been burnt. I thought I'd better follow up while he was off-balance, so I swung to my left and grabbed at the nearest thing.

It was a dead body. I sort of realised as I reached at it that it was a human body, and I realised that it must be the man who'd died of AIDS. Aaron, I think Judy said his name was. I couldn't believe this was happening, but I was in a situation where there were no second chances and no time to think. Aaron's body was on a stretcher which was at an angle, the top part resting on an empty wooden crate, the bottom part resting on the ground. He was dressed in a white T-shirt and blue jeans and there was a scarf tied around his head, as though his mouth would fall open without it. I picked him up easily, by the front of his T-shirt and his belt. He weighed about forty kilos I'd guess. His body was quite stiff but as I lifted him his head fell back in a horrifying and sickening way, and there was a crack as though a bone might have broken. There wasn't time to feel sick. I just heaved him straight at the soldier, hoping as I did that when Judy told me about Aaron's sense of humour, she knew what she was talking about.

The man was picking up his rifle. I don't think the burning spear had hurt him much. Aaron landed on top of him. Perhaps it would have been funny, in a different situation. I'd kind of run out of laughter though. I had time to see the soldier's expression of terror and disgust as he tried to roll out from under the body, and then I was running. I looked for Dr Muir, but saw no sign of him. We were both on our own now. I knew all too well that he'd risked his life for me, and that he might now be in deep diarrhoea, but there was nothing we could do for each other. Some day if we both survived I might be able to thank him.

In the meantime I just ran and ran, in a kind of stumbling, limping jog, until I was at least three k's from the incinerator of horror. Then I kept walking, as fast as my poor tired stuffed-up legs would travel.

At least I had a definite mission now, a goal. If my mother was in Simmons' Reef, I was going to find her. I couldn't remember having a stronger sense of purpose at any stage since the beginning of the war.

15

I ARRIVED AT SIMMONS' REEF AT THREE O'CLOCK IN THE afternoon, after six days and nights. It had been a wild trip. So much had changed while I was in hospital and the camp. The war was burning along, throttle all the way out, black smoke pouring from the exhaust. When I was hiding in a ditch by the side of the road, up to my hips in water, cold and hungry, hoping the passing convoy of trucks and tanks wouldn't see me, it was hard to remind myself that all these soldiers racing around the country were good news for me in the long run.

I didn't think much about acts of sabotage, or attacks on the enemy. Without the support of Homer and Lee I didn't have the nerve to try much on my own. Plus I had no weapons. The truth is, I didn't have the nerve for anything more than staying alive. Not that there were many opportunities for sabotage anyway.

Things got quieter approaching Simmons' Reef. It seemed to be in a bit of a backwater; always had been as far as I knew. A freeway went right past it, but that had been so heavily bombed, you'd be lucky to get a bike along there now. The military traffic seemed to be detouring west, over the Wyndham River. I wished I had a radio, so I could call Colonel Finley. If the New Zealanders knew that there were convoys going along those back roads they could drop a few bombs on them, to slow the party down a bit.

But maybe the New Zealanders knew anyway. They

sure were active. There wasn't a day when a whole lot of Kiwi bombers weren't thundering overhead, or when the lighter faster fighter planes weren't racing past like whippets. Even better was the fact that I hardly saw any enemy planes, and the ones I did see were old and slow, lumbering along in complete contrast to the groovy new Kiwi planes. I guessed the military help from Japan was making a difference.

On my first full day of freedom, skirting around Cavendish, I saw an almighty explosion towards the eastern end of the city. The sky went red, from one horizon to the other, like it had been sprayed with blood. Then came the huge slow dark cloud, more like a toadstool than a mushroom. I wondered who'd blown up what, but I didn't let it slow me down. I figured at worst it would be a good distraction, would mean fewer soldiers searching for me.

After all that Simmons' Reef looked quiet and peaceful in the afternoon sun. I had no idea what day it was, even what week it was, but we were moving into autumn and the leaves were changing colour. I hadn't scored a lot to eat in the six days. The first two days all I got was fruit stolen from orchards, but by the third day I was so desperate that I sneaked up on a row of motorbikes by the side of a road near Kerrie. I couldn't work out where the riders were, but they were nowhere in sight. I wriggled up to the first bike, peeping around in every direction. I shoved my hand in the saddlebag. There were a few spanners and screwdrivers, and an empty paper bag. But there was also a long cool aluminium cylinder. I slid it halfway out and took off the top, closing it again quickly when I saw the bowl of rice inside. That was enough for me. I pulled the whole thing out and retreated fast through the grass, like a snake going backwards. I just hoped I wouldn't meet a real snake in the long grass.

Hungry as I was, I still didn't dare to open the container until I was at least three kilometres clear of the bikes. My mouth was watering so much I was dribbling. At last, burrowed under a bank of earth and bushes, I felt safe enough to open the cylinder properly.

It was a very neat arrangement: three bowls, each on top of the next, and each with different food. Below the rice was a bowl of vegetables, mainly some spinachy-looking stuff, and bok choy, and something like celery. It was in a beautiful sauce, oyster I think, with maybe a touch of garlic. Below that was a bowl of beef. The sight and smell of the meat had me drooling like a faulty garden sprinkler. I'm so carnivorous.

I ate half of each bowl, although it was so difficult to stop. My stomach felt full but I wanted to keep going. The flavours were intense and powerful after weeks of food that tasted like rat droppings.

By the time I got to Simmons' Reef I'd eaten the rest of the three bowls, dumped the aluminium cylinder, and was well and truly ravenous again.

At least I forgot my hunger for a while as I looked at Simmons' Reef. It was a pretty town, running along the side of a range of hills, with lots of yellowing English trees and a couple of old churches poking their spires up in the foreground. The only thing that spoiled it was the big blocks of flats at the eastern end, that Mrs Samuels had told me about. But to me those flats didn't look too ugly. I'd come a long way to have this view, and right now it was quite attractive.

I started moving closer. It would be a long time before darkness set in, and I couldn't wait. I had a deep intense longing to see my mother, and I also had a terrible niggling uncertainty about the way Mrs Samuels spoke. The fear she left me with had haunted me for nearly a week now. Had something gone wrong with my mother? Had she been beaten, or tortured? Had she been injured, crippled, brain-damaged? The only consolations for me were that the reality of what was in Simmons' Reef could hardly be worse than my imaginings, and that whatever I found, whatever had happened, couldn't affect my love for my mum.

I followed a gully down from a bridge and then walked up the sandy bed of the river. There wasn't much water, so it was quite easy. I realised as I got closer to the town that I could follow the river right in there, like a road. Although I was getting excited, and impatient, I had to check myself and say, "Come on, slow down, take care, don't get caught now, when you're so close."

So at each bend I snuck into the bushes and moved forward gingerly, holding the branches apart and peering at the view, making sure there were no nasty surprises. I made good progress for a while. But just as I started getting confident I came to a grinding halt. A couple of fishermen were in the next stretch of water, casting their flies over a long deep pool.

I swore at them under my breath. This would happen. Teach me to get smug. I should know better, after all this time in the war. I waited for a while, hoping they'd move, but they looked quite happy, and then one of them caught a trout, so I figured they'd be there until dark at least. I withdrew along the river, still cursing, and climbed the bank.

I found myself in a park, in the outer reaches of the

town. Nice park too, with a statue of a mother and daughter in the middle, and gardens radiating away like spokes of a wheel. Surprisingly the gardens still looked to be in good condition — someone had looked after them. The statue was kind of knocked around though. In the distance a few kids were using the playground stuff. Two of them were spinning on those whirligig things, and another was on the monkey bars.

I kept in the shadows of the trees and made my way along the banks of the river, close enough to see the heads of the fishermen below. I was planning to get back to the river but at the next bend it curved away from the direction I wanted. I could see the blocks of flats ahead, two or three kilometres, so I figured it'd be better to strike out directly for them.

It was the first time I'd been in the streets of a town since we'd hung out in Stratton. That seemed a long time ago. Simmons' Reef wasn't as big a town as Stratton, although it was a lot bigger than Wirrawee, but the main thing that struck me was how it was so undamaged. I guess there'd been no reason for the enemy to destroy it or New Zealand to bomb it. It certainly wasn't a major military target. This was the way Wirrawee could still have looked if it wasn't for the bad luck of being on the road from Cobbler's Bay to the big city.

The only difference here between the old days and now was that the people in the streets were a different nationality. I had to remind myself to be alert. These old grandmothers watching the toddlers on the footpaths, the men talking in the front gardens among a haze of cigarette smoke, the children playing soccer in someone's wide driveway were my enemies.

I didn't know the rules for this town though. Each place seemed to have its own rules. From listening to people in Camp 23 I'd learned that in one town prisoners could stay in their old houses, in another everyone was sent to a prison camp in the Showground or the footie oval, in another they were sent right out of the district. There didn't seem to be any logic to it. Maybe it depended on who was in charge of each area.

As there was no sign of my own people in the streets I assumed they were restricted to the end of town where the flats stood. So I couldn't walk confidently out in the open, hoping I'd be taken for another factory worker. Just like it had been all the way through this war I had to skulk along, keep in hiding, treat every noise and movement as a threat to my life.

That wasn't so difficult. My real problems started when I got to the eastern end of the town. It was obvious the prisoners were kept here. Mrs Samuels was right. A high-wire fence had been put up around the whole area, and the only gate was guarded by a couple of women soldiers with rifles. Inside I could see people who looked more familiar to me, doing the same kind of stuff the people outside were doing, but doing it in a much more restricted and unattractive area.

It seemed it should be easy enough to get in, compared to the other stuff I'd done during the war, but the more I looked at the situation the more I realised the problems.

I waited and watched for an hour and in all that time not a single person came in or out. That was bad enough. But when someone did eventually arrive and go through it was a careful and complicated business. A minibus pulled up with a dozen prisoners on board, and two soldiers. One of the guards from the gate got on the bus and did a head count, then looked at some papers she was given. I was too far away to see, but I think they were probably security passes or identification cards. I didn't have anything like that.

The only good news was the approach of darkness. It couldn't come fast enough for me. I was in such a state of exhaustion and excitement that I was in danger of losing my common sense: I was so tempted to run straight at the gate and crash through, ignoring the fact that I would have been shot down in the first dozen steps.

It seemed weird. After all, these buildings were a prison, more or less, and here I was trying to break in. Break into a prison. "Good one, Ellie," I thought. "Trust you to do everything backwards."

Staying in the shadows I went for a tour of the complex. I couldn't do a complete circumference because on the other side there was no cover: a newer suburb stretched away down the hill. There was no obvious way into the high-rises from any point.

It was too frustrating. I couldn't believe it was so difficult. I felt more impatient with every passing minute.

I slouched against a tree, angrily, watching the suburban houses in their neat lines facing each other across their neat streets. I would just have to wait for full darkness. Somehow I'd have to ignore the terrible hunger that was making my stomach feel like an echo chamber. I could hear the rumblings and gurglings, all too loud in the still evening air.

And it wasn't just food I was hungry for.

Then below me, in the streets, something funny happened. A woman came running out of the front door of a house. She was calling, not just calling: shouting. I suppose there would have been a dozen people in the street, doing the usual sort of stuff people do in the early evening, walking, talking, playing. For a moment every single one of them stopped, like they'd been frosted. Then they ran towards the woman. It was like a dance: it could have been choreographed. The woman stood in the middle of the road, waving her arms and talking nineteen to the dozen. I watched, puzzled. Behind me a bell started ringing, an urgent irritating noise. More doors opened, and more people started coming out into the street. Then, behind me, in the blocks of flats, there was sudden chaos. I heard people yelling, screaming. I strained to hear what they were saying, but I couldn't make it out. I moved quickly back into the trees. I didn't know what was happening but I didn't like it. I ran around to the other side to see what was going on there. People sprinted out of the flats, towards the sentries at the gates. The sentries unslung their rifles and dropped to their knees, aiming at the crowd. The people stopped suddenly, and gathered in a group, facing the soldiers. They were shouting and at last I could make out the words:

"The war's over, you bloody idiots," was the first thing I heard.

My skin got goose bumps everywhere. I took a few more steps forward. Had I got it right? Had I heard correctly? The words I'd been waiting to hear, all this time? In the distance a siren wailed, like an angry bunyip. The sentries hadn't moved, and when a man stepped forward to talk to them, one of them fired a shot. She aimed to miss, I'm sure — she could have shot him easily if she'd wanted — but it was a frightening moment. Everyone backed up fast.

The sirens sounded closer and suddenly they were right

on top of us, screaming so loudly I put my hands over my ears. Three police cars thumped to a stop, one by one, in front of the gates. A dozen or so soldiers piled out of them, and formed a line across the brow of the hill, dropping to one knee and aiming their rifles, the same as the sentries.

As they did that an officer, who'd been in the front seat of the first car, walked forward. He halted about ten metres short of the gate and held up his hand for silence. He got it.

"Obviously you have heard some news," he said. He had a pleasant voice, heavily accented, but he spoke excellent English. "I don't know how, considering that radios are illegal. The fact is we don't know yet if the announcement is correct. Until we do know, my troops will confine you to this area. As of now, all exit passes are cancelled, all work parties suspended, and all privileges withdrawn. I'm sure you will understand the need for these precautions. I am now instructing my troops to shoot without warning anyone found outside this fence."

It was as soon as I heard those words that I got my great idea. The only light came from the buildings and the police cars, and I thought it was dim enough for me to have a chance. As the crowd inside the fence, subdued by the officer's speech, but still talking excitedly, started to fade back towards the high-rises, I came out from the shadows.

"Excuse me, sir," I said to the officer.

"Yes, what is it?"

"I heard what you said about shooting people found outside the fence. I got out just before you arrived. I think I'd rather go back in now. I think I'm safer in there."

I said it with all the confidence I could muster, staring

him straight in the eye, but at the same time trying to look like a contrite naughty little girl. Trying almost to make a joke out of it.

"Very sensible of you," he said. "How did you get out anyway?"

"It was total chaos when the news came through," I said. "The sentries didn't know what to do. But I was the only one."

"You'd better be," he said. "All right. Hurry up."

Ignoring me as I walked towards the gate he began giving the troops the big speech, in their own language, I suppose about how they had to kill us if we put a foot wrong.

As I approached the gate I heard very clearly, above the hubbub of chattering voices, a woman say clearly: "My God, it's Ellie Linton."

Everyone seemed to go quiet at once. I realised straightaway the danger it put me in. The last thing I wanted was to attract this kind of attention.

The two sentries at the gate had their backs to me. I assumed the soldiers behind me were listening obediently to their officer. So I took the risk and put my finger to my lips, to tell them to ignore me. It seemed like a long time before they got the idea. It seemed like five minutes. It was probably ten seconds. But all I could think about was how cruel it would be if I got this close to my mother, only to be arrested and dragged away. Ripped out of her arms, almost.

At last some bright guy got the idea and started talking loudly again. I kept walking at an even pace, counting the steps as I got closer and closer to the gate. My back felt like I was being microwaved. I was only a couple of metres from the sentries.

Then I heard the officer's voice: "Just a moment, young lady."

I panicked. I was too close to turn back now. The sentries, startled by the officer's voice, were turning. I accelerated and ran straight through them. The sentries yelled out something, the officer yelled out something else. Ahead of me the crowd separated. Behind me I heard the sound of rifles being cocked. That's one sound you can never mistake. Doesn't matter how much noise there is around you, the sound of a rifle being cocked penetrates right through to your bones. To my right, the crowd threw themselves to the ground; to my left the rest went down equally fast. It was almost funny. Like a crop of wheat hit by a gale. I went to the ground too, but unlike the others I kept rolling. I heard someone yell, to the officer I guess, "Don't shoot, the war's over," then after a pause, he added, equally loudly: "It'd be murder if you shot anyone now."

I was still rolling, kicking up dust. I fetched up against a concrete block, hitting it hard. It was a doorstep. I was up, twisting and scrambling through the door before my conscious mind even understood what it was. I found myself in a long dark corridor, cool, but smelling of a million different smells, most of them unpleasant. I didn't know what to do so I kept going. My footsteps echoed in the long concrete tunnel. At the end was a stairway, so I aimed for that. There was a lot of yelling outside, but as I started up the steps the noise from outside was cut off completely, as though a wall had come between us. I just kept running. I didn't even know if I was in the right building, but something kept me going. Up, up, up and despite my exhaustion and hunger and my bullet wound and my bad knee I didn't feel any pain at all. I got to the third floor and at last started to think again. On a board at the end of each corridor was a long list of names. I guessed they were the names of the people living on that floor. I scanned down the list. There were so many changes — names crossed out and written over the top of other names — but I knew our family name would jump out at me pretty strongly, if it was there. It wasn't. I headed up to the next floor.

It wasn't there either, but I wasn't discouraged. I went up again, to the fifth floor. I'd completely forgotten what was happening outside; didn't give it a thought.

My mother was listed in Apartment 5A12, along with a heap of other people. But all the apartments were like that, a crowd of names scribbled together in the same way that the people must be squashed into the rooms. I ran along the corridor, looking at the letters and numbers on the doors. It wasn't easy, because half of them — more than half of them — were missing. A lot of the doors were damaged too. This place looked like it had seen some hard times. I still couldn't work out the lettering and numbering system. On one door was 5A17, but the next one was 5A22. I turned a corner to the right and the very first door was 5A12. I felt a tremble run through me, a deep, deep shiver like an underwater earthquake. I paused, said some sort of prayer without words, opened the door and walked in.

If you don't believe in destiny, how do you explain that of all the huge numbers of people in those flats, my mother must have been about the only one actually home? I suppose it was the way the war affected her. But there were plenty of other people who'd suffered terribly in the war, and they were outside, milling around the front gate.

A lot of things had changed during this war. But apparently my footsteps weren't one of them. My mother came out of a side room like a snake had bitten her. The light in there was dim — I found out later it was always like that because the authorities were too stingy to supply enough electricity for the apartments — but dim light or not I could see how pale her face was. No, not pale, white. As white as vanilla ice-cream. She grabbed me by the arms, so tightly she left bruises. I can still feel the pressure of her hands. "Hey, take it easy," I said. "It's only me." She was terribly thin. She's always been thin, but now she looked like one of those concentration camp photos. I put my arms around her. She started making these kind of whooping sounds, a bit like — I don't mean to be rude — a bit like koalas during the mating season.

It wasn't the way I'd pictured our reunion. I thought I'd be the one falling into her arms. I lowered her into an armchair and squeezed in beside her, half on the arm of the chair. It was a battered old chair, and it barely coped with both of us.

"I'll get you a cup of tea," I said, but I didn't get up. I'd started remembering the shambles at the gate outside and I was wondering what was happening out there.

"I thought . . . I'd never see you again," she said. Her voice was really croaky, like an old lady's. She sounded like her mother.

"We did say we were only going for five days," I said. "We got held up. Sorry."

She was trembling so much, and it wasn't getting better.

"Hey," I said, realising I sounded a bit like Mum when I said it. "Come on. It's OK. You're OK. It's over now."

"How are the others? How's Homer?"

There was no gentle way I could answer that question.

"They didn't make it," I said, holding her closer and feeling her body shake.

She gave a sob and put her hand to her mouth. Homer had always been a big favourite of hers.

When she didn't say anything else I asked: "How's Dad? Do you know where he is?"

"More or less. He's mucking out stables on a stud near Absalom. Last I heard, he wasn't too bad."

"Oh God," I breathed. At last I could let myself hope that he had survived.

There was a noise from outside. I jumped up nervously. With the briefest of knocks, a couple of people hurried in. I recognised one of them as Don Murray, a farmer from Wirrawee, but I didn't know the woman. She was short and dark-skinned, and she gave me a great warm smile.

"It is you," Don said. "Fantastic! This is just wonderful. The first good thing that's happened in this whole damn war."

"What's happening outside?" I asked nervously.

"It's under control," he said. "We convinced the officer that it wouldn't be a good idea to shoot you. Every last one of us assured him we'd testify to the UN that he was a murderer. He's basically not a bad bloke. He didn't take much convincing. Mind you, he doesn't seem to know who you are. I don't think he heard the dickhead, excuse my French, who called your name out. He knows something's a bit suss; he's just not sure what. But you're safe now."

"Am I?" I asked, feeling a sickness in my heart. "With everyone in the place knowing I'm here? I don't think so."

To me it was like a replay of Camp 23.

"Even if the war is over, I don't think I'll be safe as long as there are enemy soldiers around."

Don came to a shuddering halt. "Yes. Yes. I see what you mean. Well, you'll be safe until the morning. No-one's allowed out till then. But if the radio's right, and the war is over, I don't think they'll come in here looking for you. I'd say you're safe for as long as you want to stay. Though why anyone should want to stay in this Godawful rat-infested apartment block I have no idea."

The woman who was with him tugged his sleeve. "Let's go, Don," she said. "I'm sure we're in the way here."

"What?" Don said, looking puzzled, and then gradually realising what she meant. "What? Oh yes. Of course."

The door closed behind them, and I went into the kitchen to make the cup of tea I'd promised Mum. It took a few minutes to find the stuff, although God knows it wasn't because there was so much to choose from. The kitchen was as neat and clean as scrubbing could make it, but it sure was short of food and drink. The only reason it took me so long to make the tea was that I had to open at least a dozen empty containers before I found a cupful of tea-leaves.

When I went back to the main room I found Mum slumped down in the chair, with her eyes closed. I got a terrible fright. I put the cup down quickly and ran to her. When I lifted her she woke straightaway, but I couldn't control the pounding of my heart. I sat beside her, shaking like a Saint Andrew's Cross spider.

"It's all right," she said, putting her hand on my arm, "it's going to be all right now."

But she was so shaky and weak that I had to become like a nurse. I made some soup out of some old soft spuds.

At least there was plenty of salt and pepper. I put her to bed, then, because it was such a narrow bed that I couldn't sleep next to her, I got in at the other end. For the first time in the war I slept without dreams, and when I woke the sun was shining and the war was over.

16

For two reasons we were in the first lot of people sent back to the reclaimed territory. One was that people with illness or disability had priority. Mum qualified under that, because she'd been really ill. A nervous breakdown I guess you'd call it. Don Murray told me, that morning after I arrived, that she'd hardly said a word for four months.

That's why Mrs Samuels had been so guarded when she spoke to me, back at the prison camp.

Irrationally, in the middle of my concern about Mum, and my fear that she might get worse, was my anger that she wasn't there for me. Instead of fussing over me and nursing me, which was the picture I'd imagined all through the war, she dragged herself around the place looking awful, and somehow I had to find the strength to look after her.

She had no energy, no stamina: she kept fainting all the time. So she sure qualified for the first bus, just on those grounds alone.

The other reason we got selected was that the committee in charge of flats wanted me out of there, for my good and for everyone else's.

"If they know you're here, there's a chance they'll try to abduct you. The sooner you're gone, the better."

I sure was happy to go. I found the overcrowded and smelly apartments extremely depressing and with every fibre of my being I longed to be home.

We left on a convoy of buses, on a Tuesday morning. It was a wonderful moment. The people who couldn't get onto this first convoy gave us a huge send-off, cheering and clapping and throwing flowers. As the buses started up everyone sang "Auld Lang Syne." That song had never meant much to me before. It always seemed like such an oldies' song. But to hear it that morning, from people who had been through so much together, who had suffered in this war for so long, brought the tears to my eyes.

Then they sang the Maori Farewell as we headed out of the gates, and I bawled.

It seemed that now the war was over I could let go a little. I had the window seat, next to Mum on the aisle, and I rested my head against her and let the tears run onto her sleeve, in a steady flow, like a quiet spring. In my head I was going, "Fi, Homer, Lee, Kevin, Gavin," in no particular order. I remember hearing once that when someone close to you dies, it's like you've had a limb amputated. It never grows back, it never gets fixed, but after a while you learn to live with three limbs instead of four.

I didn't know where that left me though. All the friends I'd lost, it was like I didn't have any arms or any legs.

But under the grief something else was stirring. I wasn't yet ready to look at it, but I guess I did have a sense that my life would go on. For better or worse I had survived. Maybe that was the main reason I was crying, because I had survived.

We went home via Stratton. At that point the buses were going to split up and go in different directions, but everyone on our bus was from Wirrawee, so that's where we headed. We knew already that Wirrawee had been included in the area handed back under the peace treaty. That was the good news. The bad news was that Wirrawee was on the very edge of the reclaimed territory, so we didn't know how much of the countryside would be returned. In other words, we didn't know whether our property was on the right side of the new border or the wrong side.

I was again amazed at the damage we saw as we rolled along. Time and time again we had to make major detours because of destroyed bridges or roads with huge craters in them or unexploded bombs. But that was nothing compared to what we found in Stratton. I'd seen more damage in Stratton every time I'd gone there, but now there was virtually nothing left. Street after street was a mess of rubble. Hardly a building was left standing. Only in the outer suburbs were there occasional streets that were reasonably intact. I didn't think there was much chance Grandma's house had survived.

I couldn't help wondering how much of this damage was indirectly — and sometimes directly — the result of what Homer, Lee, Fi, Kevin, Gavin and I had done. It was frightening, horrifying — and exhilarating. I sat in silence staring out the window.

I'll never forget the homecoming to Wirrawee. By the time we arrived we were all tired and hungry and fed up. But we still managed to raise a cheer as we went past the 60 k's sign. Everyone crowded to the windows to have a look. Most of them hadn't seen Wirrawee in over a year.

As we pulled up outside the Post Office a few people started coming out of houses to see what was going on. A day earlier these houses had been occupied by our enemies. The colonists had been evacuated already, no doubt complaining bitterly as they went, no doubt feeling hard done by and victimised. The few prisoners left in the Wirrawee Showground had been released at the same time. They'd wasted no time reoccupying their homes and farms. It was these people who came into the street now, wondering about the big bus pulling up in the centre of town.

Before we got to Wirrawee if you asked anyone on that bus how they felt about a party you'd have got a poor response. But when we arrived something possessed us. A charge ran through the bus, through the crowd. For one night we forgot the war, forgot the suffering, the deprivations, even the friends and family we'd lost. Sometimes you've got to give yourself credit just for enduring. And we had endured.

Mum and I at least had something very specific to celebrate. Our property was confirmed as being in the returned territory. We were right on the edge, right on the border of the two new countries that now had to exist side by side, where for over two hundred years there had been only one, but for now we were happy enough with that. We didn't want to think too much about the problems it would bring.

Just after dawn, as people sat around fires that had been lit in the middle of the main street, still talking, still reminiscing, still asking each other questions that no-one could answer, we heard another big vehicle grinding its way towards us, coming down the hill.

"It's a bus," someone yelled. "Another bus."

We all jumped up and ran to the end of the street, if only to stop the bus rolling straight into our fires. Sure enough it was another load of "returnees." And waving to us from a window near the back, with unshaven face and dark-rimmed eyes, was my father.

"What are you bludgers doing? I thought you'd be home, getting a killer in."

They were his first words. Typical.

He and Mum hugged, then it was my turn. He's never been a good hugger, my dad, but he put up with me, rocking me backwards and forwards like we were in some sort of slow waltz. I clung to him like a little baby. Eventually we separated again, but not by much. I kept one hand resting on his back, using the other to wipe my eyes.

He already knew most of Mum's news, having been kept in touch by the people transferred from one place to another. It had been a pretty good grapevine, carrying news backwards and forwards across the country.

Just an hour later came the next bus. It brought a problem I knew I'd have to face eventually, but which I'd pushed firmly to the back of my mind. Not just pushed it firmly to the back of my mind but locked it in, sealed the door with cement, and thrown away the key.

Homer's mum was on that bus.

I didn't even see her until a couple of minutes after I'd hugged some other people. Then I saw Dad bringing her over.

Not for the first time in the war my nerve failed me. I clung to my mother.

"Mum, please, I can't face her on my own."

But my mum started trembling so badly I knew I'd been wrong to even ask her. And then Mrs Yannos saw our faces and she started to tremble too. She put both her hands up to the side of her head and pulled on her hair as if she was demented.

She cried: "Ellie, Ellie, what are you going to tell me?"

I just shook my head, staring at her. I couldn't speak, couldn't say the awful words.

Mrs Yannos went completely off her head. She sat on the edge of the footpath, feet in the drain, sobbing and hitting herself, then she keeled over and lay on the grass, sobbing.

In a way though it helped me find some strength. To see her in such a state was so bad that I pulled myself together, rather than give way like she had.

We tried to get her up, but she wouldn't be lifted, so in the end Dad and I sat beside her, hugging, with me stroking her.

It brought everything home to me again, just when I was hoping it might gradually go away. I'd hoped time might heal a few things, but I knew that morning there was no hope of that.

Without my friends, I would always be alone.

The day was pretty bad in most ways. Everything was a shambles. There were arguments all the time, and total confusion in every area. For instance, we wanted, naturally, to get out to our place and see its condition. We were determined to sleep there that night. But we didn't have a vehicle, and the vehicles in town were in hot demand. It was one o'clock in the afternoon before we managed to hijack a Mitsubishi Triton one-tonner and even then we had to agree to take eight people in the back, and drop them off at various places along the route. Not that we minded of course, but it was frustrating. Everyone was tired and crabby, and no-one could agree on anything. We didn't know yet that this was going to be the pattern of the next few months, but I suppose if we'd stopped to think about it we could have worked it out.

We didn't get home until right on dark, not just because we had to drop people at different places, but because at each farm we got out and sympathised and gave advice and made optimistic comments. It was a long process, and because we were at the end of the road there was no-one left to do it for us. So we arrived home alone, and any comfort we needed we had to provide for ourselves.

I don't want to be a whinger, and the fact is that our place was in pretty good shape. Whoever had lived there, and left just twenty-four hours before, had taken pride in the house and done their best. But somehow you can't bear to walk into your own home and see so much changed. Little things and big things. The fridge in a different part of the kitchen. Dad's office turned into a bedroom. All the books dumped in a shed out the back.

And of course heaps of stuff had gone. Basically, anything of value. We'd expected that, so the shock maybe wasn't so bad. God it hurt though, when you suddenly realised another precious belonging couldn't be found. I didn't mind about stuff like videos and CDs and TVs. "Never cry over anything that can't cry over you," Dad said. I knew the jewellery would have gone, but it still upset me. And then there were the odds and ends that were nowhere to be found, even though with some of them you had no idea why they would be stolen. For instance, my photo album, my bookends that Fi had given me, my mask that I made in Year 8. I was proud of that mask.

Maybe they just got chucked out.

Mind you, we'd gained a few things too. There was a new tennis-table in the dining room, and quite a lot of food in the pantry, and most amazingly, a brand-new header in the barn that we figured we'd have to give back when we worked out where it was looted from.

I'd thought that when we got home we'd go hammer and tongs to put everything back together, to get it all into good shape; not just the house and the sheds, but the property itself. But it didn't quite happen like that. I guess we were a bit shell-shocked. Mum and Dad argued a lot, usually about something totally trivial. Mum spent hours sitting in the vegie garden, just staring at the mountains. She took it for granted that I'd do the housework, whereas, like I said, I'd always taken it for granted that once the war was over she'd look after me. I didn't complain but I wasn't happy about it, and I did a pretty sloppy job. With Dad wandering around the paddocks and Mum sitting in the vegie garden having her Great Depression, I don't know whether they even noticed that I was doing most of the work. I thought it was so unfair. There I was, still limping, still a mess on the outside and an even bigger mess on the inside, and there were my parents lost in their own worlds.

Of course there were lots of good moments, especially the times when we were nice to each other again, when we hugged or sat side by side holding hands or walked together or talked about the stuff we'd seen. At those times I could believe that eventually we'd get back to the way things used to be.

When there was any time to stop and think — and I didn't want any time to stop and think so I made sure there wasn't much — I was amazed at the changes in me. Even little things. After a couple of days the first TV station came back on air, and it only operated between five p.m. and nine p.m., but I started watching the news every night. Partly because I thought I'd better start taking an interest in all that political stuff, partly because there was nothing else on, but also because each day important announcements were made. The only trouble with that was, you couldn't rely on the announcements. On Tuesday night they announced that schools would reopen in ten days; on Thursday they said, "Sorry, we don't know when they'll open." On Saturday they said fighting had flared up in one of the border territories; Sunday they admitted it was a mistake.

The day after that, the Monday, the first people from the United Nations War Crimes Commission arrived and announced they'd be calling for people to come forward to give evidence. I wondered if anyone would ask me about Colonel Long. I certainly wasn't going out of my way to look for him.

The biggest immediate change was the resettlement. It had to be done, and it had to be done quickly. Twenty million people had to fit into an area that used to have six million. We knew we'd lose most of the farm; the question was how much, and which parts. We were pretty confident we'd keep enough to be viable, because obviously farms and farmers were going to be needed more than ever, and Dad's experience would be worth a bit. But the freedom I'd once had, to roam across the paddocks on the motorbike, or to go skinny-dipping in the dams: well, I could kiss that goodbye.

In the Wirrawee area Fi's mother got the job of dividing up the land. She was hardly in the best shape to do it but she said it'd take her mind off Fi a bit, so maybe it was a good idea, I don't know. There was no way she could do it without making everybody unhappy. Each day her proposals were put up at the Post Office, so you could object if you wanted. I think she went too far with us, to show people that she wasn't biased in our favour, or maybe even because she was mad that I hadn't taken better care of Fi, or that I'd helped blow their house to smithereens. We ended up with only a couple of hectares of farmland — part of Nellie's Paddock and part of Burnt Hut. Plus the wetlands, which we could only use if we drained, and just as we were considering doing that Fi's mum slapped a preservation order on them so we couldn't touch them. A covenant, it was called, which meant we still owned them legally, but we weren't allowed to change them in any way.

As if that wasn't bad enough they announced that people like us had to provide shelter and food to whoever was allocated the rest of our farm, while they started building their houses.

When I had a few hours free I got a lift into Wirrawee to try to track some people down. It was a long list. On top of it was my Stratton grandmother, who we'd been looking for since the first few hours of peace. We'd had no news of her at all, and Dad and Mum were frantic trying to find her. Then there were the New Zealand commandoes, Monique and Issa and Judy from Camp 23, Nell Ford and Mrs Slater, who we'd talked to in Wirrawee Hospital, Mrs Alexander, whose ride-on mower I'd destroyed . . .

The main ones for me though, apart from my grandmother, were Lee's brothers and sisters, and Dr Muir. I was terribly worried about Dr Muir, because I didn't know how he could possibly have escaped from the soldiers at the incinerator. I didn't think I could stand it if I'd caused something terrible to happen to him.

I didn't get far with my searches for the out-of-town people. I added my notices to the huge boards outside Tozer's that were put up for exactly that purpose, and registered their names with the Red Cross office in Barker Street. But the Red Cross people were only interested in family reunions at that stage. Dad had already got them looking for Grandma, but they said it would be a week or two before they could look for friends.

They did tell me that Nell Ford had died in Wirrawee Hospital, about six months before the end of the war.

The good news was that Mrs Slater and Mrs Alexander were fine. Robyn's parents were fine too, if you call moving and breathing fine. If that's all there is. They were still functioning, but you felt that inside was bare and barren. Worst of all was the way Mr Mathers grabbed me and hugged me when I visited. He nearly broke my ribs. I could feel his desperation. I knew I couldn't be Robyn. I had enough trouble being myself. And I knew I couldn't take on two extra parents.

With stuff like that to deal with, I had very mixed feelings about going into Wirrawee. Every street I walked down, every park I passed, every shop and every corner reminded me of Robyn or Lee or Fi or one of the others. That roundabout was where Robyn fell off her bike and got a bloody nose; that milk bar was where Homer and I nicked a packet of Stimorol and then, ashamed, took it back; that house was where Corrie bit Travis on the ear when we were in Grade 3 and he tried to kiss her at Simone's birthday party. I felt like I was in a Luna Park of memories, surrounded on every side by the laughter and tears and cries and happy shouts of ghosts.

The other major problem about going into town was the number of people who wanted to stop and talk. I mean it had always been like that — if you wanted to buy a loaf of bread in Wirrawee you had to allow half an hour minimum — and sometimes that had been annoying and sometimes it had been nice, but now it was embarrassing and ridiculous. I felt like a freak show.

It was a difficult time, and made much worse by the fact that I'd expected the end of the war to be some kind of paradise. No matter how many times during the fighting

I'd told myself that life after the war would be different, and difficult, deep down I'd still kidded myself that we could return to normal. Better than normal: the longer the war went, the more I remembered life in the old days as being pretty much perfect.

Then a few things happened. The first was that I got news of the feral kids who had gone back to New Zealand with Ryan. It had been impossible to get any messages through to New Zealand, because the telephone lines were reserved for the military and for government business. When they were opened to civilians for three hours a day, you still couldn't get through, because of the heavy demand, and the problems with lines and equipment damaged during the war. The Wirrawee Exchange didn't seem to be a high priority.

I tried a few times, whenever I found myself near a phone, but in the end I only made it because of my powerful friends. I was in town again with Dad, trying to buy herbicide from the limited amounts available, when Heather from the Post Office ran down the street to catch me.

"Oh Ellie," she puffed, "I wish you wouldn't walk so fast. Oh, let me get my breath back."

I waited, wondering what I'd done to deserve being chased down the street.

"Oh," she said again, "I'm so glad I've caught you. There's a very important military man in New Zealand, been trying all morning to get you. Says it's urgent. Said he didn't know you were free until last night, when he saw a newspaper article about you."

"Did you get his name?" I asked, hoping against hope that it might be . . .

"General Finley? Does that sound right?"

"Colonel Finley? Seriously? Oh my God, I can't believe it."

We both started hurrying back to the Post Office.

"Yes, he's really been quite demanding. Quite impatient. I've never talked to a General before. I hope they're not all as rude as that."

"He's not a General, only a Colonel."

"Well, I'm sure he said he was a General."

Turned out I was wrong, because when I finally got through I learnt that Colonel Finley had scored a promotion. I congratulated him, but as usual he wasn't interested in small talk. However he certainly wasn't rude to me.

"Now, Ellie, I'll only say this to you once, but if there's anything you want, you just have to ask. What you've done will be recognised more officially in due course, I think I can say, but in the meantime you can make outrageous demands and I'll guarantee that they're met."

He sounded so genuinely delighted that I'd made it through the war that I was touched. I hadn't blamed him for sending us back from New Zealand, or for pushing us into action. That was his job. But I never thought he was interested in us as people, just as fighting units he could allocate wherever he wanted.

"Oh Colonel, I mean General, I've got two big questions. The first is, what happened to those kids we sent back with Ryan?"

"Why, they're fine. They've been fostered here for the time being, but in the long term we're hoping to reunite them with their parents. If their parents can't be found, well, you might like to think about adopting one yourself."

"Good God," I thought. "I'm a bit young for that."

But it was another sign of how much things had changed, that someone my age could seriously be considered for adopting a kid.

"What's your second question?"

"Have you got any news on Iain and Ursula and the rest of the group?"

"Ah well, that's very interesting. The short answer is 'No,' but the other side are playing some complicated games at the moment. As you know, the peace settlement allowed for a full exchange of prisoners of war, but it's not happening at the speed it should. They won't even give us lists of names. So some people we know about, some people we don't. We know that your friends are held in one of the prisons, we don't know where, but Iain and the others are such tough cookies that . . ."

And we got cut off with no warning. It was typical, but infuriating when I'd had such a clear line to the Colonel — I still thought of him as that. Try as we might, and as Heather did, we couldn't get the line back. The biggest frustration was that we hadn't even mentioned Homer and the others. I wanted so much to tell him about our last attack, and how it had ended.

The call put me in a much better mood though. On the way home Dad commented that it was the happiest he'd seen me since he got back. I was pretty rapt. To hear that the ferals were all right, and on top of that to hear Colonel Finley saying that Iain and Ursula and their team were probably prisoners — it was more than I'd dared hope for.

And I still hadn't forgotten my promise to Casey.

While I was in such a good mood I decided to do something I'd been putting off since I got back. I wanted to take a walk — or go on a pilgrimage, whatever — up to Tailor's Stitch, so I could look into Hell again. I know I didn't want to go right down in there. I just wanted to stand on top, say a prayer maybe, chuck a flower in, something like that. It was my first time since we'd left so long ago with Ryan and the ferals, apart from a quick trip with Dad to get the Land Rover. At least the whole area was still designated as crown land, which was lucky, seeing every spare scrap of country was being swarmed over by human rabbits.

I suppose I was a bit stupid to go up into the mountains, considering the warnings that had been broadcast about what the army called "hot" areas — areas not cleared properly of enemy soldiers. Of course nearly all the enemy troops and colonists had gone voluntarily — well, sort of voluntarily; most of them were furious — but we'd all heard stories of the ones who wouldn't go, and the trouble they gave. Some were fanatics, determined to defend their new homes to the last breath, some were stupid, and hadn't realised the war was over, and some were simply off their skulls.

Because everyone was so busy clearing and building and planting and repairing I knew I'd have the whole of Tailor's Stitch to myself. As far as I knew no-one except Dad and me had been up there since the war ended.

God it was a beautiful morning. There was a little mist, but as soon as it lifted you knew it would stay perfect all day. The sulphur-crested cockies screamed at me, the kookaburras laughed like machine guns, the rosellas flew like red arrows through the trees.

I had to walk, because there was so little petrol, but I'd underestimated how much I'd lost since the war ended:

how much energy, how much strength, how much stamina. Halfway up I was struggling, and it was only willpower that got me to the top.

On Tailor's Stitch I could take it easy at last. It was the first time since the war ended that I felt a little real peace again. I lay in the sun, thinking that as long as the bush survived there had to be some hope for the world. The prison at Stratton, the hospital in Cavendish, the internment camp, the block of apartments in Simmons' Reef were at last starting to fade into the distance. I could feel the smell of them being baked out of me by the sun, a last reminder of the summer gone.

I got up again after a while and headed to the right, towards Hell, picking my way along the little track for a couple of k's. It felt weird to be walking it in broad daylight, not worrying about being seen or attacked. It looked so different under these circumstances.

When I got directly above our old clearing — as far as I could tell anyway — I stepped down farther, below the ridgeline, wondering if I could pick the campsite from here. Our camouflage should protect it well enough, but I thought I'd be able to work out where it was, even if I couldn't confirm it.

I guess I was there ten minutes. Eventually I thought I'd got the right spot, just from picking up the contours of the land, especially where the creek would be flowing.

Wiping the hair out of my eyes I turned and went slowly up the rise. I walked over to the right, to the edge of the steepest cliff, the part of Satan's Steps where Kevin cut the rope and sent the soldier falling to her death. Prompted by some ghoulish feeling I peeped over, hoping there'd be nothing to see, but somehow compelled to look anyway.

There was nothing. Just a tree with a broken top, a white branch sticking up like a human bone. A eucalypt with a compound fracture.

I turned away, wondering why I'd looked in the first place. Just as I turned I heard a loud rattling noise behind. It took a moment to realise it was the sound of footsteps. Running footsteps.

I whirled around. A soldier was coming straight at me, an enemy soldier. I knew straightaway that she was the soldier we'd captured that morning on the top of the cliff. She was young, twenty or twenty-one maybe, but I knew she was mad. I could see it in her emaciated body, her quivering arms, her bared teeth. Most of all I saw it in her eyes. They simply weren't human, had stopped being human quite a while ago.

They were lit like they were radioactive. That lurid green light you get in some city streets late at night, when everyone's gone home.

She'd looked pretty crazy that morning when we'd killed her friends. If she'd been roaming around on her own up here ever since, then I could understand her being completely out of her tree. And she knew I was one of the people who'd shot her buddies. She recognised me. I saw that in her eyes too.

It seemed that the Hermit had returned. Another crazed person, sent mad by the death of people close to her, was running around in these mountains.

I didn't have much time to decide what to do. She was five or six paces away, running straight at me, running hard, taking giant strides. My fear of heights had gotten worse during this war, mainly after my fall down the cliffs into the Holloway Valley. As she charged I felt myself lock up, felt the strength leave my limbs, leeched away by fear. I knew that would be fatal for me and I tried, as fiercely as I could, to get my strength back. I thought briefly of Robyn. She had discovered the courage when she needed it.

With the woman three metres away I found some energy flowing into my limbs. I don't know where it came from. The second I'd taken to recover might just have cost me my life. The woman was about to crash into me so hard I'd go flying backwards. Over the cliff.

There wasn't time to get right away from her, to run. Instead I dropped low and tried to dive at her feet, keeping as low as possible, hoping that if I kept low enough she would go over the edge but I wouldn't.

It kind of worked. It certainly took her by surprise. She went down, but sideways, almost landing on my head. I grabbed her around the knees, and I clung on to her legs, like a rugby tackler, but she kicked me off. I got a knee in the chin as I rolled free.

Then I was up again and at her, hoping I'd be quicker to get to my feet than she was, hoping again to get the advantage. In fact we were both up at about the same time. She had her back to the cliff, and I tried to ram into her hard enough to send her over, but she locked her arms around me, and I knew if she went over I'd go too, held in an embrace that would take us all the way down to death together. I twisted free and tried to get lower, to tip her up from underneath. But instead she got me around the waist and started to turn me, to get me into a position where she could push me backwards.

I felt her strength then. The strength of a maniac fighting for her life. I'd read *Great Expectations*. I knew how strong mad people can be. She got me around and started forcing me backwards. I was still quite bent over and I could see my boots gouging tracks in the dry soil as she forced me along, inch by inch.

The tracks got deeper, the momentum slower, as I dug my heels in, harder and harder. But no matter what I did, I still kept going, closer and closer to that edge. I didn't know how close I was, but it could only be the length of my shoe away.

I had to risk everything on getting my knee up, and into her groin. It was the hardest decision of my life, because I knew that by lifting one foot off the ground I'd lose half my traction, and in that instant, if she was quick enough, she'd have me over the edge and gone. But as I went back another inch, as I felt the void below me, I drove up with my right knee.

She gave a yelp, like a fox, and for a moment her grip eased. For that one awful moment I hung over the cliff, about to drop. I think my point of balance was already over: it was sheer mindpower that brought me back up, lifting me away from the fall I should have begun. I staggered forward, pushing the woman away, then headbutted her in the stomach. But not hard enough: I didn't have enough momentum; she was able to grab me easily around the waist again, and again start to turn me towards the cliff.

At least this time her grip wasn't quite as good. Now I was grateful for all those wrestling lessons from Homer. I twisted and shoved at the same time and sent her sprawling back. But she was up and at me again with that terrible speed she had shown before. I stepped to the side, only half a step, and caught her and tried to push her to the edge while she was slightly off-balance. She brought up an elbow and hit me in the cheekbone. I let go, just as a reflex reaction, and she used both hands to try to throw me over, gripping my right shoulder. I recovered by spinning around and getting under her and driving up towards her face. That took her by surprise and for a moment I had her, driving her backwards, as powerfully as I could. I got her right to the edge. For a moment I thought she was going over and I guess I hesitated, weakened, held back.

I think she sensed that. She took me by surprise then, dropping suddenly very low, even lower than I'd done when she first ran at me. She was going to get me somewhere round the knees and just flip me straight over her head and into space. She could do it too, because her centre of gravity would be so low and mine would be off the ground.

At that moment the ground under her feet crumbled. I saw her stagger and start to fall. I nearly reached out a hand to help her, but knew if I did we would both go. Instead I pulled away. She was staggering backwards, windmilling her arms to try to get her balance. I kept reversing, flinging myself as far from the edge as I could, not sure how much of it was going to collapse. But the whole time I was staring into her eyes. I saw the knowledge come into those mad eyes, the knowledge that she was dead. She reached out her right arm, as if to plead with me. She opened her mouth. A sob came out of it. She started to fall. I could still see her eyes. My God, those eyes, I'll see them every day and every night until I die. Green eyes, staring at the horror of the thousand-foot fall that she was beginning. Staring into the horror of her death. Seeing the rocks in her mind, knowing she would be falling onto them, her body smashing into the unforgiving ground.

As she disappeared from my view she started to scream. She screamed all the way to the bottom.

I knew then the answer to my question; the question I'd asked myself many times during this war, and many more times since it ended. When would I be able to put the war behind me? When would I be able to forget it? And I knew now that the answer was simple.

Never. I never would. Some things end. But war never does.

17

Our telephone still hadn't been reconnected when one of our new neighbours called in a few days later with a message from Heather at the Post Office. Apparently it was the General again. And apparently it was even more urgent than last time.

I sighed. I wasn't at all sure I wanted another urgent message from the General. I still associated most of his messages with danger and unpleasantness.

But it was like Judy in Camp 23. You didn't ignore messages from General Finley. Even me, who wasn't an enlisted soldier, who wasn't under his command in any sense of the word, didn't dare ignore him. I guess it was the strength of his personality.

The nearest phone that was working was all the way in at Shannons'. There wasn't enough fuel to take the Land Rover but I didn't mind walking. I told Mum where I was going, and set off.

To pass the time I started trying to guess why he might be calling. I'd gone less than a kilometre when a funny little thought wandered into my head. I was remembering the last time I'd spoken to General Finley; the last time I was in Wirrawee in fact. And something struck me. Maybe it should have struck me before. When I'd been talking to him about Ursula and Iain he virtually said that he didn't know. It was like he had no idea whether Iain and Ursula and the Kiwis were alive. But then he'd said something along the lines of "we know your friends are prisoners," when in fact he didn't know about Ursula and Iain.

And would he have called the Kiwi commandoes my friends? He might have. Sometimes people used expressions like that kind of loosely. But on the other hand he might have been referring to some other people.

I couldn't allow myself to feel any hope. Just couldn't. But I realised my feet had started moving faster. Suppose General Finley knew that someone out of our group was still alive? Someone out of Homer and Fi and Lee and Kevin. And suppose he just assumed that I knew that too. That might explain the way he'd spoken on the phone.

Another thing; contact with him had been pretty much impossible, true, but how come he hadn't asked me anything about Homer and the others? I'd been a bit disappointed with him, that he hadn't. But if he knew they were prisoners, and assumed *that I knew, too* . . .

Suddenly I was running. I had to: it was all I could do with the excitement and adrenalin and fear pumping through my system. I knew it was only the faintest of chances, and I knew if I was wrong it would be devastating, but I also knew that if any of them had by some miracle survived, then I could too: I could cope with all the confusion and depression and tension of this post-war world. And what about Gavin? Oh how I wanted to see him again. He was so young and his life had been hard, and he was such a feisty character. He deserved a second chance at life.

But then I remembered it was no good asking General Finley about Gavin, because it wouldn't have meant anything to him: General Finley would never have heard of Gavin.

I was pretty rude when I got to Shannons', just burst

in, said, "Can I use the phone?" and grabbed it. Then I went through the usual infuriating and frustrating business, calling over and over again, getting every possible recorded message, from "All overseas lines are currently in use, please try again later," to "The number you are calling is no longer connected." I ignored them all and just kept hitting that redial button.

Every ten minutes one of the Shannons poked their head in the door, took a look at my red, frustrated face, and retreated again. I'd say it was three-quarters of an hour before I at last heard the ringing tone. I'd become so used to hanging up on every call that I almost hung up again, automatically. Luckily I didn't. I waited, sweating, thinking, "If only I still had our radio, to call up New Zealand anytime we wanted."

A man answered, and when I told him my name he said: "Wait on please; I'll find him for you."

Almost immediately General Finley's voice was in my ear, as usual getting straight to business.

"Well, Ellie, we've tracked them down for you."

My heart stopped as I said: "Who, exactly?"

I actually had my fingers in my mouth.

"Well, everybody really."

"For God's sake," I screamed at him, the infuriating tears starting in my eyes. "Who?"

Unlike just about every adult I know, General Finley didn't launch into a little speech about how you get on far better in life if you show some basic courtesy, and how when you scream at people you don't achieve anything.

He started reading a list of names beginning with Homer, Lee, Kevin, Fi, Iain, Ursula, Bui-Tersa, Kay and then a half-a-dozen others whom I didn't know or didn't remember, but whom I guessed were the other New Zealand commandoes.

I wasn't listening too hard after the first six.

At the end he added: "There're three of our people who have now been confirmed killed or died of wounds. There's also a little boy with a hearing disability, who apparently was caught with your friends. I can't work out from this list which one he is. There's a hundred and forty-three names. But Fiona said you'd want to know about him."

"Is he all right?"

"Apparently. They've all had a hard time, and the youngster has been with your friends in an adult prison, so I don't imagine he'd be in the best shape, but they're being examined by one of our doctors today."

"When can I see them?"

"We're rushing them back. I'm not sure how far Wirrawee is from Absalom, where they've been held, but I'm told they'll be in Wirrawee at 0800 tomorrow."

Eight o'clock in the morning. Seventeen hours.

An afternoon and a night. One sleep. A sleep I wouldn't be having. Seventeen hours.

It seemed so fast. One minute they were dead; the next, they were brought back to life, the next they would be standing in front of me.

I rang Fi's parents, who were the only ones on the phone. I can't remember what I said to them, can't remember a word of the conversation. Then I stumbled out of the Shannons' house and started running all the way to Kevin's. The farther I ran, the lighter my feet became, and the last three kilometres I didn't even notice. I wish the Olympic trials had been on that day. I would have blitzed them.

It was two o'clock in the morning before I got home, and even then I only went back because I knew Mum and Dad would be out of their minds with worry. It was lucky my news got me off the hook. If I'd had any other excuse for being so late I think they would have really cracked.

It was funny being on curfew when such a short time before I'd been out all night launching attacks, killing people. I quite liked it though. Made life feel more normal again. Made me feel like I really was home, back with my parents, back to the way it had been before the war, when I was just a kid.

Mum and Dad wanted to talk, when I told them the news. But I'd had enough talking. I'd talked and listened and talked some more at the Holmeses' and again at the Yannos's. I'd never had so many hours of talking. We'd screamed and laughed and babbled and hugged and talked and talked and talked. God sure knew what he was doing when he gave human beings language. Without it we'd have been stuffed. Or we would have had to do a lot more dancing.

So I went to bed. I didn't sleep, surprise surprise. I tossed and turned, I wriggled and squirmed, I tumbled and twisted. I rolled over to a new position every thirty seconds. One minute I was a tight little ball, the next I was sprawled across the bed.

Round about 3.30 in the morning I realised what I was feeling as much as anything. Terror. Terror? How could that be? Terrified of the people who were probably closer to me than my own parents? Well, that scared me for a start. I didn't want anyone to be closer to me than my parents. I got a shock when I realised, there in the darkness, just how close Fi and the others had become to me.

But that was something to think about long-term. It wasn't really that which had me kicking and flailing around the bed.

No, it was the fear that they would come back as monsters. That whatever had happened to them in those last few weeks of the war, and even since the war ended, might have been so horrible, so bestial, that they would come towards me out of a kind of hellish glow, with a green light shining from their mad eyes. Like the woman up on Tailor's Stitch.

After going through so much together we had suddenly been separated. They had a whole lot of new experiences they'd shared, and all those experiences excluded me. The prison they'd been in might have set a new low. General Finley said they'd had a tough time. Just how tough was it? Enough to change them forever, so they would come back as strangers? Was it worse than Camp 23?

Worst of all, would they blame me for being caught? Had I done anything wrong? Should I have gone in a different direction, that night in the bush when I ran away from the truck stop? Should I have found Lee and the others again? Should I have led the soldiers away from our packs? Did I do the wrong thing by jumping onto the train? At the time I felt I had no choice, but maybe I was wrong about that.

I got up about 5.45 and sat in the kitchen shelling peas. Very good therapy, shelling peas. Normally anyway. This morning I felt too tired and heavy-eyed and sluggish and stupid.

Eventually Dad got up and came in, grunting something at me that sounded vaguely like "Good morning." He put some toast on, put the kettle on, got out the poor variety of jams available these days. When the toast popped he spread me a slice with Vegemite. If I'd had to do it myself I wouldn't have had any breakfast, but seeing he'd gone to the trouble, and seeing it was right there in front of me, I ate it. And I did feel a bit better.

"Are you nervous?" he asked.

"Yeah. Don't know why. But I am."

"I thought you were. Guess you don't know what shape they'll be in."

"Yeah, that's right."

There was much more to it than that, but I couldn't be bothered explaining. Once you're a teenager it's like your parents so often just don't get it, and that's one thing that war doesn't change.

Although when I came stumbling back from Tailor's Stitch, bruised and grazed all over from the fight on the cliff top, they were great then. They held me and petted me and let me cry. Afterwards Dad took me into Wirrawee to report it. I had to write out this huge statement and answer heaps of questions, and I was glad I had Dad there. He's good with stuff like that.

We'd only talked about the war a few times, I mean, like sat down and had a full-on serious conversation. That's the kind of the family we are. We talk about stuff, and always have, but there's stuff we don't talk about too. We referred to the war all the time of course, how couldn't you? But apart from one conversation that went till after midnight, our second night back in the house, we didn't go on about it. It seemed so incredibly unreal, so totally unbelievable, that I could have done the things I did, killed so many people. I think I was scared that if I started talking about it too much it would create a gulf between me and my parents that we would never be able to bridge. So we kind of played it safe, talked about other people, about the present and the future rather than the past.

Mum appeared and as soon as I'd cleared away the breakfast stuff I went and started the Land Rover, and drove it round to the front door, just to give them the hint.

The drive into Wirrawee seemed to take longer than any of the trips we'd done during the war. Even when we'd walked there. I drove, Dad sat beside me, Mum in the back seat. The only time anyone spoke was when Dad looked at a mob of cattle in a paddock on the left of the road and said: "You can't beat hybrid vigour."

I parked half a block down from the Post Office. We were way too early of course. A few minutes later Homer's parents arrived, with George driving, then I realised Kevin's parents were there already with their two little boys. They were parked on the other side of the street, another block up. Fi's parents and Victoria were the last to arrive.

I felt sad that there was no-one I could tell about Lee. I'd still had no word about his little brothers and sisters.

Gradually, as eight o'clock got closer, we all got out of the cars, and gathered outside the Post Office. The mood was strange. I don't think too many of us had slept. No-one said much. You could see the suppressed excitement in their clenched hands, in the way they gazed down the street, in the nervous dancing of the kids. Most of all in everyone's eyes. But there were so many other things in their eyes too. So many shadows. All the parents looked about twenty years older since the start of the war. Everyone, adults and kids, looked thin and tired and sad and hungry, even on this special day. It was just the way people were now. Maybe it would change again as time went on, and they would start to look like they had a year and a bit ago. I couldn't wait for that to happen. I wanted to wipe away the worry on their faces, and see their cheeks fill out again.

I still remember the screaming of brakes as the bus stopped. It was like a knife into my heart. I saw faces peering out of windows, but I couldn't see anyone I knew. Then I saw Kevin, looking gaunt and unshaven, waving at me from the back. Suddenly I knew it was going to be all right. I waved madly at him then ran around to the door. I nearly knocked Fi over. She looked so exactly the same that it was disconcerting. Even with the scar on her face, it was like this war hadn't changed her at all. We hugged, but only briefly, before Victoria, sobbing and wheezing, clutched her. Homer came off the bus but he was engulfed in people before I could reach him. He gave me a huge grin, then disappeared into a human knot of half-a-dozen bodies. Someone grabbed me from behind: it was Kevin, hugging me with his big hands and long arms. When he let me go I saw Lee behind him, waiting.

Perhaps that's what had made me most nervous. With no-one else there to meet Lee I knew it had to be me. I felt like I had to be mother, father, sister, girlfriend to him, to welcome him home. It seemed like an awful lot of roles for one person. I didn't think I could fill all those vacancies. He deserved to have all those people there, and then some. He should have had an avenue, a whole town of yellow ribbons on old oak trees. Instead he only had me.

I tried to be everything I could to him. I hugged him, kissed him all over his smooth face, held him tight. As I did, it struck me that Lee was in many ways our true hero. Lee was the one who did the dirtiest jobs, quietly, without fuss, without going into big emotional scenes. He was so efficient, so reliable, so brave. Wherever we fell short, he made up the gap. I'm not just talking about the red-hot moments, when enemy soldiers were shooting at us, when we were within a moment of death. I'm talking about the sourer times too, when we were so tired we could hardly remember to breathe, or we were so bored we'd pick at each other just for something to do, or so distressed we'd wish a soldier would come along and blow us into oblivion with an M16. At all those times Lee stood strong. He was like the Wirrawee grain silo. You could see the grain silo from miles away, tall and reliable. It stood for Wirrawee, and it gave you a safe comfortable feeling to know it was there. That was how I'd felt about Lee during the war. Most of the time anyway.

"Do you know anything about your brothers and sisters?" I asked when we separated. I was wiping my eyes.

"More or less. I know they're OK. They're in a refugee camp, a couple of hundred kilometres away. I've got to ring General Finley as soon as I can. He reckons he'll have the full details by the time I call him."

"What about Gavin?"

"He's been with us. Didn't you know? They took him to Stratton this morning to see if they could find his rellies."

"Oh thank God for that. Is he all right?"

"Gavin? He's indestructible."

"So where have you guys been hanging out?"

He laughed. "How long have you got?"

I had plenty of time that day, but no-one else did. Three hours later Lee was whisked away in a car to get his brothers and sisters. It was three long days after that before the five of us actually got together. By then I think they were quite glad to get away from families that clung like scarves. For more than a year we'd dreamed of seeing our families again, but once we'd done it, well, three days was enough.

We met at Homer's, down at the creek. It was nice there. I walked from our place; Kevin walked from his. Fi and Lee got a lift out with Fi's mum, who had to inspect some new subdivisions. That was her excuse anyway. I think she could have inspected them anytime, but she took pity on us, and agreed to drive Lee and Fi.

It was funny. We were sort of awkward. An arranged meeting like this wasn't the way we normally got together. We brought whatever food we could scrounge, but it was difficult with the rationing being so severe. All that time we'd spent during the war, having to live off the land; you'd think we'd be pretty good at scrounging food. But it was different now. Obviously we didn't want to steal food off our friends and neighbours. I found some late blackberries and made a pie which went OK — the blackberries were all right, I mean you can't really stuff up blackberries, but the pastry was kind of gluggy.

The highlight was some freeze-dried ice-cream that General Finley had sent from New Zealand, to Lee. It was in a pack called Astronaut Ice-cream, because it was supposed to be the same stuff the astronauts used on their space missions. The flavour, believe it or not, was Neapolitan. When you opened the pack — and that took about five minutes because it was sealed so tightly — you found these three separate packs, one pink, one white, one brown. They looked like pieces of chalk, and they sure were dry, about the driest substance I've ever picked up. I took a piece of the chocolate and put it in my mouth, while the others watched with interest. It was weird. It felt like fizzy stuff, like sherbet, until the moisture of my mouth gave it a bit more flavour. Then it tasted quite sweet and nice, but it didn't taste like ice-cream.

On the pack they said it was "all natural," but when I read the ingredients it had stuff like monoglycerides and diglycerides, potassium sorbate, ascorbic acid. They didn't sound too natural to me.

After lunch I got up and wandered into the creek, up to my knees, then a bit farther. Once I got used to the cold I dog-paddled down to a deep waterhole where Homer and I had often swum when we were little. Next thing Lee surfaced beside me, like a sly serpent from a burrow under the water.

"Where are the others?" I asked.

"Asleep."

He started undressing me, which wasn't difficult, as I wasn't wearing much. I watched my shorts float slowly away. I didn't try to stop them. The water washed around my body like an endless loving caress. Like Lee's tongue. I didn't feel cold now. I didn't feel passionate about Lee, like I had the other times, but my body was responding. God was it ever responding. When my undies drifted after the other bits of clothing I felt for the waistband of Lee's shorts. They weren't there. He was already naked. I slid up against him, and over him. I've never felt the pleasure more intensely. It was sweeter, stronger, sexier . . . and then disappointing. Without a condom I couldn't keep him in me; I had to let him go and make up for it in other ways.

Afterwards was such a joke, trying to get my clothes back. It took about twenty minutes of deep diving to find my T-shirt. While we were making love I'd had no self-consciousness about being naked, but now, after we'd both relaxed, I was half and half — half-embarrassed, but half just laughing because it all seemed so dumb and silly and funny.

As we walked back through the shallow section of the creek Lee tried to take my hand, but I wouldn't let him. I ran on ahead. I didn't know what I felt about him or us or what we'd just done. This wasn't the time or the place. I'd have to think about it later. The war was over. I wasn't sure what else was over.

When we got to the others they were still sprawled on the sand, asleep or barely awake. Lee and I were in an extremely relaxed mood, and we spread this among the others, with generous lashings of sand and cold water.

And then, when they were sitting up and swearing and laughing and chucking anything we could find at each other, then finally we talked.

"So what the hell happened at the truck stop?" I asked Homer. He was making himself comfortable against a tree trunk, three or four metres away from Fi.

"What happened to you? We'd thought you'd been killed out in the bush somewhere. We'd given you up as a hopeless case."

"I grabbed a train."

"On that train line we found with Gavin?"

I nodded.

"You actually jumped onto a train?"

I nodded again.

"Ah. We never thought of that. That was about the only thing we never thought of."

"So, come on, tell me, what happened? Did you stay together? When did you get caught?"

"Well we got away from the truck stop, thanks to you."

"How do you mean?"

"They followed you, when you yelled out," Fi said. "That was wonderful, Ellie, that you did that."

"Yes," Kevin said. "We talked about that a few times after we were caught."

I was blushing like a cherry.

"I saw them chase you up a hill," Lee confirmed. "Nearly all of them went after you. We only had a couple left to worry about."

"But they followed us a long way," Fi said. "It must have been two or three kilometres."

"Yeah, I think even Gavin was getting worried," Homer said.

"So how did you get rid of them?"

Homer took over, in one of his favourite roles, the storyteller.

"We were belting along, but the more tired we got, the more noise we made. So I thought, 'We've got to get a bit more creative here.' I dropped back till I was next to Lee, and I said: 'You want to hide, let them go past you?' He's quite bright, Lee; I think he'll do well for himself. The next minute he ducked behind a tree, without another word said. I was a bit worried that I hadn't mentioned the second part of the plan, which was that he'd get them from behind. I thought he might just stay around the back of the tree for the rest of the war, but luckily he worked it out for himself."

"What did you do?" I asked Lee, feeling the familiar stirring in my stomach as I spoke, wishing I didn't have to ask, but knowing we were in this together. I couldn't leave Lee to spend the rest of his life with the knowledge of another dirty job that he'd done on his own, and no-one to share that knowledge with.

"Used a knife," he said looking away.

And that was all I could get out of him. I don't imagine it helped him much in dealing with it.

Homer described how they kept running as best they could for most of the night. Eventually it was Gavin who couldn't go on.

"He was disgusted with himself," Fi said. "But his little legs just wouldn't work anymore. We found a bit of a hollow, halfway up a hill behind some fallen trees. We had to carry him up there."

"When she says 'we' she means 'me,'" Kevin explained.

"I wouldn't say anyone slept well," Homer continued. "We were too scared, and we even spent an occasional moment wondering what might have happened to you. Of course we didn't even notice you were missing for a long time, but eventually someone pointed out that we were one short."

"Thanks." I chucked a handful of sand at him.

"When it got light we crawled farther into the bush, where it looked safer. Our big worry was dogs. We knew no-one could see us from the air, and ground troops would have taken a month to find us, but dogs would have smelt Kevin in thirty seconds flat. I could smell him myself, a couple of kilometres away. Luckily no-one turned up, and when it got dark we set off for Cavendish again via the place we'd stashed our packs."

"We were bloody hungry by the time we got there," Kevin contributed.

"Yeah, I'll say. Not for the first time in this war, but

we were feeling the strain. Especially without our trusty leader. We snuck up on the packs slowly, but there was no sign of anyone around. We were rapt that your pack was missing, even if you did have the last bag of licorice allsorts. We were a bit confused though. We figured, 'If she'd had time to get her pack, she must have been feeling pretty safe, she must have lost the soldiers. But why wouldn't she hang around and wait for us?' So we hung around and waited for you, but after a while it became obvious that this was going to end up as one of those 'Unsolved Mysteries' on TV."

Homer left his tree and shuffled a bit closer to Fi, but she didn't look at him.

"We thought you might have grabbed your stuff because you'd seen a good target you could attack in a hurry," Lee said.

"Actually when I think about it, someone did suggest you might have gone down to the train track," Homer said. "But there was no evidence you had. We didn't know you'd gone off on a joy-ride, like it was Puffing Billy."

"I was sick of walking everywhere," I said.

"Well, there seemed to be some problem with the train line, because although we hung there for a day and a half, we didn't hear or see a single train go past. Eventually we hauled ass again, leaving a nice little love letter from Lee to you, that suggested a few meeting places in Cavendish, should we ever get there. I suppose the letter's still sitting under the tree."

"I suppose it is."

I shifted into a more comfortable position, and found another gumleaf to tear into tiny pieces. "What did you do then?" I asked.

"After we gave up on you? We thought about detonating the train line, but it seemed a bit pointless with no traffic on it. It wasn't a centre of gravity anymore. I'm starting to form the impression that there may have been some damage done to it by an irresponsible young vandal, farther up the line, but we didn't know that at the time. So we just put our packs on our backs and started walking. We've walked a lot of kilometres in this war. I tell you, I don't care what cars are going to cost now that the war's over, I'm getting one, and once I've got it I'll never walk anywhere again."

"They say there'll be no new cars for sale for at least two years," Fi said. She rolled over on the sand and lay on her back, a couple of metres away from Homer again now.

"Well I'll get a bike. Anyway, we walked all the way to Cavendish, El, and it took a while. But the good thing was, we could see the effect of blowing up the servo. They had ten times more security along the road. Guys riding shotgun on the trucks, tanks escorting all the convoys, patrols racing backwards and forwards. Guess Ryan was right when he said we could tie up a lot of troops.

"So we kept away from that and got to Cavendish about nine o'clock one night. Poor old Gavin's legs were dropping off again. He was losing interest in the war pretty fast. Fi and Kevin and Gavin holed up in a Scout Hall in the first suburb we came to — Rennie Park it's called — and Lee and I went for a bit of an explore.

"It's such a boring flat ugly city, Cavendish. I don't care if I never go there again. We found one good target, a power station, and a couple of other possibles — a hotel they'd turned into some kind of officers' club, another servo, and a bank. So we headed on back and convinced the others that blowing up a power station would make General Finley, or Colonel Finley as we naively called him then, very happy indeed. It didn't take long to talk them into it."

"What exactly do you mean by a power station?" I asked.

"Well I mightn't have the right word. One of those big paddocks where they have massive power pylons, and the whole thing's got a big fence around it."

"Oh OK. Good target all right."

"Reckon. The only problem was that as well as the fence, they had half-a-dozen soldiers guarding it. Which at least showed how much they valued the place. Convinced us all the more we should knock it off."

"Tough gig."

"Yeah. Well we worked out the coolest plan. Lee still had his uniform from the servo, so we decided we'd borrow a truck and Lee would drive it up to the front gate. He'd stop the truck a bit short, get out and go towards the sentry, holding a bunch of forms in his hand, like he was there on some big-time official mission. And at that moment we'd blow the truck sky high."

"Oh yeah? How'd you plan to do that?"

"No problem," Kevin said. "Well, no major problem. As Lee got out he'd light a thirty-second fuse and start counting. He had to reach the sentry as he got to thirty. Then he'd dive off the bank as the truck exploded into smithereens, and we'd come over the slope beside the road, blasting away with every weapon we had. We'd have wiped them out before they'd stopped blinking."

"Jeez," I said. "I can't believe you're still alive to tell me about it."

"It was a great plan," Homer said firmly. "It would

have worked." He wriggled closer to Fi and put a hand on hers, but she didn't seem to notice.

"Well, except every enemy soldier for ten k's around would have come for us like bees at a honeypot," she said.

They'd obviously had this argument many times before.

Homer shrugged. "Everyone agreed to it," he said to me. "Kevin and Fi did the charges while Lee and I went for a truck. We got one from a milk bar a couple of suburbs away. The driver left the keys in the ignition when he went inside to buy something. We just hopped in from the other side and took off. Good truck too. Just a nice size. It was a Nissan or something I think."

"Mitsubishi," Lee said.

"Whatever. We kept to the back streets in case anyone followed us, or in case we ran into a patrol, but things were cool. I think everyone in Cavendish was so busy dealing with the D-Day stuff that normal life was suspended.

"That's what we thought, anyway. Maybe we convinced ourselves of that a bit too easily. We got back to the hall and parked the truck behind a shed, where you couldn't see it from the road. But there was one thing we didn't think of."

"Helicopter?" I asked, being a smart-ass.

Homer looked seriously annoyed. "Did someone tell you that?" he asked suspiciously.

I laughed. Fi took her hand back and smiled at me and said, "See? I told you we needed Ellie."

I got the impression this was the last thing Homer wanted to hear. He kept going with his story, but kind of grim-faced.

"We heard the helicopter and we thought it'd just pass

over on its way to somewhere, so we weren't that worried. By the time we realised it wasn't going away it was too late. I wouldn't exactly say we panicked but we weren't happy. The first thing was to get rid of the weapons and explosives. If we were going to be caught we didn't want to have those on us. Kevin basically saved our butts. There was a stage at the end of the hall where they have Gang Shows and stuff I guess, and in the corner he'd found a little trapdoor that opened into a storage space under the stage. We shoved everything in there, then we dragged an old cupboard across to cover the trapdoor. Fi did a bit of dusting, so you couldn't tell the cupboard had just been moved.

"I mean, I know this probably sounds like half an hour's work, but it literally took about a minute.

"Then we were prepared to break out. I suppose we could have tried to keep the weapons and shoot our way out, but we just saw that as a fast route to suicide.

"We squeezed open the back door; well at least I did, with the others looking over my shoulder. And I saw a very ugly sight. An enemy soldier had his face about one metre in front of me, with a bloody great rifle pointed up my nose."

"And at that moment," said Kevin, joining in, "the door at the other end crashed open and three soldiers came racing in. They smashed straight through the door, just like in the movies. And for us the war was over."

"It was awful," said Fi. "But it was almost a relief in a way. There was nothing we could do. And being caught wasn't really our fault. I mean we shouldn't have parked the truck there, but once we'd made the mistake we were dead ducks. At least we didn't have to feel guilty about not shooting it out with them. They had us cold."

"And they didn't find the explosives?" I asked. "They couldn't have, or you wouldn't be sitting here now."

"Right," Homer said. "That was our only lucky break. We sweated while they were bringing our packs out. We had to wait outside, with our hands in the air, and we could hear them inside, kicking stuff around and generally vandalising the Scout Hall. Honestly, nothing's sacred to these people. But they weren't trying too hard. The place looked so bare and empty. There was a bit of gym equipment, and a box of old uniforms, and not much else. It was obvious we were just passing through."

"Is that what you told them?" I asked.

"Yeah, it was good because they fired all these questions at us while we were standing together under the trees, so we heard each other's answers, and we knew what story to stick to. They started with Fi, because she's so sweet and little, and she said we'd spent the war hiding in Stratton, but when the fighting got too scary we bailed, and now we were on our way farther outback, where we hoped it'd be safer." Homer turned ninety degrees and moved like a centipede until his head was resting on Fi's right leg.

Fi continued the story, patting Homer's hair as she talked. "And we stole the truck because we were tired of walking. We looked as pathetic and childish as we could, like we were just naughty kids. Having Gavin actually helped quite a lot I think, because to anyone who doesn't know him he looks pretty harmless. And when they realised he was deaf they were quite impressed."

"So instead of shooting us on the spot, which must have crossed their minds as a possibility, they took us to the local military lockup. We spent the night with soldiers who'd been busted for different crimes," Lee said.

"It was awful there," Fi said. "They really were the dregs of the army. I think half of them got themselves put in the lockup so they wouldn't have to fight."

"Seeing half of them were deserters, that's a fair deduction," Lee said.

"Well, interesting first chapter," I said, stretching and yawning. "What happens in the second part?"

"A riveting saga of sex and violence," Homer said. "Actually, not a lot of sex. In fact no sex at all, unless there's something these guys haven't told me. But enough violence to satisfy even Lee's sadistic appetite."

There was an awkward pause. Homer realised, I think, that he'd said the wrong thing. Lee had done more than his fair share of killing during this war, but it was hardly what he wanted. Maybe he was prepared to do it because some of us were too squeamish. Perhaps lately it was because he wanted revenge for the deaths of his parents.

But no-one said anything, and Lee just looked away. Homer sat up again, cleared his throat and hurried on. "Well, the next day we got taken to a prison for any old riffraff they happened to pick up. Before the war it had been a Catholic school, Our Lady Help of Christians. Unfortunately Our Lady wasn't much help to us. The place was a hole."

"The girls' section was OK," Fi said.

"That's because there were only a dozen of you," Homer said. "The guys were packed in like a rugby scrum. A mixture of nationalities, personalities, nasty habits . . ."

"Nasty habits? Such as?" I wasn't sure how seriously Homer meant it.

"Such as fights, bashings, people being totally selfish. Some of it was pretty bad. I got my head kicked in just for being Greek. A bloke in the next wing got knifed and died, I don't even know why. And some of it was trivial, but it all adds up, you know? For instance, one day a guy in my wing got a whole heap of stale biscuits, as a present, because he fixed a guard's computer or something, and he pigged the whole lot. Didn't give one away. I know it doesn't sound like much, but if you're starving, if you haven't had a meal for forty-eight hours, it's a lot. And he had about a kilo of the bloody things. The only good news was he got sick as a dog from eating them all."

"Yeah," Kevin said, "the guy next to me set records for dobbing. He got me three times in my first week. Dobbed me in for nicking a cigarette lighter from a guard, for slipping a note to Homer, for vandalising a telephone. I was totally innocent on the telephone, but I still copped a bashing every time. Lee fixed him though."

I grinned at Lee, but I was kind of anxious, the way Kevin said that. "What did you do?" I asked him.

He shrugged. "Nothing you'd want to know about."

"How did you go generally?" I asked him.

"Not bad." No-one said anything for a minute so he was forced to say a bit more. "Look, it was a bloody awful place, but I don't want to dwell on it for the rest of my life. The war's over. I've got other things to think about."

It sounds kind of rough, written down like that, and he said it fairly aggressively, but I was on his side. He had a new war to think about already. His brothers and sisters were his responsibility; he still wanted an education, a career, a life. Out of all of us he had the toughest future. And he was on his own. We might be able to help a bit, from time to time, but basically it would all be up to him.

It was a long afternoon by the time I told them my

story. I got a bit emotional towards the end, mainly because of Dr Muir. From the moment when he whispered to me at the incinerator, no-one has heard from him or seen him again, and I can't help feeling he must have died, and that it was my fault.

On the way back to the house, we stopped and looked at the daffodils Homer and his brother George had put in a few years ago. They were peeping out of the rich earth, worth every penny of the ten cents their mum and dad paid them for each bulb they planted.

Lee knelt and took one between his fingers and gazed at it intently, as if trying to read its secrets. Fi picked a dozen to take home. Homer used a stick like a golf club and knocked a couple of flowers flying. Kevin said, "You should have put in jonquils. They smell better."

I smiled, watching them. Maybe war didn't change people much after all.

Lee stood up and came past me. Suddenly he grabbed me and danced me around a patch of anemones.

"We survived, Ellie, we survived."

EPILOGUE

It all got really strange. Every second person I met said, "God, you can make a fortune now." We did get approached by at least a dozen publicity agents wanting to talk about business deals, especially film deals. Most of them seemed OK, like they weren't totally tacky or anything, but it was weird to be even talking to them in the first place. As well as that we got direct calls from heaps of companies. Money was so short we figured we couldn't be too precious about earning some, especially in US dollars, so we did quite a few interviews, including the one with the American *60 Minutes*.

Dad and I used the money for turkeys and geese. I never thought I'd see the day we'd go into poultry, but with the small amount of land we had left, we couldn't keep going with sheep or cattle. Nearly everyone else went into chickens or vegetables or both. Dad figured that turkeys and geese would be better, for the simple reason that they were different and people'd get sick of chicken pretty fast.

But like everyone else we had to diversify, so we put in spuds too, and Mum started a mustard business with Homer's mum.

It's amazing to me that we've adjusted to the new life so quickly. I guess humans are an adaptable species. I wouldn't say it's been easy, and there have been lots of depressing and ugly moments, with people not able to accept change, but in general I'd say we're taking three steps forward for every two back.

Really, there's no point my writing about all that, because everyone knows what it's like.

The only other thing I want to do, to finish off this record, is to say what's happened to Homer and Kevin and Lee and Fi and the ferals.

Kevin went back to New Zealand. His mum and dad had been wanting to get off the land for some time before the war, so they took the compensation and went to live in Cavendish, where they opened a place that sells and services chainsaws and mowers, stuff like that. Kevin didn't seem to be getting on too well with his parents, and after a few months he got a free plane flight to New Zealand, through General Finley, and off he went. He planned to give some talks to schools again, like we'd tried that other time, but I think mainly he just wanted to get away from home. I hope he does better with the school talks than we did. I don't know though. I haven't heard from him in ages.

Chris' parents are still overseas. I don't know whether they'll come back at all now. I wrote to them, in Ireland, but I haven't had an answer.

Fi's family went to the city. Her mum was too stressed after doing the land redistribution and as they said to my parents, they felt there was no future in Wirrawee. They never commented once to me about how we'd wrecked their house. Typical. I'd rather they had said something.

Fi's going to a private school, all girls. We talk every few days, now that the phones are up and running, and she's coming to stay next holidays.

Of all the people in the world Fi has become the one I

feel most comfortable with. It just seems like we're going to be friends forever.

That's how it's worked out between us girls, but it hasn't been the same with the boys, none of whom have any contact with each other. It's a bit sad, but I think they needed a break. I still see Homer every day at school, and most weekends, and we've gone back to that same sort of friendship we had before the war. But we don't often talk about the war. I suppose when I think about it more, when I really look at it honestly, we don't have the same sort of friendship: it's just that I'd like to believe we do. I'm a bit nervous with him somehow; like there's too much that's happened for me to deal with properly, and I'm too aware of other stuff that's getting in the way.

To be really really honest I think I like him too much. I just need to work out what the next stage of our friendship will be; where we go from here. It's all complicated by Fi. She says she wants to end it, that she doesn't love him anymore, but she can't bring herself to tell him. She doesn't want to hurt him. He still talks like he's got this big thing going with her, but I get the feeling he knows deep down that it's over. When I told him Fi was coming to stay with me he didn't look as excited as you'd expect. I mean, he was pleased, but he sure didn't act like Romeo when he sees Juliet on the balcony.

Strangely I don't feel the way I used to about Lee. It just died suddenly, some time, without my even knowing it. That day they got back to Wirrawee, when everyone was hugging like writhing masses of sawfly larvae, I think I still loved him then, and perhaps I did the day at the creek, but that seemed to be the end of it.

He's gone to live in the city, with his little brothers and

sisters. They've been helped quite a lot by a programme for war victims. They've been given a little apartment, and Lee's doing an accelerated course to get into uni early. He rings every couple of weeks, but I can't say I enjoy the calls that much. I think they're more important to him than they are to me. I know he gets lonely and depressed an awful lot.

Casey and Jack and Natalie all got reunited with their families. I haven't even seen them, but I had a few cute little letters from Casey. I'd love to see her again, only travel's so difficult and expensive.

I suppose it sounds awful, like I haven't done anything about her, I haven't kept the promises I made in the little patch of bush near the creek in Nellie's or even as I forced her into the helicopter. Well, that's true, I haven't, and I don't want to make excuses for myself. But I will. It's the way things happen I suppose; in the heat of the moment, in the passion of great danger or great love or great anger, you say things, you make promises. Then the circumstances change. I wasn't totally neglectful with Casey; I rang General Finley quite a few times about her, and I wrote to her. But once I knew she'd found her parents, I was out of the picture. Obviously she was better off with them than with me.

As for Gavin, well, wouldn't you know it, we've ended up with him here. In fact it's pretty crowded at our place, because Corrie's mum, Mrs Mackenzie, is living with us too. After the war Mr Mackenzie walked out on her, and I guess with their house destroyed there wasn't much for her to come home to. She's been very ill, with nervous shock and stuff, the same as Mum, and like Mum she looks about fifty years older, but she seems a little happier.

The funny thing is that Mum and Gavin get on so well. Lucky they do, because Gavin infuriates everyone else at least ten times a day. Dad takes him out into the paddock most mornings but loses his temper with him well before lunchtime. You can always tell, when you see Gavin backing away and Dad yelling about the broken eggs or the broken tail-light on the tractor or the broken irrigation pipe or the screwdriver that's broken because Gavin's been using it as a chisel.

I think Dad secretly likes him though. Whenever he goes to do a job he looks for Gavin, and he's always a bit disappointed if he's off playing footie or at Homer's place.

I don't know how long we'll have Gavin. They're still searching for his family. The last time I talked to the Red Cross they said there was a report that his mother had been murdered by enemy soldiers during the war, and they couldn't find his little sister. But we haven't said anything to Gavin yet, and we won't until we know for sure.

He hardly ever asks about them.

I suppose it is possible that General Finley's suggestion about adoption might come true yet, but not quite in the way he suggested. If we end up with Gavin permanently I guess most of the work would fall on Mum and Dad. I'm not planning on being here much longer.

Gavin is seriously difficult though. All that killing and violence, why wouldn't he be? Why wouldn't we all be? He's so aggressive, and loses his temper so easily. The school's always complaining about him beating up other kids. I'm trying to teach him to calm down, to play normal again. Today was good. We built a haystack in the shape of a fortress, and stuck flags in the turrets. The flags are pillow cases we pinched out of Mum's meagre supply in the linen closet, and I don't know what she'll do when she realises where they've gone.

He's propped my only remaining teddy up as the guard at the entrance, with a long stick for a spear. He does have an imagination, Gavin, no doubt about that.

Despite the fact that he annoys Dad he's pretty handy. He's quick at fixing things, even if mostly they're things he broke in the first place. But he's thorough. And he's excellent at handling the different poultry. I think he likes bossing them around.

I wish Gavin could go and talk to Andrea, my counsellor from when I was in New Zealand. I wish I could go and talk to her. Maybe one day. We've chatted on the phone a couple of times, that's all. I know General Finley said he'd obey my every wish, but it wouldn't be fair to ask for something as selfish as that. There're heaps of people with bigger problems than me: people who are seriously schizo as a result of the war, and I can't jump the queue. Anyway, things are too busy here.

Well, I'm nearly finished. I'm sitting at the desk in the office. I want to knock this off then get outside. It's a nice day. Mum's painting the outside of the house, with a bit of help or hindrance from Mrs Mackenzie. She's been painting it yellow, which I thought was a terrible idea, but I must admit, from a distance it looks good. Up close I'm not so sure.

From here I can see the old fountain, where there used to be a statue of a lady with an umbrella, before someone vandalised her during the war. I can see the white bridge over the creek, the fake stone goanna at the foot of the gum tree, the carport with the grapevine growing over it, the flat green stretch of grass leading to the little waterfall, the Japanese maple and the old barn and the Dumpmaster and the rows of hydrangeas and the duck dam with its stone bridge and little island and wire arch of wisteria. And I know I'm home.

In a way though it's an illusion. It looks so safe and familiar and comfortable. The truth is that everything's unstable. No-one knows if the peace will last, if the settlement will hold. Already there are lots of problems. Accusations and counteraccusations. "Incidents," they call them on the television news.

As if that wasn't enough to remind me of the war, there are constant reminders all the time anyway, all over the place. Little reminders and big ones. Damaged buildings, damaged fences, damaged gardens, damaged trees. Damaged roads and bridges. We're still waiting for a new bridge in Wirrawee, and not a day passes at school without some smart-ass giving me a hard time about it.

Damaged people. People bursting into tears for no apparent reason, then you find their mother or father, their brother or sister, was killed during the occupation. Different faces in some shops, in some houses, because the person who used to work or live there is dead.

Yesterday I found another souvenir, another reminder. I found Kevin's little Corgi, Flip, whom we'd had to abandon at Corrie's place, in the first week of the war. I didn't find much of her. She had apparently made her way to our place. I don't know how or why. She couldn't have followed our scent, because we came here in the Land Rover after dumping her, and she'd hardly have tracked that. But it seems like she made a little nest for herself under our shearing shed, in the way dogs do when they're sick or injured. I guess that's where she died, because I found the remains of her coat, a pathetic mess of reddish hair, and her dark brown leather collar, that I bet Kevin made himself. It even had a little brass disc with her name on it. Kevin might have engraved that too. Probably in Metalwork class at Wirrawee High.

I don't know what happened to our remaining dog, Millie, the only one to survive when Mum and Dad didn't come home from the Show. I guess she died somewhere, probably within a day or two of my finding her, that terrible horrible no-good day when we came back from our happy little camping trip to Hell. She was in critical shape the last time I saw her.

Not long ago Mum said, "Do something for yourself, Ellie," so this is what I've been doing. I went down into Hell, on my own, which was not exactly an easy thing to do. But no-one else wanted to come, which isn't surprising seeing I didn't think I ever wanted to see it again either. I went because I wanted to get all the writing I'd hidden in the Hermit's hut, and that was a powerful enough motivation to drag me down there. Then I rang Andrea in New Zealand and got her to send me the stuff I'd done there, that I'd given her to look after, and then I sat down and started writing this last part. And I swear to God, once it's finished I'll never pick up a pen again.

Well, maybe if we ever get back to the point where we can afford a computer, I don't know, I wouldn't mind trying my hand at a novel or something, seeing I've given myself so much practice with all this stuff. It wouldn't be bad being an author, I reckon. Better than digging up spuds.

Sometimes I say to myself: "A lot of people died because of you in this war, girl. You'd better do something special with your life, to make up for all those deaths."

So yeah, I'll be out of here pretty soon I reckon. Now that I've had some time at home again, now that I've had a good drenching from the mist that rolls off the hills, and the mud in the duck dam, and the dew off the long grass in the gully, I'm ready to leave. I don't know where to, but probably America. I'd love to see it, and with the help General Finley's offered, and if I agree to do a couple more interviews over there, I reckon I can make it.

School's the only problem. Homer and I are doing an accelerated course that they brought in especially for people like us. Not as accelerated as the one Lee's doing, but then he's smarter than us. Still if I get through it I could graduate in two months. It's a hell of a lot of work though, and it's been so hard to get into work mode after a long time with no mental activity. I wish now I had read some of those set texts for English, like *My Brilliant Career* that Robyn was reading in Hell, way back, when we told her she was wasting her time.

Once the exams are over, I should be free. A different kind of freedom.

The old stories used to end with "They all lived happily ever after." And you'd often hear parents saying: "I just want my kids to be happy."

That's crap, if you ask me. Life's about a hell of a lot more than being happy. It's about feeling the full range of stuff: happiness, sadness, anger, grief, love, hate. If you try to shut one of those off, you shut them all off. I don't want to be happy. I know I won't live happily ever after. I want more than that, something richer. I want to go right up close to the beauty and the ugliness. I want to see it all, know it all, understand it all. The richness and the poverty, the joy and the cruelty, the sweetness and the sadness. That's the best way I can honour my friends who died. That's the best way I can honour my parents, who brought me into this world. That's the best way I can lead a life I can be proud to call my own. I want to experience everything it has to offer: LIFE!

ABOUT THE AUTHOR

JOHN MARSDEN IS THE AUTHOR OF MANY ACCLAIMED international best-sellers, including *Letters from the Inside* and *Winter*. He has won numerous awards, including the Christopher Medal and Australia's Children's Book of the Year Award. The first book in the Tomorrow Series, *Tomorrow, When the War Began*, was named an ALA Best Book of the last half-century. He lives in Australia. Visit him online at www.johnmarsden.com.